MW01167105

A Crown in the Dark

A.J. YANG

This is a work of fiction. Names, characters, businesses, events, and incidents are the products of the author's imagination. Any resemblance to actual persons, living or dead, or actual events is purely coincidental.

Fifth Avenue Press
343 S Fifth Ave
Ann Arbor, MI 48104
fifthavenue.press

Fifth Avenue Press is a locally focused and publicly owned publishing imprint of the Ann Arbor District Library. It is dedicated to supporting the local writing community by promoting the production of original fiction, non-fiction and poetry written for children, teens and adults.

Printed in the United States of America

First Printing, 2023

ISBN: 978-1-956697-12-4 (Hardcover)
ISBN: 978-1-956697-13-1 (Paperback)
ISBN: 978-1-956697-14-8 (Ebook)

Cover and Map Art: David Curtis
Editor: Gabriella Jones-Monserrate
Layout: Ann Arbor District Library

To Mom and Dad, for whom I am eternally grateful.

THE WITCH ENCAMPMENT
MAARSO
Cheusnys Cave
AHUIQIR
TILLKASEN FOREST
TEGAK
Greensbriar Manor
Tontin's Cabin
PHEORIRYA
Saelmere Castle
Yllalin
Shylseserin
ILYVALION

PROLOGUE

CATARINA

WHERE HAD IT ALL GONE WRONG? My father's study smells of dust, leather, and of the oranges he always kept in a bowl on his desk. A rug lays on the wooden floor, looking as comfortable as if it had been there for eternity. I lie on it and absentmindedly draw shapes through the soft material. The silken strands are pleasantly cool to the touch. A book lies splayed open at my side, forgotten. Mahogany bookshelves surround us, every inch of each book covered with fine-bound paper. There is a sword, nestled in its embroidered leather sheath, resting high up on an otherwise unadorned shelf on the wall. My father watches silently from where he sits by his table piled high with rolled maps and thick ledgers. I stand to pull the sword down from its perch. I run my hand down the long, graceful length of it, admiring the delicate stitches of pale flowers with their sage-green stems. With one swift motion, I unsheathe it.

If my father has any feelings about his eight-year-old child brandishing a weapon in his study, it does not show on his face. The hilt of the sword is a plain brown leather, which has seen an age. The blade is bitingly sharp. I press the pad of my finger into it and a small bead of blood blooms out of my skin. I watch as it drips down my finger and along my wrist.

"Catarina, did you know," my father starts, not seeming to notice the tiny rivulet of red running down my arm. He is sitting with his legs curled under his thick robes. A gentle snow is falling outside. Fat snowflakes brush up against the glass panes of the great window beside us. He touches the blade, then slides a hand across my shoulders.

"When I was a boy—before my own days as a warrior—my grandfather told me the story of this sword. It once belonged to a demon general slain in battle by our ancestors long ago. A great and terrible war it was." Sensing a story, I snap my head up to look at him. I point at a painting that hangs above the fireplace.

"A demon like those?" I ask. The painting is brittle with age and shows a flickering scene of bloody, brutal war. Humans and tall, horned creatures clash in a hurricane of toiling bodies. Blades meet claws and arrows meet fangs. The demons each have a pair of wide, feathered wings, all in various stages of injury throughout the canvas. Fittingly, it is painted in thick crusts of dried oils, all shades of dry red and mauve and unfathomably dark black hues. Just underneath the canvas sits a tiny gold inscription, which reads *Cheusnys Battle* and is screwed into the frame. It is so large a canvas it seems to crouch menacingly on the wall rather than hang from it.

"Yes. A demon like those," my father replies. We sit in silence. I thought he might tell me more, but he only stares at the sword in my hands and pats my head like a father does.

"If you're so interested in all this history, you can ask your aunt Iesso. She seems lonely these days," Father says. I nod absentmindedly; I'm only half-listening. I don't understand why my father keeps that painting there, forever watching over all who stepped into the study with the terror-filled eyes of the humans and the glowing ones of the demons. If we'd had such a horrible time during the war, why did he want to look at a painting of it in the room where he spent the most time?

"Are they bad?" I ask.

"Hm?" he asks. He has been looking at the painting and even now, doesn't take his eyes off it.

"Are demons evil creatures, Father?" I repeat, more confidently than before.

"Yes." A wrinkle puckers his forehead now. I wonder if I have made him angry. The moment passes and eventually he is smiling again. "Pray you'll never meet one, Cat."

I look back at the painting. Flashing teeth and lashing tails and hateful eyes—the winged demons are lunging toward the cowering humans with such force, I think maybe someone not pictured in the canvas has thrown them.

"Do you think they know they're evil?" I ask. Father is silent again. The furrowed brow returns.

"I suppose it's a matter of perspective. Why do you ask?"

First, I panic. My father has never asked me a question before with that look on his face, and I wonder if I have said something wrong. Maybe I missed something in my history lessons with Aunt Iesso and my father meant to test me. Maybe I have asked something only adults should ever wonder. *Why do you ask?* His question fills me with a thousand emotions. I don't recognize a single one of them.

"What if they're like people? What if they're like us?"

I can see his mouth moving quietly as if practicing what he is about to say. The playful mood I was in has changed, and I suspect so has his. Another unfamiliar feeling spears me, though. It's like a kind of joy at the thought that something I have said could surprise a man like Father, who I thought knew everything. Then I feel guilty for feeling this kind of glee.

"You can't say that, Cat," he says in a hushed but harsh voice. "They're not like us. You know that."

My gaze finds the painting once again. "But, what if—"

"No," he says firmly. It all spills from him again in a desperate burst. "No, no, *no*." His wide hands plant down on my shoulders to shake me. It surprises me enough that my neck has no time to prepare and snaps sharply back with the movement. *What's wrong with you?* his eyes seem to beg. But the words he decides upon are different.

"Demons are nothing like humans, Cat. They don't have hearts," he says.

"Oh."

There is a silence between us that makes me squirm. I do not know how a creature could live without a heart, and the question is so big that it tires me.

"I think I'd like to fly, too," I say suddenly. He laughs, the sound squeaky from relief. I pretend I don't notice.

"Then fly you shall, my darling." His broad hands wrap tightly around my waist as he lifts me into the air. I laugh, and then I am thrusting my hands out to mimic the wings of the demons in the painting and my father is spinning and I ask no more questions about the painting watching us from the wall.

That night, a thunderstorm rages outside my window and rips hard at the trees beyond the castle. Rain pours down in sheets and pounds against the roof. I squeeze my eyes shut and press myself farther into the warmth of my bed, hoping to force silence around me. Finally, I sit up in frustration, slowly slide off my bed, and leave my room to wander.

The hallways of Saelmere Castle are tall, cold, and empty. The candles were blown out by the servants long ago. I can't even smell their smoke anymore. My bare feet tap quietly against the glossy wooden floor, and my blush-pink nightgown swishes around my ankles as I swing my arms around myself. I hum a tuneless melody. I've always enjoyed solitude. While some people thrive off of human touch and human interactions and humans in general, I am most at ease knowing that alone, nobody will know if I make a mistake. Nobody can find fault with my appearance, or personality, or abilities, as if I'm a prized racehorse ready for auction. I was born knowing myself, my aunt Iesso always says. I am told I came out of the womb as a solemn babe, crying only when touched and sleeping through the quiet hours of the night without waking.

I run my fingers down the twisting rails as I pad down the stairs. The path to the kitchen is muscle memory after walking it so often growing up. Even at this hour, a warm, comforting light spills out of the open doorway. The smell of something sweet baking in the oven greets me as I step over the threshold. A maid is taking a large pie from the masonry oven. She might be the only other person awake in the entire castle. She gasps when she finally sees me.

"Lady Catarina," she says, dipping her head. "Should you not be in bed?"

Her voice is not chiding, instead, full of warmth and humor. She smiles gently as she brushes away stray strands of wispy, graying hair. A grin takes over my face. I like the way she calls me *Lady*. It makes me seem far older than I am. Like a grown-up.

My gaze travels to the dessert resting on the table and she laughs at my expression.

"Of course, darling." She cuts me a thick slice of pie and tops it with fresh whipped cream from a pitcher. I cut into the pastry with a fork as she slides a steaming mug of honeyed milk toward me, because I can't resist a bite before I go. Then I carry the rest of my food back up the stairs, walking slowly and carefully to avoid spilling. The hallways are even darker now after spending time in the lighted joy of the kitchen. I reach the open window I like most in the castle and slide down the wall next to it, leaning my head against the cool stone. I am alone and eating sweets and there is nothing else on this cold, snowy night for a child like me to want.

And then a loud creak throws me out of my contented, satisfied haze. Many years later, I'd realize that *this* was when my life began to rot around me. The beginning of the end. Up until this, I had only been a girl with pie in her hands. My heart is fluttering. A cold fear settles into me as I look around for the source of the noise.

My head whips around. A dark figure emerges from the top of the staircase. For a moment, I think it is only my father. I had seen him not hours before, and I wonder if he has returned to finish those stories he half-told. The hope sours when I look closer. Whoever the man is at the top of the stairs, he is not my father. He doesn't belong to this castle at all. He is holding a wickedly serrated knife. The pie in my stomach turns to lead, and I carefully put the plate and mug down so they don't clink. He looks around, doesn't see me, and then starts in the opposite direction of where I'm sitting. I stand while keeping my eyes on his retreating form. He has broad shoulders and wears a black cloak that flares out behind him as he walks. I am having trouble breathing. Maybe he is only a servant or a guard. Maybe I am overreacting. But then he pushes open the door leading to my mother and father's bedroom at the far end of the corridor. The guards who usually flank the doorway are nowhere to be seen. It is just me in my sleeping gown, my silly slice of pie congealing on the windowsill, and the tall shadow of a stranger watching my mother and father sleep. I stand rooted at the spot even as he enters the room.

"Who are you?" My father's voice rings through the silence, as loud and sudden as a violin string snapping mid-note. His voice is strangled and pitched. Hearing him afraid makes me afraid. Immediately, I know. *That man is not a servant*, I think. My vision plunges into blotchy hues of red as the world around me seems to tip, my nails digging into the flesh of my palm. My body sings at the thought of violence even as my mind actively repels it. I sprint wildly down the hall as though every muscle in my little body is screaming at me to do it, even as my eyes well up with tears.

I can barely see the room around the strange man's back, but it looks just like it always does. Except my father is bound by his ankles and wrists on the carpet, unable to move except to follow the man's knife with his eyes. The man stands above a tall woman in a white sleeping gown, her hair loose around her shoulders, and he holds a knife to her throat as she trembles on the floor. My mother. Her eyes are wild, and when she sees me stumble into the doorway, she shakes her head furiously. Her eyes beg me to leave. But I don't. The man turns to look at me, and as soon as my eyes meet his, as soon as I see the cold, dark *nothing* that lies there, I know that he will not hesitate to kill every single one of us.

Then I know nothing at all. I stop thinking. I lunge to grab my father's sword from where it rests on the dresser. The strange man reacts to my movement and tries to grab my arm, but I am faster. In one fluid motion, I twist and drive the sword clean through his chest. The point of the blade spears through him and comes out the other side with a wet, sickening sound. I am surprised by how long a second of pure, horrified silence can feel as all four of us in the room stare at the man's chest. My mother and father's faces are shapeless moons in the corner of my vision. I only see the hilt of the sword in my hand and hear the garbled strain of the man as he tries to say something.

His mouth opens and closes but he says nothing, only stares at me, wide-eyed. He falls beside the bed. His mouth stays open as he dies. All this time, my mother and father say nothing. I would remember this later and realize how strange that was, but for now, I am grateful for the silence. I wrench the bloody sword out of him and saw at the ropes tying my father down until he pulls his hands out from underneath him. Once he cuts my mother free, she crawls desperately to me and holds me tight in her arms. I can feel her shallow, shuddering breath against my neck. She doesn't let me go until the sun rises: a bright, golden ball cutting through the terrors of the night. But as I feel her tears slide down her cheeks and onto my own, I still feel no fear, no shock. That feeling of the blade sliding through his flesh has burned itself into my memory and I refuse to think about anything else. I think only of the sensation of breaking through his back. I reimagine the look on his face as he realizes how close the hilt is to his stomach. The image of his death trapped in that wide scream sits on my eyelids and I see it every time I close my eyes.

How final his death was. How *satisfying.* A slow smile stretches across my face.

TONTIN

The queen is an absolute wreck. She looks like a ghastly quilt of shredded thoughts, sewn sloppily together with fraying thread. She rocks back and forth in the armchair before me, glossy nails plunged into the roots of her hair.

"Someone needs to help her," she murmurs, so quietly that it could've been my imagination.

"Hm?"

"There's . . . no." The queen is stammering as she thinks out loud. "This is good. *Good.* Shows strong character."

Instantly, I am more cautious.

"What happened?" My voice is carefully neutral, something I've mastered after years and years of mollifying the queen's fits of rage or despair. News of the assassin had seared through Pheorirya as quickly and fiercely as a wildfire. Although it'd been a week since the incident, there was no soothing the queen. There had been plenty of assassination attempts before. The royal family had recovered quickly enough from those. So why was this one different?

"Nothing." Her back straightens suddenly, one slender hand coming up to wipe away the twin trails of wetness coming from the corners of her eyes. "I want you to train her for her Embracing ceremony. Catarina, I mean. I can tell her gift is very strong, Tontin. I trust you."

"How do you know such things? Has her gift begun to show?" I ask. I don't acknowledge the subject change because I know the queen will be angry if I persist. I hadn't seen any sign of a gift when I briefly caught a glimpse of the Princess herself this week, but perhaps the queen had seen something I hadn't. Considering how unusual it is for a girl of Catarina's age to not have even a flicker of the royal magic that runs through the veins of the monarch and his family, I assume the queen's nervous manner is a result of an encounter with her daughter.

"No. She's always just been a powerful girl, you know that."

Powerful is one word for it. Many of the servants would prefer to use another word. I have heard them whispering in the halls even when I am in full prophet garb. They know better than to let royal gossip befall the ears of a member of court and yet it doesn't stop them. The queen tries for a smile, and while her efforts are applaudable, I only shake my head.

"Simone, what has happened? What has shaken you about this assassination attempt that others have not?" I ask. This time I am not smiling. I am her Royal Council and I need to know.

"Nothing!" she repeats, more harshly than before. "I don't know what you're talking about."

I let out a sigh, bracing my hands on my knees before pushing myself out of my armchair.

"I don't want to train her," I say. If she won't tell me, I'm guessing it is because the news is dangerous somehow. Royalty forgets that avoiding a risk usually means someone like me taking it instead.

"What?" Her head jerks up and her eyes are slits.

"Ask your sister. She needs work."

"Iesso?" The queen looks up at me. She is as doe-eyed as she was in her youth. A dangerous contrast to her true nature.

"Yes. Iesso. It'll be good for her. Iesso is gentle. She can soften Catarina."

Falling into this familiar banter seems to calm the queen, just as I'd known it would. I laugh internally. Decades upon decades of being constantly surrounded by the Winyr family has made it impossible to not know their nuances by heart.

"I'll ask her later," I say. She hesitates, then nods and briefly places a hand on my arm.

"Thank you, Tontin. Like I said, I trust you." The queen's voice still shakes, but it seems as if she's calmed a little. I slip out of the room silently and close the door behind me. The weight of the queen's words bears down suddenly and heavily upon my shoulders the instant the door shuts between us. She'd said that Catarina's gift was strong, but how could it be strong when it was nonexistent? Gifts—the elemental powers that all royals would eventually develop, usually by the time they could walk—were always revealed to the public on their coronation days. And yet, despite Catarina already being eight years of age, there is still no sign of her gift. Quite contradictory to her parents, as both often boast that they'd been blessed with their gifts from birth.

I stroll down a long hallway with my hands clasped behind my back. I let out a weary breath and roll back my shoulders. The Queen of Pheorirya isn't one for dramatics nor exaggerated stories. Something had clearly happened. But why had she been so hesitant to tell me? That is the reason my heart refuses to settle. *Queen Simone tells me everything.*

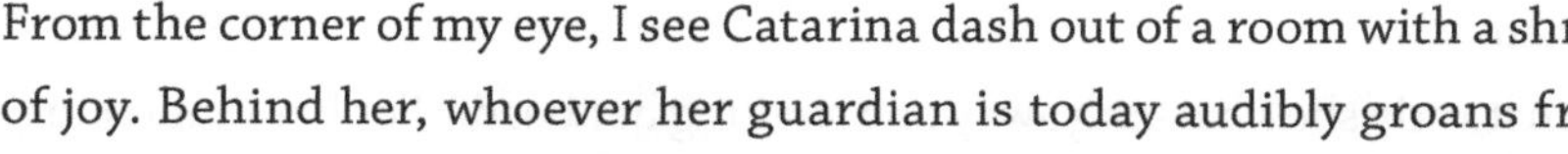

From the corner of my eye, I see Catarina dash out of a room with a shriek of joy. Behind her, whoever her guardian is today audibly groans from inside the room and runs through the door shortly after to chase the small slip of a girl.

"Catarina!" the woman, who I now see is Iesso, calls. The two turn into a corner, both laughing now. They have similar wide, happy smiles. The blood relation is strong in the Winyr line. I watch them carefully, especially the girl. She seems completely normal. A happy, carefree child. So why was the queen so distressed? Several moments later, Iesso returns around the corner with a defeated look on her face and her hair loose around her ears. She shrugs sheepishly at me as she passes by, and I suddenly whirl, remembering what the queen had told me.

"Have you seen signs of Catarina's gift?"

She shakes her head.

"No. But her tutors say she'll develop one before long. They claim she's a passionate girl."

Her words, while undoubtedly meant to be reassuring, worry me instead. *Passionate? What could that mean?*

"Do you know what happened? With the last assassination attempt?"

"No," she replies. "But I know how distraught my sister was." She peers at me, clearly trying to see if I have any information of my own. Iesso and I share a similar subtle language for dealing with royalty, though she herself is one. We both like to talk in code.

"Quite unusual for her character, no?" she asks.

"I agree."

"I'm more than slightly concerned. Do you think it could've involved extortion?"

I hadn't even considered that possibility, but instinct reminds me that it was something far more personal. The queen has been through enough to become unaffected in the face of a threat.

"Perhaps. I actually spoke with her just now," I say, brushing my fears away and pasting a smile on my face. "She wants you to begin training Catarina."

Instantly she's backing away and shaking her head. "For her Embracing? Tontin, you know I can't do that."

"Why not?" Of course, I know her answer already, but it's habitual to ask anyway.

"My own gift could hardly be considered strong. I'm not qualified. Why don't you do it?"

I sigh softly to myself. "Do you really think a girl as spritely as Catarina could tolerate being mentored by a man as old as I?"

She doesn't laugh, and my own slight smile fades. "I'm worried about her." She says it so quietly, maybe she meant for me not to hear.

"Why?" I ask. *Has she noticed the same things as I?*

"Sometimes she doesn't act like children her age. She doesn't like the things she should."

"What do you mean?"

She shakes her head. "I don't know. Do you know the story of Keres and Merikh?"

"Of course." It seems irrelevant to mention an old wives tale, but I humor Iesso.

"I remember there was one particular instance when I was trying to tell it to her. Every child I've ever met loves hearing it over and over again." She smiles faintly. "Maybe it's something about how pretty it sounds to be a princess made out of stars. The children find it charming. But Catarina took no interest in any of it." She shakes her head. "It's a stupid example. But it's just that instead, she wanted to know about demons. She wanted to know what they did to be hated by humans so much. Tontin, the things she says . . ."

"Are you insinuating something?"

"No, not necessarily. Maybe it's only curiosity driving her. It's silly. I don't know why I mentioned it."

But Iesso's eyes are wary, and my I begin to feel heavy with the possibilities of what she is saying. Suddenly, Catarina sticks her head out from behind the corner, thrusts her tongue out at Iesso, and disappears again with a laugh. Iesso looks at me. She doesn't speak, but her eyes say everything. Dread overwhelms me, making me light-headed and dizzy. Is there more to Catarina's mischievousness than just the games of a growing child?

PART ONE

THE DEVIL IS A GENTLEMAN

CHAPTER ONE
CATARINA

My mother and I match each other stride-for-stride as we glide down the long hallways of Saelmere Castle. The velvety, sparkling fabric of her scarlet gown brushes against my own and makes small *shushing* sounds with each step. Two guards walk several paces ahead of us, holding up a man hanging limp between them. The man wears nothing but a tattered gray shirt that hangs down to his knees. His black hair is damp and glossy with sweat. Grime coats every inch of him. I can smell the urine that soaks him, even from afar. My mother's cold, dark eyes meet mine, and I know better than to search for a smile from her. She hasn't smiled at me in years—not counting half-winces during important dinners and family reunions.

My expression sours. What about my father? He'd always been more affectionate with me. Why doesn't he smile at me anymore, either? Father is the warmest king to grace Pheorirya in an age, and I, his own daughter, cannot remember what it's like to hear him laugh. I dig through my recent memories, scrounging for the last time we'd been happy as a family. I love them in a way that feels more like respect—respect for the power and gravity they hold upon their subjects and respect for the physical strength they possess.

"Where are we going, Mother?" I ask, shaking the thoughts away. In the several seconds I've been lost in my own head, she's somehow already several feet in front of me. I can only see a sliver of her cheek, even when I double my pace.

My mother is beautiful. Her long, brown hair is hanging loose today and almost touches her waist. Every single one of her features is sharp and flawless. She has small, tense lips slashed with red, high cheekbones and a delicate nose. Her heavy gold crown sits atop her head and the lustrous metal catches the light. My father has always said I am an exact replica of her, but I cannot imagine myself looking anything like the cunning, sharp-witted blade that is the Queen of Saelmere.

"Treacherous actions do not go without punishment," she tells me. It is an infuriating response to my question, but soon I see for myself. As we turn the corner, we nearly collide with the men we have been following. The guards in front of us swing into my mother's throne room and drag the prisoner with them. We follow suit.

There is a crowd already gathered in the gold-gilded room. They all wear unusual fabrics on their bodies and gleaming diamonds on their hands. The women laugh and flutter their long eyelashes. They peer out from behind great, feathered fans and shift their sheer, gossamer gowns to reveal as much skin as possible, then giggle in false surprise when they finally acknowledge their exposed legs as if they hadn't been the ones to expose them in the first place. I roll my eyes. The men, on the other hand, exchange swords and daggers and talk about their prices. They are all much louder than they mean to be. The patricians of Pheorirya are a horde of royal well-to-dos who seem to spend more time lying about my castle than I do. I cannot stand any one of them. They whisper conspiratorially amongst one another now, talking of the latest woman who'd left her unfaithful spouse or of a man who had challenged another to a duel. They've all paid to witness this event my mother has rushed us to, whatever it is.

"Queen Simone has arrived," a servant announces.

Instantly, every pair of eyes snaps to me and my mother. A sense of pride overcomes me as I watch their laughter-filled faces slowly sober into expressions of awe and respect. But mostly fear. The several bolder noblewomen who eye my dress to carefully hunt for rips or spills don't go unnoticed, and I shoot them the coldest glare I can muster. My dishevelment, whenever present, has always been a favorite topic among the elite. My mother addresses none of them. Instead, she fixes her gaze straight ahead.

"Release him," she says to the guards still holding the man.

The guards throw the man and he falls face-first onto the floor with a grunt. A murmur of excitement flickers through the crowd. His wrists are handcuffed with iron shackles. My mother rolls up her chiffon sleeves, then pulls something out from under her gown. A whip. Its serrated edges gleam in the candlelight. The man on the ground lets out a terrified moan. Liquid trickles down his leg, pools on the ground, and strengthens the vile smell wafting from him. The crowd jeers and laughs with delight while pointing and shouting and calling out. My mother does nothing but stare down at him with disgust.

"Twenty lashings." She decides quietly. "Take the pain with grace, with dignity. It is the least you can do."

The look in his eyes changes from undiluted fear to defiance. He glares up through damp lashes and spits at her. The shiny, wet glob of liquid lands directly on the hem of her gown. The room inhales in a collective gasp. The onlookers shift forward in unison and their faces gleam with sick anticipation. My mother says nothing, but her lips press together and sparks fly from within the depths of her gaze. She draws her slender arm back, far behind her, looking elegant even as she prepares to bring the whip down onto the man's bare skin. The whip comes down with lightning speed and a sickening, sharp crack.

His screams fill the room, complemented by the jeers and hoots of the crowd watching. I see flashes of gold and silver being passed around as people bet on how long they think he'll stay conscious.

"It'll only be a couple more seconds now," a man near me whispers as he slips a coin into the hand of his friend. Neither of them looks away from the beating my mother is delivering.

Blood splatters everywhere and stains the marble floor red. My mother does it all emotionlessly; her expression remains the same even when the bloodied man beneath her pleads and begs for mercy. When she's done, she gestures for the guards to drag him away. Some whisper about my mother's insistence that she always be the one to brandish the whip. Others speculate that that is why she always wears red to these lashings. Already, she is bored. I avoid looking at the man's ruined, bloodied back. The crowd waves their fists, shouting insults at the man, who is now curled up on the ground. But they are not even angry. They are merely entertained, and their enthusiasm is fueled by the cheers and shrieks of those around them. I almost feel bad.

"What did he do?" I ask my mother as she wipes the blood off her whip and hands it to a servant.

"He was caught communicating with demons." She rolls down her flowing sleeves, brushing away any specks of blood and not meeting my eye.

"What exactly are demons?"

"Vile, evil creatures."

"Why didn't you kill him?" I dare to pry.

"He will feel more pain if he is left alive."

"But—"

"Stop, Catarina. I am not in the mood to discuss these matters."

I tilt my head, watching her as she leaves. Violence has never left me unsettled because it is always all around me here at Saelmere Castle. A fact of life. But this instance, and my mother's eagerness to flee the scene—to flee from *me*—disturbs me.

Later that day, when all the aristocrats have left for their fancy manors and my mother has gone off to clean the blood from her hands, I creep back into the throne room. The man is still there, shivering and shaking. Heavy chains are locked around his ankles and wrists, bitingly tight, and the other end of them tether him to the wall. I doubt he has the energy to escape even without those constraints. His back is oozing a yellowish pus. I swallow my sick. His spine is a wasteland of torn skin and bruises.

"What do you want, girl?" he asks bitterly. "Have you come to mock me? Have you come to remind me how much of a traitorous fool I am?"

"No. I'd only like to know your name." I now realize that he is young, only fifteen. Three years younger than I. Not a man, but a mere boy. From afar, he'd looked much, much older.

"My name is Cam."

"My mother says you were contacting demons."

"Yes. Yes, I was."

"Why?"

"I guess I was curious."

I tilt my head. I can sympathize with that. "Where do these demons even live?"

"If I tell you, I shall be in even greater trouble."

I frown. And then I stare deep into his eyes. He stares back, unflinching. His eyes are an odd shade of green that stands out starkly against his dark hair, filled with such a defiant light that I can hardly bear to look into them. His cheeks are hollow, his skin ashen, and blood trickles down his back and onto the floor in a persistent rhythm. Yet he still finds the strength to be defiant, and that is another thing I can respect.

"Where are you from, Cam?"

His piercing gaze sweeps over me, reading every plane of my face and every twitch of my muscles. I allow my mind to relax and school my features into cold neutrality to avoid giving him even an ounce of insight.

"I live in Tegak," he says finally. I vaguely remember the name from my studies. A city of snow and ice to the north of my city, Pheorirya.

"Well, Cam of Tegak, today is your lucky day."

"What?"

He does not yet realize his fate, I think. Blind, unsuspecting fool. I almost laugh. The dagger I'd hidden in my sleeve slides into my palm. I grip the worn leather hilt, smiling. Only then do his eyes widen, and his legs propel him backward.

"I am doing you a great favor," I whisper. Then I lunge at him to plunge the dagger into his throat. His eyes widen and he tries to scream, but blood bubbles from his mouth and trickles down his chin. I turn the blade. I don't know what it is in his neck that snaps, but the sound is loud and stark against the prison cell walls. He falls to the ground. I straddle his chest, smiling down at him as he chokes and gags and finally drowns in his own blood. The defiance in his eyes finally fades. I do not know how long I stay in the throne room, sitting on the body, but I do know I am smiling all the while as I gaze at what remains of Cam.

That night, I dream of complete and utter darkness. I look around, bewildered, but everywhere I turn, there is only black. The blackness pulls me in and pushes me away at the same time. I wander about, panic slowly beginning to build in my chest with unyielding pressure, but there is no end to my pitch-dark surroundings. The panic finally overtakes me. I open my mouth to scream for help, but nothing comes out. The dark is devoid of all sound and light. There's a pounding in my head, growing and growing, and I press my fists to my temples as if that'd make the pain go away. Nausea hits me in relentless waves, and I try to scream again. Nothing happens. I'm voiceless.

Suddenly, everything stops. The pain in my head goes away and I hear a rhythmic noise in the distance. Eventually, I can make out words. *Catarina, Catarina, Catarina.* The voice chants my name at me, suddenly all around me, filling up the deep dark emptiness. It's as if two people are speaking at once: one with a lilting, sweet voice, and one with a voice like the ear-splintering screech of nails scraping across glass. I press my hands to my ears, screaming for it to stop, for everything to go away, but once again my voice is lost in the void. *You are destined for great, great things.*

"What?" My voice is nothing more than a hoarse whisper. "Please, just leave me alone."

I know the creature—whatever the hell it is—understands because it lets out a laugh. The sound is all wrong, hollow and empty in my ears. *Why settle for less when you can have more?*

"What do you mean?"

You killed a man a decade ago. You killed another only hours ago. Do you know what that means, Catarina?

"No!" I cry. "I don't. I don't know what you want." Despite everything, the creature's words make me realize it never occurred to me to think about *why* I killed. I had only done it to feel the same joy I felt the first time, when I saved my mother and father. And now, it feels as if this voice *knows* me . . . in a sick, twisted way, too intimate for comfort.

You. Are. Destined. To. Kill.

Each of the monster's words is accentuated with a sharp sound I distinctly recognize as steel scraping across steel. It releases another wicked, cruel laugh, and the sound cuts off as my eyes finally open.

I am back in my bedroom in Saelmere Castle. Most importantly, I am safe. An awful combination of sweat and tears runs down my cheeks, and I let a wild sob out into the dark of my bedroom.

CHAPTER TWO
IESSO

"TELL ME WHY our gifts were made possible."

The young woman sitting before me is the epitome of careless arrogance, her head rolled back and legs splayed out at her wooden desk. She ignores my request and my teeth clench. Even though Catarina has long since grown out of the clumsy naiveté of youth, there are some things about her that have retained a child-like quality. Her tendency toward devastating boredom, for example.

"Catarina," I say, and her head lolls to face me.

"Hm?"

"Where did our gifts come from?"

"Witches."

"What did they do?" I feel as if I am speaking to a three-year-old, only able to coax out one-word answers. Tontin, who sits in the corner silently, catches my eye and flashes me a reassuring smile.

"They saved us from demons."

"How?"

"They cast a spell to grant the elites of our society magic."

"Good. Why?" I close my eyes, finding that it helps.

"To make sure a portion of the human population had the strength to fight away demons. So that we wouldn't die out." She looks as if she's physically restraining herself from adding something obnoxious.

"Exactly. Now tell me about Keres and Merikh."

Catarina rolls her eyes, just as I'd predicted she would.

"In what scenario would I need to recite a myth to my subjects?"

I blink but do not respond to the way she says *my subjects*. That is new. She used to just say *people*. I let loose a heavy sigh. "Catarina. Please."

"I genuinely don't understand."

"It isn't about memorization. It's about understanding our history and our magic so you can rule with wisdom when you become queen. How much of a fool will you look when you cannot recite the basics of our storied past?"

She heaves a sigh that puts mine to shame. "Keres and Merikh are two women rumored to be goddesses who fell from the sky and took over the southernmost area of Guinyth a thousand years ago. They had powers more potent than anyone had seen before, even though very few people witnessed these powers first-hand."

I smile at her.

"You're good at this," I say. She folds her arms over her chest as if I've insulted her, but I see a small quirk at the corner of her mouth. Catarina is pleased, if reluctantly.

"Are you nervous about the Embracing?" I ask.

Her eyes instantly narrow and she looks at me with an expression of something comparable to disgust on her face. Her emotions are always so quick to change.

"I know myself, Iesso. My gift will be stronger than anything Pheorirya has seen before," she says forcefully, like she's spitting each word out of her mouth.

"Even stronger than your mother's?" I ask wryly, hoping and praying that she's only kidding.

But she stares at me stonily. "Yes. Even stronger than my mother's."

"How can you be so sure of this?" I ask her, laughing, still trying to keep my tone light-hearted.

She frowns at me. "I can't imagine anything else."

"What do you mean?"

"I feel as if I'm destined for something greater." She gestures at me. "I don't need to know anything you're talking about. I already know I'll succeed."

I search desperately for any sign of playful humor, but none flickers in her eyes, and the affection I'd felt toward her dissipates instantly. Once again, Tontin's gaze meets mine, and I widen my eyes at him despairingly. He can't seem to offer any comfort this time.

"Can you demonstrate your gift?" he asks suddenly, eyes trained on her. "If you're so confident."

The shift in her demeanor is instantaneous. She stiffens, then turns to face the prophet. "I'm sorry?"

"Show us your flame, Catarina."

Her eyebrows furrow, eyes narrowing. Several moments pass before she lifts her arms into the air, stretches, and then stands.

"I'm going to find something to eat."

Her familiar confidence has returned. It's as if Tontin hadn't said anything at all. But when I watch him observe her walk out of the room, I know that his concerns match my own.

"Her Embracing is soon," I whisper as soon as I know she's out of earshot.

"I know," he replies, just as quietly.

"What does this mean?" I ask. "Is she just unwilling to show us? Or could it be that she truly does not have a gift yet?"

"I have faith in her," he says. I try to read the expression on his face. His gaze flits down. "But maybe I'm not letting myself consider the possibility that Catarina might be giftless." I shiver. He'd said exactly what I'd been thinking. My mind rejects the thought of it too. I can hardly imagine what Catarina being giftless would do to the kingdom.

"Simone wouldn't have it," I whisper to myself. "She wouldn't accept it."

"Has she truly been lying to us this entire time?" he interjects. At the look on my face, he presses the back of his hand against his forehead, eyes fluttering shut. “How could I have let this happen?”

CHAPTER THREE
CATARINA

A SERVANT SWIFTLY BRAIDS my hair, twisting the long, dark-brown locks into a graceful swirl against my head. Her touch is gentle. I sigh softly and close my eyes.

"Don't slouch, Cat." Iesso's wary voice cuts into my brief moment of peace, but a smug hint of pride bursts within me as I register the way she approaches with timid caution. I have always liked when adults look at me like I could hurt them. It makes me feel respected. Feared.

I sit in a chair pushed in front of a mirror in my bathroom, a ridiculous array of powders and pigments arranged before me on the surface of the vanity. I can sense Iesso's fingertips resting on the chair, just beside my right shoulder, and I shift to position myself a millimeter away from her. I can hear the candles surrounding us crackling with their faint warmth, and the trees sway with gentle autumn winds just outside the window above me.

My mother has pounded that into me since I was but a young child. "Observe your surroundings, Catarina," she often said. "Do not let a single detail go unnoticed." And not one does.

The servant puts a hand on my shoulder. "Stand up, my lady."

I slowly rise from the chair as if any slight movement would ruin my carefully done hair. She slips into my closet and returns with my gown. It's stunning: a graceful black embroidered dress with red rubies designed to look like flames dancing up the waist. The fabric flows down my legs and to the floor. A long train of delicate black lace trails behind me. She pulls a corset over my head and tightens the strings to hold it in place. I stare at myself in the full-length mirror propped against the wall. I hardly look like myself. The fabric of the gown hugs my every curve and makes me seem taller than I am. The servant has caked my cheeks with white powder, covering up the bags under my eyes. Dramatic black eyeliner flares near my temple. I smile to myself. Beautiful, I look beautiful.

The servant places a shimmering diamond circlet on my head. The round diamonds catch the light of the candles that surround me as I tilt my head to admire myself in the mirror. When I am accepted as the new queen, the circlet will be replaced with the crown my mother wears now. The servant coughs from behind me. She bows quickly and the fabric of her gray, shapeless dress swishes as she hurries away.

"Come, Catarina. The ceremony will be starting soon." Iesso wraps her long, pale fingers around my arm. The older I've grown, the more I've begun to resent her eternal presence in my life. It is nearly suffocating. But I smile when I realize that soon, she and her endless *tutoring* will be something of the past. I will learn only what I like when I am queen.

My feet tap softly against the pale marble floor. I count the steps I take. *Three hundred fifty-two.* I count the shallow breaths that leave my lips. *One hundred seventy-three.*

It seems as if everyone in the whole of Guinyth is in the courtroom of Saelmere Castle, but of course, there are only a handful of court members. Their wide, frilly gowns and long trench coats are ornate enough to make me dizzy. I can barely stand to look at them, but I want to be sure they all see me. I stare them all down, donning the mask of cold, unbothered detachment I've worn enough times to have it become muscle memory. They avert their eyes. A small flicker of pride ignites in my chest before dying away. I truly am my mother's daughter.

A long wooden table full of food sits off to the side, waiting to be feasted on. My stomach rumbles at the sight of the roasted chicken, round potatoes, and flutes of sparkling champagne. The chatter dies as soon as Iesso and I enter the room. My attention drifts from the food to the cleared path before me. My vision narrows and my breathing goes dangerously calm as I meet the gaze of Prophet Tontin. He stands at the altar at the very end of the room. My mentor gives me a squeeze and a reassuring smile before going to stand beside her sister, my mother. I do not return the gesture. Slowly, I walk forward, one foot in front of the other. In that moment, even with the burning gazes of a hundred people all turned on me, my cheeks stay cool and my steps steady.

I am unafraid.

We join my father, King Kairos, who already stands at the throne. Prophet Tontin stands beside him with a huge, tattered book in his hands. The five of us turn to face the people from where we stand on the marble platform in the center of the room, and I hold my head high. Soon, I will hold power over every single person in this city.

I am unafraid.

"Show us your gift," Tontin says, his powerful voice booming through the room.

My hands are steady as I slowly lift them into the air, spreading my fingers wide and throwing my head back. A low murmur ripples through the crowd and I smile. I imagine hands plunging into the depths of my consciousness, peeling back the layers of everything I am until they finally reach my core and pull my glowing gift to the surface. This is the gift that every single person with royal blood flowing through their veins possesses.

My mother has always described her gift as an ever-burning inferno in her chest. My father's gift is more a raging storm straining to be released, but no matter the person, their gift is embedded into the very material of their soul. It is a part of them, and flows with their aura. I strain, searching for the emanating warmth that my mother and father have always spoken of. But those fictitious, intangible hands searching inside me find nothing.

They move faster and more desperately now, and still, there is no special bud, no flower of light. In the throne room, I become aware of the passive noises of the living bodies around me. Sniffing, breathing, a few scratches or scuttles here and there. One person sneezes. Humiliating.

No, there truly is nothing. I squeeze my eyes shut. The silence is deafening, and the precise calm I'd forced upon my mind is breaking. My eyes finally open, and I find the prophet staring at me, his forehead wrinkled with concern and his milky blue eyes slightly narrowed with an expression I can't seem to place my finger on. The crowd's murmuring changes both in tone and volume and the bumbling prophet scrambles for words.

"Lady Catarina, please summon your gift now," Tontin says.

My mother pinches me just below my ribs. Even through the suffocating corset, her fingers hurt me.

"Hurry," she whispers, so only I can hear. "Look for it!"

Fear washes over me in overwhelming waves. I dive deeper into myself, searching every crevice, every hollow of my soul. The utter lack of anything seems to mock me. *Worthless, worthless, worthless,* it chants. My eyes fly open for the second time, at the exact moment Tontin clears his throat. No one speaks. I stare into the eyes of citizens I'd looked down upon with such contempt only minutes before. Now, it is their turn to be disgusted.

It suddenly seems as if every single one of my actions leading up to this point have been nothing but foolish acts to disguise how weak I truly am on the inside. But even as my cheeks burn hot and red, and my heart thumps so harshly in my chest that I fear I'll explode, I feel no shame. I feel only anger, not at myself, but at the people around me. Their once hopeful gazes are full of disbelief, disappointment, contempt. They make me feel frivolous. The muttering reaches a peak, and the prophet finally composes himself.

"Do you, the citizens of Pheorirya, take Lady Catarina Winyr, daughter of Simone Endrdyn and Kairos Winyr, to be your true and rightful queen?"

There is an oppressive silence now, harshly contrasting the beat of blood pounding through my head.

"Of course not!" a single person shouts, and whispers break out in the room once again. They taunt me. A few light chuckles for the benefit of the person who broke the silence is soon overshadowed by a whispering wave of commentary. The more they look at me and then at one another, the bolder they get. I see a few smiles behind hand fans and fingers, then outright laughter as the crowd begins to animate.

Why? I want to scream. *Bow down before your queen.* Obey *me.* But then they throw small stones and rotten fruit and insults, and my mother turns to her guards. Her eyes are uncharacteristically wild.

"Get them out!" she shrills.

The guards scramble into action and herd everyone out of the courtroom with their swords drawn. I can still hear their barbed words even after the guards slam the doors shut.

I am silent while my mother continues berating the guards for not moving quicker. It is only when I hear footsteps behind me that I turn around and look up into the crestfallen face of King Kairos.

"You are a disgrace to the Winyr name," my father says quietly, his gaze fixed at a point somewhere behind me. And although his voice is soft, I hear the hatred behind every word. My heart breaks at the way he doesn't even bother to look at me. He'd always been the kind parent, the gentle parent. Even without the smiles, he had been more generous with his affection than my mother.

"I'm sorry," I whisper. He shakes his head and walks away. My apologies are unheard.

I look desperately at my mother. It is the first time I have seen her truly shaken. Her hair has fallen out of its tight updo and a bead of sweat trickles through the thick layer of powder on her face.

"Get out of my face," she whispers. I would've preferred it if she'd screamed. "Get out of my face, get out of my home, get out of my life." Her clenched fist flares up in flame, and I flinch. Tontin puts a hand on her shoulder.

"Your daughter is still rightfully Queen of Pheorirya, gift or no gift," he says. I think he means to help, but his words only drive the wound deeper in me. She spins around, her hand poised to strike, but catches herself just in time.

"Prophet, the people do not want a giftless ruler." She buries her head in her hands for a moment, moaning softly. "How could my own daughter be so weak? How could a girl born into such power be so powerless? I have given her every opportunity, Tontin." She doesn't even look at me, even as she talks about me.

"There have been giftless rulers in the past, Simone," the prophet soothes. The queen does not hear him.

"The other kingdoms will laugh at us; Catarina will not be able to protect Pheorirya." She laughs, but the sound is so devoid of humor that both the prophet and I shrink away from her.

He shakes his head. "We have no other choice." I know he is right. Who else is there? It would be even more disgraceful for my mother and father to return to their thrones after failing the one, single job that every king and queen is responsible for: bearing an heir capable of protecting their home. Iesso was never suited to be a queen. Even though she is the eldest of her siblings, first in line to the throne, she flat-out refused, which made her younger sister, Simone, queen. *I am what they have been forced to settle for.* I feel something cold, dark, and powerful awaken inside me.

The feast afterward is just as glamorous as it would have been if I had succeeded, except for the lack of conversation. Across the table, I can still see the way my mother shakes with anger. My father has locked himself in his room and refuses to open the door, even for dinner. A servant warily pushes a glass of wine toward me and I pick it up, grateful for any relief the alcohol could bring. Later this week, my mother and father will leave for a manor on the rocky coast of Guinyth, where all kings and queens live after their rule for the rest of their lives. But after tonight, I doubt they will ever want to see me again. Tontin suddenly slides into the seat beside me and grabs my hand.

"Catarina," he whispers. "Relax. I need to try something."

I jerk back, out of his grip. "What?"

"I want to transfer some of my own gift to you."

"*What?*"

"I'm a magician, Catarina. My singular job is to manipulate and bend the laws of magic to my desire; I have the ability to transfer gifts between beings." My eyes widen, and he sighs in frustration. "Have you heard about the legend of the goddess sisters? Keres and Merikh?"

I nod; every royal-born child had been cautioned about them. "Their magic is deep and mysterious. One of their many abilities is to steal someone else's gift for themselves," I say.

"I can do the opposite of that," Tontin says. "I can give you some of my own." He grabs my hands.

"Close your eyes, Catarina."

I obey, a final spark of hope igniting in me. If he can give me a gift, we could lie and say I'd simply been under too much pressure at my Embracing. The citizens would accept me again. His hands heat up around my own, and I let out a small gasp of surprise. It burns like a flame.

"Relax," he orders, and I force my shoulders to loosen. His skin begins to hum. Light beams out of the cracks of our intertwined fingers. The heat becomes more intense and I have to fight the urge to pull away. But the sensation stops almost as soon as it begins. I feel nothing. I feel nothing powerful settling itself in my core, only the warmth of the prophet's hands. And even now, they're slowly beginning to cool. My eyes open, and when I look into his own, they're full of tears. I hate those tears.

"I'm sorry, Catarina." He sounds like he means it, which only infuriates me more. He stands up, releases my hands, and clears his throat. I look up at him with desperation.

"Can't you try again?" I plead. He shakes his head, already beginning to move away.

"I'm sorry," he repeats. "The magic refuses to take hold in you."

That night, a bath awaits me, full of vibrant flower petals and sweetly-scented oils. No servants are there to attend to their new queen. I slide out of the dress I had once felt unstoppable in, shoving it aside with my foot. My crown remains on as I sink into the water, inhaling the hot, misty steam. No tears slide down my cheeks despite the burning in my eyes. My mother's high-pitched shriek seems to echo through the castle. I can hear her through the walls. It was once a useful way to plan my troublemaking as a child, but now the holes in the ancient walls of the castle deliver a conversation I'd give anything not to hear.

"Iesso, how could this be possible? You trained with her for hours a day!"

"Catarina lied to me."

"What?"

Rarely have I ever heard my aunt so angry, but even through countless walls, I can hear the fury in her voice.

"She told me she'd been practicing. She claimed she'd summoned enough flame to rival yours."

Ah. There it is. My deepest, darkest secret laid bare for the world to see. Yet I still feel no guilt. Only anger, aimed at Iesso now. My mother wails louder and louder.

"My lady, calm yourself," a servant says sharply.

"Get off of me!"

I hear glass shattering and a scream.

"Simone, *calm yourself!*" Iesso snaps.

"How am I to calm myself when my only daughter—"

"My lady, it really is getting late." The servant's voice is more forceful now.

"Do not touch me," my mother barks. "Iesso, you will speak to her in the morning. This is ridiculous."

"Simone, this could be for the better. You know your daughter better than anyone else in the world. You know her temper, her attitude. Her potential gift could have spiraled out of control."

There is a long moment of silence.

"For the *better?*" My mother's voice is so loud, her words are barely comprehensible.

"My lady, it's time to go now."

A little later, someone forces the door to my chambers open and I sit up to meet them. My heart is pounding fast. My father storms in, and I am almost knocked from my bed with the sudden gust of wind that he shoves toward me. His gift. Something I've seen a million times over, something that is now a stark reminder of what I could not contrive.

"You are an ignorant, selfish child," he spits out. "Your mother and I have given you anything and everything you wanted for twenty years, and this is how you treat your family? Lying about having a gift? What did I do to deserve this?"

He stumbles to an armchair and collapses into it, tearing at his hair. His eyes are wild and he licks his lips repeatedly. I try to go to his side, but he thrashes his arm out at me.

"Get away from me, you stupid girl."

My hands flutter around helplessly, unsure of what to do.

"No, no. Everything will be fine. I just need to speak with other prophets. I can speak to some witches too. Maybe . . ." He trails off from his rambling and looks up at me. And with no explanation, he gets up and staggers out of the room.

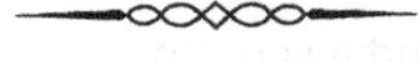

I creep out of my room into a silent hallway. The sun still sleeps and the sky is a drab, slate gray. I am wearing nothing but a thin cotton nightgown, but even the faint rustling sounds of the cloth pound in my ears as I walk. Ignorant selfish child, ignorant selfish child, ignorant selfish child. My father's words are a chorus of hateful whispers in my head and in my heart. I reach the room my parents share. I push the door and it swings open without a sound. They haven't left, yet. Clothes are strewn in every corner of the room, lumps of black amidst the shadows. I drag my hand along the smooth walls, feeling my way through the darkness. I don't dare light a candle for fear I will wake them. My fingers brush against cool, hard metal. I prod farther. My father's blade, the one I'd admired so much as a child. I reach another hand to my left, and I am met with something silken. The bed. I can hear my parents' soft, steady breathing. And then the anger

sparks in me again, brighter and hotter than any flame could possibly be. Never again, I think. Never again will I let someone else make me feel so inferior. My fingers close around the hilt.

Never again will I allow myself to be so weak. I lift the sword.

Never again will I be powerless. And I drive the point of the mighty blade into my parents' hearts, one after the other. Red seeps into their white bedding. They do not have a chance to scream before they drown in their own blood. Just like Cam from Tegak.

The dream feels uncomfortably real. Someone touches my shoulder and I jerk awake. A young, frightened girl stands at my bedside, her brown hair pulled into a tail at the nape of her neck. Not a single hair is out of place, and she stands with her shoulders thrusted back and her back is so stiff that her posture looks almost comical. Her eyes narrow as a soft huff of laughter leaves my lips.

"Your Majesty, my name is Ellanore. I will—"

"Get. Out. I do not require your presence, nor do I want it."

She lets out a tiny, strangled sound, and tears fill her eyes as she whirls and runs out of the room. I massage my temples, then press the heels of my palms into my eyes. *Annoying girl.*

It is too early to be awake and yet the pale sun already glares mockingly at me from its place in the sky. I force myself to slide out of bed and I stumble to my new wardrobe. I open the aging brass doors and fabrics of every color in the rainbow spill out. They are a mess of brilliant blues, vivid amaranthine, and fiery scarlets. All mine. I smile. *My mother's gowns,* I realize. The smooth fabrics still smell like cherry blossoms and spiced pear.

I slide into an emerald gown embroidered with a dragon made of golden thread dancing up the side of it. I pull my hair from its loose braid. I'm struck by how much I suddenly look like my mother, just like my father had always said. Beautiful. My eyes narrow. I'd thought the same thing before my Embracing. Perhaps I only *look* like a queen.

I wander to the washroom and dip my hands into a basin filled with warm water. I splash it all over my face and let out a soft sigh at the sensation. I look up and catch sight of myself in the mirror in front of me. There are dark circles below my eyes, but as I peer closer, something is amiss. My eyes look different somehow. I gaze into them for a long time, searching. Then, there! A tiny black dot in my left eye. The longer I stare at it, the larger it seems to get. A shudder runs down my spine, but I shake away the feeling. Just a speck of dirt.

I crack open the great oak door of Saelmere Castle's meeting room. The room is full of chatter and laughter and good friends exchanging the latest canards of Pheorirya. But as I step into the meeting room, everyone's gaze snaps to me and the room is silent. No one stands to greet me.

"Queen Catarina has arrived," a servant says from beside me. "Bow before Her Majesty." No one moves. My gaze sweeps over them, locking eyes with every single person who laughed at me during my Embracing—every person who *hurt* me. "Bow before Her Majesty," the servant repeats shakily. I can feel his gaze fall upon my back as he stands there, quivering. Still, nobody moves.

Something in me snaps. Within seconds, I've walked the length of the room. My hands lock around the throat of a young woman. She is several inches taller than me, and yet I lift her into the air as if she weighs nothing. She lets out a scream. Her hands clamp down on my arms, frantically pulling, and I can feel her pulse racing beneath my fingertips. I realize just how easy it would be to snuff out the life that beats frantically, desperately there. *If I just squeeze a little harder—*

"Release her!" someone shouts from across the table.

I meet the petrified gazes of everyone at the table, squeezing the woman's throat even harder. "Then bow before your queen."

Every single person surges upward from the table in one singular, fluid motion. Everyone bows. I let go of the woman and she collapses to the floor, her fingers fluttering to her neck. Five deep purple bruises mar her skin. They will not fade for days.

"I'm terribly sorry." I pull a chair out from the table and settle into it, smiling. "I do hope this gathering may proceed without any more interruptions."

There is silence then. Awful silence, but I am patient with them now. *Time is such an odd thing,* I think. *It belongs to everyone. It belongs to no one. And yet it is the most abundant thing in the universe.* I remain sitting perfectly still and smiling serenely, because I know I will not be the one to break first. I can feel the exact moment the frustration and silent fury of everyone else in the room reaches its peak, then boils over into resignation.

"Of course, My Queen." A muscled, tall man stands, his hands curled into tight fists at his sides. His words are clipped, wrestling out through a clenched jaw. "My name is Regan Grimsbane. I am the Head of Weaponry and Defense."

I dip my head in the barest acknowledgment of his words. They go around, introducing themselves. Maritess Riddle, Head of Relations. Ulrich Cromwell, Head of Strategy. General Lilura Tenebris. Their eyes are fearful, darting between me and the woman I'd grabbed. Her eyes are unfocused, and her fingers still hover over the bruises spreading across her skin. I leave the room after I have blissfully eaten every single thing on my plate.

Night is falling, and the sky is a shade of dusty, pale pink. Stars are already starting to peek out from behind the wispy clouds. A servant pulls a thick red cloak over my shoulders as I stride outside.

"Your Majesty," she whispers as she dips her head in a shallow bow.

I dismiss her with a wave of my hand. I slide down the trunk of a tree somewhere in the gardens behind the castle and let my eyes flutter shut. Leaves of brilliant reds and golds swirl around me as they fall from the trees above. The cool air plays with my hair before blowing it across my face. It is peaceful here.

"Your Majesty."

My eyes fly open. I look up. A figure stands above me. I scramble up, dusting off my gown. He wears the simple, brown attire of a servant. But he stands with his back too straight like a military man. His eyes are bright and proud, even as he dips his head in a bow. I look at him closely and wonder if he may not be a servant at all.

"I did not ask for company."

"I was instructed to escort you to dinner, My Queen."

"And I am ordering you to leave me."

"I'm afraid I cannot do that, Your Majesty."

"What is your name, servant?"

"Philan, Your Majesty. Philan Lin."

I can detect no accent in his voice, but he pauses more, thinks about his words more carefully than a native speaker would.

"Well, Philan Lin." I lean closer to him. "Get out of my sight."

He looks at me sideways. "Your Majesty, please follow me."

"I am not obliged to do anything you tell me to do. So, tell my advisors that I will not be dining with them."

Then he laughs. Loudly, with his head thrown back. "What kind of game do you think you're playing, Catarina?"

"What? You address your queen so intimately? Are you in the mood to be flayed?"

Does he not know I can have him burned alive for even looking at me too long? Despite my words, the boy continues.

"Why are you trying so hard to make everyone hate you? What do you gain from this?" Philan asks. I clench my fists and toss a glance past his shoulder, wondering if any guards are close enough to drag him away from me by his hair.

"I don't see how this conversation has anything to do with dinner."

"It has nothing to do with dinner." He agrees. "I'm simply curious." He regards me again. "You truly are fascinating," he says.

"We're done here," I reply.

He laughs again before turning on his heel and leaving without another word.

That night, I toss and turn in my bed. No matter which way I angle myself, the soft, silk covers feel either burning hot or bitterly cold. I squeeze my eyes shut and let out a frustrated groan. I can hear every squeak of the wooden floors below me. I can hear every murmur of the servants around the castle. All the tiny noises blur into one, swirling around my head in endless circles. Then, suddenly, my mind goes blank.

Sit up, my darling.

I sit up, though I don't remember telling my muscles to move.

Get dressed.

I slide out of bed and throw on my cloak. I try to dig my feet into the plush carpeting, but my legs cannot be stopped. A hot, flashing pain streaks through my head, but when I scream, nothing happens. I no longer have control over my body.

Run.

I start running faster than I have ever run before. I clear the halls in seconds, rushing like a spirit past rooms inside which unsuspecting servants sing and clean and shout at each other. I sprint out of the castle and into the stables. It hurts to run this fast. The horses whine nervously at the sight of me, with my flushed cheeks and wild eyes. I am thrilled and terrified by the way they neigh and stomp their feet at me. I swing onto the horse closest to me and slash the ropes tying her in place using only one hand. In this moment I realize I am holding a knife.

We ride hard and fast, and my hair streams out behind me in a long brown ribbon. The night around us is suffocatingly dark, even on the main road out of the castle. It is still achingly cold. Last night's snow still glistens under the moon, but I am going far too fast to appreciate the beauty of the land. I dig my heels into the horse's sides and she snorts. She is going much, *much* faster than any horse should be able to. The part of me that remains myself, suffocated beneath the weight of the voice in my head, attempts to pull back on the reins, but my arms are locked tight.

Several minutes later, a flicker of light catches my attention. It's not far away. My fingers unconsciously tug slightly on the reins, pulling the horse toward the light. I lean forward and strain to see where it's coming from. The horse's fur is slick with sweat and her breathing is ragged, yet she runs as fast as ever. I can now tell that the light is coming from a carriage. I recognize it immediately, gilded with gold and engraved with the royal emblem. It's the carriage my mother and father use.

Suddenly, the horse stops, and I am almost flung off her. Distantly, I am aware that my thighs burn from clenching her body so tightly, and my shoulders ache from being so tense, but I am already sliding to the ground and sprinting toward the carriage.

I slide to the ground and start sprinting toward the carriage. It seems as if my feet hardly touch the cool, dew-covered grass. My arm shoots out and I leap onto the roof of the carriage, carried by a sudden, supernatural burst of strength. I land with a thump that should have shattered my legs on impact, but I am unhurt. The knife reappears in my hand as I crawl to the side of the carriage. I hear a small gasp from inside the carriage and a head sticks out of the window.

Kill them. Kill them both.

"*Catarina?*" my father asks. "What are you doing?" He pauses only to look down at my hands and then adds, ". . . My darling?"

I dive into the carriage. His mouth is open with shock, but he makes no move to stop me. His eyes shine with something like delight. It's a surprised joy to see *me;* the daughter about to murder him. Was his anger at the Embracing forgotten, then? He trusts me so damn much. The space inside the carriage is tight and small, so much so that we are all looking at one another directly in the eyes. Mother and Father look like paper dolls, stuck in their open-mouthed shock.

My mother's hand grabs my own. "Catarina, what are you—" My knife slices through her throat, and she collapses silently. Slowly, I turn to my father.

"Stop the carriage!" he screams to the driver. Every fiber in my body is horrified and begging me to get out of the carriage or to drive the knife into my own chest instead. But then my leg kicks out against my will and my foot catches him squarely in the face. He attempts to sit, but my knife flies out of my hand in a perfect, twisting arc. The knife finds its mark in the hollow of his throat. He slumps down, as dead as my mother, and a violent repulsion shudders through me.

"What's happening back there?" the driver calls, and the carriage slowly shudders to a stop.

He doesn't even have a chance to fight back. I kill the driver just as easily as I'd killed my parents. I toss all three bodies off the side of the road. Their blood smears a dark trail across the grass, but there's nothing I can do about that.

You may go home now, sweet girl. The voice in my head is pleased, and a feeling of pride warms me. Finally someone appreciates me. Finally someone is proud of me.

The horse I'd ridden before has collapsed in the grass, dead from exhaustion. I regard the corpse with an unflinching indifference that scares me. *Is this who I am?* I ask myself. *Yes,* the voice in my head replies without as much as a moment of hesitation. *It is.* With steady, methodical hands, I slice through the harness of one of the horses still tied to the abandoned carriage. He rears up, his eyes wild, but my touch calms him. When I get back to Saelmere Castle, I am finally able to sleep.

The smell emanating from my own body wakes me the next morning and the unbearable itchiness of my skin makes it a painful consciousness. When I open my bleary eyes, it takes me several moments to process the sight before me. I rub my eyes over and over again, mouth gaping open, cold sweat breaking out across my chest. Drying, flaking red-brown stickiness coats the entirety of me and the bedsheets around me. Blood. As soon as I realize this, a bitterly cold wind seems to sweep through the room and prickles uncomfortably at my skin. The feeling is oddly familiar. My vision goes dark again.

You did well, the monster says.

"What did you do to me?" I am horrified, utterly horrified.

My dear, whatever do you mean? She does not reveal her body, but I can almost hear the smile stretching across her face. *I did nothing to you.*

"Why am I covered in blood?"

Why are you so quick to judge, Cat? Are you accusing me of having something to do with that? You hardly know me! Her voice is dripping with honeyed sarcasm.

"Who are you?"

I am nothing but a pitiful demon, she sings. *An innocent, harmless, pitiful demon.*

"I don't believe you."

Shadows emerge from the darkness to caress my face with evil talons. I shudder. They radiate nothing but cold, dark power and promises of destruction. Death, I realize. Her shadows are death.

How could you not believe me? she asks, pasting a look of false offense on her face. *After all, I have done nothing to harm you or anyone you love.*

"What are you doing to me?" My voice is the barest of whispers.

My darling, did you not have a dream only last night, where you fantasized of killing your parents? Why are you not happy now?

"Who are you?"

The demon cackles. *You shall find out soon enough, my dear Catarina. Be patient.* Her shadows swirl faster and faster as she fades away into the darkness.

I have so many great things planned for you.

CHAPTER FOUR
PHILAN

"The queen's parents are dead!"

"What?"

"Queen Simone and King Kairos have been murdered!"

"Bandits? Thieves?"

Shouting voices traveling through the castle wake me. Instantly, any lingering sleepiness in my body vanishes, and I throw aside my sheets to run to my bedroom door and fling it open. Dozens of people are already starting down the hallway, eyes wide with curiosity, most still wearing their night clothes.

I grab the arm of the man closest to me, pulling him toward me. "What's happening?"

"Someone killed Queen Simone, King Kairos, and the driver in their carriage last night," he whispers. "There's speculation that there's a rebel group of underground, machete-armed assassins going around and murdering people for fame." I roll my eyes, not buying the sensationalism, but he barrels on. I almost don't believe the king and queen are dead by the way that the crowd is chattering excitedly.

"It's been confirmed that the three were murdered by hand with a blade," he says.

I freeze at that. *A crime that messy could only be personal. Greedy assassins would've just shot them from afar.*

"There's a rumor that Catarina was the one who did it."

"Catarina? Her own parents?" I ask.

He smiles smugly at my shock. "A maid claimed she saw her being escorted away by two guards. She was coated in blood."

I want so badly to scoff and dismiss this man's words as ones of someone craving attention, but a part of me feels something is amiss. Cold-blooded murder might be something Catarina Winyr is capable of. She'd nearly strangled an adviser of hers the day after her coronation. The only thing missing is a motive. Why would she murder her parents?

Because she'd been furious at them during her Embracing ceremony.

The thought dawns on me slowly, before turning my blood to ice. I tear away from the man and join the throng of people shoving their way down the stairs. My heart sinks as soon as I push into the courtroom. General Tenebris, Tontin, two guards, and a blond-haired maid stand in the center of the room. On her knees between the two guards with two swords pressed to her neck is Catarina. She's absolutely drenched in blood. Just as the man had described.

"She is a *murderer,* prophet," the blond woman insists, arms crossed tightly over her chest, hugging herself in an effort to self-soothe. Her eyes are wide and frightened, and I realize she must have been the one to discover Catarina in this state, one of Catarina's personal maids.

Tontin gazes down at Catarina with eyes as cold as ice, utterly silent and still. As if he doesn't know her.

"Catarina Winyr. What do you have to say to Ellanore's accusation? Did you or did you not murder your parents?"

"I did no such thing," she snarls through clenched teeth.

One of the guards behind her adjusts his sword so that it cuts deeper into her neck, and if it hadn't been for her visible wince, I wouldn't have noticed.

"Stop," Tontin orders, addressing the guard. He bends down so that

Catarina's eyes meet his. "My Queen. You are covered in blood that we could easily identify as your parents' if we wished. But we don't want to do that. So just tell us the truth."

Her gaze shifts to look into the general's eyes. "I did not kill them."

The general's expression remains unchanged as she turns to Tontin, who nods once.

"Throw her in the dungeon. She will be executed in one week's time."

What? My eyes widen, darting between the general and the prophet, to try and understand their decision. The queen has just denied the accusation. The guards burst into action, lunging forward and hauling her to her feet roughly. But Catarina doesn't utter a word. It's as if she hasn't even heard the sentence bestowed upon her. The guards begin to drag her away and the crowd of people charge after them, screaming and continuing to throw things at her. I follow, watching her grit her teeth as item after item strikes her body. The guards do nothing to shield her.

"Kill her now!" the people in the mob roar. "We don't want a giftless queen anyway!"

Finally, we arrive at the staircase that leads to the dungeon. The crowd tries to surge forward but is held back by more guards who come storming out of nowhere. The guards throw Catarina down a short flight of stairs and the jeers of the crowd do nothing to drown out the sickening thump of her body hitting stone. I watch as the two guards saunter leisurely down the stairs toward her. General Tenebris appears with a sword in her hand.

"Get the hell back!" she roars at the raucous crowd. People in the front begin to retreat in fear, crushing me between sweaty bodies. Through their pushing shoulders, I can just barely make out the clang of cell doors slamming shut and the guards reemerging from the dimness of the dungeon.

I want to say something to Catarina, I want to see her, but it all happens so fast that I don't get a chance to say anything at all as I'm swept away by the crowd and back toward my responsibilities for the day. Rumors of Catarina and her death sentence run through every crevice of the castle, each more absurd than the last. The other servants seem to think the deaths of Kairos and Simone mean a half-day for them. But as I clean out one of Catarina's old closets, I think of the way her face had seemed to be frozen in time. How did she feel? Was she afraid? I snort, picking up a dress made of fabric so expensive that most could only dream of ever touching it, let alone wearing it. The young woman never really seemed afraid of anything. Mostly, she seemed irritated by the whole ordeal.

The next morning I stand there, holding a bowl of soup in my hands and watching Catarina sleep. I cannot help but notice her features. Her long brown hair is disheveled and still crusted over with dried blood, but her face is clear and peaceful, and her eyelashes are so long. Beautiful. I had seen her beauty before, but never in sleep. It makes me just as sick as her for even allowing the thought to pass through my mind, but the blood coating every inch of her only makes her more perfect. And despite the things this woman has allegedly done, I realize with a start that I feel no fear, not even disgust. In fact, this makes her all the more intriguing. *I want to know her.* Her face is content despite the conditions in which she lies.

I stare at her hands for a long time. The skin is soft, the nails glossy and perfectly shaped. *The hands of an innocent*, I think. I close my eyes and squeeze the bowl of soup and listen to her steady, soft breathing before I force myself to wake her by tapping the spoon against the bars of the cell. She awakes with a groan, then presses both heels of her palms into her temples as she attempts to sit up. I show her the bowl in my hands.

"Breakfast time," I call, not unkindly.

When she shifts, I can't help but notice the necklace adorning her throat. It sparkles even in the gloom of the dungeon. My eyes widen at the sight of it. The chain itself is studded with diamonds arranged to look like tiny, delicate leaves, both sides sweeping down in elegant curves to join in the middle in a cluster of flowers. That necklace alone could pay a gentleman's upkeep for a year. Suddenly, I know what I need to do.

She rubs furiously at her eyes, finally managing to push herself off the dirt floor. Catarina hesitantly picks up the tray I slide under the cell door. The metal bowl is half full of thin soup with unidentifiable objects floating in it. Absolutely disgusting, even to my own eyes. But she seems too hungry to care and gulps it all down. I don't even know if she recognizes me from our conversation the other day. I don't know how she feels about anything except for what is directly in front of her. The woman is a steel trap.

I watch her silently. "What happened?" I ask eventually, trying to keep my tone nonchalant. Her eyes narrow anyway.

"What?" Anger floods her face like a tidal wave, and the metal bowl slips from her fingers and clatters to the dirt floor. "I don't need your *pity*."

My brow furrows as I try to read her body language: a stiff back, widened legs, and clenched fists. So defensive. Does she think I'm going to attack? Does she think I am down here to mock her position?

I hold out a hand between us, as if that'd make her trust me. "My Queen, with all due respect, you are in no place to negotiate. You may not need my pity, nor anybody else's, but you do need help," I say.

"Who the hell do you think you are?" she says menacingly. "I am your queen."

"And *I* am the banished King of Tegak, at your service." I sink into an exaggerated bow, eyes on her the entire time. I relish the sight of her widened eyes, but she seems quick to recover. Then her mouth curls into another snarling frown.

"*Of course* you are." The viciousness with which Catarina paints over the words could make even the most war-torn general flinch, but I force myself not to. My surprise overpowers my fear of her. The fact that she doesn't think anything of me and doesn't question why I'm here startles me into silence for a moment. I would have thought she'd be more suspicious of my motives, but Catarina is strange in this way. Even stranger now.

When I raise my hands for the second time, a single snowflake drifts from my fingertips and into the air. Catarina's eyes snap to it, widening. She opens her palm and allows it to fall into the center. As she stares at it, I can't help but smile. Such a beautiful, tiny, delicate thing in the midst of such grime. Even I can't help but be amazed. My mother always said my gift was a beautiful one. But her eyes narrow and her mouth presses into a harsh line. It's an ugly expression. I can only suspect why she's looking at me in that way. To watch a man she'd once believed to be a servant present a fully formed gift after failing her own Embracing must be torturous, but I only have time to feel guilty for a moment before her gaze turns murderous. She crushes her fingers over the snowflake, which hadn't melted despite her body heat.

"Just because you are a king does not mean I trust you," she says softly.

"You have no choice but to," I reply. "In fifteen seconds, I am going to unlock this door, Catarina." I pull a set of keys from my jacket and jangle them in front of her. "I do not care if you decide to come out or not. I am simply offering you the choice." She watches silently as I lower the key to the lock. With a screech of iron against iron, the cell door swings open. She stands there. I hold my hand up in a *right this way* gesture, but her legs seem rooted to the flagstones on which she stands.

"Why are you helping me?" she whispers.

I gesture impatiently. "Does it matter? Now, are you going to come out or not?"

She carefully steps out of the cell, eyes locked on me. And then, in a flash, she darts forward. I don't have time to brace myself before she's somehow behind me. My head is squeezed under one of her arms, wired with sturdy muscle. One leather boot comes down, hard, on the back of one of my knees, and I collapse with a soft grunt. She shifts so that her weight is pressed entirely on me, and I feel the distinct stab of pain of something sharp pressing against my neck. From the corner of my eye, I can see that she's taken a metal hairpin from her hair and held it against me.

"What are you planning, Catarina?" I ask softly. I stay completely still underneath her. She digs the point of the pin in harder, and I can feel a sharp bite and a hot drop of blood well and slide down the column of my neck.

"I don't trust you."

"Have you ever trusted anyone?" I reply. My elbow flies out and down, landing on the inside of her arm. She releases me, crying out in surprise. I slide out from under her, flicking the pin out of her hand and laughing quietly. "You are careless, Catarina. I expected better."

Her cheeks go up in flame. I circle her, clicking my tongue and shaking my head.

"What a strange person you are," I say. "Why do you do it?"

"Do what?" she asks.

"Why do you try so hard?"

I don't elaborate, but from the look on her face, I know she understands what I mean.

"You don't know what you're talking about."

"Hm." I lean in closer, and she flinches away. Her eyes are a soft shade of sienna, the beauty of which I hadn't noticed previously. "I don't believe you know what you're talking about, either."

I pull something from the inside of my sleeve. A simple, unadorned knife. "For you, my darling." I press the brown leather hilt into her palm.

"What do you want me to do with this?"

"I think there's something odd running through your veins, Catarina. Something deep and dark and something that you want to *hide*. But today, I want you to unleash it. Let it free." She tilts her head at me, still confused, and I heave a dramatic sigh. No one ever understands my jokes. Though, I have noticed the uneasy spell that drops over the people of the throne room whenever Catarina enters. Even before she brutally murdered her parents and left the kingdom defenseless, people gave her a wide berth. My father always told me people like that, the ones who repelled others for reasons unexplained, must have something foul in their blood.

"I'm breaking you out," I say. When she smiles at this, I smile, too.

"We're going to rip this place apart," she whispers.

"Then we're in agreement," I murmur.

I hold the door open for her at the top of the dungeon stairs as she slips out, silent and graceful as a cat. There are two things I learn about Catarina Winyr in the span of thirty seconds. One: she is fast. A maid pokes her head around the corner, only having enough time to widen her eyes and open her mouth to scream before Catarina descends upon her with a gleaming blade. I admire her handiwork as she rises from her crouch. Catarina leaves a long, thin, slice across the woman's throat. The cut is so clean, it doesn't begin to bleed until a second later. Two: I was right about the odd thing running through her veins. There's something in her eyes, like a little black worm that wriggles when she thrusts the knife.

We are unstoppable as we make our way out of the hall, swinging and stabbing as we go. It takes people just a second too long to register what we are doing. That helps us kill them quickly. Servants, guards, and maids all fall beneath our twin blades. I am panting and bloody and exhausted by the time I finally reach the stables at the entrance to the castle, but when I look back at Catarina, I stop. She's glowing. I look her up and down, slowly, taking in every soaked square inch of her. There's a half smile on her face that looks forgotten there. Like she doesn't even notice she is happy at a time like this.

"There is no going back from this, Catarina," I say. "Perhaps it could be argued that, when you killed your parents, it was not your fault, but all of this," I gesture around then down at my billowing sleeves, now richly stained red, "is a choice you can't get out of."

"I know. Let's go."

I reach the nearest stall, take the reins of the massive horse within it, and guide it out. Catarina swings her leg over its warm body. She ignores the way the expensive dirtied silk of her gown strains and then tears.

We veer our horses silently out of the stables and out into the wild forests of Pheorirya. The humid, sweetly scented air brushes against my cheeks and dances through my hair. The sun is bright and warm, and I want to bask in it forever. I look over at Catarina and see her face is filled with the same contentment. I watch as she inhales deeply and closes her eyes, and for a moment, I can't imagine how the person I'm seeing right now could be the same person who had killed her way out of her own home only minutes before. The heat of the sun ensures the blood dries crusted on our clothes but sticky on our skin. We ride in silence for what seems like hours. I'm sure Catarina has noticed my frequent glances at her out of the corner of my eye. The next time she sighs loudly, I speak up.

"I know you didn't kill your parents. Purposely, at least." For the first time since we left the castle, she looks at me.

"Why? You have no reason to believe I didn't. I don't even know why you helped me. Or what a person like you is doing here anyway." She sounds almost annoyed.

"And I also have no reason to believe you did, either." I don't address her other questions, even if she did somehow say them as accusations.

She looks at me for a long while. "What are you saying?"

I smile. *Too smart for her own good. Did* you have a reason to do what you did?" I say.

"I didn't." I see from the way she winces that her words sound unbelievable even to her own ears. But I only nod and she smiles at me.

"You know . . ." I say.

"Hm?" she asks.

Our horses' hooves pound against the forest floor, dry leaves crunching with every step. The sun has reached its pinnacle at the very top of the sky, no longer the pleasant warmth it once was. Its scorching rays pound down at our skin, and I pull my hood up over my face, grimacing. Even though the thick, wooden material does nothing to cool my body, it does shield me from blisters and rashes.

"You're a strange person."

"Why, thank you. You've said that twice now."

I laugh. "No, no. I didn't mean it like that."

She smiles a little. "Then how did you mean it?"

I pause, considering how to phrase my next words. "I don't think I have ever seen someone kill so easily. Those guards and servants back there, I mean." I make sure to keep my voice light, nonaccusatory. "Weren't you close to any of them?"

"None of them cared about me."

"Did *you* care about them?"

"I think I used to."

"And you stopped because . . ." I trail off, waiting for her to finish my sentence.

"Because they stopped caring about me."

I almost want to laugh at the absurdity of that logic. I've never killed anyone for mutual dislike. But then I think for a moment what it would be like to be giftless in a world that only values one's power, and part of me sympathizes with her.

"Have you killed before yesterday?" I ask.

"Yes. A boy named Cam from Tegak." Her words are blunt. When I look up, her dark eyes are on me. I recognize something flitting through them: *fear.* Fear of me? Or what I will say to her confession? I smile.

"You remember your first kill?" Catarina asks.

I tilt my head. "Yes," I reply slowly. "I do."

"Who was it?"

"It wasn't a person. It was an animal. A doe."

"Why would you bother remembering a creature you killed during a hunt?" Her eyes are strangely bright, as if anticipating my answer. I don't hear any sarcasm in her tone.

"No, it wasn't during a hunt. I found her when I was playing in the woods, caught in one of my father's traps. I was trying to free her, but when I finally undid the metal clamp, she just laid there. Her eyes were wide and panicked like she wanted to run, but all she did was stare."

She turns to look at me. We are trotting slowly through the path in the forest now. I can hear the horses' heavy breathing from where we sit side-by-side.

"Then I noticed her leg was broken. Nearly severed in two," I say.

"She would have never survived," Catarina mutters. "So, what did you do?"

"I put an end to her misery."

"Oh."

"She knew what I was doing, Catarina." She's looking at me now without a furrow in her brow. She tilts her head and I wonder if she is trying to be gentle.

"And why did you think that was so special? It was just an animal," she says. The question is phrased quite rudely, but something in her eyes makes me think her intention is good.

"Because I hated my life. And that moment made me feel something besides self-pity, I suppose. The right thing to do was right there in front of me even if it was hard. I liked how simple that was."

"What a dramatic story," she whispers. But I can see that she understands what I'm trying to say. "Why did you hate your life?" she asks.

I run a hand through my hair. "I couldn't stand the idea of becoming king, even as a young boy. I didn't like what it made my dad. I didn't like knowing that every choice I made could kill or save a thousand people in a second. I didn't want to wake up every day with a dozen councilmembers standing around my bed, asking me for orders. So, I stopped trying. I refused to participate in my studies. I missed all my trainings with the court swordsmen in favor of my own practice. I was a complete ghost until my father caught wind of it. He threatened to kill my sister if I didn't start taking my eventual rule seriously. That's when I knew what I was doing was right. I didn't want to become the man he was."

"So you ran away."

There's a funny expression on her face now. A corner of my lips curls upward.

"Yes, I ran away. Why are you smiling like that?"

She snorts. "I think you and my aunt would've been very close friends."

I say nothing to that, but hope it is a compliment. The words flowing between us have gotten more comfortable, almost easy-going. It's nice to have a person to talk to, even if I've known this person for hardly a few hours. We continue on, the silence between us now pleasant instead of stifling.

The wind has begun to carry the scents of the city to us, and I inhale deeply. I can smell the distinct odor of the fish markets, of fragrant smoke mixing with roasting meat. The familiarity of these things is comforting, and it feels as if a weight on my chest I hadn't even known about has been lifted, knowing that home is near. The forest has begun to thin around us, and I can't stop the uncontrollable smile that overtakes my face. Out of nowhere, the trees clear, revealing a long, winding cobblestone driveway that leads up to a manor. Emerald vines crawl up the gray brick walls, twisting around elegant windows and curling around stone gargoyles with bulging eyes and outstretched claws. *Home.*

"Greensbriar Manor," I tell her. "Home sweet home."

I watch her careful eyes comb across it to take in every little detail. I wait for her to make some sort of snarky remark about décor but she doesn't. A woman runs out through the wooden gates wearing a brilliant smile. She wears fighting leathers, blades strapped around her waist, and has a shine of sweat dripping down her face. Her hair hangs loose down to her shoulders, raven black and glossy. At the sight of her, I immediately arc my leg over one side of the horse and leap down to meet my sister. I forget Catarina is with me.

"Philan!" She collides into me with a joyful shriek, then wraps her arms around me and buries her face in my neck. I laugh freely and loudly, the first time I've heard the sound from my own throat for months.

"Zhengya," I say, laughing again and crushing her to my chest. She pulls back, finally noticing my traveling partner. I hesitate to turn around. I'd rather not see whatever expression is on Catarina's face.

"Who is that?" Zhengya asks sharply.

In a flash, twin blades slide into Zhengya's hands, and her smile evaporates. She holds herself with a widened stance and firm shoulders. Our training is identical, but her energy is completely different than mine. I usually try to look like every fight I'm in is boring and beneath me. My gaze is lethargic, but Zhengya's is steely, unsympathetic. I've always liked that about us because we were trained by the same people, but we turned out complete fighting opposites. I peer closer at her, observing the sharp angles and planes of her face that I remember were slightly rounder in childhood. A scar curves along her eyebrow, another at the left corner of her lip. I wonder what Catarina makes of my sister.

"*That* is the Queen of Pheorirya. Catarina Winyr."

Zhengya snorts. "Catarina," she repeats, as if testing out the name on her tongue.

"And why would we, mere hoi polloi, be blessed by the presence of a queen?"

Catarina's back stiffens, and her fists clench around the reins of the horse. I look between Zhengya and Catarina. I stay as silent as they do. She laughs, noticing even the slight shift of both my expression and my body.

"We're not hoi polloi, Zhengya. Also, she murdered her parents," I say and look at Catarina sideways. My sister does not respond right away. Zhengya looks oddly at Catarina now, not making any comment about my dry words. *Does she not believe me?* I wonder.

"Get off your horse," she says. "I want to see what you look like."

I nearly hold back a chuckle. I can only imagine the barbarically vicious response Catarina will bestow on my sister for trying to command her. Instead, Catarina moves. She obeys, slowly lowering herself to the damp, grass-covered dirt. Under both of their mutual gazes, I feel completely and utterly invisible. Have they forgotten I'm here?

"Look me in the eye, girl," Zhengya says.

And Catarina does. They stare at each other for three long beats more before she nods slowly. "Good," she says. Without even waiting for an invitation, Catarina has turned and followed Zhengya into the manor. I still stand outside, my hands trembling as they grip the horses' reigns tightly. I am alone, watching their backs recede into the building.

CHAPTER FIVE
CATARINA

I CAN TELL THAT THE MAIN HALL of Greensbriar Manor was once magnificent, with two sprawling staircases taking center stage in the foyer. Each curves gracefully up to what I am sure is another opulent floor. Tapestries depicting scenes of battle line every inch of the gold-gilded walls. The intricately marbled floors must have cost a fortune. It would have been grand a century ago. But now the wood that makes up the stairs is rotting from years of moisture damage. Each step sags like a tired smile. The tapestries are covered with so much dust, their colors are almost indistinguishable and there is a faint smell of old, wet hay coming from them. The marble embedded in the floor is cracked beyond repair. And yet, there are almost unnoticeable details that make it clear this decrepit manor is a home. A handmade wreath of dandelions twisted together with vine adorns one wall. Next to the rumbling fire in the marble fireplace, a book lays splayed out across an armchair with a brightly colored, hand-painted bookmark sticking out of it. A pair of pink slippers sits on the first step of the staircase, abandoned. Zhengya strides away into the manor without another word. Whatever it meant that she looked at me the way she did when we met outside seconds ago, she seems to have forgotten it, and me, entirely.

"My sister," Philan says suddenly. "Zhengya is my sister."

"Hm."

He looks back at me and something like a smile flickers across his face. He starts toward a door I hadn't noticed before, swings it open, and gestures for me to follow. It's a stone staircase leading downward. I follow him down it. The walls are narrow, and I shiver in the damp coldness of the space. This is far too similar to the dungeon in Saelmere Castle for my liking. The walls grow closer as the spiraling staircase gets darker. Or is it just my imagination? Finally, the hallway opens out into a cozy looking room. Someone has strewn pillows and blankets across the entire floor, and three people lie draped in different positions across a large green couch opposite me.

One girl, her finger poised to turn a page of the book she's holding, looks up lazily. "Who's this?" she asks. The two people beside her give me a scrutinizing look.

"Catarina, these are Soren, Brienne, and Liserli."

Brienne looks up at me, a warm, unashamed smile curving her lips and brightening her entire face. She seems like the kind of girl you'd often catch daydreaming. As she puts down her book and stands to shake my hand, I peer more closely at her. She has soft eyes, so different from Zhengya's sharp ones. Her hands are the only thing rough about her. They are covered in calluses that scrape across my own smooth skin. A fighter's hands. Brienne leaves the couch and ascends the stairs and I follow, turning only to glance at Philan and the two others now laughing, hugging, and talking. My heart tightens a little at the sight, but I look away quickly. I don't know the last time I was hugged.

"This is Greensbriar Manor. Soren, Liserli, and I used to work for King Hanying and Queen Liuxiang. We were spies," Brienne says. *Philan's parents,* I assume. He hadn't mentioned their names, hadn't mentioned anything about what they were like. She continues. "And then he was exiled from the city. The three of us, along with Zhengya, decided to go with him." She looks down, inspecting her nails. "Zhengya would've killed us if we decided otherwise."

I blink at her. Are all of them being held here at Zhengya's whim, against their will? It couldn't be. They seem happy.

"What do you do now?"

"Nothing. We do nothing." She speaks nonchalantly, but something about her voice has changed. Her smile has faded. She looks away often but doesn't ever seem to fix her wide eyes on anything in particular. I wonder if she feels like she should be somewhere else.

"Whose home is this?" I ask.

She waves a hand flippantly. "It was an abandoned manor we found in the woods. Soren enjoys renovating things." I recall that Soren is the one with curly, dark hair and even darker eyes. He strikes me as a strange, quiet person. Brienne points at the ceiling.

"You see that uneven patch? A tree fell on the roof and broke clean through." She laughs. "Soren climbed up in the middle of the night and fixed it while the rest of us slept."

I look around, beginning to see more signs of Soren's work. There is a chunk missing from the wall that's coated with plaster and a shade of white that doesn't exactly match with the rest of the wall next to a very clearly hand-built dresser.

"How do you and your friends make a living?"

She brightens again, her eyes glowing. "We steal."

I do nothing but stare at her for a moment. And then I laugh, the unfamiliar sound escaping my lips before I can stop it. Brienne looks at me in wonder.

"I didn't think you were capable of doing that," she says. Instantly, the faint smile curving my lips disappears, and she blows air through her teeth. "That's what Philan was doing in your home."

"He was *stealing*?"

"Yes."

It seems so ridiculous, the thought of Philan running about, stealing from my mother. Even more ridiculous considering who he is. Or, used to be. I feel the urge to laugh again but squash it down. I don't know why I do.

"Did he succeed?"

"Yes, of course." She smiles mischievously. "You rich people never see it coming." I snort, and she gestures at me.

"Come, come. Let me show you about our humble abode."

I feel a pang of sadness as she takes me around the manor. Every little aspect of their home reminds Brienne of a memory she shares with her friends. In the kitchen, she sees a rusting, scratched knife and recalls how Zhengya once gave Philan a haircut with it because they didn't have scissors, and because of it, he wore a hat for a month. In the training hall, she laughs and tells me that the three targets they have were constructed from the wood Soren stole from the closet of a nearby duchess's estate.

"He used the fabric from all the dresses in the closet to make those curtains," she tells me, pointing out the brightly-colored lengths of silk hanging from the windows. I can picture everything she's saying with such clarity that all of a sudden, the strange, mismatched manor becomes a place of surreal beauty, and Soren's look of wonder when we'd first arrived makes perfect sense. I feel a horrible hunger when I look at it all. I want what Brienne and her friends share: all this joy, comradery, and warmth. But beyond the jealousy is the desire to become a part of their happiness. So, I smile at Brienne's enthusiasm. I allow myself to take a deep breath. It feels like the first one I've taken since the Embracing ceremony.

Several hours later, Brienne and I are splayed out on the floor of the manor's living room, talking of our own lives. Zhengya enters the room abruptly, as if she had always been there and I was a fool for only noticing now. I'm taken aback by her. I think I'll be taken aback by her every time she walks into the room. Her features are stark, each sharper and more striking than the last. But the way her graceful movements handle the edges of her frame is astounding.

"Come eat," she says, and I'd be a fool not to notice the way her gaze lingers on mine for a split second longer than necessary. Soren, Liserli, and Philan are already sitting at the rickety wooden table set up in the dining room when we walk in. The space could've once been the image of opulent grandeur, with the tiny delicate painted flowers on the wall and the crystal chandelier hanging from the ceiling. But now, the chandelier is merely a gold-painted skeleton and the flowers on the wall have faded away into ghosts. Six chipped porcelain plates painted with red tulips lay across the table, each placed carefully at the five seats. The sickly, thin slices of meat that lay across each plate are garnished with a dollop of chunky green sauce. But Liserli is already diving into her food. The others follow suit, but I poke hesitantly at the meat. Soren's gaze meets mine. His eyes narrow as he watches me.

"Not to your standards, Your Majesty?" he asks. Back at Saelmere Castle, I would have flogged him for using that tone with me. Brienne's gaze flicks between us before she lets out a loud, high-pitched laugh and grabs my arm.

"Don't mind him, Catarina. He's just being cautious," Brienne says.

I freeze. "Cautious?"

Soren scoffs. "Don't pretend you've had a perfect track record. We know all about your parents' deaths."

Zhengya's eyes snap to him, nervously. "Don't say that."

He glances at her. "Why? We have every right to question a newcomer. Especially one with blood staining her hands."

"I didn't do it." My words ring out, squeaky, unconvincing even to my own ears. But Zhengya looks at me with something other than contempt.

"What do you mean?"

"I wasn't myself. Something was in me, making me do it. Or someone I don't know was making me. They took control of my body." I'm surprised by my own honesty. It didn't occur to me to lie to the five of them.

"That's what she told the court in Pheorirya, too," Philan says quietly. Everybody has put their forks down. It feels like their gazes are boring holes into me.

"Catarina." Zhengya chews on her lip as she looks at me. "You have to understand that 'Someone took control of me' doesn't sound believable."

My fist clenches around my fork. Didn't she think I knew that already? Even as I said it, I knew it sounded like a lie a child would tell. It sounds like I'm telling ghost stories even now.

"But it's *true*," I respond. I hate that I sound like I'm begging.

"It might be." The second half of her sentence is left unsaid. *But nobody thinks so.* I blow air through my teeth, and Liserli picks her fork back up with unnecessary enthusiasm.

"Let's just eat, shall we?" Liserli says.

Later, Philan is sitting on the front porch of the manor, twirling a long, gleaming blade in his hands. He has changed from his brown, shapeless servant disguise into a loose white shirt and dark pants.

"Catarina." He doesn't turn to look at me when he says my name.

"What are you doing?"

Finally, he looks at me through stray locks of dark hair, the exact same shade as his sister's, and pats the cement beside him. I sit and stare out into the distance. The sun is beginning its descent below the horizon and soft pink light has washed over the land, bathing everything in a sweet glow. Cicadas call to one another in their own strange, chirping language, and sparks of light around us signal the arrival of fireflies. This is a wild place. I was never this close to the forest when I lived in Saelmere Castle.

"I have not seen you use your gift," I say suddenly. "Besides in the dungeon."

He stiffens beside me. "I don't like to."

"Why not?"

"It reminds me of a life I don't want to remember." His blade is still spinning in his hand, drawing swift, silver figure eights through the air. The movement is entrancing, and for a while, neither of us speak.

"Do you fight?" he asks.

"I was required to take lessons in Pheorirya." I had neither enjoyed them nor attended on a regular basis. My eyes narrow as memories of childhood flit through my mind. I spent my time growing up escaping Iesso, Tontin, and my father's chiding yet affectionate reprimands, running through the halls with a smile that could not be banished from my face, and tripping and stumbling over the folds of my gown. It was a raucous and happy childhood for everyone until the people around me started looking at me like I was going to hurt them. Ever since Cam.

"Will you spar with me?" Philan asks. I don't know if I'm relieved or angry at the interruption of my thoughts. The question is genuine, but I still flinch.

"Why?"

He lifts a shoulder in a wordless shrug and stands, offering me a hand. I do not take it and rise on my own instead. He unsheathes a second sword I hadn't noticed swinging at his side and gives it to me. Together we stride across the cool, damp lawn. The sword is heavy in my hands, the design so very different from the weapons I'd handled in Saelmere Castle. Pheorirya's blades were lighter and more delicate. Nothing about the steel in my hand is delicate. It is designed for brutal violence. I find that I prefer it much, much more. Philan stops when we reach the center of the lawn. He lifts his arms, carefully positioning his body until he has achieved his fighting stance.

"Attack," he orders. With a roar, I surge forward, letting the momentum of my body carry the blade down, down—steel crashes against steel, and the vibrations shoot up my arm and sing through my blood. I stagger back, shocked at the strength in his thin arms. In that microscopic moment of weakness, he brings his sword down toward my side in a flash of silver metal, and I am forced to duck away. The stinging pain in my hand sharpens my mind. Across from me, Philan is grinning wildly now while sweat drips down his chin.

"Again," he says. With a hiss, I lunge at him again. This time, he dances past my defenses as if I am nothing more than a clumsy, uncoordinated child. A slash at my waist, and I throw myself to the ground. I'm unable to defend myself in this position.

He laughs. "Again," he demands. Philan's blade is soaring toward me in a shining arc of silver. It's too quick. I abandon my blade and retreat. A stone finds its way under my heel and I fall backward with a cry.

"Again."

"No." My voice comes out in a snarl.

"Why not?" he taunts. "Scared?" I don't answer. I can't look at him, but I also can't stand the way it makes me feel like I'm afraid of him. I roll over to stand and I stalk away to hide my tear-streaked face from his sight. I walk too fast to hear if Philan has said anything to me.

Later, Zhengya finds me sitting pressed against the side of the manor with my head hung between my knees. Moisture from the soil seeps up into my clothing by the hem of my pants. My ankles are cold and damp, but I don't move to relieve them. She settles herself beside me wordlessly. We sit there in silence for about five seconds before she stands back up.

"The grass is wet as hell."

"I know," I say.

She offers a hand to me. "Are you going to stand up?"

I take it, brushing uselessly at the backside of my pants as I push to my feet. She throws her arms into the air and stares up at the sky. Stars have begun to show, and they look like a million twinkling specks of light against a plane of navy blue.

"You know what I do when I'm angry?" she asks, grinning at me. Her smile is so wide and genuine that I can't help but smile too.

"What?"

"I arm wrestle."

"With your brother?"

"With myself."

"What?"

She laughs, swinging her arms about her and closing her eyes, lifting her face upward. I drink in her smile hungrily, wanting to copy her every movement to see if I can make myself smile the same way.

"It's nice. You should try it," she says. She hasn't even shown me how, but I like that she trusts me to figure it out.

"Right now?" I ask.

She lifts her shoulders. "Why not?"

I sit back down on the ground, cross my legs, brace one elbow on each knee, and press my hands together as hard as possible. It's the closest thing

I can imagine to arm wrestling myself. The only thing that surprises me about the moment is that I am not angry, nor embarrassed. It all seems to wash away, leaving nothing but a blank slate, if only for a moment.

Zhengya sits back down beside me, watching.

"I like to do this because it's not possible to win. When you realize you can't win, you feel silly but also free. You forgive yourself. You let yourself go."

I don't answer her. I don't know how. But she's right; the force I'm applying to my palms feels good. As I'm sitting there talking to Zhengya, arm wrestling with myself, I feel a little bit of that smile I wanted from her spreading across my face.

That night, Liserli patiently shows me how to turn on the bathwater.

"It only works if the handle is at a specific angle," she explains. "Soren says it took fifteen years off his life trying to fix the water system." Brown water spurts out of the rusting tap and sprays into the dusty marble bathtub. After several seconds, it clears and Liserli steps back.

"Have fun!" she calls as she leaves. I can hear her laughing quietly to herself as she pulls the door shut and I sigh. I gingerly step out of my clothing, leaving it piled on the floor beside the bathtub. I spot a small bar of soap laying on the sink beside me. Even after my harsh scrubbing and soaping leaves me clean, I stay in the water. I'm paralyzed by memories of the day. Soren's words from earlier had shaken me to my very core, and only now has it occurred to me to think about my position. What am I going to do now? Not to mention how utterly powerless I am. In the hands of the voice in my head which could make me *do* things and in the hands of this band of thieves who are always laughing at me when they aren't suspicious of me. In Pheorirya, I'd had power borrowed from my parents' position and the gifted blood coursing through me. Or, at least, we all *thought* it had been coursing through me. Here, I am nothing. Here, I'm not even a thief, just a stowaway hiding from the kingdom I am supposed to be ruling.

The little burst of joy I'd felt before with Zhengya is reduced to ashes, instantly overpowered by the sputtering frustration clawing at me. The thoughts follow me as I finally drain the water, dry myself, walk across the hallway, and slide my legs into the sheets of my new bed. The blankets chase me into my dreams, swirling and swirling and swirling into typhoons of muted grays and endless black.

I am back in that carriage, the knife in my hand and my parents staring at me, utterly horrified.

"Catarina?" my mother whispers. Her hand is clenched tightly in my father's. They are terrified of me.

"Kill them now," that voice in my head demands. The muscles in my arm burn as I resist the temptation to drive my blade into their chests. I will *myself to fight it, to fight the voice in my head. But I am too weak. With a scream of frustration, I give in to the voice. My body betrays me and my arm lurches forward and my blade slices across the necks of my parents.*

"Why?" my mother whispers as her eyes flutter shut. I cannot answer the question, I do not even know *the answer to the question. Blood is everywhere, coating the windows and dripping down my face and soaking through my clothing.*

I awake with a scream. My limbs are tangled in the sheets and my nightclothes are soaked through with sweat. I cast a frantic look toward the window. The night is thick and devoid of stars, and I feel heavy, sinking, as if I am drowning in my parents' blood. The feeling in the dream is here now, in my waking mind. I stumble desperately toward the window. As soon as I throw open the window and the cold night air hits me, nausea roils through my body. I lean over the side of the windowsill and vomit all over the stone wall of the manor. When my stomach calms and my vision clears, I can finally make out the view before me. The forest is breathtakingly beautiful, moonlight gracing the tree leaves and outlining them in silver.

"Catarina?" a voice asks. I turn around, my eyes so bleary with sleep and tears that I can hardly make out the person striding toward me. "What happened?"

I finally recognize the voice. It is Zhengya, carrying a candle in her hands. She sets it down on the dresser and comes to stand beside me. To my surprise, I feel her rubbing her hand down my back in long, comforting strokes. Considering she'd commanded me off my horse just hours ago, I am confused by the action and tense my back.

"Are you okay?" she asks.

"No."

"Do you want to talk about it?"

"No."

And she does not pry.

This is not the Zhengya Lin I met yesterday morning. This Zhengya is gentle. In her voice I hear care. I turn to face her for the first time. With a start, I realize her eyes are no longer the same shade of ice blue they'd been before. Now, they're dark, as black as her hair. She catches me looking, and the corners of her lips twitch upward.

"They were glass eye covers. I'm not white," she says. She's smiling at me now. I stare at her, dumbfounded. Then I have to bite my fist to keep from laughing. We stand there for a long, long time, with my head resting against her shoulder and her hand still traveling up and down my back. I don't even think my aunt Iesso has held me like this in years. Much less my mother. But this feels different than when they used to hold me. I wish I hadn't thrown up earlier now that Zhengya is so close to me.

"Do you need anything?" she asks finally.

"No," I say. It's the only word I've said since Zhengya arrived in my bedroom.

"Will you be okay?"

"Yes." No, not today. No, not tomorrow. But someday, I will be.

"All right." She sighs and moves away, which leaves the side of my body and cheek cold. She stands and takes the candle in her hands. "My room is right next to yours. Just call if you need anything." She starts to move away but I catch her by the arm.

"Thank you," I whisper hoarsely.

"You're welcome," she whispers back. And then she is gone.

I stand at the window for several more minutes, perfectly still and perfectly silent. *I wish I'd asked her to stay. I need someone to stay.* The tears resume. They do not stop this time and now they're huge, gasping sobs that shake my body.

I hurl myself out of the bedroom, suddenly unable to bear looking at the silken curtains covered with golden tassels, or the elegant wooden furniture, or the barely-lit candles. I run down the stairs until my bare feet reach the cold marble floor again. I am blindly fumbling my way through dark halls and pushing through door after door. I run into the biggest room I've seen yet. It looks like some great hall. I'm so distracted by the view that I don't notice pain in my side until it's blinding. My hip collides with something solid and rock hard, and in that instant, it is enough to make me want to scream. I nearly beat my fists against whatever this object is, and then cry some more. But as my palms slide tentatively across the surface of my aggressor, feeling a fuzzy, woolen cover lying upon graceful curves and bends, I realize what it is. But it's ridiculous and I haven't thought about one in weeks. *A piano.* I rip off the cover and, although there is no music laying on the rack, my fingers find the keys and I begin to play.

As soon as the first note echoes brightly into the silent manor, I can't stop. My fingers fly across the keyboard, knowing exactly where to land. My father had taught me to play, his calloused yet gentle hands folding over my own to teach me the notes. I remember him as I send notes bouncing loudly off the abandoned walls of the great hall.

"Do you know the greatest part about music?" Father once asked me as we sat, side by side, on his worn piano bench. I shook my head. "One can do no wrong, one can do no right. And yet, it can paint the air with color and communicate what words cannot." He played the opening to a lullaby then, asking me to listen. "What do you hear, my darling?"

The melody was simple yet beautiful. "I don't know. But it's pretty," I added lamely. He nodded solemnly, as if my answer was precisely the one he'd been looking for.

"Do you know what I hear?"

"No," I said, a bit sheepishly. He spread his arms wide, closing his eyes, as if the music was still playing in his head.

"I hear a mother's lament," he said, and then repeated the same opening.

I listened harder the second time he played and gasped a little as I understood. Yes, I thought. A mother's lament. This time, I could hear her quiet crying in the soft, persistent chords my father played with his right hand. I could hear her grief. The left hand had been playing something else, but those mournful church-bell chords never ceased to stop. After several lines, he looked back at me with a grin, and began to sing in a rich baritone. There were no lyrics to the piece, but that didn't matter to him. He created his own, humming and tapping with his feet when he couldn't come up with words fast enough. I'd always wondered why he never sang more. I loved listening to him more than anything else in the world. This was just one of many differences between him and his partner. He was creative and caring, and appreciated the tiny beauties of the world. She was brutal, and frank, and thought the arts were a waste of time.

As I play now, I'm sure nothing about the melody I render is the way the composer intended it to be. Everything is loud, noisy, all fortissimo. I am furious as I pound out harsh, clipped phrases. Finally, the piece ends. For a moment I sit there with my head bowed and my breathing ragged. I think back to what my father had said so many years ago. *A mother's lament,* he'd said. *A mother's lament,* I'd agreed. But what had she been lamenting? The death of a child, perhaps? *No,* I think. *The lullaby had been a sad one, but not in the crushing, soul-consuming way. The mother did not lose a child.* The flowing motifs had had a darker, more fierce emotion laced in them. *Anger,* I realize. *Anger, frustration, and a little guilt.*

I look down at the keys and my fingers and I restart the piece. But this time I play softly, and as I do, the mother's fury, sorrow, and grief become my own until the music runs through my blood and I am utterly consumed.

CHAPTER SIX
ZHENGYA

MAYBE VISITING THE BEDROOM of the girl who killed her parents and ran away was an unwise thing to do. She could have killed me under the cover of night, and nobody would have discovered me until morning. I already regret being kind to her. It's not like Catarina has earned my trust, especially not after the outbursts I've seen from her and the way Philan described her to me when she was out of earshot. But I recognized something in her grief. She tilted her head back when she cried like she was trying to hold the tears in. It was a stubborn attempt to convince the world around you that it couldn't hurt you no matter what happened. I did that when I cried, too.

She'd looked so young, so lost, yet far too mature for her smooth skin and nimble limbs. A girl who did not know who she was. I'd been genuinely curious when Philan brought her to us yesterday and when I'd ordered her to look me in the eye. Everything about her is a contradiction. Catarina looked frail and her hair had torn out of its tight updo and left stray pieces drifting into her face. I'd heard lifelessness in her words. But then she had stood her ground and met my gaze. I'd felt the same years ago as a teenager, convinced I was worthless and useless and capable of nothing but drinking my woes away. The difference between me and Catarina is that I know my place in this world. I know my strengths. I know my weaknesses. I know whom I love, and I know whom I hate. I want to help her learn the same things.

Someone is pounding away on the piano on the first floor, and I know instantly that it is Catarina because nobody has touched that piano in years. Soren had dragged it to the manor only months after we'd moved in, claiming that he'd found it abandoned in a landfill. Although I'd never played the piano a day in my life, I'd known just by looking at it that Soren lied. It was too beautiful a thing to be stolen. Its glossy black finish and energetic keys looked too precious to be abandoned.

Catarina suddenly stops her frenzied, wild playing, and I sit up straight in my bed and tilt my head to hear better. *Has she stopped?* Then she starts again. I've never heard anything like the rhapsodic notes she coaxes from the great hulking instrument. My breath catches in my throat. I slide out of bed and creep toward my door. Slowly, I open it and stand there. I listen to her play. This hallway is directly above the living room in which she plays, and I could see her if I just leaned over the railing a little. But I am perfectly content with keeping my eyes closed and savoring the music. Soon her fingers begin to falter, and the flowing lines are interrupted by halting, sporadic breaks. I lean over the railing to look at her.

She is sitting there with her head flung forward and tears streaming down her face. Still, she hammers the piano keys, even as the music is mangled with her shuddering sobs. Finally, she stops and presses the heels of her palms to her eyes and cries. *Truly* cries. Still wiping at her tears, she suddenly stands and begins striding swiftly toward the stairs. The only issue is that I am still standing at the top of them. I quickly retreat to the safety of my bedroom and shut the door silently behind me. I slump back into bed. I hear her go back to her own room as well, and she doesn't make another noise.

The four of us decide to meet that night. We're quiet when we arrive, although it's near dawn enough that the birds have begun to chirp. Liserli,

Brienne, Soren, my brother, and I sit in a circle on the floor of the living room, our expressions perfectly identical. *Confusion.* And one floor above us, Catarina lies unconscious after her weeping piano breakdown. It's all enough to make my skin itch.

"Philan," I say. "Did you hear the way she cried last night?"

"I only heard piano." He snorts quietly. "Thought I hallucinated it. She's pretty good, right?"

I ignore his question. "Something happened to her."

"What an astute observation," Philan mutters under his breath.

Liserli twists a strand of hair around her finger repeatedly. She chatters when she gets nervous and now is no exception.

"She kept starting up playing piano again right when I thought she'd be done, over and over," Liserli begins. "I've heard her in the hallways, whispering to herself about something in her eye when she thinks no one's around. What is this darkness she keeps talking about in her sleep?" She looks incredulously at my brother. "Did you bring a dangerous person for us to take care of? Is this what a murderer looks like?"

I shake my head, already frustrated at the two of them. They hadn't seen her cry like I had last night.

"No. That's beside the point," I interject. "Philan, tell us about what happened before you brought her here."

He thinks for a moment. "Her parents left for the coast several hours after her Embracing ceremony. They were found dead later that night in the middle of the road by two travelers, along with a dead horse with no visible wound. Prophet Tontin was saying that he believed she rode out on that horse and caught up to them. She was found in her bed, absolutely covered in blood."

"How did her parents die?" Brienne asks warily.

"Their throats were slit."

I watch my brother's face carefully. I know Philan well enough to see the exact moment that something clicks in his mind. His jaw sets and he looks down as if he'd see the realization at his feet. "What does that mean to you?" I ask.

"Nothing," he says. "It's just that every time she's killed, it's been in that way. The same clean throat slit. Like a professional." I pause at that. So, if she was killing, was she doing it for fun? I didn't think a murderer-for-leisure would take the most efficient route of death for his victims. Philan was looking at me with his eyes narrowed, so my face must have been giving a bit of my thoughts away.

"She needs to go," Liserli says suddenly. "I won't let a woman with such a destructive nature stay here and endanger us all."

"I thought that the instant she stepped foot in this manor," Soren says, folding his arms across his chest. "And you all ignored me."

"No." I force the word out through gritted teeth, suddenly wrathfully angry with my friends. I picture Catarina with her eyes still puffy from crying lying in her bed while all of us down here plot her exile. Philan and the others look like villains to me right now.

Liserli looks at me in utter horror. "What? Zhengya, have you not heard a word your brother has said?"

"I heard him perfectly."

"So why on *earth*—"

"She needs help."

"She's going to *murder* us," Soren interjected, his eyes wild as they flicker between me and Liserli.

"She needs help."

Philan covers his face with his hands and groans. "You need as much help as she does, Zhengya."

My fists clench. "How on earth could you live with yourself if you shunned a girl in need of support, not the opposite? If the people she's grown close to are turning their backs on her one by one, she has every right to lash out."

Brienne's eyes narrow at me. "Zhengya, do you hear yourself? She *murdered her parents*. And I agree, she did seem like a good person when I talked to her. She had a sense of humor, she was genuine. In another life, I would have invited her to bake a pie with me. But I don't think that quite makes up for the fact that she's been acting strange at night when we're all *asleep* and *vulnerable . . .*"

"Stop. We don't get to be who we are and still judge her. Or did you forget you were spies before this? Now exiled from your own kingdoms? She might be innocent, and she might not be in control of herself. She. Needs. Help." My voice comes out whiny and I know it, but it's the only way I can get out what I've been thinking. I must sound obstinate enough, though, because it takes more than a petty jab to make Soren blow out an exasperated breath. He's usually so composed, but now he shakes his head violently at everything I say.

"You're acting like a child. Now isn't the time to debate ethics," Soren snaps.

"Now is *exactly* the time to debate ethics. I said *no*. She isn't going anywhere," I repeat.

And as Brienne's shoulders slump and Liserli heaves a sigh and Soren looks down, I thank the universe for my father's hereditary bull-headedness. But Philan, with the same skeptic obstinance running through his veins, frowns at me with an expression only a brother could muster.

"Then you're going to be the one to care for her, Zhengya. To help her with her healing process, or whatever it is you feel that you need to accomplish. And keep *us* safe," Philan says to me, in an older-sibling scold I loathe.

"Like you kept us safe when you brought her here in the first place, Philan?" Soren says quietly, but sharply. His eyes glitter, a little dangerously. "We never did talk about why you brought her—"

I choose to interrupt Soren then. "I want to help her get rid of the darkness she muttered to herself about," I say quickly. "We've all heard her talking about it, and I think we can agree it doesn't sound like Catarina's in control of herself. She might have done something she didn't mean to." I don't look at Soren this time. My argument is threadbare compared to his. But I don't let it go.

"Do you really think that's possible?" Liserli asks softly. Her chattiness has died now that Soren and Philan are locked in a reciprocal glare. "To lose enough of yourself to kill your parents, and then recover? Pretend that everything is all right? That you've become a different person? Even if you do help her, she *still killed her parents*."

I look Liserli straight in the eye. "I don't know. But I choose to have faith that it is. And I choose to have faith in the humanity within us all."

"And what if that humanity fails you?" Soren whispers.

"It won't."

Several moments pass before Liserli leans forward and offers me her hands, palms upward. "I trust you, Zhengya."

The others offer me solemn nods, and tears prick at my eyes as I'm yet again reminded of my love for these people. "Thank you," I breathe.

Soren grins at me lopsidedly. "Don't get us all killed."

"I won't."

CHAPTER SEVEN
CATARINA

I WATCH AS THE SUN finally rises above the horizon, flooding my room with pale, early morning light. I've stayed at my spot at the window and haven't moved the entire night after returning from the piano in the living room. My joints are stiff from inactivity. Finally, I limp over to the washroom and stare into the mirror. The black dot in my eye has grown. It now takes over half of my iris, the black stark against the hazel. I drag a hand over my face in frustration, but what is there to be done?

When I step into the hallway, Liserli is walking past. She looks at me through her lashes. Her hands twitch by her sides. I pause and just look at her for a second. Can she see that I've been crying? That's embarrassing.

I turn my face away and ask, "Where have the others gone?"

"I believe some are in the training hall," she responds too quickly. And then Liserli is on the move. I realize only after she leaves around the corner and is too far to call that I have no clue where the training hall is. I start down the endless stairs, counting each step and each retraction of my muscles and each blink of my eyes. On the fifth step, a headache starts to grow in my temple. On the seventh step, I have to clutch the smooth gold railing for support. A wave of nausea washes through me, and I let out a soft groan but continue. On the ninth step, black spots dance in my vision, and I squeeze my eyes shut. It feels as if I'm falling. I flatten my palms against the stairs to remind myself I'm still standing, I'm still myself. There's a ringing in my ears now, and I stiffen in fear. I can no longer feel my feet, and I have to force my eyes open to make sure they're still planted firmly on the ground.

By the time I stagger to the bottom of the stairs, the world is lurching, and I can hear a woman softly laughing in the back of my mind. I fall to my knees and gasp like a fish out of water. With each passing moment, more and more air escapes from my little fish lungs and my throat flutters fruitlessly to try to keep my heart beating. She is the one who is doing this to me, I realize. This woman lurking in the shadows. The stranger in my dreams. Daydreams? Darkness seems to pulse from my body, wrapping around my skull and squeezing until I am letting out moans of an awful mix of pain and fear. *No*, I correct myself, *Nightmares*.

"Catarina?"

I hear the voice. It must be Liserli come back again, so I picture her broad face and perpetually furrowed brow. But I can't open my eyes, much less find the strength to pull myself out of this strange whirlwind of darkness. My limbs are thrashing, my head is jerking back and forth.

"Catarina, *stop,*" that voice begs. No, it's different. It's not Liserli. But I'm only thinking about how I can't see. My hands scrabble at the wooden planks of the stairs for something to bring back my vision. I wonder if it will last forever or if my eyes have gone. I hear a scream, and I can't tell if it's my voice or not. Someone's hand locks around my arm, and I wrench myself away, but this person is strong. I feel myself being lifted into their warm embrace, and a little while later, I am set down. Something sharp pierces my arm. Numbness spreads, and everything begins to fade away, but all I can think is one thing. *The darkness is back.*

"Catarina." Someone is saying my name. "Catarina, wake up." Her voice is so commanding, I swim through the dark, murky fog to reach for her. "Wake up!"

I do. I curl myself around her voice—the light reaching out, through the mist, to *me*—and I haul myself out of the darkness. My eyes fly open. Slowly, I begin to make out the people around me. I am lying in my bed with the sheets tucked tight around my body. Zhengya is leaning over me, her eyes gleaming with victory. Did something happen, or does she always look that smug? I don't hate it. Liserli stands beside her, holding a mug of steamy lavender tea. Nobody else is there, and the room seems strangely silent. *Silence . . . silence.* It reminds me of the dark thing in my mind, the shadows, the—

"The darkness has returned." The words float out of my mouth without my consent, as if those of someone else. I clutch my head in my hands, rocking back and forth, pulling on my hair even as my scalp shrieks in protest. I've never heard my voice sound like that before. Deep and rough, like it turned my throat inside out. Zhengya's firm hand lands on my shoulder and shoves me back.

"Stop," she hisses. The word is angry but desperate. Her voice is strangely soothing, and my screams die down into mutters as I fall against the pillows with a choking cry.

"The darkness is coming," I chant quietly. "The darkness, the darkness, the darkness . . ." I repeat the two words until they turn to ash in my mouth, meaningless syllables and sounds. When I say them, I hear other voices saying them with me. Liserli and Zhengya rear their heads back at this. I sit up. Liserli pushes the tea into my hands and I swallow it all in one long gulp, ignoring the way it burns my throat. I savor the way it burns my throat. It dulls the pounding in my head to a distant roar. Liserli reads the look in my eye, taking a kettle from the dresser, and pours more of the honey-colored liquid into my cup. Once again, I drain it all. But then I am writhing again. I drop the cup on the bed and it stains the sheets but I am already kicking to get out of my own skin.

Zhengya watches me with those piercing eyes. "Catarina," she begins.

I pull at my clothes, which suddenly seem suffocating. "Nothing," I say. "Nothing, nothing, nothing."

They watch me for a minute more. Worry creases Liserli's forehead, but I cannot discern the expression on Zhengya's face. She runs a hand through her hair, something like anger flitting through her eyes.

"Leave," I whisper, and they obey gladly.

Liserli offers me a small half-smile as she sets the kettle of tea back on the dresser. "If you need anything, just call for someone," she says as she turns.

Zhengya stays for a moment longer, still watching me. And then, she too strides out of the room. I immediately throw my legs out of the warmth of the bed and stand. For a moment, my knees threaten to buckle under my weight. It is a long, painful walk to the bathroom, but I grit my teeth and force myself to stay upright. I stand before the mirror and gaze at my reflection. Sure enough, the black stain is larger still. The edges of the spot stain the white of my eye a sickly gray.

Catarina, Catarina, Catarina, the voice in my head chants. I've come to expect it now.

That evening, I force myself to get out of bed and go outside. The darkness has completely disappeared from me, leaving nothing but emptiness in its wake. I want to feel something again. The air is balmy, the evening sun is warm against my skin, and the breeze is just enough to stir my hair, but I can't bring myself to smile. I clench the sword in my hand so tight that my knuckles go white. Philan is sitting on the porch, a spot I've come to recognize as his, fidgeting absentmindedly with a twig. His own sword lays beside him.

He looks up at me, surprised. "What are you doing?"

"Fight me."

"What?"

"I want to spar."

"No, you're not—"

"I don't care," I say. I hate how easily he'd defeated me last time, I hate how it made me feel.

He stands finally, drawing his blade. "All right," he says, and strange relief fills the pit gnawing at my chest.

I do the same, eyeing him. He makes the first move by slicing at my side. I block it, but suddenly, my muscles are turning to jelly. A familiar, unflinching wall of power, nauseating power, power that is not mine, has returned to me. Philan notices and immediately puts down his sword.

"You shouldn't have come tonight. You're not well enough."

The darkness swells inside of me, and I can feel it taking control. But I am ready this time. I can feel it wrapping around my mind, searching, prying for weaknesses. I allow my anger to fuel me, and with a half-scream, half-roar, I squeeze my eyes shut and *force* the darkness out. But within an instant, as I am paralyzed with shock at the belief that I'd truly succeeded, it returns. I push back, but it is no use this time. I can almost hear the monster's voice, laughing at me, mocking me, making fun of my pathetic attempts to fight its grip. My mind goes blank, with only one word clear. *Kill, kill, kill—*

"Philan," I say slowly. The shadows are seething now, angry at my defiance. Their icy cold talons dig into me even harder. "Get away from me."

He doesn't move. I raise my sword, and he only stares at me in confusion. "What are you doing?"

"Get. Away."

He does not move. The shadows win the battle raging in my head and I am utterly lost in their control. *Kill, kill, kill.* Fire sings through my blood, courses through my veins, and spreads through my body. Wild, uncontrolled energy warms my muscles and they tense as if bracing for a fight. I lift the heavy blade of my sword. When I'd sparred with Philan the first time, the weight of my weapon had been a hindrance. But now I can feel the damage that it could inflict, and I relish that. I suddenly understand how to use the sword's weight to my advantage.

"Scared now, prince?" I ask, charging. My voice isn't my own. It is dark and cruel and—

He throws up a shield of ice in defense, but it melts as soon as my blade connects with it. He ducks at the last possible second and rolls away. Suddenly, I know exactly where to strike. I know exactly where to feint. I move with cold, calculated grace, as if the blade is a part of me.

Good girl, the shadows purr. *Wonderful girl.*

I glow in the light of the praise coming from inside my head. Philan throws a look at his sword, which still lies several yards away. I laugh in delight and kick it even farther from his reach.

"Catarina, what are you doing?"

I hear every terrified tremor in his voice, even as he tries to steady it. I raise my sword high above my head and smile. Never before have I felt so free, so alive, and I don't want it to ever end. I tell the darkness inside me that I take back everything I ever said. This new power is the best thing that has ever happened to me.

I knew you'd come to your senses, it purrs back.

No, what am I doing? I feel like there is an army of voices in my head, each screaming something different from the other. Some want me to kill Philan, others want me to run away. Some want me to turn the blade on myself.

You know exactly what you're doing, darling.

Something in Philan's eyes changes, and he lets out a snarl. "Catarina," he growls.

"Philan." I say his name, hoping he can hear the desperation, the terror hiding behind the coy, taunting tone that is not my own.

"You've gone crazy," he says. He doesn't seem to hear me.

He sprints for his sword and I wait for him, knowing I wouldn't have been able to get to him in time anyway. He grabs it, and without waiting for me to make another move, he ducks past my swings and grabs my neck. I scream. Icy pain shoots across the surface of my skin, spreading across my body. I fall to the ground, clawing at the collar of ice he's created, but it's stuck fast against my throat.

"Take it off!" I scream. Philan stares down at me in cold fury, but there's obvious confusion in his face.

"Your eye," he says suddenly. My lips tighten. I am not ready to share my secrets with anyone yet. I want to savor the freedom the monster can offer me for just a little longer. I'd just come around to liking it.

"I don't know what you're talking about," I manage to choke out. Philan gives me an almost sympathetic look, and the shadows controlling my mind force my lips to twist into a savage snarl.

"Sorry," he says. The hilt of his sword comes swinging down at my head and the world goes black.

I awake in a dimly lit room. As my eyes adjust to the lighting, I see it is not my bedroom. It is a room made with walls of rough-hammered stone. They must be foundational to the manor. There are rusted manacles hanging from the far wall with the chilling remnants of what looks like human hair wrapped around the shackle of one. It's a goddamn dungeon.

I almost want to laugh but the throbbing in my head is too painful. I stand slowly, and my joints creak in protest at the movement. There are three empty cells around me, and a set of stairs, which I assume lead up to the main floor of Greensbriar Manor. I notice a dusty, cracked mirror on one of the dirt walls, and I limp over to examine my face. A purple and blue bruise blotches my right temple, probably where Philan hit me with his sword. Then, my gaze slides down to my left eye and my breathing turns ragged. It's gone completely black, tendrils of that inky stain beginning to spread to my other eye. I wonder how long I've been down here. Bits and pieces of my memory start slowly coming back. Nausea, then a ringing in my ears, and then nothing. I can remember nothing after that. I slump to the floor as I realize what must have happened.

"No," I whisper. There had been a collar of ice on my neck. My hand drifts to my throat, but it's not there anymore. Nothing is left besides a faint, aching pain. I relax a little, but before anything else, there is something I need to do. Shards of the broken mirror on the wall have fallen to the dirt below it. Slowly, I bend and scoop one of the slivers into my hand. For a moment, I can only stare at it. My hands are shaking. The voice in my head has dwindled to almost nothing.

Catarina . . . Catarina, the monster in my head hums chants quietly. She's taunting me. I'm afraid of the shard of mirror in my hand. Part of me knows why, the other can't quite believe this is happening. I rip at my shirt and wince when one of my fingernails tears at the effort. The pain lances through my fingers and up my arm, but I pay no heed to it. If anything, it clears my mind and readies me for what is to ensue. Hopefully, once this is over with, the thing residing inside my mind will finally be gone. I want to be able to rest.

I steady my hand, inhale sharply, and before I can convince myself not to, I plunge the shard of glass into my left eye. At first, I feel only a dull pressure and a hot *pop*. Then pain roars through my body and brings me to my knees. The cold, harsh stone scrapes against my bare skin, but I don't notice. A scream of pure agony tears itself from my throat and tears and blood stream down my cheeks. I clasp my hands to my eye, which gushes blood that pools at my feet in torrents. Only then do I realize that the blood that pulses from my eye is not ruby red. No, it's *black,* black as night and the shadows that rule it. The sight only makes me scream louder. I continue to stare at the puddle in horror for much too long before coming to my senses. Stifling another cry, I start to wrap the torn cloth around my head. I feel my head lazing forward as I fight unconsciousness. Suddenly, I hear footsteps pounding down the stairs, and then Philan is standing there with his hands on the bars of the cell door. He gasps.

"Catarina—" He sees me kneeling there, covered in black blood, the shard of glass still stuck in my eye. I want to move toward him, but my muscles are frozen. *I* am frozen. "What did you do?" he asks hoarsely, unlocking my cell door. He hurries over to me, peeling back my makeshift bandages to see the damage. "*Why?*" It is all he can muster. I force myself to speak.

"There is a monster inside me. Hoping it's gone," I whisper, hoping he understands. But from the blank stare he offers me, I don't think he does. *Why doesn't he ever understand?* In my delirium, I reach down and drag my fingers through the pitch-black blood I've just let from my eye. I hold them up to him as proof. I sway on the spot.

"You need help." He'd said the same thing to me in Pheorirya. He says it like we don't all already know. Like there isn't a shard of glass sticking out of my eye.

He offers me his hand, but I shake my head. "No, I—"

"Catarina."

I notice he's shaking so hard that he has to press his hands together to attempt to hide it. "No," I whisper again. "I can't."

"You can't what?" He's begging. I can hear the desperation straining his voice.

I don't know how to respond to that. I can't hear myself think over the voices in my head, I can't allow you to help me, I can't feel my fingers nor my toes anymore. That last thought hits me like a physical blow, and suddenly the world is tilting.

I thought you were smarter than this. The monster laughs. *Did you really think that by gouging your eye out you could get rid of me? Catarina, I* am *you.*

I turn around, trying to stay calm. "Show yourself, then," I demand.

The monster cackles. *As you wish, darling.*

I am suddenly cold. No, not just cold, freezing. I wrap my arms around my body, but it's as if all the heat in the world is being sucked away. For the first time, the darkness wavers a little. At times it's more a murky gray than endless black. It feels colder by the minute. I can almost feel my heart slowing, my blood turning frosty, and my limbs locking in place. Then I can't feel my arms or legs. Something is forming before me, and I can barely manage to lift my head up to look at it. It is made of smoke and ice which whirl and twist into an insubstantial shape. The smoke fades and a woman appears. Her hair is as pale as her skin and her eyes are icy blue. Two huge black feathered wings unfurl from behind her back and jut out into the darkness. I finally recognize her feathered wings, her twisting horns, and her lashing tail from the painting in my father's study. A demon.

Do I meet your standards, darling? The monster reaches out a cold hand and caresses my cheek. Although I cannot feel her fingers, I shudder, backing away.

"Don't touch me."

I can do whatever I want with you. In fact, I could make you gouge out your other eye, right now. Then, you would forever be mine, here in my dark realm.

"What are you?" I hiss.

The monster laughs. *What do you think I am?*

"A demon." The words come out flat and emotionless, so contradictory to the heart that flutters a million times a second in my chest.

Precisely, darling. If you really want to know more about me, fine. My name is Victoire Liverraine, and my favorite food is human flesh. Are you satisfied now?

"What are you doing to me? I would never attack Philan."

She laughs again, her sharp white fangs flashing in the dim light. *How do you know that, Cat? Didn't you kill your mother and father without an ounce of humanity in your heart?*

"That wasn't me." My voice is quivering so badly I can hardly form the syllables. "That wasn't me."

She laughs. *Keep telling yourself that.*

She suddenly disappears along with the darkness. My eyes burn with the sudden brightness of the world, even with my eyelids squeezed shut. No, not eyes. Just one eye, I remember. I slide my fingers slowly up my face, terrified of what I might find. I feel soft, worn leather with a furred interior. I sit up and cast a cautious look toward the small mirror on my dresser. Someone has tied an eye patch around my head. I smile a little. It suits me. Perhaps I'll even grow to like it. I stretch, my stiff muscles relaxing a bit. I wonder why I don't feel pain. Maybe it was the demon's eye after all? Am I cured?

"You're awake," someone says from the corner of the room. I whirl, fear beating in time with my heart. I expect Victoire to be sitting there with her red-slashed mouth and paper-thin skin. But it is only Zhengya with her legs propped up on a pillow and a book lying open on her stomach. There are dark circles under her eyes. She stands slowly and puts the book down.

"I'm just curious, Catarina . . ." Zhengya begins in a measured tone. She looks like she's physically restraining herself by putting her hands on her hips. Like she'd lunge at me any second and wring my neck. "Why did you gouge your own eye out?"

Her dark hair is wild and unbrushed like she'd had a restless sleep. She quickly runs her hand through the strands when she sees me looking at it, but the fire in her eyes doesn't diminish. Her question is so casual, I can't tell if she'd been attempting to make a joke of it or if there was really no other way to ask that. I laugh nervously anyway. She sighs. Zhengya strides across the room and plants two hands on the bed before me, her expression unbearably sober.

"You're unreal," she whispers to herself, letting her eyes fall shut. "A damned nightmare."

"Thank you *so* much."

She opens her eyes, leaning in. "You need help." Why does everyone keep saying that?

"No," I say softly. "I know exactly what I'm doing."

She rolls her eyes. "Do you want to know how long you've been out?" I shake my head, but she continues on anyway. "Four days. We pumped you full of all the painkillers we had. I don't even know how you're coherent right know."

I fight the urge to rub at my eyes. "Where did you even get painkillers?"

She throws her arms in the air, letting out an exasperated snort. "*That's* what you're worried about?" I lift a shoulder in a shrug, and she runs a hand through her hair again. "We stole them. Clearly."

"Thank you," I whisper hoarsely.

She sits down beside me. I can see how tired she looks from this distance. "I honestly wish I could put you through the same hell you put us through these past few days." I don't reply and look down at my hands instead. She sets a small bottle down on the dresser next to the bed.

"Antiseptic," she explains. "Liserli and Brienne spent seven hours straight in the library, researching methods of eye surgery and aftercare. Flush the socket every morning. Change the dressing twice a day. Normally, implants and sewing would've happened to repair what's left, but clearly, we don't have the resources."

I'm far too tired to feel guilty. She leaves shortly after, heaving a great sigh and pushing to her feet. Liserli had tied back my curtains, allowing watery sunlight to filter into my bedroom, but I untie them so that the windows are covered again. With a sudden cry of frustration, I fling myself back into the bed and curl my body amid the pile of plush pillows. I let myself think only of the points where my body connects with the bedding.

"Catarina?"

I force my remaining eye to flutter open. Soren stands above me, all cheery smiles. "You fell asleep," he says, placing a glass of water on my dresser. It takes several seconds to realize who he is.

"Thank you, Soren."

"Philan told me to stand outside your door, just to be ready if anything happened. But I didn't hear anything for hours, and I got worried. I can give you privacy if you want."

"Yes, please," I say. "Thank you."

He walks away quickly, leaving me all alone.

I wander the empty halls. Saelmere Castle had never been as silent as Greenbriar Manor is now. Even in the manor, there had always been faint chatter coming from somewhere within the walls or the sound of water running. The utter lack of sound in the manor now is chilling. *Where have the others gone?* I force myself to ignore the prickling sensation at the base of my spine.

Something in me wants to contemplate this demon, *Victoire,* polluting my consciousness and controlling my decisions, but I force myself not to. I inhale until the point of pain, and then I release it all. My mind goes blissfully free of any thoughts of *anything,* and I sigh softly, grateful for this sweet silence. Fifteen more steps, and then I reach a set of two large, oak doors leading to a room that I recognize as Greensbriar Manor's meeting room. Both doors are slightly ajar, but not open enough for me to see what lies within.

I don't remember what I was thinking of before this moment. All I know now is the distinct metallic stench of blood hitting my nose. The moments before horror, before tragedy, before death are just as ordinary as any other. Plain, simple, and *normal.* But then I push open those two doors, and the normalcy disappears entirely.

At first, I can't locate the source of the smell. But then my gaze lifts to the chair at the head of the long wooden table in the center of the room, and my body goes utterly rigid. A man is slumped there, his dark hair dyed with his own blood and his hands clamped around a small dagger he never had the chance to use.

Philan. All the air in my lungs rushes out of me, leaving me breathless and panting as I sprint to him. His neck has been sliced open in a fashion that's all too familiar to me, and his eyelashes flutter pitifully, but a single glance at the gash is enough to determine all I need to know. *He will not survive.* I am suddenly furious at the unfairness of it all. *Why has he, of all people, been chosen to die today? He was good. Kind.* Although it's futile, I rip off my own shirt and press the fabric against his wound. He groans a little and shifts away from me, but I hold him still.

"Shh," I whisper. "It's all right."

"No," he gasps. "Don't worry about me. Go find Brienne and Zhengya. They're in danger."

"I don't want to leave you."

"Stop." His hand comes up to shove weakly at mine. "I told you to go save Brienne and Zhengya. So *go.*" His eyes are aflame, an inferno of sheer, burning will. I bow to that will and murmur in agreement.

I can hear the faint sound of metal crashing against metal the second I step out of the meeting room. Even here, in the hallways, I can't clear the scent of Philan's blood from my nose. I run down the halls, dread weighing me down, a leaden weight greater than that of the sword I'm holding. The sounds of battle are getting closer and closer. And then I spot them. Brienne lays on the floor, blood spreading in a bright red halo around her head. Soren kneels on top of her with his boot pressed against her chest and a sword in his hands aimed to plunge into her heart. His eyes are black with something wild and inhuman.

And there is something about it that I recognize. This time, my rage is ice cold and razor sharp. Swift and nimble, I cross the floor in long strides and collide into Soren from behind. He falls forward and I hear the satisfying crack of breaking bone. He lets out a scream and collapses, blood spurting from his shattered nose. In that moment of weakness, Brienne drives her knee up and into his stomach. Another scream. He reaches desperately for his sword, but I reach it before he does with a wicked, triumphant smile. And then I slam it into his thigh.

He clutches his leg and cries out repeatedly. I shakily walk over to him. In one fluid motion, I yank the sword out and he falls back with a groan. Brienne joins me, her hand pressed to her head.

"Are you okay?" I ask.

"Mm," she mutters, wincing.

"Good."

I want nothing more than to rush back to Philan's side, but something stops me. I reach down, flipping Soren over on his back and prying open his eyelid. Completely black.

Oh God, I think.

Is this really happening to someone other than me? I flip up Soren's eyelid again to confirm that I haven't gone completely out of my mind. Sure enough, his eye is jet black. I feel odd about it. I don't like it that someone else might be tortured and possessed as I am, sure, but the reason I don't like it is disturbing to me. It feels like betrayal. Victoire had made it seem as if I'd been one of a kind. Irreplaceable. After the Embracing and what happened with my parents, I was looking to feel anything but wretched and disposable.

But if Soren has also been under a demon's influence, has Victoire lied? Did I mean anything to her as she'd promised? Bile rises in my throat. Or have I been totally useless like the citizens of Pheorirya thought me to be? And why did I care what the evil demon possessing my body and making me do monstrous things with it felt about me? I can't waste any more time. I turn on my heel and run back in the direction I'd come from. By the time I return to Philan's side, he is on death's doorstep. His gaze is blank, like he is looking somewhere far away from here.

"Philan," I whisper. His eyes slowly turn to me, the deep shade of obsidian glazed over and glossy. I stifle a sob, peeling back my shirt, which he still holds to his neck. The gash is a terrifying shade of red, the wound angry and festering.

"You'll be all right."

"Is my sister safe? Is Brienne safe?"

"Yes. They're all safe." I realize only after the words leave my mouth that I haven't seen Zhengya. But now isn't the time to tell him that.

He sighs and slumps farther down in his chair. "All right, then," he breathes. "Thank you."

"You're welcome," I say. But he doesn't get a chance to answer. I feel him exhale once. His warm breath mixes with my tears. And then nothing. He falls back against the chair, and I stagger back too.

No.

No, no, no. His face is frozen in an almost serene expression and his eyes are open. I shudder and reach out a shaking hand to close them. My vision tunnels until I see nothing but his unmoving body and the blood that surrounds us. The door of the meeting hall bursts open, and Zhengya is standing there. I fall to my knees with a scream of surprise and shame. Zhengya's hand flutters to her mouth, and then there are more screams.

But after the bellowing grief and shock there is silence. Furious, seething silence that pounds through my head and my blood and my veins—I dive deep into the depths of my own mind, fueled by the anger that pulses through me. Victoire's dark, thrumming presence is nowhere to be found. I roar, pushing aside memories and thoughts and a twisting tendril of black curls around me, bringing with it the aura of suffering and death.

Catarina? It asks. *Why are you searching for me?*

"Victoire."

Are you angry *with me?* She sounds delighted.

I scream, plowing my fingers through the shapeless mist. It does nothing but separate and reform again.

"Show yourself," I snarl. "Let me see your face."

Victoire materializes before me, her red mouth curved into a wicked smile.

My darling Catarina, she purrs. Shadows swirl around her in a whirlwind of darkness. A crown of black, twisting thorns adorns her head and her long, pale hair is loose. Her icy eyes shine with promises of pain.

"You did this. You brought death here," I rage.

Why do you constantly feel the need to accuse me of such things? She asks, pressing a hand to her chest. *I have other matters to attend to besides playing with you mere humans.*

"Soren killed Philan today."

I am aware.

"Soren would never—"

How do you know that, my darling? There are evil, evil people in this world with evil, evil intentions.

"What. Did. You. Do."

Victoire's eyes flash dangerously, and she clenches her fists. *I have grown weary of such talk,* she whispers. Shadows flood me, and I scream, bracing for the pain.

But there is none.

Instead, my eyes fly open, and I am thrust back into reality. My heart is pounding frantically in my chest.

When I finally stumble back up the stairs and down the hall and into my room, I collapse on the bed. I am too exhausted to remove my blood-soaked clothes. I immediately fall asleep. Victoire does not visit my dreams. Even demons need to rest sometimes.

I awake to a sore throat and a heavy tongue. The thick blankets of my bed are tucked tightly around my body to the point of discomfort. Bright sunlight spills down at me from the open balcony window. So contrary to this dark and heavy thing that weighs down on my soul, this thing that I have not felt in a long time. Guilt, I realize. This feeling is guilt. I lie there for what seems like an eternity listening to my heartbeat and counting the soft, shallow breaths that escape me. I do not realize my nails are digging into my palms until the delicate skin breaks and dull pain shoots up my arm.

There is a half-filled glass of water resting on my dresser and I reach for it, downing it in one swallow.

"Catarina."

I whirl. Zhengya stands there, dressed in a blood-smeared shift. I had not even heard the door open. Her eyes are red and puffy with dark circles below them, but tear-free.

"Zhengya," I say. Even I am surprised at how emotionless my voice sounds.

She narrows her eyes at me. "Can I sit?" she asks, gesturing at my bed.

"No. You'll get blood on the sheets."

"Can I sit on the floor, then?"

"No, you'll get blood on the carpet." I regret the words the instant they leave my mouth. From the way she goes deathly still, her hands clenching into fists and unclenching again, I know that I have gone too far.

"Catarina."

"Zhengya." I stare at her, unwilling to break down. She stares back.

"I see why my brother had to rescue you from your own people now," she breathes. Even though her voice is the barest of whispers, it feels as if each word is a slap across the face. But I exhale slowly, letting them slide away with my breath and not allowing them to bear any meaning. "You just ruin everything that you cross paths with."

This time, I cannot force myself to let the words slide away. "Leave," I hiss.

"No," she snarls back. "This isn't your bedroom, and this isn't your *home*."

I shut my eyes, pretending that she isn't here, that this is nothing more than a nightmare. "Leave," I repeat.

And finally, she does.

CHAPTER EIGHT
IESSO

WITH EACH PASSING DAY, Pheorirya descends further and further into a bottomless pit from which it'll never be able to be rescued from, if left neglected for even a day longer. Without a leader, even a bad one, my city is in ruins. But as I lay curled in bed, trying to escape all these crushing realities, my mind keeps circling back to one thing I know for certain. I do not want to be queen. How could I compare to my sister, or even her daughter? Both, despite flaws of varying magnitude, were women of unimaginable power, regardless of their gifts. Or lack thereof. I almost want to laugh. Who am I? I am a woman of subpar power, unable to accomplish anything even remotely political. And for all my fifty-one years of life, it's worked out perfectly fine. I've been happy to let Simone steal the spotlight all for herself because she deserved it. Now I almost feel resentment toward her for leaving me and dumping what used to belong to her on my shoulders, and I feel guilt for *still* not wanting to bear that responsibility. *You'd hate me right now, Simone,* I think. *I'm so sorry.* Someone knocks softly on my bedroom door and I fling a hand over my face and groan.

"Come in."

Tontin appears in the doorway with dark bags under his eyes and his hair mussed. "Iesso. You need to get up."

"I can't."

He sighs, massaging his temples. "You're acting like a child right now. You've spent enough time grieving, Iesso."

"I *can't*."

He watches me silently, motionlessly. When my skin begins to crawl under the weight of his condescending gaze, and the silence between us grows as thick and suffocating as syrup, he finally shakes his head and begins to leave. We've done this every morning since the murders.

"Wait." I sit up straight and push aside the layers upon layers of blankets I'd buried myself in. He turns back around, and I pull self-consciously at my knotted mess of hair. "What did you come to tell me? Was it just to convince me to get up?"

"The general is hosting a meeting of sorts."

"Regarding what?"

"Catarina. I told her that I thought you might have information about Catarina's sudden transformation."

"Sudden? You think this is new behavior?" I scoff. My mouth pulls into a tight, bitter line, and a persistent memory nags at me.

"Why did you kill this boy?" Simone had nudged the dead boy's limp hand. His eyes were still open wide, his lips frozen in a scream. I remember I had tried to glimpse the queen's dark eyes, from where I stood in the shadows in the corner. She was not angry, I realized.

"You said it yourself. 'Treacherous actions do not go without punishment,'" Catarina replied with her chin tilted defiantly upward. The two stood in the middle of the room, utterly unaware of my presence. As they'd always been.

"Hm. How did you kill him, Catarina?"

"I stabbed him."

My sister's face revealed nothing of what she was thinking. "Whose weapon did you use?"

"I used one of Father's swords."

The queen nodded at two servants behind her. "Clean this mess up."

They obeyed, and the queen took Catarina's hand.

"I'd like to take you somewhere," she said finally. "To see someone."

A servant helped Catarina onto the back of a tall, white horse, while her mother swung herself onto a black horse clad in velvety embroidered blankets and a saddle covered in gold tassels. My own mare was completely bare save for a plain brown saddle and thin reins. Simone snapped a small whip, and with a whinny, her creature galloped forward. I followed suit. She had changed from her deep red gown into black, elegant trousers and tall leather riding boots. Even in these simple clothes, she still managed to look the part of a majestic queen.

I'd learned to ride at a very young age, so I handled the reins with ease, but my mind refused to settle down. Pure, unadulterated fear had flickered through Simone's eyes when she saw the dead body in Catarina's arms.

My sister was never afraid.

"Where are we going, Your Majesty?" Even as her daughter, Catarina had always been expected to address her as the queen. My heart ached for the girl. It would've taken a fool not to notice the maternal affection she craved and needed. I'd seen her staring out the window at the children of servants and maids frolicking in the courtyards with their parents, visibly jealous of the way they laughed freely and chased one another around and screeched with youthful joy without fear of being reprimanded. Her mother accepted nothing but stiff, formal, perfect maturity.

"When all babies are born," the queen said carefully, "they are taken to see Prophet Tontin. He has the ability to judge the futures of all he lays his hands on."

"Was I brought to him as a child?" Catarina asked.

"Yes."

"What did he see in my future?"

"Many great things, if I recall correctly." It was a vague, ambiguous response.

"So why are we going now?"

Her head turned slowly to face her daughter. "I am worried for you, Catarina."

"Why?"

I stayed silent.

"How have you been doing in your studies?" She looked away again, turning back to the path before us.

"All my tutors say I am the finest student they have taught in years. I am exemplary at arithmetic, poetry, world history, writing . . ." Catarina trailed off. It was a rehearsed response she could've said to anyone asking the question.

"Have you been doing well? In general?"

"Yes, My Queen."

Suddenly, Simone stopped her horse. I pulled back the reins to halt my own mare.

"Catarina, please do not do that again."

"Do what?"

"Kill people without thinking. Your actions today were reckless and I still, quite frankly, am bewildered as to why you did it. Now, I must contact King Hanying and Queen Liuxiang and inform them that one of their citizens has been killed by my daughter, of all people. We will be lucky if this doesn't end in war, girl."

"I was only trying to—"

Simone's eyes flashed dangerously, and sparks flared at her fingertips. I watched as Catarina's throat worked, swallowing back tears.

"Yes. Yes, Your Majesty. I apologize."

I tell Tontin what happened that night and he now looks pensive. "I wonder why the queen didn't tell Catarina about my prophecy. It might have helped her control whatever is happening to her," he mumbles. I shake my head.

"She has had these outbursts before, Tontin. Surely you know that," I say.

"I do." His face is grim.

"What are you going to do with this information?"

"I'll let the general know. But really, there's nothing to be done, Iesso, nothing we can do to change the past. Simone is dead, Catarina is missing, and we still have no leader." He looks pointedly at me. "The general is scared of rebellion. The people of Pheorirya demand a ruler, and if they do not receive one, they will create one of their own. I have every faith that her prediction will come true if someone doesn't do something."

"Tontin, you know I can't."

"Why not?" My mouth opens and closes soundlessly, and he narrows his eyes at me. "You're a coward, Iesso. You blame it all on lack of experience, but you're just a coward."

I want to muster up the anger that both Simone and Catarina had always seemed to hold within their bodies but the only thing I feel is weariness. How many times have I been called a coward in my life? *Far too many to count.* But now that I've angered Tontin, there's no stopping him.

"Iesso, why can't you do this *one* thing for your city?" His voice is soft, but somehow, it's worse than if he were shouting at me.

"Please leave. Please." I shut my eyes, not wanting to see his reaction. And at last he does.

Late that night, after most of the castle has retreated into their bedrooms, I slip out and into the city. Pheorirya itself is far from asleep. The lampposts lining the streets still twinkle, bathing the cobblestones with their yellow glow, and the vendors selling their wares have only just begun to pack away their stalls for the night. Peals of laughter still occasionally ring out and dozens of people gather outside small cafes to chatter about their days. *If I blur my eyes, it seems as if everything is well.* But when I wander farther away from the castle, it's clear that the disorder of Pheorirya has been meticulously shielded from my view. I spot two men wrestling in the alleyway surrounded by a crowd of people watching in glee. Both of their noses have been broken by the other's fists, and their blood streams down and mixes in one current of red on the ground. There is no militia to stop them. Nor the three thieves who leap through the smashed window of a bakery and run away from a woman with a rolling pin and her hair undone. Nor the plume of smoke rising from somewhere deeper in the city.

Could I run away, like Catarina did? I wonder. Nobody had initiated a search when she disappeared from her prison cell. The resources needed would've been a waste. And in the general's words, whichever city she escaped to would be doing us a favor. Would people come searching for me if I vanished? I turn abruptly on my heel, seeking the safety of Saelmere Castle.

CHAPTER NINE
ZHENGYA

SOMETHING HAS CHANGED in Catarina's face. I want to ask her what happened in Pheorirya, but she'd never tell me, and the only other person who might have known is dead now. *Dead.* The irreversible finality of his death, of death in *general* has not yet hit me. At first, I'd felt nothing but numbness. And because the numbness protected me, I welcomed it. But then the numbness faded. Philan, my brother. It seems impossible that he won't share the rest of my life with me. I pace my room with my hands clenched into fists one second and wrapped around myself the next. My footsteps seem to thunder in the empty room and fill my senses. When I focus on that sound and forget the rest, I can convince my mind that all is well.

All is well.

All is well.

All is well. You don't feel like Philan died because he didn't die. He can't be dead.

I almost believe it. Almost. The familiar sensation of magic begins to prick at my fingertips with such surprising force it's almost painful. I shove it back down within me with a shriek of frustration. I need to do something to expel everything inside of me.

But what can I do? Scream until someone comes to rub my shoulders, soothe me, and ask what's wrong? Cry until my eyes are so dry and raw that even blinking hurts? I fall to my knees, the frustration I'd felt earlier turning into hopeless misery. The disparity between the two, and the suddenness with which they have shifted, is enough to make my stomach clench. Everything around me reminds me of my brother. Looking up, I see a cloak of his that I'd stolen and never bothered to return draped over an armchair. Looking down, I see the cartoon face he'd drawn on the floor when we first found the manor, claiming it'd keep guard over me forever. And looking to the side, I can see his handprint etched into the paint of my walls, a result of his disregard of Soren's shouts to "get the hell away from the wall" during renovations. Each memory drags me further and further down until I'm curled into a pitiful ball on the floor with tears soaking my face and shirt and sobs shuddering through me. *Let this be a nightmare,* I beg silently, staring up at my ceiling. *Let me wake up and see his face again.* The birds outside my window sing as brightly and loudly as ever.

Hours later, I stoop over Soren's garden. Sweat trickles down my face and coats my neck in a thin sheen. Flies swarm around us. Their persistent humming is enough to drive a person to violence. The rough wood of the shovel digs into my palms as I scoop mound after mound of dirt. Catarina works silently beside me, her eyes focused on the ground before us. She has not spoken a single word to me since last night, but I've already decided to forget our little moment earlier. Her casual manner must have been a form of grief. I have to believe that. Because how could I not? She has nobody else left in the world willing to give her the benefit of the doubt. Soren, Brienne, and Liserli stand behind us, silent.

The grave is finished. I straighten my back, which makes my joints pop in protest, and then I feel someone's dirt-crusted hand slide into mine. Catarina stares straight ahead, her gaze steely and focused.

"I—" I stare down at our intertwined hands.

"Yes?" she asks, impatiently.

I'm sorry, I'm so sorry. I want to scream the words until she understands how true they are and realizes that I'd called her crazy out of *concern.* Not disgust. But my mouth refuses to form the words and my throat suddenly feels as if it's been stuffed with wool. She shakes her head, looking away. Our hands stay joined. Soren, Brienne, and Liserli hold Philan's body between them, wrapped in a clean, white sheet. I feel Catarina's gaze pinned between my shoulder blades as I walk forward jerkily and place a hand on his body. Cold and stiff. My hair falls forward in a dark sheet as I shake my head and remove my hand.

"Goodbye."

Then they place his body into the grave. Somehow, the ache inside me releases its iron grip on my heart just a little. I can breathe once again.

Catarina and I walk down the hall, side by side, silent, our clothing still stained with dirt. When I look over at her, I see her brow is furrowed. Greensbriar Manor is silent. I hear no soft voices, no crackles of fire in the hearth, *nothing.*

Soren is sitting on the floor of the innermost cell of the dungeon. His leg, wrapped in hastily tied bandages, reeks of infection. I settle on the floor across from him, on the other side of the bars. Catarina remains standing. He does not look up to meet my gaze, nor hers. Still, I don't let any hint of the inferno raging inside me flit across my face.

"You killed Philan," I say.

"Yes," he replies. Softly, blankly.

"Did you enjoy it?"

"No."

"Was it against your will?"

"Yes."

I look up at Catarina, willing her to say something. I don't trust myself to say anything else, for Soren's own good.

"Who forced your hand, Soren?" Catarina asks.

"The nightmares are getting worse," he whispers. He looks at me. His eyes are dull, lifeless. His dark hair is a damp, matted mess atop his head, and he rakes a hand through it.

"There is a woman named Minerva."

"What does Minerva look like?"

"I . . . I don't know. I've never seen her face, but I hear her voice in my head all the time. It's like she's whispering commands at me that my body can't ignore." His eyes glaze over once again, and he falls back against the stone walls.

"I hear you," he murmurs. His eyes are focused on a point I cannot see.

"What?" I demand.

"I hear you," he repeats.

"Soren—"

"I HEAR YOU!" he roars. He shoots to his feet, and even when his injured leg buckles beneath his weight, he does not fall. His dark eyes are focused and filled with predatory intent. I don't let myself flinch away.

"What are you saying?" I hiss. Soren screams, lurching toward me and grabbing the cell bars in his fists and shaking. The entire room shudders with the force of it. Catarina yanks me backward, both of us falling against the cell directly across from his. His entire body is quivering, trembling.

"Stop," I whisper. "*Stop.*"

He flings an arm out of the cell, tearing at my loose hair. I jerk back, horrified, but his grip is tight. He scrapes his nails down my arm as I finally wrench myself away. His eyes are crazed now, as wide as they are petrified. White foam is frothing at the corners of his lips. Is this what Catarina looks like when she kills? I hate that I wonder, but I can't help it.

Even as I feel Catarina's gaze fall on me, I don't look over at her.

"I HEAR YOU! I HEAR YOU! I HEAR YOU!" he screams, his head whipping back and forth so violently that his eyes roll back in his head. His voice is filled with such terror that I shudder and wrap my arms around myself.

"What do you hear, Soren?" Only sheer will keeps the tremors from my voice.

"I hear her," he whispers, before falling back against the wall and shutting his eyes. His burst of strange energy has faded as quickly as it had come.

"Minerva?" Catarina asks. "Soren, what is going on?"

"Yes," he breathes.

"Who. Is. Minerva."

"A creature," he whispers, his eyes vacant and his face slack. "I've never seen her, but she has described herself to me. She's a winged, horned creature of night and mist and darkness and . . . and shadows." He looks at Catarina standing beside me. "She is not of this world, Catarina."

Catarina isn't breathing anymore. "Her power is death."

Catarina's face goes deathly white.

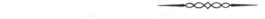

I sit at the very end of the long, glossy wooden table in Greensbriar Manor's meeting room. Liserli has placed a pot of steaming tea and three empty mugs in the center of the table, but nobody has helped themselves to it. Catarina sits beside me while Brienne sits at the other end of the table. Brienne is fiddling with her hair and touching her clothing, looking desperately like she could use a distraction.

"Where is Soren?" she asks finally.

"He isn't stable enough to be around others," Catarina says.

More silence. I close my eyes, desperate to be anywhere else. I listen to the near-silent crackling of the fire in the hearth. I listen to the gentle tapping sound of Brienne's nails against the table. I listen to Catarina's steady, even breathing.

"Tell me something," Catarina says so softly that for a moment, I don't realize she's speaking to me. "About Philan."

"Like what?" The words come out hopelessly dry and emotionless, but it doesn't seem to discourage her.

"Like why you came here."

I consider refusing, but then Brienne sits up straighter in her seat and I realize that she's never heard the full tale either. I heave a deep sigh but grant her request.

He and I were fifteen and fourteen, respectively. Philan sat down, stiff backed, at the dinner table. There was something wrong about the smile he offered me, but I ignored it as I began to eat. But then I noticed the way his finger shook as he slowly reached for his knife and fork and the careful way our mother watched him cut into the dull slab of meat on his plate. Her gaze seemed to sear through him. I could see the way his shoulders trembled and the wicked way she smiled. I caught his eye.

"What's wrong?" I mouthed. He shook his head.

"How has your training been, my son?" our father asked him, flashing him a small smile. Philan tried for one of his own and failed. Our father was completely oblivious to the way our mother was looking at him.

"I have progressed very much."

"I would expect so. You are a good son, Philan. You will make a fine king one day."

"Yes, Father." And in the way only a sister can tell, I could see he was lying.

My mother finally opened her mouth, and the meat turned to ash in mine.

"Did you know," she started.

Our father stopped chewing and turned his attention to his spouse. "Yes, my darling?"

"Your so-called 'good son' tried to—"

Philan's knife fell from his hand and clattered to the floor. He stooped under the table to pick it up but stayed with his head bowed for much longer than it took to pick up a knife.

Our father frowned, his gaze dropping to the fallen cutlery. "What's wrong? What's going on?"

Our mother smirked at Philan. She couldn't be described as beautiful, but there was something striking about her large, dark eyes. They were too wide for her severe, pinched face. She could hold the attention of a room in the palm of her hand without ever saying a single word, only drawing on that icy, bitter aura of hers. A queen through and through.

"Your son was caught trying to leave our city today."

Our father frowned, not understanding. "Why is that of any concern? He is free to go wherever he likes." Philan's cheeks turned bright red as our mother opened her mouth to continue.

"Hanying, he was trying to escape. Permanently. I think our son would like to avoid his royal duties."

Carefully, ever so carefully, our father put down his fork. He looked at Philan for a long time before he spoke.

"Philan?" The dams holding back the river of his anger were quivering, cracks already splintering across them. It was like saying Philan's name alone made him angry.

"I'm sorry." His voice was trembling. It cracked when he said the word "sorry." I glared at my mother for putting us all in this position by obviously introducing this news so we could argue about it. Our father was rarely, so very rarely angry. Our mother had always been the hot-tempered, irascible one. He'd always been the lamb. But all Philan could do was shirk in the face of his frigid, bitter anger. A storm of mist, ice, and snow gathered around him, frothing and churning.

"My son." His voice was soft, dangerous. "My son, why do you run and hide? Do you not want to be king?"

"Of course he doesn't want to be king. That would be too much responsibility for our Philan. He'd rather spend time laughing with his little friends," our mother said. She looked at my brother in distaste with her lip curled. I always wondered why she took so many opportunities to look visibly disgusted by her children. It's like she liked doing it.

"This is your son, Hanying. Cowardly, spineless, and unable to face his own weaknesses."

"Do you think you deserve punishment for your actions?" our father asked, turning his burning gaze back to Philan.

"No, Father. I do not believe so."

"Liuxiang, Zhengya, leave us." Our mother pushed away from the table before flashing Philan one last taunting smile. She exited the room in a whirl of frilly skirts, and I could do nothing but follow. Two hours later,

Philan came to my room with red welts all along his back and his lips twisted into a snarl. We escaped that night, caught in our emotions and carrying nothing but the clothing on our bodies.

When I finish speaking, I can't look at anything but my hands curled in my lap. "I can't help but think . . . how unfair is it, that despite all that we escaped, he still ended up dead."

Brienne offers me a soft noise of sympathy and I wince, desperate for a change of subject and uncomfortable in the sudden lack of sound in the room.

"What do you know about demons?" Catarina asks abruptly. I look at her, offering her a small smile of eternal gratitude for the subject change.

"Very little," Brienne replies.

I agree with Brienne with a short nod. "Does this have anything to do with Soren?"

Soren's crazed expressions and wild, uncontrollable shrieks had had the same animalistic, unhuman quality as Catarina's. To hear her confirm it, or at least imply it, both comforted and disturbed me. And though I'd never questioned the existence of the demons, they'd always seemed like hellish fragments of nightmares. Far away, and never able to harm me or anybody I loved. But one look into Catarina's face sends a tremor through me. She's *scared* and unable to hide it. I can see her chewing on her bottom lip and darting her eyes through the windows of the manor as if a demon would come for her right this second, afloat on great black wings.

"Yes," she breathes. "It does."

Brienne's gaze flicks between the two of us, worry now creasing her forehead.

"What happened?" she asks.

Catarina closes her eyes. "On the day of my Embracing, I wasn't able to summon a gift."

My eyes widen. Oh. Of course, I hadn't seen any signs of a gift. Why hadn't I thought of this before? My eyes stroll down the long waves of

Catarina's brown hair, and I frown. Probably because I was too distracted by her. She doesn't look at either of us.

"My parents were furious, as you can imagine." Her words are so filled with bitterness that I shudder, terrified of what she's about to say next. Philan had already told us that she'd killed her parents but he'd never explained why.

"And I was furious, too. I was furious at them for humiliating me in front of my people, I was furious at my people for suddenly turning against me, when only days before, they were throwing massive parties to celebrate the coronation of their much-anticipated queen."

Oh God. I already know what she's going to say next.

"That night, I dreamt of murdering my parents. The next night, a voice came to me in my sleep. It urged—demanded—I get out of bed, mount a horse, and chase after the carriage my mother and father were taking to their retirement. It told me how to slide through the window, land inside, and kill them. I couldn't resist it. I tried. Of course I tried as hard as I could. I saw myself kill them."

Brienne laughs, but the sound is squeaky and high-pitched.

"Catarina, be serious. Please," she begs. And she's really begging, I can tell. For it not to be true. For this not to be what's happening to our Soren, too. Catarina doesn't reply. Her gaze is pinned at her own hands in her lap. "Catarina?" Brienne asks.

"The voice in my head belonged to a creature named Victoire," Catarina barrels on. "A demon. She was the one instructing me to kill."

"What did she want?" I ask, fighting to keep myself calm and steady.

"Do they gain some sort of sick pleasure in tormenting mortal minds?" Brienne asks. I can tell she still can't truly wrap her head around what Catarina is saying. But something deep down in my chest knows that it's all true.

"Perhaps," she says. "But that can't be their only objective."

"Do they hope to lure in humans? For prey?" I offer.

Silence. Once again, I turn my attention to the flickering of the flame in the fireplace. I count the crackles of the wood, needing something to pass the time. *Crack, crack, crack.* Three, all in rapid succession. Brienne inhales sharply and I jerk out of my trance.

"Maybe they are running out of . . . food," she murmurs. Nobody wants to think about what demons eat for food. Not if they eat people and the old tales have been true all along.

"Perhaps they seek to invade Guinyth and harvest from us." That is a sharp turn from Brienne's earlier pleas for Catarina to be joking. Did she think demons were coming here to eat us? Through Catarina and Soren?

"They must have an entire land to hunt on," I say, crossing my arms tight across my chest. "I don't know much about demons, but I do know that they have their own world. Whatever that means. Why would they want to come here?"

"But they are the only predators in that land," Brienne whispers. "They are the hunters, not the hunted."

"I didn't know demons had their own land," Catarina says. I hear the edge in her voice and look pointedly away. There is something like hunger in her voice when she talks about demons, and I don't like it.

The day slowly drags on. We talk for a little longer after that, but the conversation soon goes in circles. Liserli comes in with a fresh pot of lavender tea, and this time, all three of us gratefully gulp down the sweet, warm liquid.

I trudge slowly back up to my room, collapsing on the bed and inhaling the fresh scent of the sheets. There is nothing I want more than sleep, but . . . Victoire. Catarina knows the name of her demon. Do they have a relationship? Does the demon know why they took Philan? There are too many impossible questions in my head. Questions that, hours ago, I never would have thought I would ask. It is too much, and it paralyzes me. I lie there for what feels like hours. I do nothing but count my inhales and exhales. It is almost habitual now. *Four hundred and twenty-three.*

Then, there is a soft knock on the door.

"Come in," I mumble. Catarina enters. She has changed out of her robes, and her long brown hair is pulled into a neat ponytail. A thin sheen of sweat covers her forehead. I sit up too fast. Blood rushes to my head, and my vision goes blurry.

"Zhengya," she says. A shudder runs up the back of my neck at the sound of my own name.

"Yes?"

She scratches at a spot on the back of her hand. *She's nervous,* I realize. "Would you like to train with me?"

Somehow, I know my answer to her question is important.

"Okay," I breathe. I am unsure what else to say, but my answer is satisfactory enough to her.

"Hurry," she says. For some reason, I find that funny. Like she wants me with her as quickly as possible. Or is that wishful thinking? And then she leaves as fast as she had come. I slip out of my sleeping clothes and into a light shirt and dark pants. I dig through my closet before finding a pile of training armor. I stare at myself in the mirror as I attempt to scrape my matted hair back. I haven't cared for it since Philan died and it's a mess of tangles. There are dark circles beneath my eyes, and my face is as thin as it is pale. I look like a wraith with my loose clothing flowing around me and my haggard, cadaverous appearance.

Greensbriar Manor's training room is a completely white, empty hall with nothing inside besides a chest filled with breast plates, other assorted armor, and a rack of wooden training swords. Catarina stands there with her back to me. A brown cloth bag filled with rice is hanging from the ceiling, and she lobs her fists at it repeatedly until her knuckles are marked with red. Her breath comes to her in soft huffs, and the muscles in her bare, uncovered arms flicker as sweat drips down her. I am mesmerized.

"Catarina," I say. At last, she notices my presence and turns, lowering her fists. They are wrapped in some sort of gauzy white bandage that has done nothing to protect her hands from the roughness of the makeshift punching bag. Liserli has given Catarina a metal-plated eyepatch, handmade and no doubt for training, which Catarina wears now. It makes her look ferocious.

"Zhengya," she replies. I have grown to like the sound of my name on her lips. All of our encounters start like this, with her saying my name and me saying hers. She likes the sound of her name on my lips, too.

"You can take a training sword from that rack over there," I say. She turns her back again, lifting her arms and resuming her own training. As if she's forgotten that she's been the one to invite me here.

I stride across the room to choose a sword. The dull, wooden blade is burdensome in my hands and the rough hilt scrapes against the callouses of my palms. Years of training have made my hands unfit for those of a princess. I wonder briefly how Catarina's hands are. I turn back around to train, but before I can say anything, something is flying toward my face. I twist out of the way, but not in time. Catarina's fist collides with my cheek in a flash of color, and pain explodes through my body in a shock of stinging fire.

"What are you doing?" I snarl, cradling my face in my hands. I can already feel the bruise blooming across it. And yet, I know she did not hit me with the full brunt of her strength; I'd seen the way she'd punched at that bag.

"Attack me," she says simply. Her legs are widened, braced in a defensive position. I consider her before lunging. Gracefully, like a small silver fish leaping through a river, she dances out of the way. I slash at her again, but she is fast. She reaches the training rack and takes a wooden sword for herself. Another slash at her waist, but she steps aside and brings her sword down at me. I hold her weight for what seems like an eternity, our eyes locked and our breathing ragged. And then I twist away, escaping only with the grace of my years of sword training experience. She does not relent. A sudden rough cut at my thigh and I barely block her blade in time. Her swordsmanship needs work, but her raw instinct is unmatched. This girl could be a monster in her own right even without a demon nestling in her lungs. Or wherever demons live when they possess someone. I find myself smiling.

"You are slow," I finally say, watching as she lowers her sword and lifts her hands in surrender. "Quick-witted, but slow."

I watch her mouth clench tight. My muscles ache and my lungs scream for air, but I savor the pain. It's distracting. We train until night settles over the manor, thick and heavy and bringing with it a dull exhaustion that muddles my mind. I don't think about Philan for hours. I don't think about Soren, or the demon in Catarina, or the way Liserli and Brienne cry together in the library when they think no one will notice. I only think about the way my muscles scream and how Catarina moves to strike. Liserli watches from the doorway. As the sun sets, she demands we eat dinner. She's made a hearty beef stew, and even though it's gone cold, Catarina and I devour it all in minutes.

Afterward, she walks me back to my room. "Goodnight, Zhengya," she says.

"Goodnight."

Catarina lingers there for a moment, as if deciding whether or not to say something. And then she turns and strides away.

I almost wish she'd stayed.

CHAPTER TEN

ZAHIRAN

THE SERVANTS QUARTERS of Liverraine Castle are my least favorite place in the world. Dingy and dark, with a perpetually damp smell no matter how many rose petals the others try to place on the floor. My room alone has twenty-four cots packed together on the floor, and not a single one is left uninhabited at night. But now, during the day, the other handmaidens are all gone about their duties. I stare up at the stained ceiling, hands folded behind my head as I lie upon my own mattress. Something, a broken spring, is digging into the space right between my wings, and I sigh as I roll over to avoid it. The irony of the situation is utterly hilarious if I let myself think about it. I could've been lounging in a gold-gilded bed right now if things had played out the way they were intended to. The way they were supposed to.

But then again, if I am still truly destined to wear Ahuiqir's crown, truly destined to rule, then I continue to have faith that it'll happen. *The blood in my veins is still as royal as my mother's had been,* I remind myself. My family's fall from glory could've been a little more glamorous, though. A grand battle, at least. Or a fierce duel between my mother and Victoire. I snort at myself. My mother had only worn the crown for several years before Victoire had snatched it all away, stealing her life and consequently, her crown. I don't even particularly want to rule. But Victoire had tilted my world on its very axis. She shredded the gleaming future laid out before me with her claws.

I want her dead.

Another servant girl pokes her head into the room, sticking a thumb behind her.

"Queen Victoire is calling for someone to clean her room," she says. "I'd do it, but I promised Liza I'd help her in the kitchen." I nod, and she turns to leave. "I'd hurry if I were you," she says. I allow myself to lie there for a moment longer before groaning and dragging myself up.

I hurry down the lengthy hallways of Liverraine Castle while running my hands over my hideous brown dress to smooth the fabric, vowing that the instant I take back my role as queen, I'll buy myself an elephant's weight in new clothing. But despite everything, Victoire and I have always seemed to share the same taste in interior décor. I can't help but marvel at the elegance of everything in the castle even after all the time I've been here. It's efficiently, viciously beguiling, just like the Queen of Demons herself. But it also reminds me far too much of what I could've had.

The layout of the castle itself is nothing short of a masterpiece. The exterior was designed to be made entirely of black stone, rough, cold, and unwelcoming. It is fitting that the capitol of the Kingdom of Demons be pitch black and ominous. But the interior is lavishly decorated, following the same black theme yet garnished with overstuffed red-fabric furniture. Inside the castle, everything down to the door handles is opulent. This is all directly in contrast to the depravity I witness here on a regular basis. I turn corner after corner, allowing myself to get lost in my own thoughts. The steps to Victoire's bedroom are muscle memory at this point. When I finally reach the massive door charmingly adorned with a stuffed human head mounted above it, it's already thrown open. I take a deep breath and let my eyes flutter shut, willing calm to wash over me. I smooth my face into a neutral blankness. I become Zamara: the obedient, submissive servant girl.

Victoire sits at a desk in the corner. She hears me and looks up, eyes narrowing, and regards me with a look of something like disgust.

"There you are. Took you long enough." She stands, putting down whatever she'd been working on. "I have a conference with General Kizmet. Make sure to dust the bathroom well."

She sweeps past me and I swallow the lump in my throat. Her words, while innocent enough, carry enough threat to motivate me to spring into action. She'd killed her last maid for not dusting her bathroom properly.

I make my way into the room with a deep frown etched into my face. There isn't a single part of me that isn't whining in protest, but I shake off the feeling and remind myself of my goals. *Victoire will be dead before the year's end.* Even after I force my face back into a neutral position, I can't stop my hands from clenching into fists at my side and a hiss of frustration from sliding through my teeth.

Before I enter the bathroom, I make sure to briefly glance around the room for any bits of personal information I can steal, the movement reflexive and unconscious. I've been snooping for years. Nothing catches my eye and I turn back to my cleaning with a sigh.

Hours later, the entire bathroom is spotless, my fingers are numb and quivering from clutching cleaning utensils and the sponge is stained brown and in tatters. I lean back on my heels to admire my work. As I do, resolution steels me further and further. By the time I've pushed to my feet, disposed of all the waste, and begun to stride out the room, the anger welling in me is as strong as it has always been.

CHAPTER ELEVEN

TONTIN

I SIT WITH MY HEAD IN MY HANDS. Iesso is seated in the chair beside mine in the meeting room. We wait for the other leaders of Guinyth. None have shown up yet, and the air between us is charged with electric tension. I know she feels guilt; I'd watched her slip out of the castle last night and return with a face crumbling with despair. But Iesso has yet to say a word to me about agreeing to be queen. I truly don't understand her sometimes. Iesso had basked in the shadow of her sister for decades, watched her reign over Pheorirya with grace and efficient brutality, attended every strategic meeting and diplomatic visit. Had she taken in nothing about the way of being a queen from that? I don't have time to contemplate. There is a knock at the door, and Iesso shoots up so fast that she nearly knocks her chair over. Our eyes meet, and a blush heats her cheeks.

"I'll get it," she says quietly.

She opens the door, stepping out of the way to reveal just one woman. I squint for a moment, taking in her graying hair, wickedly long and sharp nails, and midnight blue robes. *Ah.*

"Yseult A'tess," I say, spreading my arms and pasting on a smile. "It's been far too long." The clan leader of the Coven of the Hyacinth ignores me, instead picking a chair and settling down into it.

The political history between witches and humans has been long and complex. Even after our alliance in Cheusnys Battle, the clan of iron-hearted women and men and their leader had never seemed particularly friendly. But somehow, I still hold faith that she doesn't dislike me. I've never given her a reason to. All the memories that I have, with her present, entail stiff political gatherings with countless documents to sign and clipped, formal exchanges.

"Tontin, thank you for inviting me. I will say, I almost didn't come." Her silvery hair gleams with every shift of her body.

And although I don't know Yseult A'tess well, with just a single glance, I can see that there's something in her character that would've prevented her from missing this meeting, despite her crude words. She carries herself with steely discipline and unbreakable will. Completely ignoring my invitation would've been out of the question.

"Oh?" I ask, still bearing that cheery, false smile.

"Drop the act. Please. I know why you asked all the rulers in Guinyth to come here, and I only came to tell you this: nobody is going to unite with you."

My heart plummets, all of my optimism from before draining away. "Why do you say that?"

"Would you unite with a city on the verge of social and economic collapse?" The witch stares hard at me, forcing me to meet her gaze. "All your problems would become their problems. And because of this, you'd drag them down. Be honest with yourself, prophet. Pheorirya is only one city, and the ruin of one is infinitely better than the ruin of two. No ruler is willing to take that risk."

"Is that the only reason?" Iesso asks softly.

"Every damn person in Guinyth has heard about your niece."

My blood runs cold.

"Nobody is willing to associate themselves with such a deplorable woman. And Iesso, know that I say this with no personal ill will for you nor your loved ones, but your entire family has been tainted by her name."

"Have you at least considered it?" I beg.

"I welcome any citizens of Pheorirya fleeing their current situation into my clan with open arms," she stays stonily. "But I will not extend my generosity past that, and frankly, you shouldn't expect other cities to do so either."

"Is there anything we can say or do to convince you otherwise? Catarina has been taken care of, and all we need is a leader. Please, Yseult."

Her green eyes flash in sudden anger. "Have you not heard a single word I've said? What do you expect the rulers of Guinyth to do? Rule Pheorirya for you?" She suddenly looks at Iesso. "Why can't *you* be queen?" Iesso's eyes dart to me, then back to the witch.

"I was never one for . . . leadership," I say.

Yseult laughs. Neither Iesso nor I join her, and when she realizes that Iesso has been completely serious, she goes deathly still.

"Iesso. Tontin. I have no idea how you plan to run a city with such childish mindsets. Begging for aid. Have you not tried to rule? Have you made no declarations to the public of comfort and safety?" She leans in closer. "Remember, there is a reason all of Guinyth's cities are separate. They wanted to be independent. I will not sit here and babysit your royal insecurities."

I lean forward to reply, but the witch cuts me off. "Wait. I have a question. Iesso, why do you refuse the crown? Why were you 'never one for leadership?'" Her eyes widen slightly.

"I don't know, I just—"

"Iesso." She says the word nonchalantly, and her voice hasn't increased in volume, but the threat laced through it is apparent.

My gaze darts toward Iesso, awaiting her answer. She fidgets with her fingers by twisting them together only to unravel them. The movement is so incredibly juvenile that I'm suddenly mortified that Yseult, the famed, battle-hardened woman that she is, is here to bear witness to our seeming incapability.

"I don't want to make a fool of myself," Iesso finally blurts. "The citizens of Pheorirya loved and respected Simone as queen; it couldn't have been more abundantly clear. And you've heard the stories, haven't you? When my sister announced Catarina's birth, the entirety of Pheorirya rejoiced, but not only for the expected reasons. When I stepped outside, all I could hear was the relieved murmurs of the citizens celebrating the fact that there was now an heir to the throne. And the fact that I was no longer next in line."

Yseult's wise eyes sweep over Iesso, not even a hint of sympathy in them. "Do you truly believe that all rulers were thrust into the world already bearing the confidence and poise needed to lead their cities?"

"Yes, I—"

"Well, you're wrong."

Iesso's mouth opens and closes as she struggles to think of how to reply.

"I cried myself to sleep every night for weeks after becoming clan leader. I locked myself in my chambers, refusing to eat or drink or do any of the work that was slowly piling up. Why?" She looks Iesso straight in the eye. "Unreasonable insecurity. I imagined that behind closed doors, they whispered about how their new clan leader wouldn't be able to amount to anything and how they'd need to appoint a new leader. And with each passing day that I refused to fulfill my duties, I knew that they resented me more and more."

Silver tears glisten on Iesso's cheeks, but Yseult continues on, pretending not to notice when she lifts a hand to wipe at her eyes. "But I found that when I eventually forced myself to emerge from my tent and face reality, every single person in my clan supported me. They hosted a massive feast that night, in honor of me. They danced and sang and told me how brave and strong I was, and how grateful they were for me. And look at me now." She lifts her arms, gesturing at herself. "I've become everything I once feared I wouldn't."

Iesso shakes her head, tears flowing freely now. "But—"

Yseult shakes her head. "Nobody will be able to offer your city help if you refuse to try first." She gets up then, declining the cup of tea that a servant offers her with a flick of her hand. "I must return to my clan now."

"Thank you for your time," I say hoarsely, and Iesso echoes my words in a hardly audible breath. The witch sweeps away without acknowledging that we'd spoken. We sit there for an hour more. Iesso's gaze is fixed at the ceiling, arms folded across her abdomen in a position of unconscious self-protection.

Everything the witch had said was true. I try to read the expression on Iesso's face, but her emotions are now carefully guarded. I suddenly feel like an ungainly, clumsy teenager again, blundering his way through life in need of supervision and guidance. And from the bit of red that still stains Iesso's cheeks and ears, I can tell that she feels the same. Not a single person walks through the door after Yseult.

Finally, Iesso brushes away a tear and stands. "We're making fools of ourselves, Tontin."

I don't move. "Sit down, Iesso."

She turns to look at me, eyes glossy. "Why? What's the point?"

"I want to tell you something. You already know Catarina and her mother visited me after Catarina killed that boy. The demon-consorter from Tegak. You were there, but you stayed outside with the horses."

Instantly, Iesso's attention is completely on me again. "Yes . . ." she hesitates.

"I've never spoken about what I saw in her mind that night."

I tell her about the unexpected, unannounced arrival of herself and the queen, with Catarina in tow, at my private cottage by the sea. Of what was asked inside and what I saw and what gave me pause, even then. But recounting the tale is more painful than I expect. I'm surprised to find I remember it as if it was yesterday.

My home was, and still is, perched precariously on the very top of a wind-swept cliff. Foam-crested waves pounded against the rocky shoreline below me, and the wind carried with it the scent of sea salt and clean pine. It is still my favorite place in the world, somewhere I retreat to every chance I get. That particular day had been exceptionally beautiful, the sun's glow illuminating my entire study.

"Tontin," someone called from outside the house. My head snapped up from the book in my lap. I'd have recognized that sharp voice anywhere. I answered the door, the old, rusting hinges shrieking in protest as I did so. I spread my arms and put a gracious smile on my face.

"Welcome, welcome, Your Highnesses." Simone and Catarina stood there, looking out of place. Three horses were tied to a tree in near the door. Iesso's horse nuzzled her as she waited beneath the tree with them. Simone and Catarina slipped through door silently. Catarina's eyes were as wide as saucers, looking about as they settled into two worn, antediluvian armchairs. I headed for the kitchen, searching for biscuits and tea things, and located them in a dusty cabinet. When I entered the sitting room, Catarina was still taking in her surroundings. I watched her eyes travel slowly over the abstract paintings with colorful shapes and designs lining every inch of the bright yellow walls, the tattered books covering every solid surface, the massive grandfather clock ticking away steadily. A small smile curved her lips. It must've been a welcome contrast to the unsettlingly perfect tidiness of her mother's castle.

"Queen Simone, it's lovely to see you, as always." I placed two steaming mugs of tea before them along with a plate of biscuits. Catarina reached for the tea eagerly and brought it to her nose to inhale the sweet lavender scent. I looked at her, smiling warmly. "And you, my dear. I have barely seen you since you were but hours old, red-faced with all your screaming. What a powerful pair of lungs."

But her mother interrupted me. "It is lovely to see you too, Tontin, but I'm afraid we have not come today for tea and chatter. I would like to ask you for a favor."

"Anything, My Queen."

"Will you look into her future again?"

My expression sobered. I could hear my voice change from host to prophet. "Is there any particular reason why?"

Simone casted a glance at her daughter, blinking rapidly. "No," she replied finally. "Not at all."

She had always been and would always be an awful liar. There are certain small, unnoticeable things she does that I have grown to recognize over the years: rubbing her fingertips together when she's worried, blowing air through her teeth when she's angry, and blinking more times than she needs to when she's lying. I already knew about the incident with the boy from Tegak. I nodded my agreement, though, placing my hands upon the top of Catarina's head and glancing down at her for her consent. She nodded, and I rubbed her tense shoulder in reassurance. Carefully, she put down her tea and biscuit, settling into her armchair.

"All right, then. Inhale, child," I told her. She obeyed, breathing in deeply. "Now exhale."

She did, and I felt all her thoughts dissipate. The cool, metallic smell of my magic seemed to sweep under me, rendering me weightless and bringing me into the fields of her mind. When I opened my eyes again, the two of us were floating in dark silence. She looked around nervously, arms wrapped around herself. The darkness was not cold or foreboding. It bore down gently on my body, brushing against my skin in warm, comforting heat.

"Let me in," I said, looking into her eyes. "Open your mind to me." She stared at me, wide-eyed, but eventually, she relaxed herself enough that I could enter her thoughts. But instantly, her mind resisted, trying to block me back out, frantic white bolts of static flitting every which way. "I will not look into your thoughts," I said softly. "Do not worry."

She relaxed. The static disappeared, leaving only the warm darkness. But this time, a glowing orb containing gently swirling colors hung above Catarina's head. Catarina remained unaware of the orb, and I realized it must've been invisible to her.

"Where am I?" she asked.

"That is irrelevant," I replied. "All you need to know is that here, you cannot lie, neither to me nor yourself. I am going to ask you several questions, and I just want you to answer them to the best of your ability."

"Will it hurt? Can you tell me when it'll be over?"

"No, my child. It will not hurt one bit. And it'll be over as soon as you want it to be. Remember, you cannot lie here. So do not try to." I could tell that my words hadn't made a difference in calming her, but when she spoke, her voice was surprisingly steady.

"All right."

"As I promised, I will not look into your current thoughts, but do you permit me to take a brief look into your memories?"

She nodded silently, and I raised my palm to her. The orb above her head floated toward me and settled itself into my cupped fingers. When I stole a glance at Catarina, she was looking at me in utter confusion, and I realized she still must not be able to see the orb. I peered more closely at it.

"Show me," I whispered, and the shifting colors slowly began to take shape into specific memories. They told the narrative of her life, with Catarina as a child, as a teenager, and finally, as an adult. Some things remained the same, like her adoration of the horses in the stables and her mother's lemon cakes, her hatred of her father's mathematics lessons. But others changed over time. The first time she looked at a girl with something other than platonic affection, the moments that formed her mindset about the world, the way her confidence levels shifted.

Specific memories jumped out at me: young Catarina lounging on a sandy lakeshore, water lapping at her toes as her mother tries fruitlessly to pick the sand from her hair. Sneaking out at night with her mare just to ride about the forest, laughing and carefree till the sun rises and her frantic father sends out a search party to locate his missing daughter.

But every once in a while, moments of pure black engulfed the orb, blocking everything else out and interrupting the colors.

"Catarina?" I asked.

"What's happening?"

"There seem to be things missing. As if there were periods in your life that you simply don't remember. Do you know why?"

"No. I don't."

"Interesting. Why did you kill that boy, my child?"

She didn't hesitate. "Because I wanted to."

"Are you absolutely certain of this?"

"Yes."

My next words were a little more fearful, a little more hesitant. "And did you enjoy killing him?"

"Yes."

My eyes widened, and I threw my hands up to end the spell instantly. We were thrown back into the mortal world, so bright in comparison to where we'd been. Catarina blinked, adjusting to the light. I moved away from her and refused to meet her gaze.

"Well?" her mother demanded. The queen's fists were curled tightly around the fabric of her gown and trembling. I refused to meet her gaze, too.

"This was a bad idea," I muttered. "I should not have agreed to this."

"What happened?"

"Please, Your Majesty. I am very tired, and I'd like to sleep now. If you would be so kind—"

"Tontin, as your queen, I demand to know what happened." The Queen of Pheorirya was furious, and the flames that threatened to explode from her skin made themselves more than clear.

"I apologize, but I really cannot." My eyes flitted to Catarina for a brief second. She wore a slight smile that rattled me to my core. "Please, just . . . leave my home."

Her mother snatched her hand in her own and stalked to the front door, then flung it open with a bang that rattled the paintings on the walls.

"You have disappointed me, prophet," she spat out, dragging her daughter outside. I watched them mount their horses and ride away from my window, still physically trembling from Catarina's words. I hadn't failed to notice the sick, twisted light in Catarina's eyes, as if she was remembering the moment she killed that man and savoring it. She seemed to find joy in the terror of both her mother and me. I sometimes would catch her smiling when everyone around her was miserable or scared.

Iesso's face is pale when I finally look at her again.

"Oh," she breathes. Her tears have vanished, but something more fearful lingers in her eyes now. "I still . . . I don't know. I still don't understand it all. She acted impulsively, but I never suspected that she could *enjoy* such a thing; she always seemed like a normal child. Mostly."

She sniffs a little, smiling to herself. "I know those lemon cakes. Catarina would eat them till she threw up, and then go back for more. Everything I remember about her childhood years is positive." But then her expression sobers a bit, and she looks away. "It all changed with that assassination attempt."

"Are you saying that something happened that night that changed her?" I ask.

"I don't think something changed in her," she whispers. "It's not possible for someone to go from innocent and good to wicked overnight. Something must have *awakened* in her."

CHAPTER TWELVE

PHILAN

I AM BURNING. Burning, burning, burning. I jerk awake. Sweat pours down my face. The air feels like sandpaper against my skin. I look around me. I am lying in a barren wasteland. Mountains of red sand and rivers of murky brown water mark the land, which is littered with pale objects. I reach for one with quivering hands. I examine it. It is smooth all over and jagged on one end. But it smells of death, and only then do I realize what it is. A human bone. I swallow a scream, throwing it far, far away from me. I struggle to breathe. Where am I? Then I look up.

I can't swallow my scream this time. The person flying above me—no, the demon—is made of shadows and darkness. Its eyes are just glowing slits, and long, curved fangs glint in the dim red light. Dark, curving wings frame its form. It reminds me of a dragon, with long, spiraling horns and a slashing tail, but it has the figure of a woman. Her pale skin is stark against the blackness of her feathered wings.

"You must be Philan Lin," she says, circling me. Observing me.

"Who are you? Where am I?" My voice quivers with the tears I am holding in.

The demon laughs cruelly. "Get up."

She pulls me to my feet, and I shudder when her sharp nails brush my skin. I look down at myself. The human I'd been before is gone. The human arms, the human legs, the human flesh are not here. Black, feathered wings sprout from my shoulder blades instead, and my head is weighed down with a pair of long, twisting horns. My skin is paler. My fingernails have been replaced with talons. I look exactly like her—like a demon.

A wail wells in my throat. "What did you do to me?" I scream.

Her smile is serpentine. "I did nothing to you. Philan Lin, you are *dead*."

"What?"

"You are in Ahuiqir. The land of demons and tormented souls."

"Who are you?" I moan, tipping forward and falling to my knees again.

She laughs again, delighting in my misery. "Give me three reasons why I should even consider telling you my name."

"Please," I whisper.

"You're pathetic." She breathes. "But I suppose I'll grant you this favor." She crouches down so her eyes are level with mine. "My name is Victoire Liverraine, and my favorite food is human flesh."

I blanch, the scant contents of my stomach coming up into my throat. She smiles at me again, her lips stretching around her fangs. "Look around you, Philan. Take in your new home."

I stand, looking around for the first time. We are in what looks to be a courtyard lined with gardens, and behind us is a sprawling castle constructed solely of black marble. But there are no flowers in the garden. Instead, bones litter the deep red soil, some with rotting flesh still clinging to them. I want to feel repulsed, but instead, I am intrigued. Victoire laughs at the expression on my face. I slowly walk toward one of the bone-filled gardens as if hypnotized. As I get closer, I realize that the soil was never naturally a red color. The red color is from blood seeping into the dirt. I reach forward and pick up a bone. It smells amazing. A sudden pang of hunger jolts my stomach. I feel a need to satiate myself. Victoire floats up behind me.

"Demons are carnivores. We were born to consume human flesh and crave the taste of human suffering. So go ahead," she whispers in my ear.

"Eat them all. I know you want to." I shake my head, but I am already reaching for another chunk of lingering flesh.

I devour all signs of carnage, one by one, with tears streaming down my face.

I stand alone in the courtyard after Victoire leaves me, still shivering even in the blistering heat. I wrap my arms around myself. The haze of fear rendering me useless begins to wear off, and I slowly grow more curious of my surroundings. And my body. I take a step forward. Even walking feels different as a demon. My legs hum with energy desperate to be let out, and my wings bump lightly against my calves with every step. *The body of a predator*, I think. That thought would've once terrified me, but now, it only excites me. I attempt to stretch and contract my wings, discovering a whole new, intricate system of muscles. Each movement is awkward and clumsy, but when I spot the shadowy silhouettes of other demons twisting through the red sky high above me, I cannot bring myself to wait any longer.

It takes me several seconds to feel out how to spread my wings, but once I do, something deep within me seems to awaken. I jump up, powered by the strength in my new legs. My wings beat once, twice, and then I'm shooting into the air. Childlike elation fills me as I watch the ground get further and further away. My wings begin moving on their own, somehow knowing exactly how to maneuver through the air. I trust them to never let me fall. The hot wind rips at my hair and sand blows in my face, but I only laugh.

Ahuiqir unfolds itself before me, revealing terracotta mountains in the distance, spindly cracks in the dry earth, and an utter lack of water. There's beauty in the roughness of it all. Guinyth had been beautiful too, but in the classic way. In the boring way. *I prefer this.*

I can hear every single thing within a massive radius of me: the chattering of two demons flying side by side and the rustling wind blowing through leaf-less trees below me. My vision is sharper and clearer. I've never felt this free before. This powerful and boundless. *I love this body*, I think.

Letting out a cry of joy, I tilt my wings and dive straight for the ground only to veer up at the last possible second. My heart pounds furiously in my chest and my lips are permanently etched into a goofy smile as I fly for the black castle I'd seen earlier.

I stand on the top step of the stairs leading up to the castle. Victoire Liverraine's home is exactly how Soren would've wanted our manor to turn out: all luxurious furniture, well-appointed fixtures, delicate embroidery on the curtains, and an overall sense of deep, sumptuous style. I feel a strange sensation of smugness at that, followed instantly by a stab of guilt. Why do I think of Soren this way? I'd always liked him, but now, the idea of having something he'd always desperately wanted is something I relish.

"You're a new demon, aren't you?" asks someone from behind me. I flinch, bracing myself for another verbal beating. But the demon before me doesn't bear the same merciless smirk that I'd begun to assume all demons did. She's just looking at me.

"You have that dazed look on your face," she deadpans.

Ah. There it is.

"Why do new demons always feel so guilty?" She leans in closer to peer at my face. "Is it some sort of chemical reaction in your brain? Why do you feel the constant need to reminisce about a past life?" She braces her hands on my shoulders and shakes, hard. "Let *go.* Ahuiqir is about letting go."

I stare at her incredulously, utterly dumbfounded. "What?"

She shakes her head at me, sighing. "I was a new demon once, too. Trust me, I know. And I've noticed a pattern in every new demon that I come across. I almost feel sorry for you. Tell me, how did you come to be here? I'm curious."

I frown and try to remember. How could I forget the way I died? My memories suddenly feel as if they're incased in a thick, sugary syrup. I panic, trying to fight my way through molasses, but the details are indiscernible.

"I think I was murdered," I whisper, and as soon I as I speak the words, the shocking reality of it all hits me once again.

"Ah," the demon says. She must've noticed the expression of alarm on my face but doesn't address it. "A classic. I'd say about forty percent of every demon in this place was murdered. Don't expect any sympathy cards."

"I—"

"I've got to go now." She smiles at me, fangs glinting in the candle-illuminated hallway. "Take care, Philan. And welcome to Liverraine Castle."

She walks away, leaving me completely bewildered. "What's your name?" I call just as she's about to turn the corner. She looks back at me.

"Zamara."

And then she disappears. Unable to do much else, I continue on.

Liverraine Castle is a true work of art. Hundred-foot columns stretch from the floor to the roof of the portico. When I cautiously push my way through the massive double doors adorned with small, iron spikes, a slow smile stretches across my face. The place reeks of feminine grace tinged with poison, with elegant furniture every shade of black and gray imaginable and deep green ivy crawling wildly up the wall. Demons hurry about, slipping in and out of doors and never stopping to talk to each other.

I walk down hallway after hallway, stopping to admire every little bit of décor: a human skull spiked to a wall, paintings illustrated by what seems suspiciously like blood, and a shelf with rows of decapitated rodents suspended in jars of resin. It's beyond obvious exactly whose home this is, as all this reflects Victoire perfectly. I let out a high-strung laugh. My old, human existence, with memories of Zhengya and all the other people I'd trust my life with already seem infinitely distant.

"Philan," somebody calls.

I instantly recognize the voice as Victoire's and involuntarily flinch. When I finally convince myself to turn around, she's already directly behind me, staring down at me. She wears her shadows like a wreath around her neck. "I have a proposition for you."

"Yes?" I ask, keeping her hands in my line of sight.

She barks out a laugh. "I'm not going to kill you, Philan. I have better things to do with you." I smile nervously and she snorts. "I want you to stay in the castle. Live here. You find great pleasure in sneaking around, thinking nobody's noticed you."

My cheeks go up in flames. "Is there a particular reason?"

"Do you need a particular reason?" Victoire asks me. Her shadows shift around, metamorphosing into different contortions and never remaining in the same position for more than a split second. I carefully shift away from them.

"I'm offering you safety. Protection."

I want to laugh. Safety? Protection? With her? I have played the game of royal secrets and ulterior motives all my life—or, well, my past life. I know when someone has a private joke they're playing on you, and I suspect Victoire has something brewing. Nevertheless, my mouth opens on its own.

"That sounds delightful. Thank you for your kindness, Victoire."

CHAPTER THIRTEEN
CATARINA

I SLIDE IN BETWEEN the sheets of my bed, savoring their cool silkiness. Sleep is a gentle creature prowling at the edges of my mind, waiting to pounce. I do not resist when it does. But when I finally see the woman straddled upon a strange creature's back, shrouded in the misty shadows I have come to recognize as being Victoire's, it is far too late to do anything but open my mouth to scream. Even then, claws made of night-kissed shadows reach for me and my voice dies away in my throat.

Did you really think I would give up so easily, Catarina? she laughs. *Your friend Philan joined us today.*

For a second, my mind goes blank. Philan? The sheer cruelty of his name on her lips makes me shudder, but I have to know what she means. "Don't lie to me. He's dead," I whisper. I hate that she even made me say the words aloud.

She laughs again and the sound is hollow and humorless. *I would let you talk to him, but he's currently . . . busy.*

Fear runs down my spine in a wave of tremors. "Busy doing what?"

She circles around me and I stiffen. *It would ruin the fun if I told you, wouldn't it?* She stops moving for a moment and looks at me.

Her gaze shifts a little, her facial features twitch ever so slightly. But when a sharp pain shoots through my skull, I am unprepared. It's as if someone is digging a knife through my scalp and searching, probing, hunting with it. I feel cold fingers wrapping around my mind, trying to pry it open. I scream and fall to my knees. My lungs burn for air. But then the pain leaves as abruptly as it came. I can breathe again. Victoire snarls at me and her eyes flash with dangerous fire.

Give in, Catarina, she hisses. *Give in to me.*

I shake my head, trembling. She falls silent for a moment, and then her arm shoots out. Her nail slices into my cheek and I inhale sharply and stumble back. Even though she had not cut me deep, the wound still burns with a strange kind of pain. Victoire's eyes widen and she steps backward, looking down at her own bloodied hand. Then, with a flare of her wings, she disappears.

Brienne nudges me awake. She must have heard me thrashing because I can see my bedroom door is open behind her and her wide eyes. Her robe is half on, exposing her bare shoulders. Had I been so loud that I woke her up?

"Catarina, I think you were having a nightmare." She is looking down at me, concern wrinkling her forehead. "You were talking in your sleep. What happened to your face?"

It is still night, and I cast a glance out the balcony window. The full moon is plump and low in the sky, and the pleasant, warm air mocks the burning pain searing my face. I finally jerk up and look down at myself. My pillow is stained through with blood, the soft cotton utterly ruined. I clamp a hand on my throbbing cheek and see my palm is bloody. Brienne does not speak a single word as she offers me her arm and helps me from the bed. She strips away the bloody sheets with deft, sure movements, and throws them to the floor.

"I'll burn them later," she says softly as she strides over to the intricately painted dresser by the wall. Her fingers brush over each drawer, and she finally selects one and pulls out a carefully folded pile of sheets identical to the ones I'd ruined. I watch as she drapes it over the naked mattress, both of us silent. "Come," she says when she's done.

I can do nothing except dip my head in silent gratitude. She rests her hands on each of my shoulders and sets me on a chair. She pulls a needle and some thread from a drawer.

"Sit still." She stitches the cut on my face closed effortlessly. Even through my pained squirming, her hands are steady. Her stitches are neat and precise. The pain is secondary only to the fear coursing through my veins. *Victoire cut me*, I think, stunned. *She* cut *me.*

"Will it scar?" I ask her. I am not worried about how my appearance may be altered; I couldn't care less. But I can't imagine having a permanent reminder of what this demon did to me. I can't imagine being forced to see it in the mirror every day. Brienne pauses.

"Probably." We sit in silence for a while more, her nimble hands the only movement in the room. "I sew a lot," Brienne says, smiling a little.

I nod. It explains the fluidity in her strokes and the ease with which she handles the needle. She finishes her work and carefully dabs away the remainder of the blood with a clean towel.

"Sleep now, Catarina," she says as she tucks away her sewing kit and begins to slip out of the room. She cannot be any older than I, and yet, her voice carries with it a motherly sort of tenderness. "You deserve to rest." Then she is gone and I am left alone.

"Thank you," I whisper into the darkness.

My eyes drift shut once again, but as I drift off, I know I'm not going to sleep. This feels like before. I panic. The blackness that presses down upon me is not the signature one of deep, rejuvenating sleep. No, I am not sleeping. I'd just escaped this. My heart sinks. My body won't move. It's too late and I feel horribly helpless. This lack of *anything*, lack of sound and sight and touch is all too familiar, and when I jerk and thrash, or at least try to, I am only pulled deeper.

But just as the pressure and the utter nothingness reaches its peak and I brace myself for Victoire's inevitable appearance, it all comes crashing down. It's suddenly as if I'm looking down at myself from the perspective of someone else. The cut arching across my cheek begins to glow with a pale light. It's a peculiar sensation to fall into the folds of your own skin. But it looks like that's exactly where I'm going, sucked down into my own reopened wound. Brienne's stitches gasp and spread wide, letting my mind drop down into the abyss.

I hear a voice, utterly emotionless. *My mother had run away after my father's death. I had a sister, but she'd been taken in by a friend. Nobody wanted to take me in, though. Nobody wanted to give a sick child a second chance—or expose themselves to disease. Somehow, the wonderful Lady Ibela and her wonderful spouse, Prince Innis, found me in the dark forest where I lay, waiting to die. They took me in. I wish they would have let me die there. Death would have been far better than the twelve torturous years I spent with them.*

I am in a different world. I'm floating shapelessly above a bedroom I don't recognize, with a massive bed and gold gilded furniture and a pristine white, beautifully-patterned rug. But everything is tinted in blue haze. A memory, I realize. And, upon closer inspection, my eyes widen. *Victoire's* memory.

Hearing the drunken, blundering footsteps of Prince Innis – who I recognize the way that one understands everything in a dream that later makes no sense – and his friends come closer and closer, Victoire locks herself in an adjoining washroom. Wine glasses clink against one another as they consume bottle after bottle. Victoire is different here. The cool blond hair, the icy blue eyes—they are there, but where are her wings? Her horns? Her shadows? Innis and his friends will reach her soon. As they always do. Her memory washes over me—it's as if I'm there, as if I am her.

"My daughter," Prince Innis calls, his words slurring together. He's not a real prince of royal blood. He only likes being addressed as one. He's merely a nobleman. "Where are you?" he calls. They are right outside the washroom door now. Victoire chokes on a sob. "My darling Eliza," he purrs, "I know you are here. Do not be rude to our guests. Come to your father."

Still, she manages to stay silent. But then he throws the weight of his entire body on the door. The wood shudders and groans with each hit and she has nowhere to escape. Finally, the door frame gives way, and light spills into the darkness of the small room. She feels naked even though she is fully clothed.

"My, my," one of Innis's friends says. Eliza can vaguely recall his name to be Urian, a drug dealer well-known for business in the city. His eyes roam hungrily over her body, and it takes every ounce of will in her heart and strength in her legs to keep from shaking. "Your daughter certainly has grown into a lovely young woman."

"Is she not a fine creature?" her adoptive father says. They speak as if she is not there in front of them. As if she is not a human, but a prize.

"She is not yet wedded to someone?" The third man asks as he slides a calloused hand across her waist. His eyes are glassy with desire. She has seen him before but doesn't remember his name. His hand travels lower, and even though every inch of her body is screaming for her to run, to escape, she cannot.

"Not yet." There is an edge of bitterness to her adoptive father's voice.

Urian smiles, but there is nothing sincere about it. "A shame."

"Dance with us," Innis coos. He pulls her into his arms and she flinches away from the reek of alcohol that stains his breath. "Sing us a song, Urian," he calls to his friend. The man, running a hand through his oily black hair, opens his mouth and begins to sing. The other man standing beside him joins in. Innis twirls her around and around, but she cannot break free.

"Let me go. Please." She refuses to let her voice quiver.

"Aren't you having fun, my daughter?"

She is swung into Urian's arms. He smells of sweat and cigarettes and urine, and he grins down at her, revealing yellowing, crooked teeth. He crushes her body against his and twines his fingers with hers. A wet kiss brushes against her cheek and she shudders in disgust. The air in the room has grown thick and damp and she does not think she is still breathing. A persistent ache is building in her temple and she throws a desperate glance at the open window. It is only across the room, but that unreachable distance seems, to her, like miles upon miles. A pitiful breeze echoes through the room but it is not enough. She longs to escape.

"Please, sir. I have grown weary of dancing now. If you'll excuse me—"

One fist locks around her neck and another slides into her loose hair. Her words are choked away with a forceful squeeze. "My darling, you are unwed, as your father said."

"Yes," she manages to choke out.

"You must marry."

"Yes," she says again. The hand he has around her neck is tightening. Suddenly, he jerks her head back, baring her throat. His lips come down to graze the sensitive skin there, and even as she writhes in his grip, it is no use.

"If you were smart, you'd marry me," he says.

"I—I cannot, sir."

"Why not?"

"I have . . . I have many suitors already." The lie comes out stammered and clumsy. In reality, she has not had a single suitor since she turned sixteen. His eyes flash with anger.

"I have offered you a life of content comfort, and yet you reject me?"

"I-I'm sorry, sir."

"Whore. You are an insufferable whore, Eliza."

She hates the sound of her name on his lips. "I'm sorry, I'm sorry, I'm sorry." She sobs because there is nothing else for her to say.

He sneers. "Pathetic girl. You may have grown weary, but I certainly have not. You will dance with me until I say you can leave."

She is passed through the hands of these three men for hours and hours, until her face is damp with their saliva and she is shaking with anger. She escapes to the armory and finally lets the tears come. They stream down her face, hot, fast, and angry. She paces back and forth, her bare feet wearing a path in the rough stone floor. The air is damp and cold, but she does not bother pulling her cloak tighter around her shoulders. The room is small and cramped and filled to the brim with rusting, dull blades that are long unfit for use. She is filled to the brim with resentment.

She doesn't know what she's going to do. She does not know how to escape this, she doesn't know anything. All she knows is that she is exhausted. Her fingers drift up to her throat. She can still feel Urian's fingers locked around her neck. She can still hear the word he snarled at her. Whore.

Tonight is the eve of her twentieth birthday, but it feels more like the eve of her hundredth. She slides down the wall and presses the heels of her palms into her eyes. As if she could force away the tears. But they come down as relentless as ever.

Her fingers close around the hilt of a dagger laying at her side. She brushes away the fine layer of dust that coats both the blade and the leather shaft. Once upon a time, this had been a fine blade. She can feel small jewels studding the leather, and as she slowly clears the grime away, she exposes the flashing gems to the dim light. She admires it for a moment. And then she plunges the dagger into her heart.

Victoire's memory blurs and morphs.

Ahuiqir is a dark, violent, wonderful place, the voice continues, as images of demons swim before me. *It's filled with the tormented souls of those who suffered so much in their lifetimes that it was too much for any other place to handle. I am the queen of them all, and of all their pain. Some lucky ones, especially tormented ones like me, get shadows. Our shadows are our way of releasing all of the pain we dealt with in human life. I had another name, once upon a time. Eliza. But Eliza was weak. I remember the way she apologized to Urian, even though she had nothing to apologize for. Victoire is much better. Victoire can protect herself. Victoire has powers. She can visit people in their dreams as a shadow and torment them. She can control them for short periods of time, polluting their minds with dark, violent thoughts. She can inflict exquisite suffering.*

And thus, Innis and Ibela suffered painful deaths . . .

A new scene emerges. Victoire is no longer Eliza. She is her demon self. Innis and Ibela are running from her, and she can smell their fear mixing with their exhaustion. The streets of Pheorirya are dark and deserted. Even the torches that line the avenues are out, every flame extinguished. A cold rain falls around them, pelting against the cobbled streets. Innis and Ibela run into a dark alley, their breathing labored and shallow. They push by mounds of refuse and fling it in Victoire's path as if that would stop her. She laughs so loud, a part of her worries she'll wake up the town. Then, she remembers she could end them all, too. She tilts her wings, soaring gracefully after them.

"Go, go," she hears Ibela urge her spouse. She smiles to herself, knowing that the alleyway leads to nothing but a dead end. *Humans are so graceless,* Victoire thinks. *It's fascinating how they always help one another up, even right as they are about to die.* Finally, they reach the brick wall, and with nowhere else to go, they turn to her. "Please, stop! Who are you? What did we ever do to you?" Ibela screams.

Victoire laughs, baring her fangs a little more than she needs to. She hears a satisfying little gasp. "More than you will ever know," she says.

Innis steps in front of Ibela, brandishing a small dagger. Victoire almost feels bad for them. Almost. "Stop! If you want to kill her, you'll have to go through me first."

She laughs again. A harsh, bitter sound. "True love, huh?" Victoire whispers. In spite of herself, she longs for that sort of unbreakable attraction between two people. That sort of love that never frays with time. *If Ibela and Innis could be granted that luxury, why couldn't she?* she wonders. She takes her time killing them that night, smiling at each scream. But as their final sighs fade away into the night, she knows that what she has done to them is only a fraction of the pain they had made her suffer through.

That lingering injustice . . . that *is what drives me now and will drive me forever,* the voice says. *Humans are ugly, foul creatures. Death is but a mercy to them.*

My heart is pounding and my hands are shaking when I awake. I wonder if I've been truly sleeping, after all. But, no, it was more real than a dream. There was more certainty to it. I had seen and felt Victoire's memories.

The morning sun beams in my face, and when I reach up to touch the cut Victoire left on my cheek, I find that it's burning hot. I let my head fall back against the headboard of my bed and press against it hard, until I feel pain, just to ensure I'm awake and in the real world. I guiltily try to recall as much as possible about my dream from last night. Does Victoire truly deserve to be as hated as she is? I always assumed her cruelty came from being a demon, not the traumas of a terrible past. Her memories were human. She suffered under human hands.

Suddenly, something heavy crashes into a wall of the manor and jostles the stone of the wall. I hear a loud scream.

I rush out the door with my cheek throbbing and my sleeping robes disheveled. The scent of magic overpowers the rest of my senses, even as I press the sleeve of my shirt to my nose. There's only one person left at Greensbriar who has magic like this. Zhengya must be using her power. Her gift smells of cold metal and silvery winds, of glacial lands and clean rivers. And although it is a pleasant smell, the sheer amount of it is enough to weaken my knees and muddle my thoughts. I throw open the door to the meeting room. She stands in the middle of a whipping whirlwind of snow and ice and frost-coated mist. Her hair is flying around her, framing her rage-contorted face. Her eyes are blazing with power I have never seen before, like a burning pale fire. The room is utterly ravaged, the long wooden dining table splintered and the glass chandelier hanging above it shattered. I spot Brienne and Soren huddling behind half of the table. They cower in the face of her gift, unable to do anything else.

"Zhengya!" I shout. Her head snaps toward me, but the vortex of winter continues around her. "Look around you," I order. "Look around you!"

Finally, she does, her gaze sweeping around the perimeters of the devastated room. She takes in the marred marble floor, the shredded silk armchairs covered in horsehair stuffing, her tearful friends, and then turns back to me. The silver fire in her eyes does not diminish. No, it flares even brighter, even higher, as she throws her arms out and opens her mouth and screams. The sound is filled with such pain and grief that I flinch away from it. Something barrels into my shoulder, and I am thrown to the ground. It is Brienne with her wide, brown eyes and tear-streaked face. A long, jagged shard of wood sails over our heads and lodges itself into the wall behind us. I inhale sharply. I could've been impaled.

"Why is she doing this?" Brienne sobs. "Why?"

"I don't know," I say.

"Stop her. Please!"

Another shriek claws its way out of Zhengya's throat. "Stop!" Zhengya screams, whirling. Her eyes are unseeing and milky with raw emotion. I force myself to look back at her. Her eyes are not on me or anyone else in the room. They are wide, so wide that they bulge from her head. White foam is frothing at her lips, exactly like I'd seen on Soren the night he was possessed. Could that also be happening to Zhengya? Her power continues to surge from her in nauseating waves. "This isn't real," Zhengya whispers. "This is not who you are."

"Who are you talking to?" Brienne demands. If Zhengya had heard her, she does not respond.

"Stop!" Zhengya screams again and presses her hands to her ears. She is shuddering. Tears are rolling down her cheeks in fat, shiny drops. She seems to collapse in on herself, hugging her knees to her chest and rocking back and forth, tearing at her hair. "No, no, no," Zhengya mutters to herself. She drags her nails down her quivering arms, leaving behind angry red lines. And then I am hurtling across the room, dodging stray shards of ice which still shoot from her body. I throw my arms around Zhengya when I reach her, pinning her hands to her sides.

"Zhengya," I hiss in her ear. "Stop."

She falls into my body and the typhoon of power dies away into nothing more than faint whispers of frosted wind. The room is quiet and desolate in its destruction. Zhengya looks small.

I force my voice into a gentle murmur. "Who were you talking to?"

"Philan." Her voice is hoarse from screaming, her eyes are gaunt and hollow. Lifeless. Brienne gasps and throws her hands to her mouth.

"How? In your head? What was he saying?" My voice is nothing more than a breathless whisper. How could she know Philan was still alive?

Finally, she turns those drawn, dull eyes to me.

"He is not himself."

"Why?" When she doesn't respond, I press. "Why isn't he himself?"

A low wail builds in her chest and she claws free from my grip. "He had shadows last night."

I smooth a hand down Zhengya's hair, trying to swallow back my own fear so I can comfort her. "Was it a dream, Zhengya?"

"I saw him. He came to me in my sleep. He has been brainwashed," she growls, pulling away slightly from me. "Brainwashed, brainwashed." She repeats the word until it fades into mindless mutters.

"Brainwashed by whom?" My own voice is shaking. Dread pools into lead weight in my stomach as I await the answer.

"He was in my head just now. He spoke with to me."

"And?" I breathe.

"He claims he is happy. Happy away from me." She fixes her gaze at a point I cannot see. "But he's lying."

"Why is he lying? How do you know he's lying?" My hands begin to shake as they hold her. Brienne and Soren inch closer, trembling and wide-eyed with concern.

"He has turned into a demon."

Brienne begins sobbing and I see Soren fall to his knees, but my head is pounding too much for me to be certain. The news shocks me as if I didn't already know.

CHAPTER FOURTEEN

PHILAN

Zhengya. Zhengya Lin. Last night, when I saw her for the first time since my death, I was disgusted by the sight. Humans are so . . . fleshy. And had I been that small and squirmy when I was human? Her face had been red and splotchy as she cried, her nose sticky with mucus as she begged me to return to her. Why doesn't she understand? I don't want to go back. How did we ever share blood? Why did I ever love her so much? I finally understand demons' hatred for humans. Pathetic, filthy creatures. Soon, Queen Victoire can teach me how to take over human bodies.

As if summoned by my very thoughts, she appears beside me. Victoire's icy eyes are alight with wicked joy. "Do you know where my husband's office is?"

I nod, having seen it during my very first day in Ahuiqir. And although I hadn't yet gotten the opportunity to meet King Fane, his reputation was introduction enough. A demon rumored to be godlike, possessing a rare gift unique to him that no one in living memory had witnessed. It was one of the first bits of demon gossip I learned after my resurrection.

"Get him," Victoire orders, her voice breathless. She hesitates. "And Minerva, too. There's news to share."

I dip my head obediently and slip away.

Minerva is another foreign being, but like Fane, her reputation precedes her. Servants gossiping amongst themselves had told me all I needed to know about her relationship with the king and queen. A rumored ex-lover of Fane's, Minerva had always been jealous of Victoire's marriage, and Victoire was jealous of the attention Fane showed Minerva. Already I was learning the little intricacies of being a demon, including the gossip. *Of course that wouldn't change even in death,* I think with a small smile. My horrible mother was right about that, at least. I briefly entertain paying my mother a visit in my new state and letting her scream her throat out at the sight of me. But duty calls.

I reach the door to the king's quarters and press down on the gold-plated door handle. Minerva and Fane are curled together on a couch in the study. One of his hands rests on the sloping curve of her waist, while the other rests just under the hem of her skirt. His eyes are dark with longing and roam freely over her body. For a moment, neither notices my presence. Minerva tangles her fingers in his hair and pulls Fane's ear to her lips, murmuring something. Her hand is drifting toward his collar. But then his gaze snaps upward and he sees me.

"Philan," he says, his voice an odd mixture of amusement and animosity. I shirk away. He knows my name already.

"Victoire . . . Victoire sent me to retrieve you both," I say.

At the sound of the queen's name, Minerva's lip curls into a mirthless sneer. She slowly stands from the couch, adjusting her dress so that it falls back over her knees before dragging a long, manicured nail over the sharp, clean edge of Fane's jaw. "Then I suppose we must obey the queen's word," she whispers, offering him a hand.

He grins rakishly, flashing those white fangs. "I suppose we must," he agrees, and I cannot help but feel as if they share knowledge I do not know.

A little while later, the four of us sit at the long wooden table of the meeting room. I cannot bring myself to meet the gazes of any of the three demons around me. Fane is the embodiment of casual grace, with his arm propped behind his head and a curl of his dark, silky hair falling into his face. And yet, his eyes are sharp and focused and pinned on Victoire. She nurses a glass of wine, her eyes shut and head bowed as she savors each slow sip. Is she aware of Fane's unfaithfulness? And if so, why has she not done anything about it? Minerva certainly doesn't seem interested in being discreet.

Minerva wrinkles her nose. "What is in that wine?"

I sniff the air, and sure enough, I can smell the distinct bitter smell of poisonous moonseed slightly camouflaged by the pungent fragrance of the wine. I thank my demon nose for its precision. Why did she put it in her own drink? I know that poison wouldn't be strong enough to kill her, but it must be causing her pain.

Fane reads the look on my face and snorts. "My darling wife has her little habits. One of them is to continuously poison herself." He doesn't elaborate any further. She finishes the glass and pours another, not even acknowledging that either of them has spoken.

"I visited our dear Catarina last night," Victoire says.

Fane drags his nails along the table, leaving behind white claw marks. "And? Get to the point, Victoire. Some of us have more important things to do."

I wince. The queen's eyes flash angrily toward him, but she doesn't move to retaliate. "I scratched her, Fane. I physically touched her."

His wings twitch a little. "In your shadow form? In her dream?"

"That's not possible," Minerva says softly. But her eyes are alight and her body leans forward now as she looks at Victoire.

Fane dismisses her with a snap of his tail. "Shut your mouth."

She instantly silences, and Victoire smiles haughtily. "Yes, in her dream."

A tendril of smoke drifts from the king's hand. "Then why the hell didn't you kill her?" he snarls.

Victoire's wings open slightly as her smile fades, and she bares her wine-stained fangs. "She was waking up. I couldn't stay."

Fane glances at me for the first time, but his eyes slide unseeingly over me. As if I am nothing more than a piece of furniture. "Didn't you visit the girl, Zhengya, last night too?"

I notice how he doesn't call her my sister, and I smile. "Yes, why?"

He pauses for a moment, thinking. "Next time you visit her, Philan, try to cut her, like Victoire did to Catarina. Just a little, don't kill her. I think it would be more torturous for her if she has to watch you slowly fade away from who she knows you to be."

A soft huff of laughter escapes my lips. "Yes, My King."

Victoire hesitates for a moment. "I think we can use her continuous love for you to our benefit in another way. How much do you think she still trusts you?"

I think back to last night. "Very much."

"Then do you think you can glean information from her about Catarina and the state of Pheorirya?"

"Yes. Of course."

Both Fane and Minerva smile wickedly. It seems that on the subject of world domination, the three of them are perfectly united. But I find myself confused. What do these infinitely powerful beings want with my brat sister and her new little toy, Catarina? Sure, it was fun to torment, but this couldn't be what they do all day.

Fane laughs at my furrowed brows. I shrug, unsure of what to do. "Ah, Philan. My apologies. I forget that there are some things you don't know yet." He leans forward, his face suddenly going sober. "What have you noticed about the lovely Ahuiqir so far?"

"The climate is dry," I say instantly. "And hot."

"Precisely. And what about the condition of the prey?"

"There's none."

He nods. "And what do you think the citizens of our city want us to do because of this problem?"

The realization finally dawns on me. "Get us food . . . humans. From Guinyth."

"I knew you were a smart one, Philan." His words are kind, but his tone is not. "We just have one teensy, weensy problem. The population of Ahuiqir is only about one hundred thousand, but there are millions of humans living in Guinyth. And while one demon would have no problem at all getting through one human, one demon would have a much, much harder time getting through ten humans. Or twenty. Or thirty. Especially shadow-less demons, like most of the ones outside of this room. But thanks to my darling Victoire, Catarina has already completed one crucial part of our plan. What do you think that step was, Philan?"

"Killing her parents," I say. It all makes sense now. They wish to destroy Guinyth from the inside out. They'll weaken the leadership and feast on the millions of citizens.

"And why do you think Soren went crazy within your old manor?"

"He was supposed to kill everyone there. Including Catarina." To try to kill off the entire Winyr line. No gifts would mean no meaningful opposition.

Minerva laughs. "And even though Vicky promised it'd work, it didn't. Evidently."

Victoire lets out a snarl, but Fane ignores both of them.

"It was only a coincidence that you were killed and arrived here, Philan, but I suppose this is for the better," he says.

"Doesn't Queen Simone also have a sister?" I ask suddenly. "Couldn't she be a threat too?"

Victoire laughs, and Fane joins her. "Iesso Endyrdyn is as good as giftless. We'll find no threat in her," he says.

I mull over what I've learned, suddenly even more enthralled with my new life. I could feast on a thousand people I once knew. My tastes would have been revolting to my past self, but now, it's like the more horrible the thought, the more delicious it feels to think it. I'm itching with anticipation to help them carry out their plans. It feels good to be powerful.

CHAPTER FIFTEEN

ZHENGYA

I KNOCK HESITANTLY on Catarina's door. For a moment there is only silence. I sigh and turn to leave.

"Come in," she calls. I instantly turn around, relief flooding me as I open the door. She's standing on her balcony, staring up at the mid-afternoon sky. I join her in looking out across the land. The sun is at the zenith of its arc across the sky and its light shines down on my upturned face. I let loose a sigh at the sensation, leaning against the railing. The city of Tegak shimmers in the distance, its weighty, brooding buildings shrouded with a thin veil of smoky smog. Sometimes I forget how close I am to what was once my home. Neither of us feel compelled to speak. I enjoy the sweet silence between us.

"Do you think I've gone crazy?" I ask finally, bitterness creeping its way into my voice. But Catarina looks at me with genuine interest. She tilts her head as she thinks about my inquiry.

"No. I think the things happening around you are overwhelming." She smiles faintly. "I have faith that things will get better."

But try as I might, I can't bring myself to believe her. "I'm scared."

"Me too."

Our eyes meet, and something deep inside me stirs. I have grown to crave wordless moments like these with Catarina. Even though I've long lost my home, I may have gained a new one in the depths of her gaze. Her eyes flutter shut when she begins to speak.

"Sometimes I dream I am flying," Catarina whispers. "The sky is cloudless, the wind is sweet, and I am smiling."

"Where do you fly to?" I whisper.

"Nowhere." She sighs softly. "I remember once when I was a girl, my father and I talked of demons. But neither he nor I was serious. I was playing with something; he was laughing, I was laughing . . ." She trails off. "And then he lifted me into the air so I could pretend to be flying. I think it was one of the happiest moments of my life."

"And then?"

Somewhere, a bird calls out and trees wave in the wind. Catarina tips her head back as if she's imagining herself flying again.

"I don't know. I think about that moment a lot. I think it makes me feel like an innocent." She opens her eyes to look at me again. "My father always told me that everyone has a reason to be evil, but we are pure in the very centers of our souls. Someone, or something, corrupts them. Strips away that innocence. But sometimes I can't bring myself to believe that."

My hands tremble as I take a deep breath. "My brother is a demon," I say. When I look down, I see that the skin around my knuckles is stretched so taut I can count the individual bones lying there. "A demon."

"It was out of your control."

"Do you think you're going crazy sometimes, too?"

"Always."

I look back out toward the horizon.

"Sometimes," she begins, and my attention returns to her. Something in Catarina's expression has changed. "Sometimes I'm not sure if Victoire is a fragment of my imagination. What is happening to us, Zhengya? Sometimes I'm not sure if this *something* inside me is real, or fake, or if I . . ." Again, she trails off, and I realize that she's shaking so hard that she's forced to grip the railing for support. Silent tears are falling from her pale cheeks. "I'm only now realizing, no matter how hard I try to hide it, I won't be able to because I am so damn terrified of everything."

I reach for Catarina's hands and cup them in my own. "Thank you," I breathe. "Thank you so much."

"Whatever for?" she whispers. I don't dare look at her. What would happen if I did? I'd break down and never stop crying and lose any bit of strength I'd tricked myself into believing I had. But when I do, I find that Catarina is smiling.

"For understanding." I turn and leave then, and as soon as I've stepped into the hallway, I miss her steely, unshakable presence.

Catarina reminds me of Philan sometimes. The way I can talk to both of them is the same; they're never too busy, like Liserli, or well-meaning but unable to relate, like Brienne. I do not regret confiding in her. But even if she could understand my deepest fears, she'll never be able to understand the degree of anger I feel toward the demons. I couldn't expect it of her, but it all drives me out of my mind with frustration, so I stalk out of my room and down the rickety stairs, then head for the Greensbriar Manor library.

When Philan and I first found the manor tucked into a small pocket of the forest, the library had already been stocked floor to ceiling with manuals for war strategies, romance novels, books full of ancient myths and legends, and anything else imaginable. I remember the first few nights in the manor; the beds had been so unbelievably filthy that we'd slept on the rugs in the library with our heads propped up by books and bodies packed together for warmth. The memory makes me smile sadly, and a new bout of energy fills me. It isn't possible for someone to completely stop loving someone else, especially family, within the span of one day. I have to remind myself of this frequently. Philan has been brainwashed. It's not his fault. It can't be, or I don't know what I'll do.

I slowly comb through the rows, running my fingers along all the spines of the aged, yellowing books. I can feel myself collecting dust on my clothing as I go. But as time barrels on, marked by the ticking of the old grandfather clock on the wall, my skin begins to crawl with irritation. How is it possible that out of thousands of books, there is not a single one on demons?

Suddenly, something catches my eye. It's a small handmade book sitting on a circular table in the corner. The curtains of the window are askew enough to allow a single ray of sunshine to stream down at an angle and hit it right in the center, illuminating it. I decide to take it as a sign, and I pick it up gingerly. I have no idea how old it is, but the spine is worn and the page edges tattered. Not a new book, but oddly plain for this once-grand collection. Both the front and back covers are a sage green with no words or decoration.

I let the pages fall open by themselves in my hands, not wanting to damage the delicate parchment. One of the pages slips out and flutters to the floor. Frowning, I bend to retrieve it. It has opened to a page with a large portrait on it. A woman's face is illustrated in astounding detail, her eyebrows furrowed and mouth open in an expression caught somewhere between pain and pleasure. But there's something off-putting about the entire thing. And as my gaze travels upward, I finally notice what is disconcerting. Both eyes are completely black.

My chest feels tight. I carefully tuck the sheet into the back of the book. Flipping to the front, I begin to sweep my gaze across the first page. Black ink dances across it in unorganized sections, lines crossing with one another and blurring into one. The paper is torn and dirty and sometimes the sporadic tears in it leave words completely destroyed. I turn to the next page. It's full of the same hurried writing, with just as many tears and illegible words. I hesitate before carrying the book to a table. I flip through with trembling hands. *Demon, demon, demon.* While I cannot make out much more, that single word is a recurring theme throughout the pages. A triumphant smile lights my face. I leave my seat at the table, returning with a sheet of paper and a pen.

Over the next few weeks, I'm in the library all day. I don't make time for meals until Brienne begs; I am much too busy rewriting the book. The mundane motions of carefully sorting each word's letters to make out its meaning is strangely comforting, which I assume is part of the reason I have become so fixated. Last night, I saw Philan for the second time since his death. Nothing about him is the same. But I cannot bring myself to hate him. He still loves me. He will forever love me, and I will forever love him. But the four, identical, teardrop-shaped scabs on my arm linger and are a constant reminder of what he did to me. Do the ones who love you unconditionally hurt you? Do they sneer at you and say they enjoy watching you suffer?

No, I tell myself. *They don't*. But this isn't who Philan is. I can still save him. He still loves me. Is this what Catarina had to endure with her demon? Her Victoire?

I put down my pen and my fingers find the dully aching spot where he'd grabbed me. I don't even realize when the tears start streaming down my face, but they do in an unyielding torrent. I shake with the sheer force of all my pent-up sorrow and anger. My hands clasp over my mouth, trying to suppress the screams that threaten to spill from me. *Make it stop*, I think. *Make it stop*.

Warm arms wrap around me, and someone is whispering reassurances in my ear. It's Liserli. I can recognize the sharp cinnamon scent of her hair, the calluses of her scarred hands. She massages my shoulders, and I feel myself slowly relax. Even when I was growing up with my blood family, comfort for a sad day didn't come as quickly as it does living here in Greensbriar Manor.

"It's all right, Zhengya. Will you be okay?" Liserli asks. She reaches past me and gently moves the pen and notebook to the far end of the desk. That gesture makes me smile. I nod, and she smiles so brightly that I want to cry again. "Good. We all have our days. You just have to learn to move on." She pats my head. "Stay strong, Zhengya. You've always been."

I stare at myself in the bathroom mirror. The girl I see is a husk of what she used to be. She's skinny and pale, and her eyes are just as dull as the hair that she hasn't washed in weeks. I splash hot water on my face until it's red, then clean the dirt from under my fingernails. The water that swirls down the drain runs brown.

I walk slowly back to the library, feeling slightly better than I had before. Hours pass, and the sun has completely disappeared from the sky, leaving behind a million tiny stars and the comforting sounds of night. Owls and cicadas and frogs call to one another in the distance. There is no sense of victory, no sense of triumph when at last I put my pen down and stare down at my work. I only feel completion and a rekindled, burning will to murder those who've stolen my brother from me. I begin to read the book. Now that it is rewritten in my own hand, I discover it is a series of diary entries.

November 30th, 1689

The battle at Cheusnys Cave has devastated us all. The mighty Tillkasen Forest surrounding Liverraine Castle has been set aflame. The attack from the humans was well planned, very calculated and precise, but we cannot give up this cave. Without it, we might as well burn our city now. Supplies are running low, along with the spirits of our soldiers. General Sabien, my brother, has been badly injured, enough that his demon blood struggles to heal his wounds. He has been in the physicians' tent for days now. The humans are sure to attack again, and I am not sure if we can survive another one. However, there is some good news: Sabien's partner, Gwendydd, has recently given birth to a son, whom she has named Fane. Children born in wartime are good luck. Perhaps this will all be over soon, and Fane Liverraine can grow up without the shadow of violence looming over him.

–Illythia Liverraine

December 2nd, 1689

My brother remains unwell. The nurses say that he burns all day and shivers all night, but I still have hope that he will get better. Really, that's all you can do these days. Have hope. So I hope that the weather will be in our favor, that Fane will grow up happy, that Sabien will recover, and that everything will be over soon. I also hope for a good hunt this afternoon. There is nothing I wouldn't do for human meat right now.

The winds are picking up now, and I can tell winter storms are coming. The spies we have sent to the human territories have not returned. It has been days. I pray to the gods that they will not attack now.

–Illythia Liverraine

December 16th, 1689

Food is running low. Too low. Gwendydd is extremely weak and unable to suckle Fane any longer, and he cries long into the night. I don't know if Gwendydd's weakness is from lack of proper food or deep melancholy. Most likely both. My brother's condition has not worsened, but it has not improved either. General Merle wants to attack the humans in two days. We are not prepared. It is hard to have hope, but I do. I cling to that positivity and I do not let go.

–Illythia Liverraine

December 21st, 1689

Evening of the Solstice

Never in my life has a winter solstice gone by like this. I am filled with both overwhelming sadness and joy. My brother passed away last night. Gwendydd refuses to leave his body, and I understand. I wept through the whole night. Despite that, General Merle led us to a victory on the eighteenth and there is new hope. Now, we finally have a chance to reclaim Cheusnys Cave as our own. I am so unbelievably tired of fighting this war. Under normal circumstances, many demons live forever, but is that necessarily a good thing? Sometimes I wish I were human; I could follow Sabien, then. They are lucky they can die so easily. But I know everything will be all right. At the end of the day, life is simple.

–Illythia Liverraine

January 1st, 1690

We caught four human spies in our stables today. They killed off two of our finest octilli. One of them was Gwendydd's precious Auralia. Never before have I seen my sister-in-law so miserable, mourning both the death of her brother and her beloved mount. Of course, Gwendydd ordered that the spies be killed on the spot. They would have never given up any information anyway.

–Illythia Liverraine

January 7th, 1690

There is something wrong with Fane. He is not a normal infant. Normal demon babes cry when they are uncomfortable. They need their mothers, and they kick and scream when they cannot be with them. Gwendydd has not been able to feed her son in two days, yet not once has a single whine passed through his lips. And those eyes of his, full of calm, calculated intelligence a one-month-old demon should not be able to have.

–Illythia Liverraine

My heart pounds in my chest, my cheeks warm with the magnitude of my discovery. *Fane Liverraine.*

My mind has turned to mush and I'm now far too tired to ponder anything. I trudge up to my room, almost collapsing in exhaustion as soon as I pass through the doorway. But I cannot seem to force myself to sleep yet. Leaving a trail of dirty clothing in my wake, I wander to the washroom.

For a moment, I can only stare at the bathtub. There are no touches of Soren's handiwork here, by my request. I wanted my washroom to retain the natural charm of Greensbriar Manor. The curtains are old, moth-eaten red velvet and barely hanging on. Despite the city of cobwebs hanging from the ceiling, it is a sunny, comfortable room. Heat rushes to my cheeks, accompanied by a feeling of disgusted shame in myself. How could I let myself be this unhinged? I'd been deciphering and transcribing for weeks only to end up with a war diary from some ancient demon veteran. Who was Fane? What have I learned that could help me get Philan? Nothing, and I lost my sanity in the search of it. Then again, I have so much of the diary to read. I muster up the energy to lean forward and pull down the rusting, brown handle, and the sound of the water streaming out of the spout is enough to drown out the roaring in my head.

The library is starting to feel comforting. I recognize the woody scent of the old bookshelves and the faint hint of crisp, sweet apples wafting from the bowls of fruit that Brienne likes to keep at each table. Eagerly, I pick up my stack of parchment.

January 9th, 1690

Rumors have spread around the camp, telling of the clan of strong witches that have allegedly decided to ally with the humans. They are said to ride upon great, winged dragons, larger than three octilli combined. If such powerful sorceresses are truly siding with our enemies, we may no longer have a chance of winning.

Some of us are considering escaping to Guinyth through Cheusnys Cave, where we might live out the rest of our days in hiding. One part of me can't imagine having the audacity to flee and leave one's own people to face their fates. But another completely understands.

So many things these days are about winning and losing, and I wish they weren't, but I cannot control such things. Sometimes, though, I imagine someone who could. Such power, all belonging to one person. It's a terrifying idea. Yet I think of it often.

–Illythia Liverraine

January 25th, 1690

The rumors are true. No time to write, fires started at north end of camp. Fane gone missing. Gwendydd badly burned.

–Illythia Liverraine

January 30th, 1690

The witches have completely taken over our camp, and Fane is still missing. They are just as terrifying as the stories say they are. Their arms are covered completely with tattoos depicting horrible, bloody battles. Their teeth are filed down into points–some sort of rite of passage after their first battle, we think, but can't say for sure. In battle, they dye their hair red with the blood of their enemies.

Gwendydd will not stop screaming for her son, even when the witches beat her until she's bloody. She has lost so many people in just two months, yet she will not back down. The bond between a mother and her baby may as well be the strongest thing in this universe, stronger than any magic could ever be.

–Illythia Liverraine

"Cheusnys Cave?" I whisper out loud.

There have always been inconsequential old wives' tales about a secret gateway between the world demons come from and Guinyth, but I had never heard it named. I never thought the exaggerated tales of my childhood could hold some truth. If there is a passage between our two lands, why hadn't demons come through sooner? My palms begin to sweat as I stand up. My gaze finds the massive map of Guinyth pasted to the innermost wall of the library. It is very old. I scan the browning parchment. On the other side of Tegak, only miles from the edge of its border, is a tiny black dot—no, a hole. A cave entrance—separated from a main traveling road by a small, lonely mountain. And next to the illustration are the words *Cheusnys Cave*. Hiding in plain sight all this time.

My heart is settled. I square my shoulders. I know what I need to do.

There are only three things I know to be true. First, Philan has been stolen from me, brainwashed by demons. Second, I want him back. And third, if he's so lost from reality that he doesn't realize what's happening to me, I'll retrieve him myself.

Nobody will convince me otherwise.

CHAPTER SIXTEEN

FANE

THE BRIGHT RED SUN finally dips below the horizon and I smile from my perch on the ledge of the balcony of my bedroom. The night has finally arrived. I feel the predator inside me stir and come to life. I can feel every slight brush of the wind against my skin. I spread my wings and leap off my balcony and into the air. It feels good to fall for a moment, and I only open my wings at the last possible second. I swoop back up, tucking them back and twirling through the air. Even after centuries, my favorite part of being a demon is and will always be flying.

Philan soars beside me, a matching, exhilarated smile on his face. If it were any other night, we'd fly well into the morning light. But eventually, we must come back down to the ground. The sun is completely gone. Bright red stars twinkle in the black sky. I gesture at Philan, and we land in a patch of forest. For a moment, we just stare at the sky. I can smell all the intertwining scents being carried by the hot wind: dry earth and dying trees. It isn't a pleasant smell, but it is fascinating how each one comes alive at night when there's little else to distract the senses. I catch a whiff of the damp, musty scent of an animal, and seconds later, I hear a slight rustle of leaves. A rare occurrence. Most have been eaten by the demons.

But we can't hunt tonight.

"Do you know what Victoire wants you to do?" I ask Philan.

He nods. He begins by lifting his claws. Tendrils of smoke drift toward his talons as if drawn in by them. They weave between his fingers, twisting, turning, and slowly get larger. The smoke fully engulfs him, and I step backward to give him space. I see his silhouette raise his arms above his head, the tornado of smoke around him reaching its greatest point. He swings his arms back down to his sides and disappears entirely.

I return my gaze to the land and sigh. Philan has potential, despite his annoyingly slow descent into demonhood. I cannot wait for the day he completely disassociates from his past life and from his sister and old friends, but his inexperience is acceptable for the time being.

Fifteen minutes later, he materializes back in front of me with his hair mussed from his journey. He bears a small, wicked smile.

"What happened?" I ask, standing up. "Did she tell you anything?"

"Nothing we don't already know," he says. "She did say there've been rumors of Prophet Tontin attempting to also call a meeting with the other leaders of Guinyth." He leans forward, eyes alight. "And apparently only one showed up."

"Who?"

"Yseult A'tess. She told him that nobody, including her witches, would be willing to unite with Pheorirya."

I laugh. "Good. Even if she wasn't necessarily right, she has enough say that the others will simply join her bandwagon."

"Victoire was right about her trusting me. She was nearly groveling at my feet."

I tilt my head at him. "I'm just curious, Philan. What exactly are your current feelings for your sister?"

He doesn't speak for a long moment. Then he says, "I feel disconnected from her. Like I never knew her. And the more she tries to remind me of my past, the more I want to leave it behind. Forget about it. I don't want to associate myself with her, or any of my old companions anymore."

"Ah," I say. I will decide if I believe him later. We take off again, headed back for the castle. I know the feeling Philan was describing all too well. The acquiring of power is such a beautiful thing, an addictive rush of adrenaline and newfound self-assurance.

"What is the next step in our plan?" he asks me.

"I believe there's nothing to do but wait and see what happens next. If all goes well, Pheorirya will inevitably fall, riddled with riots and protesters, which will sow fear in the minds of everyone else. The citizens of Pheorirya will be forced to spread out to the other cities, which will cause chaos and hopefully tension everywhere, making it easier to attack."

"When do you estimate that'll be?"

"Several months, at most, but our army has been ready for this for years."

Philan nods solemnly, and I focus my gaze back in front of me. I could've admitted that Victoire's hyper-fixation upon the Winyr family, especially Catarina, has become tiring, but chose not to. There is something about the girl that Victoire cannot let go. I feel it goes beyond wanting to feed the population of Ahuiqir ten years over. I've considered what a life without attempting to invade Guinyth would look like. Regardless, Victoire would have my head mounted above her bedroom window if I said any of this aloud. I roll my eyes. Even if discontinuing the mission to invade was on the table, my say wouldn't have any impact on Victoire's decision. It has always been that way, from the very first day she was queen. The role I'd played in Ahuiqir during my reign hadn't thrilled the citizens, but to be completely truthful, the dynamic had worked out perfectly. She likes to make decisions and I like to follow.

Philan's wing grazes my own. "What are you thinking about?"

"What?"

"You have an odd expression on your face."

I shake my head, and he shrugs.

A thin trail of blood drips from the corner of my lips, sliding down the edge of my jaw to my neck. I don't bother to wipe it away. A servant approaches me cautiously, dipping his head so low that his long, mousy brown hair flops over his face.

"Would you like me to clear away your plate?" he asks in a squeaky voice. I offer a lazy, half-hearted wave of my hand just as someone else knocks on the door.

"Come in," I call.

One of Victoire's handmaids, Zamara, enters. "King Fane," she says.

A languid smile curves my lips. "Talk." She swallows, hard, and I can smell her fear wafting in the air. Always delicious. "I won't bite, darling."

Her back straightens slightly and her eyes narrow at the floor. "Your Majesty, a letter has come bearing your name." She hands me a cream-colored envelope. I recognize the spidery handwriting immediately. Aunt Illythia.

My dear Fane,

It's been far too long since the last time I've seen you, but unfortunately I've no time for pleasantries. My spies have intercepted an alarming letter going from Pheoriya to Tegak and another city in the northern lands called Maarso. The new leaders of Pheoriya–some unimportant advisors–seem to be planning a union of cities. This can mean one thing and one thing only. Pheoriya is weakening. Fane, this is the moment we have waited so long for. We could get out of this hellhole. Killing off all of Guinyth's bastardly leaders would leave its citizens in chaos. And when there is chaos, there is weakness. We could finally live in a better world. Ending them would be so much fun.

Have you heard news of Yseult A'tess recently? I worry that her clan will once again ally with the humans, and we may not win against them again.

P.S. Visit your mother and I sometime. It gets lonely.

–Illythia

After finding me sixteen years after the witches had taken me in, both

Illythia and my mother have since become my most frequent correspondents. They send regular letters. I always feel guilt, knowing they both genuinely desire my wellbeing. I would never be able to love them the way they do me. They are more like strangers than family. I'd been raised by others. But even if I had known Illythia my entire life, I wouldn't have liked her. She'd always been a rather gentle-hearted demon, incapable of making decisions, and doing everything necessary to achieve goals. Her only excuse was that she despised the messiness of bloodshed. Not very demonic of her. But in a way, her softness is a relief from the savage, bloodthirsty nature of every other demon in Ahuiqir.

My eyes narrow as I consider Illythia's words. Yseult. Her mother had been a warrior and had helped command the clan of witches in their fight against us in Cheusnys Battle. They thought it a boon at first when they allied with the humans, but the hastily created union had been brittle and frail. I slowly fold the paper in my lap, thinking.

"Send for Queen Victoire, Minerva, and Philan," I order. Zamara slips away.

CHAPTER SEVENTEEN

ZAHIRAN

FANE HANDS VICTOIRE A LETTER. I crane my head. The cream-colored envelope is unadorned, save for the name Illythia, written in looping letters across the front. I recognize the name as his aunt's. The queen slips the letter out of the already broken envelope and scans it as Minerva and Philan read over her shoulder.

"This is good," Victoire says. "But Catarina is a persisting problem."

"Would it be possible to use Soren again?" Minerva asks, staring unabashedly at Fane, and my own heart aches for Victoire. Why is she still putting up with everything? Regardless, Minerva's question worries me. Have they already tried brainwashing a person to murder Catarina? What happens to me if the Queen of Pheorirya dies? Victoire becomes unstoppable, and I become just another reminder that usurpers are always a threat. This could mean the end of my schemes to dethrone her. I frown as they delight in the letter, Minerva squealing and Philan throwing a look over at Fane. Sometimes they remind me of evil schoolchildren.

"No," Victoire responds. "They're wary of him now. It'll be harder to catch them off guard."

Her words confirm what I'd been wondering and an odd feeling overtakes me. My mission has never been to save humankind from the wrath of the demons, but something about listening to Victoire plot their downfall puts me off. She sounds too sure. I say something before I have the sense to close my mouth.

"I beg your pardon—I couldn't help but listen in on your conversation. I have an idea," I say. I keep my hands behind my back, but I take care to still my face. If I look afraid, they will carve me up and laugh about it. Three pairs of piercing eyes turn toward me and I suddenly feel the urge to wrap my wings tight around me. But I resist.

"Talk, then," Fane says. Minerva shoots a sickly-sweet smile at me. I want to punch it off her. I can't decipher any of their expressions.

"What if we keep Catarina alive instead of killing her? She would be a huge asset to have, and even after we get out of here, she would make a very fine servant indeed. Her strength is clearly superior to most humans and she has earned a reputation as a fearsome killer. We might be able to control the masses if we use her as an agent." As soon as the words come out of my mouth, I regret them. They are all looking at one another to speak first. I have heard of the way Catarina kills. She is ruthless, a cold-blooded machine designed for destruction. And keeping her alive gives her the chance to stop Victoire's efforts. Perfect for the demons' cause and mine. I see Victoire reach the same conclusion from the slight nod she offers me.

"I agree with Zamara," Philan says suddenly. He looks at me, an odd half-smile curling his lips. I smile back at him, but my mind is racing a million miles an hour. I spoke to save myself but didn't realize how much I'd helped them by doing so. Even worse, I'm proud Victoire approves of me. Fane and Minerva leave shortly after. Victoire watches them with a faraway look in her eyes.

"My Queen," I say softly. I still haven't moved from my spot in the corner. "I can't help but notice the way Lady Minerva—"

"Don't insult me, Zamara. I know," she says abruptly. It's rare that she uses my name (albeit a false one) and not some variation of "girl" or "maid." She looks deflated. Even her shadows, normally a menacing cloud around her, have reduced to nothing more than dark, wispy strands.

I soften my gaze. "Are you all right?"

She looks helplessly at me. "I love him, and I hate that I love him. His affection for me is conditional. And yet it is the only thing I long for, the only thing I crave."

"Why can't you get rid of her?"

"Because then he'll be angry at me, Zamara. I only want him to be happy. And if he's content with Minerva by his side, yet still bound to me as my husband, I can cope."

"Don't you want to be happy too?"

"I don't want to shred what's left of our relationship," she breathes.

"Why won't he simply marry Minerva then?" I ask, genuinely confused.

"He's attracted to my power and my command over the land, but I think nothing more. If he took Minerva as his spouse, Ahuiqir would most certainly turn against him."

"Are Minerva's shadows not strong enough? And to possess the crown—"

"It doesn't matter. They all revere me for something entirely different, you know. My *cruelty*. And while she may not seem it on the outside, Minerva is a woman incapable of leadership. She has a lust for power, hence her infatuation with Fane, but not the skillset necessary."

Victoire's words are dull and emotionless, and I don't have the slightest clue how to relieve her of all she's feeling. Her astute observation of the situation surprises me. I assumed her dulled by wine and denial. Her mind is sharp and calculating, even if she is playing the part of the burdened partner. Victoire sits up in her chair and all the weakness has dissipated from her gaze, replaced in a split second with hostility.

"You should leave now."

I look at her in confusion, but there's no sign of the vulnerability she'd shown me only seconds prior. "Y-yes, My Queen."

Rather than put me off, our brief conversation only pushes me further into my plans. I wait until the cover of night. Then, I sneak into the king and queen's bedchamber, determined to find new information. The two have been nowhere to be seen for several hours; the other servants say they've gone out on a hunt. I creep across the glossy floor, stopping at the massive wooden desk in the corner of the room. One side contains Victoire's belongings while the other has Fane's. I rummage through Fane's side briefly before I come across a single sheaf of papers. Written across the top in Fane's unmistakable, elegant script is the word *Childhood.* My breath catches. For a moment, I am embarrassed on his behalf. Is this a written story of fiction he has been penning as a hobby? No. He wouldn't do something so frivolous. This must be a personal account. I take the papers with shaky hands and crouch behind the desk to read.

Cold hands unravel my tightly wrapped blankets and circle around my waist. It is the middle of the night, and I am a baby again. My eyes fly open, and I open my mouth to scream for my mother, but another set of hands clamp around my mouth. I thrash my arms and legs but there is very little that chubby baby limbs can do. I'm hauled up by the armpits. I catch a glimpse of her face in the dim moonlight. Her features are human-like, yet unnatural somehow. Her teeth are sharp as a snake's and they flash in the dim light. Her long, pale hair is braided down her back, streaked with red and carrying with it a strong metallic scent of blood. She bows her head and I shiver when her breath skitters across the exposed skin of my neck.

"Good child," she whispers.

Her friend slips out of the tent and she follows, still carrying me. The cold air hits me like a slap across the face. The witch's hold tightens on me and her long, sharp fingernails press against my spine like a constant threat. Three other witches stand there quietly, waiting.

"I've got the baby," the one holding me hisses to the others.

They nod and run off toward the rest of the camp. The witch's friend nods once at her, then runs off in the same direction as the others.

They light fires that illuminate the night in brilliant gold. The screams of the demons and the shrieks of the horses are lost in the cracking sound of wood splintering and tents collapsing. The witch hauls me onto her dragon and we fly hard and fast. I'm in awe of the magnificent creature, with its huge, dappled wings and slender, elegant neck. I steal a look at the witch. Her eyes are bright and her hair has pulled loose from its braid. She leans forward.

"Down," she whispers. The creature's wings tilt with her and we fall through the air. They flare outward at the last moment and we glide to the ground.

"Pasiphae!" another witch calls, running toward us.

"I've got the baby," the witch holding me says again. Her arms tighten around me as she slides off her mount. The other witch stares at me.

"The cursed baby," she whispers.

"No, Zara," Pasiphae corrects. "The blessed baby." The witch Zara nods excitedly. "Although he is not one of us, he can be changed. He will hold powers so great that no other will be a match."

Zara touches my arm. Her skin is warm, unlike Pasiphae's. "How do you know?" she asks breathlessly.

Pasiphae brushes her hand across my small horns as if I am a sacred treasure instead of a living, breathing being. "There have been prophecies about him. And so many signs! Do you feel the change in the air when he is present?"

That night, Pasiphae takes me to see the other witches. Thousands of them sit shoulder-to-shoulder in one hall. Their leader, Yseult A'tess, lifts me into the air. I shiver. The air here is much colder than back home. I realize with a start that I haven't wished to see my mother. But it would be a nice thing to have her hold me right now. The crowd screams their approval.

"The baby is ours!" Yseult yells. "With him, we will continue on to rule the world!" Although I cannot talk by myself yet, I know these words. Back home, it is everything they talk about. Ruling the world. But somehow, even now, I am not scared. I have never been scared. That night, the witches roister for hours upon hours, dancing around their fireplaces, screaming their joy. Pasiphae stands off to the side with Zara, who must be a close friend. Yseult still holds me tight to her chest.

"What a special, special child," she murmurs in my ear. "The world is yours, my little Fane. All yours." My eyes start to grow heavy. Her voice is comforting, and I am tired. "You do not know this yet, my darling, but you have a gift that

no other has possessed before you. Not a single human, not a single demon, not a single witch."

I feel my head loll against her shoulder as I breathe a soft, content sigh.

Yseult brushes soft, gentle kisses to the top of my head as I fall asleep. "But I promise you that when the time is right, I will teach you about it. I'll teach you to harness it. I'll teach you everything. All that we do, it is for you." My eyes slip shut. "The world is yours, my little Fane. All yours." I fall asleep to her distant murmurs.

I had been wrong about Pasiphae and Yseult and Zara. No, I hadn't been an object they'd managed to steal into their possession. They loved me as if I were one of their own. For the first sixteen years of my life, I was raised by those three women and the rest of the Coven of the Hyacinth. I learned the ways of witches. I learned how to ride a dragon, and eventually, I was given my own. When the demons came storming into my new home to take me back, I screamed. I screamed until my throat burned, raw and sore. I screamed until Gwendydd tied a cloth around my mouth. She was not, nor is she now, my mother. Yseult will forever be my guardian, the only one who truly cares for me. I have not seen her in centuries but I know she is alive. As far as we know, witches, like demons, are nearly immortal; they can die if their hearts are pierced or if they contract Ditheria Morbus, a sickness that starts with a cough and then turns the blood sour. Love is weakness. I'd learned that lesson early on in life.

Yseult had never lied to me about my abilities, and as promised, she taught me about my gift the second I was able to stand on my own. The words she'd uttered in my ear flow through me now as I close my eyes.

"Do you feel anything when you reach deep, deep down inside you, past your shadows?"

"Yes," I'd whispered.

"I want you to grab it in your hands," she'd said. "Grab it and don't let go."

And so I did.

I lifted both hands, admiring the way the smoke weaved through my fingers. But as I watched, a twinkle of warmth flickered through the darkness. Warmth that heals, warmth that nourishes. Many demons are blessed with the powers of suffering, reflecting the pain of their human lives. But a demon has never possessed the gift of life before me.

After all, we are creatures of death.

CHAPTER EIGHTEEN
PASIPHAE

I SIT IN A WOODEN ROCKING CHAIR outside my tent. All around me, the other witches of the Coven of the Hyacinth hurry about. Their feet carry them with sure, present confidence. Even the children, rare and precious as they are, work just as hard as their mothers. I watch as three young girls with loose hair and wide grins run past me, each carrying an armful of firewood. Their carefree laughter rings in my ears long after they've passed by.

It has been so long since I've felt the stirrings of sadness. It has always been too much work to do, too many things to think about, for me to waste time on my feelings. But now, as I sit and watch the youngest generation of witches leap, twirl, and dance, I am acutely aware of every ache in my heart. Even if my face looks exactly the way it did when *I* was leaping, twirling, and dancing, and doesn't reveal my true age, I feel those burdensome thoughts creeping into my mind far too often for my liking. Will I be forced to suffer silently for all of eternity, unable to express this exhaustion that nobody but I can perceive? Is this the true price of immortality? The sun beams down on me, mockingly bright.

I let myself wallow in self-pity for a while. Seeing the three girls reminded me of the shortage of witch babies this year. Children were plentiful and their powers strong when there were still male witches. The magic flowing in their veins was nothing short of inexhaustible. But that was a long, long time ago. This crossbreeding is the only thing that has kept my coven alive despite the near extinction of so many others, at least those we know of in Guinyth. And yet, my fists curl at the thought that the scarce magic still thrumming beneath my sisters' skin may die out completely. This, in addition to the recent motives of the demons spread by rumors and gossip and the tension rising in the cities of Guinyth themselves, casts an invisible gloom over everything.

"Pasiphae," a voice calls softly from behind me. I'd recognize that high-pitched voice anywhere. I turn, trying and failing to hide that grin. Yseult stands there, holding her arms wide.

"How have you been?" she asks. "It feels like I haven't seen you in centuries."

I laugh. "You saw me this morning."

"I know," she says, still grinning. "I missed you anyway."

"What did you want to talk to me about?"

Her expression is sober. "You seem different, Pasiphae. Are you all right?"

You never understand how truly exhausted you are until someone who cares, *genuinely cares,* and asks about the shadows haunting you. Tears prick at the corners of my eyes, painfully so, but I don't cry. I've learned how to stop tears even when they really want to come. I want to fall to my knees and allow my best friend to hold me, to comfort me, as I sob and scream and release myself. But I ignore those urges. "Yes," I finally say, a bit softly. "I'm all right."

She lifts her arms into the air, inhaling deeply. "It's a beautiful day, isn't it?"

It truly is. I stand from the rocking chair, twisting to stretch my body and looking across the field that the Coven of the Hyacinth has made its home. I am humbled that these thirty-two brightly colored cloth tents, which form a circle around a massive willow tree at the center and one larger tent beneath it, have made up the entirety of my life. The field itself, surrounded by a forest of emerald pine, is isolated from the rest of Guinyth.

"What are you thinking about?" Yseult asks me.

"The stupidity of life."

"Oh."

I snort at her response and shake my head. "I trust you've heard of the things happening between Ahuiqir and Guinyth, especially Pheorirya?" She nods, and I continue. "I fear for our coven. I don't want war."

"Of course," Yseult says. "Our previous involvement was a mistake." But I know from the look in her eyes that she's remembering.

"We cannot side with the demons," I whisper. "You know that."

She looks at me, mouth falling open in shock. "You can't possibly be serious."

"I am."

"Fane—"

"Yseult, Fane isn't who we knew before. He's been corrupted by the brutality of those around him."

"You're going to disregard all the history we share with him?" she asks. Her voice is nonchalant, but I can hear the threat in it. My eyes narrow in disgust. Yseult, as clan leader, will always have more say than I. But I swallow my emotions and turn and stalk away, unwilling to argue. She calls out my name but doesn't attempt to chase after me.

This night, as usual, the coven gathers in the large tent below the willow tree for dinner. Each family brings something to eat: baked goods, roasted meat, freshly picked fruits and vegetables. The children help their mothers place the food on the wooden table, giggling and squealing as they pause to bat playfully at one another. I watch them with a faint, sad smile on my face, but when I look across the table at Yseult, I find that she's avoiding eye contact with everyone.

The chatter dies away as the witches eat. Each murmurs a brief phrase of gratitude before diving into her plate.

"Pheorirya's market prices are skyrocketing," a witch beside me tells her friend. "I traded an entire hog for five yards of fabric to make a dress for Evalyn."

"I'm not surprised. People barter more aggressively during times of unrest."

Both of their gazes travel to Yseult, who pretends to be engrossed in her food. Clearly, they have the same thought process as I: Yseult's continuing love for Fane is bound to become more and more of an issue. It softens her against the demons when we need her to be steel. I watch as they look at each other.

"What do you think the clan leader would do if it came to choosing sides in a war?" the first witch asks her friend.

"She'd choose Fane," the second witch says immediately. "She wouldn't choose the demons, or their beliefs. But she'd choose Fane, and if that meant siding with them, she would." My heart sinks at her words. She's completely correct. Fane had become something far, far more to her than a means to power in the sixteen brief years he'd lived in the Coven of the Hyacinth.

"Oh my God," the first witch breathes, echoing my thoughts. She lowers her voice even more. "But do you think the rest of the coven would support her? Would *you*?"

"No," the second witch replies, just as quietly. "No to both questions. But we'd be forced to."

"But isn't that ridiculous?" the first witch asks. "We'd be fighting to destroy our own home."

"It is," her friend replies. "And—"

I excuse myself from the table then, suddenly desperate for a breath of fresh air. As I walk across the room, bits and pieces of conversation find their way to my ears. Every single witch in this room is talking of Fane and Yseult and war. I let out a gasp as I finally stumble outside, inhaling until the coldness of the night air numbs my mind.

Demons are powerful enough. If Yseult makes the decision for our clan to ally with them in the inevitable war, Guinyth will have no chance to fight back.

I cannot let this happen.

CHAPTER NINETEEN
CATARINA

SWEAT DRIPS DOWN my forehead and into my eyes. I wipe it away and throw another punch at the rice bag hanging from the ceiling. My muscles ache and my knuckles are scraped and bloodied, but I savor the dull pain. I only ever let myself go when I am training. All the frustrations and angers and fears of my life propel each flex of my muscles, each heave of breath, and each satisfying blow.

"Catarina?" Liserli cautiously opens the door. "Have you seen Zhengya?"

I pause. "No. What do you mean? She's not in the library?"

"I can't find her anywhere." She runs a hand through her hair. Her voice is casual, but her eyes dart about nervously. "So you definitely haven't seen her?"

"No, I . . . I haven't."

And then Soren and Brienne are exploding into the room.

"Oh God, oh God," Brienne is moaning.

"She's not anywhere," Soren gasps.

My chest is tight. I hurtle past them and through the door, heading for the library. Cold fear courses through my veins. "What's happened?" I ask when they follow.

"I don't *know,*" comes Brienne's whispered reply.

"Where was she seen last?"

"I don't know."

"Did you see her this morning?"

"No, I—"

"Does *anybody* have a clue as to what happened?" I interrupt, whirling around and throwing my arms out. Though I know the harsh tone of my voice is completely unjustified, I can't help myself. Brienne's words, although innocent enough, have irked me.

"What?" Brienne pants, looking at me incredulously. The three of them are halted suddenly by my outburst.

"It seems like I'm the only one who cares about her." The words rip out of me, wild and mindless.

"You're not making any sense—"

I let out a shriek of frustration then, whipping back around and swinging into the library. I've seen her spend hours there, in the days since Philan's death, poring over a single book. How could I have missed this? I curse myself. Zhengya has barely talked of Philan since his death, except for the times he invaded her mind. We'd all assumed she was taking it exceptionally well. How could I have thought she'd simply move on from her brother's death and forget that he ever became a demon? I curse my naivete, as usual.

"She must have found the way to Ahuiqir," I whisper. Ahuiqir, the land of demons and monsters and fiery wastelands. The land my father had always refused to speak about, the land I'd always been cautioned about by tutors. Behind me, Brienne and Soren are silent. My fists clench unconsciously. "Find her," I say. Nobody moves. "Find her!" This time, my voice is hard enough to make Brienne jump.

"We will," Soren soothes, brushing a hand against my shaking shoulders. "She is a smart girl. She knows how to take care of herself."

I can hardly understand him. Their voices are dimming away into meaningless murmurs and all I can hear is the pounding of blood in my head. *Why?* I demand of Zhengya in my head. *Why did you walk into the arms of someone I have no power against? Why have you done this to me?*

"Catarina." Brienne's firm voice jerks me out of my stupor. They're all staring at me as if I have completely lost my good sense. "We'll find her," she soothes. "But right now, the only thing we can do is look."

I force my lips to move. "Look for what?" My mind can't seem to process rational thoughts.

"Look for any hint she may have left behind as to where she's gone." She speaks slowly, emphasizing every word as if I am a child. My nails dig into palms. Soren and Liserli stride into the library, offering me nothing but sorrowful glances and pitying sighs. Brienne sighs and offers me her upturned hand.

"Come on, Cat," she says, gentler now.

My eyes narrow. Ignoring her hand, I slip by her without a word.

Everything in the library is made up of warm brown oak. The faint sweetness of the flickering candles on the table mixes with the musky scent of the books on the shelves. It is my favorite room in the entire manor, though I haven't visited quite as much as Zhengya did. There are signs of her everywhere. A half-drunk mug of tea on the desk. A blanket sagging off the corners of a wooden desk chair. I bite my lip at the sight of one of her leather hair ties sitting next to a quill. Soren slumps into an armchair beside me, groaning softly with exhaustion.

"Does anyone know where Ahuiqir lies?" I whisper faintly. Not a single person hears; not a single person turns to smile kindly at me and reply with something hopeful, anything at all. So I say it again. "Does anyone know where Ahuiqir lies?"

Brienne places a hand lightly on my arm and gazes at me gently. "No, I don't, Catarina. But we'll find out, I promise." Her eyes are filled with such brilliant determination that I believe her.

We find nothing for hours until Soren gives us a shout from another bookcase. A tear-smeared letter is shoved under a bookshelf.

My beloved Brienne, Soren, Liserli, Catarina:

Why is it that I can't seem to let go of all my memories? Why is it that every single time I pass by his cold, empty bedroom, I want to scream and cry and rip out the hearts of every single demon in Ahuiqir? I'm sorry, my friends. But wouldn't you do the same thing? Wouldn't you go to the end of the world to avenge your only sibling, the only family you have left?

I will have reached Cheusnys Cave by the time you read this. It will be too late. Do not come to look for me. I won't come back without my brother.

With love,
Zhengya

Soren's eyes narrow as he reads. Liserli rubs her hands together nervously. Brienne's breath comes as shallow gasps. But I smile grimly. For as smart as Zhengya Lin is, she made a mistake when she told us where she was going.

"Where is Cheusnys Cave?" I ask.

My heart beats in a sharp, staccato rhythm, in sync with the pounding of our horses' hooves. Fear settles in my stomach, as heavy as a stone, but now there is a little hope. My horse is hot and damp with sweat beneath me, panting through its mouth. I have to force away the memories that suddenly flood through me. A hot, damp horse beneath me, a knife, a carriage, my mother and father. Blood.

Brienne casts a concerned look at me. "Are you all right?" she asks carefully. I nod.

The countryside of Guinyth is absolutely stunning. Even through my barely contained panic, I can appreciate its beauty. We pass by several farmhouses with acres of yellow cornfields behind them. Two farmers on the side of the dirt road wave at us as we ride past. All of us are dressed in identical clothing: lightweight leathers, dark cloaks, and riding boots. The cloth bags weighing down our backs are filled to the brim with a change of clothing, flask of water, several days' worth of dried food, and one small dagger each that Brienne had insisted we carry. Every so often, I can hear the steel clink against the metal of the flask and my heart tightens even more.

I don't want to use it.

Heavier, larger weapons would've made me feel better, but they'd be too burdensome to carry around when we arrive in Ahuiqir. As we travel, the friendliness of the land fades. Farmland turns into untamed forest. Brienne sucks in a sharp breath beside me and when I catch her eye, she flashes me a nervous smile. The canopy above us is thick enough to blot out the sun, save for the dappling of golden light on the forest floor, which is stark in contrast to the dampness of the path.

I'm suddenly desperate for conversation. Liserli and Soren ride at the front, leaving Brienne at my side. I turn to her. "Tell me about Zhengya," I say. The request is vague, but she senses what I need.

"Philan told me that she was the favorite child out of the two of them. While Philan was in a constant state of struggle with his parents, Zhengya seemed to do no wrong in their eyes. But when Philan came to her after one particular incident with his father—I think he told you about it—she was willing to leave all the comfort and safety of their palace in Tegak for her brother and for no real reason of her own. She was furious at her parents for hurting him. She's always been protective. When I couldn't find her this morning, my gut instinct told me that she'd gone searching for him."

Tears prick uncomfortably at my eyes.

"Actually, she's that way with every person she loves." Brienne's eyes take on a wistful look. My throat aches, and suddenly I wish I hadn't asked about her. The mouth of the cave looms before us not long after that. The thick, shadowy darkness lurking within it is so deep and impenetrable, I can't make out a single thing. I can, however, hear tiny scuttling and fluttering sounds, which make me certain we are not alone in the cave. I shudder. Liserli's scarred hands are clenched around her reins so hard that her knuckles show starkly white through her skin, but she presses forward. "Stay behind me," she says.

Suddenly a flare of bright, blinding light flashes as her horse's body collides with something invisible. Blood sprays as the creature's eyes roll back into its head and it shrieks and collapses, bringing its rider with it. Brienne flings a useless hand forward as if to catch Liserli, who hits the ground with a sickening thud. Soren screams. I slide off my horse to kneel at Liserli's side.

"Don't get any closer to it," she says with fury edging every syllable. Liserli's eyes roll from the cave back to me. Brienne carefully helps her lift her head off the ground. Blood smears the dirt, dark and glossy. "Don't get any closer," she repeats. "There is a barrier. I couldn't see it, but it was hard." More blood trickles in a thin stream down the back of her skull, and she lets out a soft groan.

"Then how the hell did Zhengya get through?" Soren's eyes are filled with fear that I can only assume mirrors my own. *How is Zhengya any different than Liserli?* I realize the exact same moment Brienne does.

"Royal blood," Brienne says. "It's the only difference that makes sense. You must have royal blood in your veins in order to pass through unharmed." Then she frowns and adds, "It's barbaric." They all turn to me. Brienne reaches out a hand to touch my arm. "Catarina, you don't need to go in alone," she says quickly. "I'm sure we can find another way—"

"No. I have to."

"Are you sure? You really don't—"

"I want to."

Our gazes lock and she stops talking then, bowing her head the slightest bit. Everyone seems to shrink away from me, as if my very presence is virulent. But then Brienne swings her pack off her back and takes out her dagger. "I'll feel better if you take it," she whispers, offering it to me handle-first.

"Thank you," I breathe. I slip it into my waistband and pray it stays there.

"This, too," Soren says, pulling a torch from his pack and quickly lighting it with a match. I nod my gratitude, and he puts it in my hands.

The four steps I take to the cave seem to last forever. And yet, not long enough. I am afraid of the other side. My steps thump dully against the dirt.

Too soon, I reach the slightly shimmering barrier that felled Liserli. I lift a shaking hand to it. It wavers as my skin brushes it, warm—uncomfortably so. But I feel no pain. I hold my breath and walk through, feeling only warm pressure for a brief moment before I find myself on the other side.

"Are you okay?" Brienne asks. Her voice is slightly muffled by the barrier.

"Yes." I inhale deeply, and immediately regret it. The stench almost brings me to my knees. Soren flinches and tries to reach for me, but Liserli pulls him back. I clasp a hand over my nose and mouth, fighting back the bile that rises in my throat. Brienne moves as close to the barrier as she dares, stopping just before she reaches me. Unsmiling, we stare at each other. And then she sighs and backs away.

"Goodbye," I say.

"Goodbye," she says.

The four of us stand there in silence again, sharing shallow gulps of breath.

"Stay safe," Soren whispers. I am suddenly very fond of him. He's the only other person who knows what it's like to be used for something horrible, and he's here wishing me well instead of worrying about himself.

"I will."

"Don't die."

"I won't." I laugh.

"Come on. We need to go," Liserli says softly, pulling gently at them. I force myself to turn away, walking away before they do.

The darkness of the cave is somehow reminiscent of Victoire. A shudder runs down my spine; the humidity is suffocating. I walk with one hand trailing on the wall to the right of me – the cave is dark enough that even with Soren's torch, I fear getting lost. There's a flutter of movement above me, and I flinch, praying that it's nothing but a small creature. My boots brush by loose objects and I force myself not to look down. The hard edges feel too much like bones; the soft, spongy material feels too much like decaying flesh. Suddenly, I feel the texture of the wall change, the damp smoothness shifting into something far more jagged and rough, filled with small grooves and notches. I turn the torch towards it slowly, inhaling sharply at what I see. It's a massive collection of murals, stretching from where the floor connects to the wall, all the way to the very top, dozens of feet above me. Some images are of places – I see a dark, spiraling castle, a peaceful field – while others are of people and memories. There's a scene depicting a hunt, with an arrow piercing through the chest of a rearing stag while miniature warriors wave their arms in celebration, scenes from famous wars, a scene where a winged demon holds the decapitated head of a human. I avert my eyes. Not a single inch of the walls is left bare, except for a small space right next to what I can only assume is a shrine, made up of animal skulls stacked against one another and marking the end of the cave. The one on top is the largest, and despite how horrific it is, despite how crude, I am drawn to it. Slowly, yet not hesitantly, I place a single finger on the cold, wet bone, and a pulsing hum of magic vibrates through the air at the contact. For a second, there is nothing. And then warmth is spreading through the stone, traveling through my body and sinking into my bones. The warmth intensifies and I rush to lift my finger from the stone. But then I am no longer in Guinyth.

I am in a new cave, but this time, I can see the entrance from where I stand. My head pounds from the utter stillness of the air and I force myself to stagger outside. Even in the open air, every breath is torturous. Every molecule burns as it goes down my throat. The hazy air is tinted with a red color, along with the sky itself. The trees surrounding me are shriveled and sickly looking, their gnarled limbs reaching up to the heavens as if begging for water. A dark shape swoops through the air hundreds of feet above me, casting a shadow on the ground. I duck back into the cave to avoid it seeing me. Even from so far below it, I can feel the wind that its wings produce blow across my face. *A demon. A real demon.* "No," I breathe. "*No.*"

Is this what the warriors of the past, my own ancestors, felt when they faced these hideous creatures in those wars? Did they feel this suffocating, inescapable dread that I feel? Did they feel as if death was only millimeters away, waiting to snatch him in its claws, every time? *Breathe, Catarina,* his voice soothes in my head. *Breathe. Your body is capable; your only limitations are the ones in your mind.* Even as I force myself to draw deep, expansive breaths, my heart still stutters uncontrollably. Panic clouds me, and my gaze darts back to where I'd come from. *Calm yourself!* My father's voice sounds angry now. *You don't have time for cowardice.* I count to twenty in my head and then sprint out to duck into a thick cluster of trees and foliage. I crouch just as I hear a voice.

"What was that?" the voice calls.

I squeeze my eyes shut and press my hands to my chest to try to quell the frantic beating of my heart. *Please save me.* I don't even know what god or ghost the unspoken words are directed to, but I repeat them in my head.

"Probably a deer," another voice replies.

I hear the beating of wings and have to clamp a hand over my mouth to stifle the whimper that escapes my lips. My stomach feels as if it's being wrung out to dry over a clothesline.

"No, it wasn't an animal."

The voice is close. Too close. I hear a crunch of leaves and the wing beats stop. A second crunch.

"Whatever it is, it's not worth it," the second voice snaps.

"But do you smell that?"

A pause, and a rustle of feathered wings. "Yes . . . A human. A girl."

I can almost picture the wicked grins spreading across their faces. *Oh God,* I think. *Oh God.*

"It's all right, little one," the first demon calls, false sincerity dripping from his cloying voice. "You can come out now. I promise we won't hurt you . . ."

A wing brushes by the tree I stand behind and I force myself to steal a look. They're turned the other way. Their backs are facing me. I clench my fists at the sight of those twisting horns and lashing tails, exactly like the ones portrayed in the painting in my father's study. I take the dagger Brienne gave me and briefly consider getting my own from my pack, but it'd make too much noise and take up time that I don't have.

Save me, I think one last time. And then, before my fear can take hold, I surge forward soundlessly and plunge the blade into the first demon's back. He lets out a howl, and one of his feathered wings slams into my shoulder. The second demon grabs my hair and pulls me to my feet. I manage to pull my sword from the first's back, but the second will not let go of my hair. I kick and punch, but it is obvious that there is only one thing I can do. I twist and slice through my braid. The second demon snarls and lets the chopped hair fall from his hands in a quiet brown cloud.

"You're a feisty one, eh?" the first demon laughs. His blood pools all around us, but he shows no sign of weakening. His arm shoots out, aiming for my face, and I duck away. A curved, serrated claw slices the air where my good eye had been just a moment before. I freeze, realizing what losing my other eye would mean. And in that fraction of a second, the first demon's wing wraps around my waist and pulls me into his grip. I manage to turn enough to slice through his wing.

"Get her off!" the demon screams. His tail lashes out and catches me squarely in the shoulder with unexpected force. The other demon's claws wrap around my throat and he lifts me into the air. His breath fans across my skin, reeking of putrescent meat and smoke.

"We were going to eat you." he draws a nail across my cheek. "But we have other plans for you now."

The first demon stumbles to his feet. His dark eyes flash dangerously, and I shiver even in the sticky heat. "Take her to the castle," he says.

CHAPTER TWENTY
PASIPHAE

"Have you heard of a girl named Catarina Winyr?" I ask.

I can see Yseult's eyes are unfocused. I have known her long enough to recognize her distinct nuances; we'd grown up with each other, lived in each other's tents, and shared centuries upon centuries of memories. I see every awkward, almost unnoticeable, shift of her weight. I see every shaky breath that shudders through her. And even though I know there are things she is hiding from me, I do not ask. I have known her for far too long to make the mistake of trying to force her to say something she does not wish to say. It would be fruitless to do so.

Yseult nods, the bleariness suddenly gone from her dark-eyed gaze. "Daughter of Simone Endrdyn and Kairos Winyr, two powerful warriors. She is known for the absence of a gift, is she not?"

I nod. "She murdered her parents."

Yseult hesitates. "She did. Why have you brought this up?"

"I find it hard to believe that she did it of her own free will."

"What are you saying?" The tone of her voice is still light, almost casual, but I can hear an edge of sharpness in it now.

I fold my arms across my chest as if to physically shield myself from her words. "I'm saying that she must have been controlled."

"Controlled? How?"

"By a demon."

"By *Fane*?"

"Yes. Either him or his queen. They've done it before. Demons have been using their shadows to try to sneak back into the world of the living for centuries."

"Pasiphae, you watched him grow up. He was a good child, a good—"

"Do you think Fane and Victoire could have found a way to turn Catarina to their side?" I ask quickly, interrupting her.

"I hope not. I'd like to think that I raised him not to be selfish. He would not steal a woman's freedom for his own benefit."

"You underestimate his cruelty, Yseult," I say.

Her eyes snap to me. "What?"

My first instinct is to back down from the only woman superior to me. I want to apologize, but I force myself not to. The infamously coldhearted clan leader has fallen into the trap that so many others seem to fall into—blind love. "Think about it. Fane and Victoire are powerful, but they are not gods. There are so many people who could get in their way, but somehow, nobody has. How?"

"He is ambitious, that's all."

"He is *wicked*. He is willing to sacrifice any number of lives for his own sake. He's going to invade Guinyth, Yseult. We've heard the rumors." She starts to back away.

"You aren't making any sense, Pasiphae. We will speak no more of this." She turns her back to me, then suddenly turns back around and looks at me again. "Don't waste my time like that again."

I bow my head, unable to argue anymore. It is in moments like this that I am harshly reminded that Yseult A'tess is not only my friend, but a clan leader. A ruler. It suddenly feels as if a wall has been erected between us, and our differences in power and dominion are starker than ever.

I do not sleep that night. Even as the sun finally drags itself sleepily above the horizon, my eyes remain open and unfocused, pinned to the ceiling of my tent. When the thought had first come to me, I'd shoved it away in horror at myself. But now I allow myself to ponder, *truly* ponder what it would mean to make sure Yseult's softness for the King of Demons doesn't lead us all to death. I would have to stop her somehow or make her incapable of giving orders. Then again, the clan would just rest and wait for their leader to recover. Nothing else will do. Leadership cannot be asked nicely to step down, especially when in the midst of rumored war.

I must kill the clan leader. The thought brings a feeling of odd elation. This is what I must do to save Guinyth. Is this what the heroes in all the stories felt before making their ultimate sacrifices for the greater good? If not stopped now, Yseult will take Fane's side in the war. Yseult will contribute to the utter slaughtering of millions of powerless mortals, all for the sake of love for her son.

"What am I doing?" I suddenly ask aloud, rolling over on my mattress and pressing my face into the quilt with a groan. I think back to the dinner of the previous night and the obvious worry the witches had expressed in their quiet whispers and darting glances. "Forgive me," I whisper under my breath, unsure to whom I'm directing the words.

It is midday by the time I drag myself from under the safety of the bedclothes and out of my tent. The knife I'd been passing back and forth nervously between my hands is warm now, and the hilt is damp with sweat. But I am ready.

The sky is blue, the air is cool and sweet with the scent of blooming hydrangeas and foxgloves and violas. I take it to be a good omen.

Yseult stands only several yards away, her back facing me. She is bent over the last flickering embers of a fire and douses the golden ashes out with water. "Pasiphae? Is that you?" she asks without moving.

"Yes," I whisper. A sizzle almost drowns out my answer. A cloud of white steam billows into the air.

She turns. "What are you—"

I close my eyes. *Forgive me, forgive me.* My knife flies from my hand.

There is a thud of metal burying itself in flesh, and then Yseult cries out and collapses. Blood sprays from her lips as she gropes blindly for where the knife has wedged itself between two of her ribs. I kneel down beside her, shaking my head. My vision is swimming. My head is pounding. I cough when my rapid panting catches saliva in my throat. "I'm so sorry." My mouth feels numb and the words come out strangled, hoarse. I am weeping.

"No. You're not," comes her unnervingly calm reply. Yseult's voice gurgles as she fights the loose blood inside her. I force myself to look into her eyes.

"I definitely did *not* foresee this, Pasiphae. You deserve credit for that. But I don't think anyone would've been able to."

"Don't say that," I reply. She turns her head and even more blood pours from the wound. Yseult doesn't even flinch. Her eyes remain on mine, even as shock mars my face.

"Why not? Do you feel guilty?" I don't respond. "What do you plan to do now?" Her voice is significantly weaker now, yet she still manages to infuse her words with deadly venom. "Will you take my spot as clan leader? Will you allow the Coven of the Hyacinth to die out? *What did you accomplish by doing this?*" Again, I do not reply. She mutters something under her breath. "You are a coward, Pasiphae."

Yseult A'tess dies minutes later, and although her body spasms and contorts, she never makes a single sound. When the fire finally leaves her limbs, I close her eyes. I can't look at them. I squeeze her still-warm hand one last time, take a deep breath, and let out a scream.

I'd sooner run away without notifying anyone or spinning the complex tale of finding the clan leader dead by her tent, but instantaneously, I realize how easily they could prove that I was guilty. All it would take would be one witch pointing out my absence, and the entirety of the clan would come chasing after me. But if I can somehow convince them all that Yseult had been dead before I'd come across her . . . Maybe I wouldn't even be suspected. I could always run later. I don't have time to waver over my decision before the other witches come running, Zara at the front of the crowd. At the sight of me kneeling there, Yseult's body draped across my lap, she freezes in her tracks, then falls to her knees and lets out a horrified cry.

"Oh my God." Someone behind her gasps. More and more witches collapse to the floor, letting out moans and turning to one another for comfort. I stand slowly, gently guiding her body to the ground.

"She was dead when I found her," I whisper.

Two other witches step forward with a white sheet, placing it over the clan leader and gesturing for the crowd to back away. I step backward numbly, watching with unseeing eyes as they wrap the sheet around the body.

"We will bring her murderer to justice," someone vows heatedly, and murmurs of agreement flow through the witches. The healer steps forward and puts a hand on Yseult's cooling cheek.

"Do not waste time on anger and hatred," the old woman breathes. "Her spirit has been set free. Free from the hindrances of life and of a physical body."

The witches who are still standing slide to their knees, joining hands and bowing their heads. I slip away from the crowd to watch.

"*Take this one's soul. Take it, protect it, and let it be yours*," the witches say simultaneously. Their voices blend into one, sending off their leader into the great unknown.

Yseult will be buried under the willow tree in the middle of our camp at the first light of dawn. Every clan leader before her lies there, and for as long as they wish, her family and the healer will pray that she finds final peace. But after that period, there will be no more time to mourn. Witches are powerful in that sense. We move on and remember our dead ones' feats, but we forget our grief. But there will be no forgetting on my part. Her blood will forever stain my hands.

I do not hear Zara's footsteps as she approaches me. "Pasiphae."

I turn, startled. "Zara?"

Her brows are deeply furrowed. I've never seen her looking so pained. "Where were you when Yseult was murdered? How did you find her so quickly?" The expression of horror I know shows on my face is tellingly genuine, but I force it into one of shock instead. She continues, her voice trembling as she talks faster and faster. "I know you've been arguing with her for the last few days about what to do with the clan. You told me, and you told me you thought she was taking us in the wrong direction. Now she's dead and you found her before anyone else? Pasiphae, please tell me I'm thinking wrong."

"Zara, what are you trying to say? You're not making sense. Why would I *ever*—"

She clutches my hand, her nails digging into my flesh. "Pasiphae, stop. Please, just tell me. Where were you when she was murdered?"

"She'd just finished speaking to me. I was in my tent after that." The lie comes out easily, so terribly easily.

Her eyes soften in relief, ever so slightly. "Thank you. I'm sorry. I-I don't know why I would think that you killed one of your closest friends. I'm just paranoid; I've been asking everyone else, and they've all denied it. But it had to be someone here. No outsider could have found us with the spells on our tents." I dip my head silently, not trusting myself to speak. "I'm sorry," she says again. "I—" She shakes her head, backing away. "Sorry," she mumbles as she goes.

I must go. My dragon, Isal, waits for me at the edge of camp. Her deep purple scales shimmer faintly in the sunlight. She is an enormous thing and has been with me since birth. It is the way for all the witches.

She lowers herself, and I jump onto her scaled back. She lets out a soft huff, and I run a hand along her neck. "Up," I whisper. Her ears prick back and her wings flare out in a mighty heave. In one flap, we are in the air. The wind is fiercely cold and bites at my nose, ears, and cheeks as we fly. I welcome the sting even as I feel my skin going numb. I deserve this. I deserve to be punished for all of eternity. I clench my fists, and Isal turns her head to face me. Her pale, amaranthine eyes fix on me with keen intelligence.

Dragons are magnificent creatures with indestructible scales, slender necks and tails with serrated horns, and massive wings. They have been associated with witches for millennia. The first witches of Guinyth took one look at the glorious beasts and started the domestication process without hesitation. As Isal's dusty-mauve wings beat below me, and her muscles flex and contract, I am grateful for my ancestors' foresight. They are an incalculable boon to our kind. Every dragon, each bearing a different scale color and distinct personality, is paired with a witch at birth, making the bond between them utterly unbreakable.

I allow myself a smile and bring one hand down to stroke her side. Despite everything, I laugh a little as I look down at the land below us, speckled green, blue, and brown. No sign of the world's mundane cruelties from up here. Flying has always been a therapeutic experience. It is a completely unique, surreal opportunity to forget, to forgive, to move on. Guilt-ridden though I've been, this flight is no exception. As Isal falls into a smooth dip, following the wind and its natural flow, my heart is a million times lighter in my chest. I can *breathe*. The ridiculous urge to throw my arms up and scream with joy bubbles up from within me.

When we reach Cheusnys Cave, I slide off Isal's back and reach decisively for the barrier. It shimmers around my fingertips for a second, and then I'm through. Others would need permission, but witches do not. We were the ones who created the barrier in the first place. After the battle of Cheusnys Cave, we did a lot of barrier spells like these. I shiver. Decades of war do not just leave a person's memory. Bloody, war-ravaged scenes flood my mind. A witch lying there on the ground. Her skin is as pale as the snow around her, and deep red blood bubbles from her lips. *My mother.* The glorious Clan Leader Saskia Sandor, Yseult's predecessor. She'd died that day, from an arrow straight into her old wise heart. But I push it all from my mind. I take one last glance at Isal. Her head bobs down once, and then she lifts into the air on her way back home.

CHAPTER TWENTY-ONE

CATARINA

As the two demons drag me down a long gravel trail headed straight for a massive castle made entirely of black marble, I take in my surroundings for the first time. If I blur my eyes enough, Ahuiqir almost looks like Pheorirya. Down the street, a group of demon children are playing some sort of game with small animal bones, shrieking in delight when one of them steals a bone from another. But there's something different in the atmosphere. The adult demons who stride past us move with only the utmost focus and determination, hardly even sparing me a glance. And when I do catch the gazes of some of them, they look at me as if I'm a helpless rabbit fated for the dinner table. Ahuiqir lacks the light and warmth of Pheorirya. Or anywhere else in Guinyth.

The castle itself is a clear demonstration of that. Four massive turrets tower over each corner of the rectangular building, which seems more like a prison than a home. There's something inherently menacing about the statement the castle makes, with its unapologetically cold, pure-black stone silhouetted against the red sky. Vines creep up the sides of the castle, their dark emerald leaves intertwining. When I look closer, I see that their stems are all black, like the castle, and I wonder if they have been tampered with for aesthetic purposes or if they're a special type of plant found only in Ahuiqir. The absurd thought of Victoire flying about, injecting individual veins with black ink makes me want to laugh. If I weren't in my current position right now, I would.

Almost on cue, we arrive at the main entrance, where two guards stand watch. I'm thrown at their feet. "She attacked us," my captors report haughtily. One of the guards narrows her eyes, flicking my hair away from my face.

"My, my. I never thought I would live to see this day." A dagger appears in her hand and my breath hitches. She saunters toward me with slow, feline grace. There is a flash of silver, and blood begins to run down the side of my face, warm and sticky. She lifts the bloodied blade to her mouth, running her tongue along its razor-sharp edge. "The one and only Catarina Winyr . . ." she whispers.

"Well." A smile spreads across Fane's face. He sits on a throne created from bones dyed black. A heavy-looking crown of solid gold rests on his head. "Who do we have here?"

The guard shoves me and I fall to my knees before him with a grunt. The cold, hard floor digs into my knees, but I swallow away the discomfort. "Who are you?" I hiss.

He rises from his throne. "Do you not recognize me? I'm offended." His voice drips with cold, caustic sarcasm, and I narrow my eyes. He laughs, but the sound doesn't quite meet his eyes. "I am King Fane of Ahuiqir, darling."

I look him directly in the eye. His wavy hair is dark and thick with several strands falling into his face, and his eyes shine with keen, watchful intellect. I instantly understand why this man is idolized the way he is; they've all been charmed.

"She attacked two citizens," the guard behind me explains.

The king cocks his head at me, and with a flick of a finger, he sends a tendril of darkness curling toward me. My eyes widen, and I lean as far away as my chained arms and legs will allow. The shadow curls itself around my shoulder. At first, the affected area burns only slightly. And then the burning turns into a searing pain that lingers even after the little coil dissipates, as if he'd cut me open and poured rubbing alcohol all over the wound. I bite my tongue so hard trying not to make a sound that I taste blood, but Fane notices regardless.

"You see, this is what I love the most about pain. It is a constant in life, no matter who you are. Everyone feels it, even if they claim they're oh so strong and that nothing affects them." He leans down, smiling lazily. His shadows wreathe his body, always flowing, never unmoving. Harmless. "Tell me, Catarina. Is this pain affecting you?"

"No," I hiss through clenched teeth.

He stands and the smoke dissipates around him. I glare at him, but somehow, I cannot force the same iciness into my gaze as before. "Scared?" he asks.

I spit at his feet. "Never."

His mouth draws into a thin line, and he turns his gaze to the guard behind me. "I believe the queen wants to see her as well."

No. The very thought of seeing Victoire in the flesh makes me physically recoil. "What do you want from me?" I blurt out, desperate to keep him talking.

He looks at me, a sneer curling his lips. "I trust that you remember the day of Philan's death?"

The sound of the demon uttering Philan's name sends a white flare of anger through my chest, and my fists tighten at my sides. "Of course not," I say.

"You're acting childishly, Catarina. Would you like to say hello to my lovely shadows again?" He lifts a finger and a tentacle of that poisonous vapor waves tauntingly at me.

I clench my jaw so hard that my teeth ache. "What does Philan's death have to do with this?"

"It has everything to do with this, darling," he whispers, crouching down so that our eyes are level. "What did you think of Soren's behavior?"

"He wasn't acting like himself; he was absolutely out of his mind. He told me a demon was manipulating him. Minerva."

Fane hooks one serrated claw under my chin and drags upward so I'm forced to meet his gaze. "Did you believe him?"

"Yes," I growl, ignoring the drop of warm liquid I feel running down my neck and onto my shirt.

"What do you think was the point of manipulating one of your friends?" he asks me, clearly delighted with the conversation. "I'll give you a hint: it wasn't to kill Philan."

My brain whirrs, sorting through his words and realizing their true meaning. "Does that mean that Philan's murder was unintentional?"

"It means whatever you want it to mean." His grin is positively sadistic.

"What are you saying?"

He lets out a sigh of mock resignation. "All right. If you truly can't figure it out, I'll just tell you. Soren was meant to kill *you,* my darling. But after some reflection, we realized it might be beneficial to keep you alive. And now, here you are!" He takes a strand of my hair in his clawed fingers. "You truly make it too easy for us."

"Why did you decide that?"

He reaches for my face and I jerk away from him, disgusted. "Don't touch me," I say. Something changes in Fane's face, and he gestures at the two guards behind me once again. "Ask Victoire," he says.

"Your Majesty," the guard says.

I'm taken to an adjoining room, where a demon sits at an imposing desk, her icy blond hair falling into her eyes as she bends over her work. Slowly, she looks up, and her eyes widen as her gaze registers me. The quill she's been holding slips from her fingers, ink splattering everywhere.

My heart plummets. I'd prayed that she'd have less of an impact on me in real life than in my mind. But it's the opposite. Every fiber that makes up my body is begging me to turn around, to *run,* but I'm rooted to the floor. Victoire Liverraine. Her piercing blue eyes are just as cunning and cruel as they'd been before. Her shadows are just as dark and vile. I've met many demons for the first time today, but she is the one who feels the most real.

"Catarina Winyr, Your Majesty," the guard announces.

"Leave us now," she tells him.

I whirl around and silently beg the guard with my eyes not to leave me alone with the demon before us, but he does anyway. Victoire's long, dark gown brushes my legs as she glides past me and shuts the door to her study. When I hear the soft click of the lock falling into place, I am convinced I might not live until tomorrow. "Victoire," I whisper.

"A pleasure, as always." She finally turns to me, slowly taking me in. "I never realized how much you look like your mother."

I can't stop the shudder that runs through me at the mention of my mother, and from the smirk on her red lips, I know Victoire mentioned her on purpose to rile me.

"Why are you here, Catarina? However sad it makes me, I don't believe you came here simply to pay your favorite demon in the world a visit." But somehow, by the way she looks at me, I know that she already thinks she knows.

"Why didn't Fane kill me?"

"What do *you* think?"

My eyes narrowing, I sort through what Fane had told me. "You want to use me. Again."

She laughs. "I always knew you were a smart girl." She leans toward me, clearly delighting in every flicker of fear she senses. "And *you* are going to obey my every command. Because if you don't, I will go to Guinyth and kill every last one of your friends myself." My stomach flips but I try to steady my face. I cannot stop the corners of my mouth from trembling.

"Don't waste your time, I don't care for any of them."

"I think you are lying to my face right now, Catarina." I know that my despair is written across my face in plain, stark lines, but I can't seem to control it. "What about Zhengya? Ms. Zhengya Lin?"

"What about her?" My lips quiver as I speak, and she laughs.

"Where's the big, strong, fearless Catarina gone? What happened to her?"

I swallow, but my throat is completely dry. "I could slit that pretty little throat of hers," she murmurs, trailing a talon up my arm and taking a lock of my newly shortened hair in her claw. "I've dreamed of that for as long as I can remember, you know. It'd be *so easy.* Just a flick of my wrist, and she'd be dead," she laughs, throwing her hands in the air. "Dead! Imagine how nice that'd be. In fact, I could slit *all* their throats."

"No."

"*Yes.* Now, stop resisting."

"What do you mean?"

"I think you know what I mean. Open your mind to me, Catarina."

I hesitate for a second. A tear slides down my cheek, and I brush it away roughly. "Weren't you able to control me before?"

"Your mind didn't fight mine that night. It does now." A fierce sense of pride fills me for the briefest of seconds at her admission, and she sees it. "If killing your friends isn't incentive enough, I could also cut out that other eye of yours," she says.

I jerk up. "*No.*"

Victoire steps back, smiling. She's won and she knows it. "Then what are you waiting for, darling? You know what to do."

I'm furious at her ability to completely flip the balance of power between us in a matter of seconds. I'm furious at everything about her. "Why? Why do you need me? I asked the king the same thing, and he wouldn't respond."

"Well, Catarina. Need I remind you of the strange way your mother and father died again?"

Oh. "I'm supposed to be your little assassin." The words leave me without emotion.

"Yes!" Victoire exclaims in false delight. "I thought you'd never get it!"

I want to fall to my knees and beg her for mercy, but I realize she'd enjoy that. And my heart lurches at even the thought of complete blindness. *It'd make me even weaker.* And so I give in, allowing the walls around my mind to finally fall and revealing everything that makes up who I am.

A victorious smile takes over Victoire's face. "You won't regret this."

Victoire pushes her power forward and it reaches out hungrily, gleefully wrapping her shadows around me. I stiffen. "Don't fight back. It will only be more painful for you." she purrs.

My eyes close. I can feel the invasive force of her power searching for something to cling to. It feels slimy, *wrong*, and it takes all my willpower not to shut her out again, especially knowing that I can shut her out at all. It's the only ability I have that makes me feel in control. My body shakes with the strain of it. But then, with a click, everything falls into place. And I feel nothing. Distantly, I sense Victoire flipping my eyelid open and letting out a shriek of joy. By her command, I look into the mirror she's holding out for me. *My eye is completely black.*

I lean against the bathroom wall of my new bedroom, staring at my reflection in the mirror. The girl who stares back is not the person I know. Her lips are pale and dry, and her skin is cracked from the toxins in the air. The most noticeable difference is her remaining eye, which has gone completely black. *Just like her left eye had once been.* I sigh and run a hand through my hair. Nothing feels the same. My body is not my own, I can't even think about anything anymore. Victoire will always be there, listening. She's allowed me to have my own room for that reason: escape is utterly futile. At any second, she could change her mind about wanting to keep me alive.

My spine suddenly goes rigid as I shoot to my feet. *Zhengya. I've completely forgotten about Zhengya.* Awful waves of guilt and fear crash down on me, washing away everything and revealing nothing but vicious hatred for the demons and heated determination to *save her.* I slip out of my dirty clothes and find a plain black gown in the closet. I may as well look presentable if I am going to face Fane and Victoire. I stalk out of the room, my chin high.

A servant stops me. "You're not supposed to be out of your room," he says cautiously.

"I want to speak with the king."

He considers me for a moment. "He's in the throne room with the queen, just down the stairs."

I nod curtly. "Thank you."

As I walk down the spiraling staircase, memories flood my mind. I remember how I'd collapsed on the Greensbriar Manor staircase all those weeks ago. It's not a particularly happy memory, but I would do anything to be back home. *Home.* When had it become that? But, the word is nothing more than a daydream now. A fantasy of another life.

Fane's eyes snap to me as I enter the room. He is sprawled casually across his throne, his queen perched atop her own beside him. "What do you want?" he drawls.

I force myself not to shrink under his eye.

Victoire places a hand on his arm, shooting him a glare. "You are one of us now, darling. What do you need?" I start to walk forward, but suddenly, my legs freeze. "You haven't bowed yet, darling."

I shake my head, unable to speak. Victoire sneers. With a twist of her fingers, I find myself dropping into a stiff curtsy, although I do not tell my knees to bend. Icy cold loathing seethes in me. "Where is Zhengya?"

Fane laughs. "Zhengya Lin? Philan's sister?"

I grit my teeth. Victoire turns to look at her spouse, smiling with genuine humor. "It's not like she can escape with the girl, Fane. Tell her."

He stands slowly and prowls toward me. "You know us, Catarina. So where do you think she is?"

My heart drops. "You have her captured." My voice is dull, lifeless, and I do not say the words as a question, because why would I need to? I already know the answer.

He leans in even closer, his horns almost knocking against my head. "Smart girl. We're going to kill her. Surely you know this, too." I close my eyes, willing my heartbeat to slow and my fists to uncurl. "You're going to watch us do it, too. And you're not going to be able to do a damn thing."

With a roar, my hand shoots out to strike Fane across the face. But before I make contact, my arm locks in place. A brief flash of pain shoots through my shoulder and a force lowers my arm against my will. Victoire shakes her head in mock disappointment.

"Don't be so violent, Catarina. I thought you were better than this," Fane says and throws his head back, laughing delightedly. "I could take you to see her now."

Victoire stands and puts a hand on Fane's arm. "That would be lovely, darling. You go do that." Her eyes never leave my own.

Fane and I stride down the hallway, his hand tight around my arm. He turns a sharp corner, then drags me into what looks to be a library. The guard standing there bows deeply. "The dungeon," Fane orders.

The guard hurries over to a bookshelf separate from all the others and pushes lightly on one of the shelves. The entire wall behind it swings open, and I jump. *Just like the stories.* Fane smiles wryly at me in a way that feels too knowing. It's as if he can read my thoughts. Perhaps he can, for all I know.

Fane gestures at the gray stone staircase before us. "Ladies first."

CHAPTER TWENTY-TWO

ZHENGYA

MY HEAD SPINS. Everything hurts. All I know is that I was captured by the demons I'd read so much about. One of them shoved a single white berry down my throat as soon as they captured me, and the symptoms are only now beginning to manifest. My teeth never broke the skin of the berry, but its bitterness lingers on my tongue. It'd been one that I couldn't identify from my years of lessons on natural poisons and toxins, though I had seen illustrations of it. *It must be native to Ahuiqir.* The world begins to tilt and I right myself with a jolt, pressing both hands into the stone beneath me to ground myself. I pinch myself in the thigh. Already, I am starting to lose focus. I rack my brain. What general cures are there for poison? I can't remember.

My body refuses to move even a single inch. Saliva pools in my mouth, even as my throat burns for water. Each breath feels like sandpaper scraping against my lungs and leaving a trail of searing fire. My eyes feel heavy. They're dead weights I can't hold up. *How is it possible to feel this tired, this drained? Rest. I just need to rest.*

"Zhengya!" Someone calls my name, but I assume I'm hallucinating. "Zhengya!"

My eyes fly open. Catarina stands there, just outside of my tiny cell. Fane stands behind her, smirking. She kneels down, reaching through the bars. "Get up," she spits. "Get up!" She sounds angry and desperate. Her voice strains and is higher pitched than usual. I want to take her hand but she's too far away. She strains to reach for me again but I shake my head, which sends a fresh wave of pain washing over me.

"Can't," I force out. Catarina's expression falls. Fane puts a hand on her shoulder.

"Would you like to do the honors, my dear? Or should I?"

Catarina's face flushes a flaming red as she whips her head around to snarl at him. "If you so much as *touch* her—"

He cocks his head. "You'll do what?"

She falls silent, and I close my eyes. Poison wouldn't be such a bad way to die. "Zhengya, you've got to stand up."

Even if I could open my eyes, I wouldn't. But, I can hear the pleading in her voice clear enough to shred what's left of my decaying heart.

Fane lets out an exaggerated sigh. "Well then. This has been lovely, but I do believe it's time to get to work."

Catarina slowly rises to her feet. "No."

Fane laughs, but dark eyes narrow ever so slightly. "I'm a demon who gives credit where it's due. So Catarina, I admit that your bravery is admirable. But it's also stupid. What will this accomplish for you?"

"I'm going to die anyway," I whisper. Catarina shakes her head. She won't look at me now.

Fane gestures at me. "Exactly," he tells Catarina, leaning towards her. "Even the girl knows it. We'd be doing a moral thing, putting her out of her misery."

She shoves him, drawing a small dagger from her waistband. "I said *no.*"

But the demon doesn't even flinch. "Darling, you are human, if you've forgotten. And the queen does have full control of your mind."

What? My eyes fly open and I attempt to clench my fists, but even that simple movement makes my arms shake with effort.

"Then tell her not to interfere, just this once," comes Catarina's reply.

"Are you challenging me?"

"Catarina, stop." I hate how small my voice sounds. Her gaze flits to meet mine for a moment, but she doesn't reply. Fane takes one step back, and Catarina's shoulders sag with relief at even the slightest increase of distance between them.

"Let's make a deal," Fane says. "If you somehow manage to defeat me, I will allow you to take your friend home unharmed. But if you don't, I kill you both."

Catarina looks at the demon, and then back at me. *She's going to say yes.* I let my head fall back against the cold stone wall, tears streaming down my cheeks. "I'm going to die either way," I repeat.

"No, you're not." In one swift motion, Catarina turns and hacks through the lock of my cell. The metal gives way with a clang, and she throws the door open. "Go!" she screams.

Somehow, I push to my feet and stagger out. Fane lets out a snarl and lunges for Catarina. She turns away, slamming her knife into his side. He pulls it out easily.

"Get up the stairs!" Catarina shoves me behind her, and then turns back to the demon.

As I stumble up the stairs, the last thing I see is the determined fire in her gaze. I can't stop the tears that fall from my eyes as I run down the long, dark corridors of the castle. My footsteps are the only sound I hear. It is by some miracle that I don't run into anyone else. Not even a servant. Where is everybody? I can't focus on that. My entire body trembles like a flower caught in a hurricane. I clamp a hand over my mouth, muffling the scream of sheer agony that threatens to explode from me. I stumble out into the dry heat of Ahuiqir, looking around frantically. *The cave. I need to find the cave.*

For a moment, I sway on my feet and am reminded of how little time I have left. I duck into the scant safety of Tillkasen Forest. Sweat pours down my back. Cheusnys Cave cannot be far. I hear a persistent pulsing beat in my ears, and I can't tell if it's my own heartbeat or the wings of a demon. I can't tell anything anymore. My vision swims in and out, and I fall against a tree.

Get. Up.

I imagine Catarina's angry voice fills my mind. Gritting my teeth against the pain, I push to my feet. I turn a corner and the dark mouth of the cave yawns before me. I lurch across the barrier, through the cave, and back into Guinyth.

My legs give out just as I take my first step onto the fresh green grass of the human world. I fall forward, shuddering and exhausted. The torment of the poison coursing through my veins has shifted into a searing liquid fire. My breath comes to me in short, harsh pants.

"Zhengya!" someone shrieks. I can faintly recognize it as Soren's voice. Someone's arms wrap around my waist and gently turn me onto my back. When I wrestle my eyes open, I catch a flash of flaming red hair.

"Poison," Liserli says slowly, as if in shock. She places a hand on my forehead and then jerks backward. "She's burning up."

Brienne mops a damp cloth over my face, cleaning away the grime of the dungeon in Ahuiqir. "What happened?" she whispers.

Soren's head appears over her shoulder, and when he sees me, he physically recoils. I would laugh if I could.

I open my mouth to attempt to answer Brienne's question, but Liserli's hand covers it.

"No, stop it. Don't try to talk." A thin stream of cold water lands on one cheek, then moves to the other. "We need to get her to throw up the poison, whatever it was."

I've never been so grateful for Liserli's steady, unwavering presence. "Too late," I manage to whisper. Liserli pushes my blood-matted hair away from my face with a hiss of frustration.

Brienne looks desperately at Soren, who still stands above us, silently watching. "Soren, *do something.*"

He bends down, placing his hands awkwardly on my stomach. I groan and turn away, his touch only agitating the pain.

Liserli shoves him. "What are you doing?"

He shoves her back. "I don't *know*."

Brienne glares at the two of them. "Stop. Soren, stick a finger down her throat."

He obeys, and I gag, doubling over. Vomit spews out of my mouth and my throat burns with the acid from my stomach.

"Good," Liserli says, after several minutes of this, taking a cloth from Brienne and gingerly wiping my mouth. "How do you feel now?"

Weakness still riddles my muscles and my head still spins, but most of the pain has suddenly mollified. I sit up and accept a flask of water from Brienne. "Thank you." My voice is hoarse and shaky, but I still feel infinitely better than I had only moments before.

Soren starts to pace. "We need to get in there. Catarina—"

"I'll go again," I say. They lapse into silence, foreheads identically creased with worry as they look at one another.

"Only Zhengya can enter," Brienne whispers, reading the hesitation in Liserli's eyes.

"I know. But I don't think she should."

Soren runs an exasperated hand through his hair. "This is ridiculous. Why do these things always happen to us?"

Brienne ignores him. "Liserli, there's always been a feeling in my gut that the demons want her for something. We can't let them have that."

I push to my feet, wiping my hands on my clothing. "I don't need you three to decide my fate for me. I can do that perfectly well myself."

"You're not well enough," Liserli protests halfheartedly. Soren shoots her a look, and she sighs, looking at me again. "Are you sure? You were just on the ground dying by poison and you want to go back? What makes you think this time will go any better?"

I face her, unsmiling. My mind is clear and free from the effects of the poison. I'm sharp again. "I'm going."

CHAPTER TWENTY-THREE

CATARINA

HIS SHADOWS SNAKE AROUND my wrists and ankles. The wisps wrap tighter and tighter, and I throw my head back, my screams echoing through the dungeon. I'm bound here. But I can handle pain. I'd rather endure centuries of ceaseless torture than see Zhengya in that state again. Fane pushes me against a wall and presses my own blade against my neck.

"You're not going to kill me," I choke. "You can't. Victoire won't allow it."

He angles his head. "We have no use for you anymore. What good is a weapon when it is just as dangerous to you as it is to your opponents?" I try to slide down the wall, but he holds me tight. "She's going to die anyway, you know. Your precious friend. And so when I kill you, you will have died for nothing."

"At least I will have died honorably," I say. The knife digs into my skin even harder, and my breath comes to me in short pants.

"There is no such thing as an honorable death. Humans, demons, we are all selfish in our own ways. You only tried to save her because you knew that the rest of your little entourage would never forgive you if you didn't. And of course, we can't forget that poor Catarina Winyr is hopelessly in love with Zhengya Lin." He grins at me. "I saw the way you looked at her.

You see? Selfish, selfish girl."

His words feel like a slap across the face. "That's not true," I whisper.

He laughs. "Yes, it is."

"Do you think people kill for selfish reasons, too?" I ask, desperate for more time.

My question makes Fane pause. "Who was your first kill, Catarina?"

"A boy."

"And why did you kill him?"

"I wanted to."

He smiles widely down at me, revealing those fangs. I shudder but he only presses closer. "There's your answer, Catarina. You killed because you wanted to; I kill because I want to."

"Doesn't that make you selfish, too?"

He frowns. "I suppose it does."

"How does that make you feel?" I ask, genuinely curious.

His knife loosens a little as the sneer dies away. "I was raised out of selfishness, you know."

"What do you mean?"

He doesn't look at me as he speaks. "I wouldn't be who I am today without a group of people being very, very selfish." He leans back down toward my face, and when he speaks again, I can feel his breath. "And I think in rare occasions, selfishness is for the best."

With one flick of his wrist, the knife slices through my throat, severing the tendons and muscles and compromising my airway. With my last conscious thought, I marvel at how ironic it is that *this,* a slice to the neck, is how I was always fated to die. I'd always wondered how my victims felt as they bled out.

The darkness presses down on me, slipping through my nose and mouth and eyes, washing through me, *absorbing* me. I am swept away in the warm current. The waves are gentle but firm. Unyielding. My muscles feel unbearably leaden, moving them would be impossible. And just when I am at the end of the river of black, something jerks back at me. *Hard.*

Light pours down on me, harsh and unrelenting. As if someone has ripped a hole in this black world I am floating in. The light reaches down for me and wraps around me. I fight back weakly, but it does not release me. It pulls me up, up, up . . .

CHAPTER TWENTY-FOUR

ZAHIRAN

THERE'S SHOUTING COMING FROM THE DUNGEON. I sit in the corner farthest away from its entrance, pretending to be engrossed in a book. Moments later, someone comes stumbling out, moaning in pain, white foam crusting her lips. Tears flow freely down her face. She crashes out the door, clutching her stomach as she disappears from view. I shoot to my feet and press a hand to my mouth. My book tumbles forgotten to the ground. I recognize her as the prisoner Fane and Victoire had taken: Philan's sister. Only minutes ago, I'd seen Fane and Catarina go down. But after several seconds, there is still no sign of them chasing after her. *What is going on?* I return to my book, unable to do much else, but my heart pounds on. Zhengya looked like she'd been poisoned. She won't live for much longer without help. But why had Fane let her go? And why is Catarina still down there with him?

From the corner of my eye, I see Fane slip out of the door to the dungeon, swiftly replacing the revolving bookshelf, into its original position and wiping his hands on his coat. My heart thuds to my feet. *Where did Catarina go? I definitely saw her go in with him.* The king glances around before exiting the library. He doesn't notice me. Servants like me must be invisible to him unless he needs our services. I sniff the air, searching for the scent that will confirm my suspicions. The twang of human blood lingers in the area he'd just been in, and it gets stronger when I step closer. I stride across the room, push open the bookshelf, and descend the stairs.

Just like I'd feared, the girl is chained, slumped against a wall. Her tilted head reveals an ugly red gash in her neck. Her hair is soaked with blood, the red liquid dripping down and pooling around where she sits. I clamp a hand over my mouth in shock, backing away from the gruesome sight. But the feeling is quickly replaced with overwhelming terror and fear for me. If Fane had the audacity to kill the girl he knew Victoire wanted to keep alive, what did that say about my security in this place? If Fane even doubted for one second that I was who I said I was, I'd be dead in an instant. I glance back at the entrance of the dungeon, suddenly horrified.

My mother died here, in this castle. The thought chills me to my very core.

I'm torn between my cowardice and my selfish desire for revenge, both renewed by my memories of how my mother died. How long has it been since I first came to this castle? At least a year. When I look down at the girl, my heart hardens. *Victoire ruined your childhood,* I remind myself. *Tore apart your family.* Although I didn't know my mother for long enough to remember her appearance or personality or *anything* about her, Victoire had stolen even the potential for normalcy, and that is the cruelest thing anyone can do to a girl with her whole life before her.

I crouch next to the dead girl. But when I lift her arm, intending to check for a weapon I could take for myself, an electric shock seems to go through her and jolts me in the process. I let out a cry of surprise and stumble backward. She is motionless when I look again. I begin to stand up to leave, utterly horrified, but then she begins to shake. Convulsing tremors run through her body until her back is arched off the wall and her head is thrown back. Light emanates from her mouth, eyes, and nose. A confused grunt leaves me as I watch. There's something artistic about the way she's splayed out. It's beautiful. And then something snaps in her back. Bile rises in my throat, but I can't bring myself to look away. She's flung onto her side, giving me a clear view of the bones shifting and breaking and rearranging themselves in her back. Each crack is nauseatingly loud. New bones form from the fragments of shattered old ones and soon enough, two twin peaks begin to rise from her shoulder blades and grow wider and thicker. When her shirt finally tears, I see two small wings there, already covered in shiny black feathers. They expand outward as she continues to shudder; I see horns beginning to peek out from her tangled mess of brown hair. Her skin takes on a paler, more translucent tint, and then she goes utterly still.

My heart is in my throat as I crawl tentatively toward her, touching her arm again. "Catarina?" I whisper.

She begins to stir, and instantly, I shoot to my feet and run for the door. By the time she stands, limbs vibrating with the energy of a newly born demon, I am long gone.

In the hallway outside the library, I spot Philan. "Sir," I call.

He turns, eyes slightly narrowed in irritation. "What?"

"Do you know why Catarina Winyr was in this building?"

"What did you just say?"

My brow furrows in genuine confusion. "You weren't aware?"

"No." He steps closer to me. "Why do you ask?"

"I was wondering if perhaps she'd come to save Zhengya."

"*What?* What in the world are you talking about?"

It takes all my willpower not to laugh at the expression of pure bewilderment on his face, even if I'm just as bewildered at his reaction. Does he truly not know that Zhengya has escaped and that Catarina entered the castle? "Hasn't she been detained in the dungeon?" I can see the gears in his mind working as he struggles to comprehend my words.

"You're saying that Catarina is here. Right now. To save Zhengya."

I pause, debating how to answer. Confirming that Catarina has been here could end in someone finding her as a demon, but I want to make the demons' plans just a little harder. Catarina's transformation could be a critical setback to them; she'd be seeking revenge. *Just like me.*

"Yes. I was only asking you about Catarina because I thought I saw someone with features similar to hers in the hallway." My tone is childish and slow, something I'd mastered my very first day in Liverraine Castle. A very useful tactic indeed, and it works with Philan.

He rolls his eyes. "All right. Whatever you say."

I look back in the direction of the library, toward the newborn demon within the dungeon, most likely conscious now. And then I walk away.

CHAPTER TWENTY-FIVE

FANE

I WALK BACK to the dining hall where Victoire still sits.

"Why do you look like that?" she asks. "You're smiling like a fool."

"I killed Catarina."

"You *what?*"

"I know, we decided it might be a good idea to keep her. But Victoire, both Catarina and Zhengya are gone from our lives now. And Catarina would be impossible to control for long; she's untamable in her very nature."

She narrows her eyes at me. "She surrendered her mind to me."

"And yet, she challenged me today. With a tiny dagger and no chance of winning. Trust me, my darling. She would not have cooperated."

"I could've forced her to," she hisses, planting both hands on the table. "Fane, I could've forced her to kill every single person with a gift in Guinyth. We could've won without lifting a single finger; she was terrified of losing her other eye." Her shadows swarm around her like a hive of bees protecting their queen. Any other demon would be terrified out of their mind, but she's offered me that same look far too many times for it to affect me anymore. I shake my head firmly.

"No. You didn't see the way she looked at the girl. You didn't see her determination."

"What?" Her eyes widen. "Zhengya?"

"She has a weakness, Victoire, that she developed during her time at Greensbriar Manor." I laugh to myself. Victoire smiles too. The frigid flame in her eyes disappears as quickly as it'd burst to life.

"All right, fine. *Finally.* Who would have known? All Catarina needed was a little motivation, and she came right to us."

I look fondly at her. I'd married her because of her ambition, her ability to always get exactly what she wants, and her foxlike cunning. Even after so long in her company, she is always two steps ahead of me. The assassination of every royal in Guinyth was an idea I'd grown to like more and more as I thought about it, but it began as her idea. And the reason why our marriage has stood the test of time is because of the mutual respect for each other we share, not because we are soulmates. Besides, the concept of having a soulmate is such a human ideology. *Ahuiqir is for exploring your deepest, darkest desires.* And the deepest, darkest desire of both Victoire and me is the same: power. Together, we are *unstoppable.* Victoire and I have always been suited for each other in a way that Minerva and I could never be. She understands me. Minerva only *desires* me. But I enjoy all this attention, too. *It's good to be wanted.*

I steal a tiny sip of her wine, wincing as the sharp, bitter taste of poison coats my tongue. "Why do you still do this to yourself?" I ask.

She turns away, her expression instantly closing off. "Stop asking."

I am not in the mood to argue. "Fine. But we need to discuss what our next move is. Simone, Kairos, Catarina, and Zhengya are dead. Iesso is insignificant. Who's left?"

She tilts her head, thinking. And then a slow smile stretches across her face, baring her fangs. "The largest city in Guinyth has fallen," she breathes.

I slide a hand across the table to her, palm up. She takes it in her own and brings it to her lips. "We have succeeded, Victoire," I whisper, my cheeks aching with the width of my grin.

Her eyes almost seem to glow with eagerness. "Now is the time to attack."

"Right now?"

"*Yes*. Waiting will no longer do us any good. Every member of the Winyr family capable of doing harm is gone. Pheorirya is in shreds. The rest of the land will be in utter chaos. Now is the time, Fane."

When I see the truth in her words, my own heart begins to thump in excitement. I snap my fingers and a servant hurries over with a bottle of fresh, unpoisoned wine. Victoire wrinkles her nose at the sight of it, but both of us are too high on elation to care. I pour each of us a glass and lift mine into the air. "To success."

She repeats the gesture, and our glasses clink. "To success."

* * *

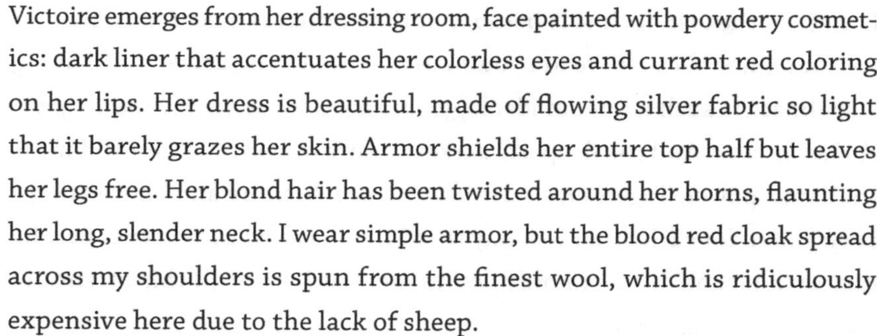

Victoire emerges from her dressing room, face painted with powdery cosmetics: dark liner that accentuates her colorless eyes and currant red coloring on her lips. Her dress is beautiful, made of flowing silver fabric so light that it barely grazes her skin. Armor shields her entire top half but leaves her legs free. Her blond hair has been twisted around her horns, flaunting her long, slender neck. I wear simple armor, but the blood red cloak spread across my shoulders is spun from the finest wool, which is ridiculously expensive here due to the lack of sheep.

"You look absolutely ravishing," I whisper.

She kisses me lightly on the cheek. "You don't look so bad yourself."

"Are you nervous, My Queen?" My hand travels to the small of her back and rubs small circles just below her wings.

She shakes her head, playing with a lock of my hair. "Not in the slightest."

Our feral grins are identical.

* * *

Thousands of demons astride octilli stand before me. I could never get used to a view like this. The fur of the massive creatures—a cross between panthers and dragons—gleams in the light of the scorching, bright red sun above us, the silver armor of the warriors even more so. It hurts to look at them, and before long, my eyes ache. But I don't look away. The creatures' roars of anticipation, accompanied by the cries of the warriors and the beating of fists against chest plates, are a symphony.

"My warriors!" Victoire bellows. "We have been waiting for the opportunity to invade Guinyth for centuries. Millennia, even. Why is it that the people who live there get to experience luxuries like clean water and healthy prey, and we don't? This ends today!" A rumble of agreement rolls through the crowd. She raises her sword into the air, and I follow.

"Let us march, my demons! Let us claim what should rightfully be ours!" I shout. The cheers of my people fill my ears and warm me to my very core. I throw my head back, bathing in the sound. I stand beside Victoire and put my hand on her shoulder. "Come, my Queen," I whisper against her skin. "We must prepare."

We walk to the stables together, where a servant has both our octilli saddled and ready. When I move to mount the creature, it snarls, and I snarl back. Gracefully, it lowers itself to the ground. *Bowing* to me. Another servant comes forward holding a rack of weapons. I take a long, wicked looking sword and tether the sheath to my waistband. My eyes shine with dangerous joy. It's a feeling I haven't felt in a long time. Victoire takes her time choosing her weapon, eyes combing over everything with intense precision. Finally, she selects an elegant bow and a quiver of arrows. She runs a hand across the flexible wood with an odd smile on her face. After a moment's hesitation, she tucks three small throwing daggers under her armor. We ride out of the stables, our weapons lifted high into the air. The army of demons bellow their support, crashing their swords against their armor.

When we finally arrive at Cheusnys Cave, I turn to the demons. "I grant you all access to the cave," I declare. A slight shimmering mist seems to fall over their heads and settles onto their skin. This will shield them from the magic of the barrier. In organized squadrons, the army begins to trickle into the cave.

CHAPTER TWENTY-SIX

TONTIN

I PULL A CLOAK over my shoulders and head to disguise myself and stride out the main entrance of Saelmere Castle. As soon as I open the gate separating the castle and the city, the stench of smoke mixed with rotting meat, human waste, and alcohol nearly gags me. The rioters, who'd started off as loud but harmless protesters, have now made an absolute mess of the city. Not a single shop has been left unscathed, each one cleaned out and barely standing. When I pass by where a bakery had once stood, my mouth falls open in horror. The building has completely burned down. Ashy black smoke rises from still-burning embers. Both the baker and his wife sit on the floor outside the ruined business, a metal tin with several coins between them. Once one of the wealthiest families in the city, their clothing is now tattered and their faces marked with grime. It is suddenly hard to draw breath. I reach into my pocket and empty all the coins I carry with me into the tin.

The baker's eyes flutter open. "Prophet," he whispers, voice scratchy from the smoke.

"I'll fix this," I whisper fiercely. "All of this."

His wife awakens beside him. "Pheorirya is falling. There are whispers we are on the verge of civil war," she says softly.

"I know."

"We need a ruler, prophet."

"I know." I've heard this countless times over the course of the past several weeks. They're right.

"What can you do at this point, prophet?" she asks helplessly. "Everything is stolen and burned down. Money is no good. Nobody has anything left to sell."

"I'm sorry," I say again, rising to my feet. "I'm doing everything I can." I hesitate. "But I swear on my very life that I will fix everything."

The two nod, exhaustion dragging their eyelids down again. I turn to leave, but then turn back. I pull my cloak off and gently drape it over their bodies. The baker opens his eyes again. "Thank you," he mouths. They have every right to be angry.

A damp, sweaty body collides into me, knocking me backward. I fall, hard. A man stands above me, clutching a torch in his hands. His yellowing, chipped teeth gleam as he grins down at me.

"Look who I caught," he mocks. "Everyone's favorite interim ruler." He reaches down, grabbing me by my collar and hoisting me up. "What's your plan, Tontin? You've promised safety and reconstruction from the very hour Catarina was arrested." He leans in close, his hot, damp breath fanning across my cheek. "So where's our safety, huh? Where's our reconstruction?" One hand lets go of me to gesture at the city behind us. "You have ruined us."

"I'm trying my—"

"Lies! Our numbers have grown strong, Tontin. Your decaying government will stand no chance." His torch is dancing dangerously close to my body now; I can feel its insistent, searing heat against every sliver of exposed skin. A bead of sweat slides from my temple all the way to my chin. He presses it even closer, sick pleasure gleaming in his eyes.

I let out a cry as my robes catch on fire. The golden flames are beautiful for a moment, almost hesitant. And then they begin to spread. They crawl up the back of me as I yank myself out of the man's grip, throwing myself to the ground and rolling around desperately. I must look so small writhing there. Suddenly, icy cold liquid splashes over me, dousing the flame and drenching my body. I let out a gasp and spit out a mouthful. With a roar, someone collides into the rioter still standing above me, tackling him to the ground. The baker's fist flies into his face, bashing his nose until blood spurts out in a crimson arc.

I sit up, looking down at my robes. There is a hole singed in the deep blue fabric, but I am unharmed. The baker rises from the rioter, fury still etched in his face. He offers a bloodied, bruised hand to me. I take it and grunt as I climb to my feet. "Thank you," I say.

The baker nods. "I trust you, Tontin. I don't believe our city could be snuffed out this easily. Pheorirya has stood through much worse."

The rioter struggles to get up, wiping his newly crooked nose with a dirtied sleeve. "Pheorirya will survive. Just with a new government," he says.

"Your 'new government' will never work," I hiss. "What will it be based upon? Every man for himself? Whoever acquires the most power through bloodshed becomes ruler? How will the new royal family be decided?"

"We'll be independent. We'll separate from the rest of Guinyth and become our own country. We'll grow powerful, especially without the meddling of an obsolete, old-fashioned royal family and their prophet. The bloodline has grown weak! Catarina didn't have an ounce of flame!"

"That was an anomaly."

"It might've been. But her offspring would've been affected by their mother's incompetence. And every batch of little, pathetic princesses and princes thrust into the world after that would be more and more inept." He sneers at me. "And you know it. We're saving ourselves, Tontin. Embrace the change and *let go*."

The baker punches the rioter right in the center of his face. He collapses, finally unconscious. I look down at his unmoving body and feel absolutely nothing.

"Don't listen to the words of an impulsive man," the baker says, putting a hand on my arm. "You don't need the opinions of anyone else, especially that of your enemy."

I look at him in gratitude. "Thank you for everything."

"Just remember that we all want normalcy again." He walks away, returning to his wife's side on the floor outside their ravaged shop.

I return to Saelmere Castle, suddenly infinitely lonely. *I need someone on my side*, I think as I return to Saelmere's gates.

Iesso descends upon me the instant I step foot into the castle and pushes me toward my office. "There's been development, Tontin, hurry! Where have you been?" I sit down at my desk heavily, sighing. She pats my arm and gives me a small smile as she slips away. "Someone will come to update you."

I brood on the rioter's anger, the baker's destitution and, yet, loyalty. The only thing we can do is look for a new ruler. Could we look for Catarina? But how would my city look with a murderer as its queen? I wonder how she's doing. Although I could never and *will* never forgive her. Such potential wasted. I sigh, falling backward into my chair. How could the daughter of such a cunning queen and her wise, kind king turn out the way she had? I'm too old for these things.

A pile of account ledgers sits, untouched, on my desk. Surely that is work better suited to the Master of the Treasury than to a prophet. I refuse to make eye contact with the ledgers. A council member bursts into my room. I can never remember his name, but I always associate him with a rodent, with that pinched, narrow look.

"Your Majesty," he squeaks. "Queen Aideen of Maarso has agreed to help us, but she says that she will not agree to a joining of our two cities."

"I've told you many times. Do not call me that. I am not a king."

He ignores me and pushes an envelope into my hands. It is sealed with the Maarso royal coat: two dragons twisting around a quiver of arrows. I tear it open and scan over it quickly.

Prophet Tontin,

I hope this letter finds you well. As I promised, I contacted several other cities regarding your cries for help. None of them are willing to help until order is restored in Pheorirya. My guess would be that the fear of war in your city is what's stopping them, and frankly, it is the reason I am so hesitant as well. The only job of kings and queens is to keep their people safe. And that is what I am doing. I am so sorry that I'm unable to do more.

With love,
Aideen Rathfall

The council member clears his throat, and I hand the letter back over to him. "What is your name again?" I ask bluntly.

He frowns a little. "Frewin, Your Majesty."

I rub my temples, too tired to correct him. "As you can see, we're in trouble."

He looks at me, his round glasses almost sliding off his long, curved nose. "So what do you propose we do?" he asks.

I ignore his question. "Get General Tenebris. And the rest of them."

He turns to go, but stops. "May I ask why?"

I shake my head, allowing my hands to fall into my lap. "I don't know what to do."

General Tenebris throws the door to my study open. "Tontin."

I peer behind her to look for Frewin, the rat-reminiscent council member, but he is nowhere to be seen. "Lilura." I speak carefully, watching the way she slowly drags a hand down her face and rolls the hilt of her sheathed sword between her hands. But no matter how hard she tries to hide it, I can see concern furrowing her brow.

"Creatures have been spotted at Cheusnys Cave," the General says.

Still, I remain calm. "What kind of creatures?"

"Demons. Great, winged demons astride massive panther-like animals." Her voice is even.

"How long do we have?" I stand, willing my hands not to shake as I do so.

"Hours at the most."

My heart plummets a million miles. "Gather the army. Move all regiments to the center of the country. We'll stand in defense."

She doesn't move. "Tontin—"

"Now!" I shout. Finally, a flicker of the desperate terror breaks through my carefully crafted walls and infuses itself into my voice. She rushes out of the room, and I follow.

It is utter chaos outside. Servants run every which way. People are slumped against the wall, crying, and Iesso stands in the middle of it all, screaming for order. I inhale slowly. "Stop," I command. If I have learned anything at all, it's that fear is the greatest weakness of humanity. Fear drives people crazy. It forces away all rational thought and welcomes carelessness. The only thing that could drive fear away, even just for a moment, is hope. Everyone in the hall freezes, turning to look at me. "There is no need to panic. Our general and the Head of Weaponry and Defense are already working on this problem."

"So what do *we* do?" someone in the crowd calls.

"We will make sure that every citizen of Tegak and Pheorirya are safely evacuated," I say. A complete lie. There is no way that we can evacuate hundreds of thousands of civilians, given what little time we have, but I barrel on. More people will die if I do not lie. "However, if you would like to be a part of the army that fights off these creatures, you are welcome to speak with General Tenebris now," I offer.

Nobody moves. Dread pools in my stomach, as leaden and heavy as stone, but I swallow it away. "All right." I gesture at Regan Grimsbane, the tall, muscled Head of Weaponry and Defense. "Grimsbane, get Maritess Riddle and Ulrich Cromwell. Tell Riddle that she is to ride to Maarso and request that Queen Aideen allow our citizens to stay there. And tell her that if the queen says no, offer money, get on your knees and beg, anything."

He nods, not needing any further instruction. "Yes, sir."

"If she has time, she also needs to go to Tegak and find out what's going on over there. But Pheorirya comes first, always. And instruct Cromwell to help the general. Rounding up an army will be no easy feat. If you have time, which I doubt you will, help evacuate the citizens."

He nods again and runs away. There is so much to be done. Someone taps my shoulder. Iesso stands there, her hands covering her face and her thin shoulders shuddering. "What are we going to do, Tontin?"

I almost laugh at her. She lowers her hands. The rouge coloring her sharp cheekbones is smeared over her pale gown, the dark kohl painted in a delicate wing over the top of her eyelid now stains her under-eyes, making her appearance wraith-like. "Tontin?" she asks shakily. This time, I *do* laugh. The sound is slightly maniacal, slightly delirious, but I don't care. Her eyes widen, and she wipes furiously at her tears.

"What do *you* think we're going to do?" I ask her, clutching her manicured fingers in my own calloused ones.

"I don't *know,*" she sobs, tearing at her hair.

"We are going to fight. And we are going to win."

"So what do you want me to do?"

I let out a sharp, harsh snort. How did Simone Endrdyn live with a woman like this her whole life? The two are complete contradictions of each other. Although I'd always been fond of her, and sympathetic to her insecurities, I'm suddenly furious at the fact that she can't seem to accomplish anything without someone else's instruction.

"Get yourself together, Iesso. We are going to do this one step at a time. You need to go and evacuate all those people. Don't worry about anything else." I speak to her like a child, slowly and clearly. Somehow, it seems to help. She sniffles once more, wipes fruitlessly at her ruined gown.

"Okay," she breathes. "Okay." And then stumbles away.

CHAPTER TWENTY-SEVEN
ZHENGYA

I RUN THROUGH THE HALLS of Liverraine Castle. It is a miracle I returned here without running into any demons on the way from the cave. Where has everyone gone? Why can I hear nothing except my own labored breathing? Everything is empty. I shiver, running my hands up and down my arms. My footsteps echo through the eerie silence, bouncing back and resounding in my ears like drums. My head still pounds from the remnants of the poison coursing through my veins, but I press a palm to my temple and continue.

"Catarina!" I call out weakly. I am afraid to be loud, but I want her to hear me. No answer. I peer into a kitchen. A pot of stew bubbles on a stove, the thick liquid spilling out and long forgotten. I put the fire out with a flick of my wrist.

"Zhengya?" a voice echoes from somewhere.

My heart leaps into my throat. "Catarina! I'm here!"

I turn a corner and collide with someone. Shadowy wisps of energy surround them and great wings flutter on either side of the collision. I can't get a close look, but it's enough to confirm my fear. *A demon.* My legs instinctively widen into the fighting stance I've shifted into thousands of times and my hand lands on the sword hanging from my waist with a slap.

The rest of my mind, the *thinking* part of my mind, goes blank. *What do I know about demons? What are their weaknesses?* My gaze darts frantically to the demon's dark eyes. One is already covered by a black eyepatch. *Could I stab the other eye? Would she be weakened enough for me to attack her?* Her skin is soft, more human-like than I expect. I've seen demons illustrated with black scales, glowing red eyes, and hunched bodies. Of course, I've seen real demons before, but I'd never touched one.

"No, stop!" The demon's eyes widen as she thrusts her hands up, protecting her body. "Zhengya, it's me."

The sword slips out of my hands and clatters to the floor. The world around me is starting to sway, and she lunges for me, but I step backward from her touch.

"Catarina?" I whisper. "Is that you?"

Catarina nods, and I suddenly feel dizzy. She looks the same as she did before, with that unruly brown hair, but I see the black feathered wings hanging awkwardly from her shoulder blades shift every time she moves. Two twisting horns protrude from her head. "I died. After you ran, Fane killed me," she says, as if that's any explanation. "And then I came back. Like this."

I pick my sword up from the ground, my eyes pinned on her even as I bend down. Her skin hasn't turned scaly, her remaining eye is still warm brown, and her spine is still upright. But none of those facts offer me even a drop of comfort. I can't bring myself to trust her. *She'd never hurt you*, a part of me whispers. *She saved you from certain death.* But that was when she was a human. She's a demon now. And demons cannot be trusted. I think of Philan when I look at her. She is different now.

"Zhengya, it's *me*." She looks at me desperately, seeing my hesitation. She attempts to reach for me but I take another step away. Hurt flashes through her eye, even as she attempts to straighten her back and steel herself. My fist remains clenched around my weapon and sweat continues to trickle down my back in a steady stream. Tension lies between us, thick enough for me to feel it prickling at my skin.

"Where are all the other demons?" I ask skeptically, like Catarina might not tell me the answer.

"I overheard them talking about invading Guinyth. If we leave now, we'll be able to get to Pheorirya before them," she says. Her tone is careful, and her eye flickers between both of mine. I don't know how she manages to keep herself so calm.

"*What?*"

She shifts impatiently, and as she does, her wings knock against the backs of her knees. I know her well enough to catch the flash of anger that streaks through her remaining chestnut eye. "We have no time to talk. The more time we waste, the closer the demons get to our cities," she says.

"But—"

"*Now.*"

We start through the halls, and when she notices my ragged breathing and pale, sweat-soaked face, she sighs and sweeps me into her arms with terrifying ease. We swing into the stables, hopeful there will be octilli left behind. Every single stall is empty. Catarina curses under her breath.

"What do we do?" I ask. *I hate this feeling.* Unknowing panic, desperation, *fear.* Why am I scared of everything these days? She looks down at me, and I realize how close our faces are. But if she notices, she does not let it show.

"We're wasting time," she whispers.

"I—"

"I'm going to carry you."

We lift into the air and my fingers dig into her wrists. My legs dangle below us, useless.

"Are you okay?" Catarina calls.

I squeeze my eyes shut, willing my stomach to still and my limbs to stop shaking. "No."

She laughs a little and I close my eyes. *I hate this feeling too.* Guilt, regret, self-loathing. "I'm sorry," I whisper.

"For what?"

I look up at her. Her gaze is fixed straight ahead, her hair is whipping about, and her cheeks are flushed against the biting cold of the wind. She dips her head to look down at me.

"I left you alone with Fane in that dungeon," I say. "I didn't even try to help—"

"I didn't want you to," she says, looking back at the horizon.

"You sacrificed yourself. You saved me."

"Yes."

"Why?"

"Because I wanted to."

"What does it feel like?" I whisper.

She looks down at me. "Being a demon?"

"Yes. I can't really . . . I don't know how I feel about it." I watch Catarina carefully for her reaction to my words, but she doesn't seem insulted. She tilts her head, thinking. "I feel stronger, like I have more control over my body."

"What about your mind?" I can hardly believe I'm asking a *demon* these questions, but my curiosity is overriding my sense of self-preservation.

"There's a part of me that would love to eat you right now," she says.

My mouth falls open in horror, and her faint smile reveals her new fangs. I know that she's at least partially serious. And she knows it too. With a great sigh, she shifts me into a more comfortable position.

"Let's stop talking about this," she says.

The tension returns, stronger than before. We refuse to meet each other's eyes. She tilts her great wings, and neither of us utter another word as we fly toward the mountain where Cheusnys Cave lies.

CHAPTER TWENTY-EIGHT

IESSO

I STRIDE OUTSIDE Saelmere Castle, pulling the hood of my cloak over my hair. Rain has started to fall, and lightning streaks through the air with thunder that shakes the earth. For a moment, all I can do is stare up at the sky, letting cold drops land on my face and dampen my skin and slide under the fabric of my clothing. One or two soldiers half-heartedly try to herd the panicking citizens into orderly lines, gesturing haphazardly with swords, but their efforts are in vain. My jaw tightens slowly as this scene of chaos unfurls before me. I feel the prickling sensation of my fire burning at my fingertips.

My gift is nowhere near as strong as my sister's was, but it's there. Hers had been an unending inferno completely at her will. Always coming to her easily, always there for her to tap into. Mine is more reserved. I need to search for it; it doesn't come naturally. If Simone's power was a fire-hearted lioness, mine is an elusive kitten: small, timid, yet completely capable of baring its claws on occasion.

And on *this* occasion, my fire is aching to bare its claws.

The frustration that had been slowly simmering in the pit of my stomach unleashes itself, completely uncontrollable. And as the fire lances upward, coursing up my arms and into the sky, I find it freeing. The flame grows and grows until it becomes a great plume of gold expanding into the sky, searing through the gray rain until the court goes completely still, Every pair of eyes turns to me. When the fire reaches its peak and I'm left utterly drained, I finally allow my arms to swing back down to my sides. The fire dissipates instantly, leaving behind only a faint cloud of smoke and the metallic twang of magic.

"Now that I've got your attention," I begin. My voice is soft, but they absorb every word. "Get into two lines. One with the children and the elderly, and one with the capable young." They obey, shuffling slowly into their lines, grateful for clear instructions. I point at the soldiers.

"You two. Take these people to the edge of Maarso. If Queen Aideen agrees, get inside the city. It won't be any safer, but it *is* farther away from the cave, where the demons are coming from."

I watch them bow and hurry away to carry out my orders, waiting to feel a hint of pride. But instead I am filled with dread. This group of a hundred or so people will survive. I'll make sure of it. But what about the next hundred? Or the hundred after that? There is no way to tell. I bury my face in my hands, but remember the prophet's words and straighten. *There is work to be done.* He'd scared me with his sudden angry outburst. But it was exactly what I'd needed. I look out at all the people shuffling into their respective lines, a sense of grim satisfaction finally coming over me. If there was anything Simone and I had in common, it would be our authoritative ability. But she'd always been able to outshine me; her confidence left an impression on people. I'd always been in her shadow. I look around, suddenly self-conscious about my own outburst. Someone's hand lands on my shoulder. I whirl, coming face-to-face with Tontin.

"Are you wallowing again?" he asks. "You get a certain look on your face when you are." I shake my head, but his lips press into a knowing, disappointed line. "Look around you, Iesso. Look at what you can accomplish when you put your heart into it. You've got a spark in you. Find it. Use it! Self-pity will only leave you comatose again."

I offer him a smile, but it feels as stiff and fake as plastic. He doesn't seem to notice, though, and only gives my hand a squeeze before leaving. I retreat to the side of the castle and slide down the brick wall until I'm seated and curling in on myself. My head spins, refusing to settle down. I can't identify any of the emotions darting through me, each one as swift and unpredictable as a hummingbird. I shut out the rest of the world, all the sights and sounds and smells, as I begin to descend into my own head.

I feel as if I'm being tossed about, a helpless bird trapped in a hurricane. I don't want to be told what to do. Being queen would render me trapped for the rest of my life, unable to do anything but be a queen. Forced to marry, bear children (if I even can anymore), sit upon the throne and give orders until my children come of age to succeed me. After that, I'd be kicked out, forgotten, all my good deeds and accomplishments completely wiped from the minds of my people, who'd immediately look to my eldest for the next set of good deeds and accomplishments. It all sounds like my own personal hell. That's yet another defining difference between me and Simone. I want to be free, to live and breathe and exist as a normal human. But what kind of a person would I be if I left my city to rot? What kind of person would I be if I abandoned my people when only I could save them? A selfish one. I must choose between my own happiness and the happiness of Pheorirya. And I hate that.

My hands begin to shake, and I bury my head in them. *Could I run away like Catarina did?* The thought spears through me suddenly, and the fact that I even stop to consider it for more than a second disgusts me.

Tontin is too old. Even if he did become king, death would steal him away after far too little time, and there would be no children to succeed him. I am the only one left.

What about the general? Nobody would be there to take her position.

I am the only one left. I feel like a soft-bodied insect who must bear the weight of the entire world on my shoulders. I am too small for what I must do.

"Iesso?" I feel someone's shadow fall upon me, shielding me briefly from the rain. When I open my eyes, Tontin stands there, eyebrows furrowed in concern. "Are you all right?"

I push to my feet, offering him a small, twitching smile. "Yes, thank you. Just dizzy."

CHAPTER TWENTY-NINE

PASIPHAE

A SINGLE BIRD sings in the treetops above me, its lonesome song echoing through the otherwise silent forest. But then someone lets out a scream somewhere in the distance, and the bird explodes out of the tree. A crash. More screams. The demons must have crossed paths with the first line of warriors.

After leaving the coven, I'd spent weeks wandering aimlessly about the forests around Tegak and Pheorirya, waiting for the demons to arrive. I regretted not keeping Isal with me. My dragon would have been so helpful to my cause, but much too conspicuous. Even now, my feet are blistered and cracked within my disintegrating sandals. With so much time on my hands, I've been able to reflect on what I want for the future. I've decided to kill Victoire Liverraine as a last act of penance to the spirit of Yseult. I almost laugh. Penance. *I* killed Yseult. I know there is no penance for that.

An odd sense of jealousy begins to brew in the pit of my stomach as I realize that Zara has most likely become clan leader, the role I'd been in line to occupy after Yseult's death. In normal circumstances, clan leaders are chosen by the previous leader. But, considering Zara's friendship with Yseult and her popularity among the other witches, I have no doubt that she has been given the title. As for the other witches, they'd already be moving on with their lives and new leader, as per tradition. The realization makes my mouth pull into a bitter line. In only a few years' time, I will be as good as dead in their minds.

And so, when news of the demon invasion spread like wildfire, along with tensions throughout the country, I was relieved. Excited, even, to set about achieving my new goal.

But now, as the realities of war are suddenly infinitely closer than they'd been only yesterday, my palms are slick with sweat and my pulse beats against my skin like a drum. I look up at the sky. Then I plunge back into the thick brush. It only takes several minutes of walking before the sound of steel slamming against steel reaches me. As I push past one last row of trees, I see her. *There she is.* My eyes narrow as I creep forward. Victoire is busy fighting off a horde of warriors, her back turned. *Perfect.* I sling my bow back over my shoulder and draw a knife from my pack, legs aching from keeping me so close to the ground.

Before I can even react, a demon leaps out of the shadow and lunges for me. Her jaw is open wide and her eyes glint with malice. But then, an arrow from behind whizzes past my ear and sinks deep into her chest. I let out a gasp of horror and leap backward as she falls at my feet. Her eyes are still open. I can do nothing but stare at her. She looks just like my mother, with graying hair and cold, war-hardened eyes. I am taken back to that fateful day. Bloody images flash through my mind. The arrow sticking straight out of her heart. Her calm, unafraid eyes, and the way they slowly drifted shut. The way Yseult pulled me away from her body. The way I screamed for her to let me go.

"What are you doing?" someone snarls, pulling me out of my trance. A warrior shakes me by the shoulders. A deep gash runs along the side of her temple, and her arms are crisscrossed with cuts. "Snap out of it, soldier." I nod slowly, distantly. She slaps me, hard. "Get out there."

I nod again, rushing away. Victoire's blond head has moved farther into the crowd. I've wasted too much time as it is.

There are bodies everywhere. Bodies with twisted wings and bodies with human features. I must wade through piles of severed limbs and twitching figures and half-eaten corpses, fire burning in my eyes and in the very pit of my stomach. My knives flash endlessly as the world around me seems to fade away and all I can focus on is myself. The aching of my muscles dies away to something utterly distant, and my vision seems to tunnel, only capable of focusing on one target at a time. But where one demon falls, another takes its place. My body begs for me to rest; my throat screams for water. Purpose drives me. Yseult drives me, even in death.

And then, as if on cue, Victoire is right before me, her blond hair dyed crimson with blood. I don't bother being discreet this time. With a shriek of fury, I leap forward and drive my knife into her wing. Once it's in, I drag the tip downward. She screams and whirls to me, but I'm already grabbing her horns and twisting hard. We collapse to the ground, rolling and rolling until I grunt and dig the heel of my foot into the blood-soaked soil.

"You—"

I kick her sword out of her reach and drive the point of my knife into her neck.

Victoire freezes instantly, eyes narrowed. "Who are you?"

I laugh humorlessly. "Do you really not recognize me, sister?" I shove my hair out of the way so that she can see my face more clearly.

Her face clouds with confusion for no more than a split second before her eyes widen with realization. "Pasiphae."

I lean in closer to her, my gaze never leaving her eyes. "Yseult said you died in a forest only miles from our camp," I whisper. "I didn't believe her. I refused to believe her. I looked for your body for years, Victoire. Or, rather . . . Eliza." She looks stricken but says nothing. "And when I finally accepted that you were truly and utterly dead, I wandered the world, seeking refuge in tiny, unnamed kingdoms until I swallowed my pride and returned home to the clan. Our mother came back, too. But you know what happened? She was killed in Cheusnys Battle." My voice starts to shake, and my grip on the knife loosens. "I did not know you had become a demon, but because of *your* demonkind's stupid war, we lost the only family we had, along with so many others."

She interrupts me now. "I did not die in the forest. I did not die of fever."

I pause. "What?"

"I was taken in by a nobleman and his wife."

"How did you die then?"

Her eyes narrow. "I killed myself."

"Oh," I breathe. "I—"

"Don't pretend you care, Pasiphae."

I clench my free hand in a fist, fresh anger flaring once again. "You're right. I don't. Do you remember Yseult A'tess?"

"How could I for—"

I put a finger over her lips. "Well, she sent me here to do one thing."

"And what's that?" Victoire breathes shakily, and for the first time, I see the fear that lies in the depths of her eyes. They are the exact same shade of icy blue as mine.

"I'm supposed to kill you." The lie comes out convincingly enough, and her eyes widen yet again. For a moment, we only stare at each other.

And then, she opens her mouth to scream. "Fane! Philan! Help me!"

CHAPTER THIRTY

ZAHIRAN

Pasiphae and I watch as my mother bends over our father's unmoving form. He lies on a small mattress, the sheets tucked tightly under his chin. He lets out a wet, rasping cough, and my mother, a cloth over her nose and mouth to keep her from contracting Ditheria Morbus, presses a hand against his forehead.

"Water," he rasps weakly. She hands him a glass of water, watching as he drains every last drop. "Get them out," he whispers, gesturing at us. My mother throws a look at us, as if she'd only just realized we're there. She locks us out despite our protests. We sit side by side right outside the tent they are in, drawing idle shapes in the dirt. Pasiphae has always been an artist, and even now, when her mind is preoccupied, the sketched shapes seem to spring to life beneath her fingertips.

"Is Father going to be okay?" she asks, letting her head fall against my shoulder. Witches stride by us, murmuring whispers of pity.

"Be strong," one says in my ear, patting my head. I nod numbly, and she moves away.

"Yes. He will get better soon," I tell Pasiphae. I am unsure if I am convincing her or myself. Another cough interrupts us, and my sister reaches for my hand. She is terrified. I am, too. My father's coughing continues on long into the night. My sister and I have always slept on the couch, my head resting on one armrest

and hers resting on the other. A quilt is spread across our bodies, frayed from years of use. I press myself deeper into the worn material of the couch, not wanting to hear my mother's frantic muttering from the other side of the tent. I feel the weight at the other end of the couch shift as Pasiphae sits up.

"Eliza?" she asks softly.

"Yes?"

"I can't sleep."

"Neither can I." I feel her hand reach toward me, and I reach for hers. We sit there in the darkness for a long time, our hands intertwined and our shallow, irregular breathing synchronized. "Do you think you can sleep now?" I ask finally. There has not been a cough from my father in a while.

"Yes. I think so," she replies.

I release her hand, falling back against my side of the couch. And then a wail pierces the silence: My mother is screaming.

I throw the quilt off my body in an instant. My bare feet pound against the cold ground as I run toward the sound. There is not enough light to make out anything, but I can see the dark figure of my mother kneeling by the bed and roaring into the night. One hand is ripping at her graying blond hair, while the other is resting on my father's chest. I stare at him for a long time.

He is not breathing.

"Mother?" my sister dares to ask. She stands by my side now, her hand reaching for mine. Slowly, my mother's crazed, tear-streaked eyes turn to us. I cannot tell if her expression is angry or agonized or a mixture of both. "What has happened?"

"Get out of my sight."

"What?" I ask, stepping toward her. "Mother–"

She flings her arm out, and it connects with my face. I fall backward in shock, landing hard on the ground. "Get out of my sight," she snarls. "Do not make me repeat myself."

"Why?" Pasiphae's voice is high-pitched with frantic confusion.

"Because your father is dead. He is dead, dead, dead, and he will never return." She rocks back and forth, still ripping at her hair.

The soft, hushed voices of the other witches carry over to me as I sit crouched in the corner of the room. "Perhaps his body was simply weakened by something first. Something the healer missed?" They don't want it to be Ditheria Morbus; no one does. My head is pounding and cold sweat soaks through my tattered clothing. I watch as they slide a blanket over my father's body, unceremoniously dumping it in a wheelbarrow.

"Clan Leader Saskia." One of the witches stops to bow before my mother. "Idris Sandor will be remembered as a brave, brave man." Even though her voice is soft with sympathy, she will never understand. My mother does not respond. She is sitting at the small dining table, her head buried in her hands and her hair loose and unkempt. I have never seen her like this. She's always been the calm mother, the fearless warrior, the flawless clan leader.

The aching in my head and the feverish feeling in my cheeks does not leave. A witch stays behind that night to look after my mother, who has not spoken a single word in hours.

I curl up in a ball on my side of the couch and Pasiphae takes her place on the other. "Are you okay?" she asks softly.

"No. Are you?"

"No."

The witch looking after my mother shoots us a look, pity shining bright in her eyes. Yseult A'tess, one of the most respected members of the Coven of the Hyacinth and one of my mother's most beloved pupils. A woman of great potential and high-reaching goals. The witch slides a glass of water into my mother's hands. "Drink," she orders softly. My mother does nothing but stare at the water, her eyes unfocused and glassy.

Yseult sighs and settles onto the couch beside me. "How are you feeling?"

"I'm freezing," I say, and then, a wet, rasping cough escapes my lips.

She leans in closer to place a hand on my chest, frowning in concentration. A moment later she jerks away. "Pasiphae, get away from her." Each word is carefully spoken.

My sister stands slowly, confused. "What? Why?"

Yseult points at me. "She's sick too." My mother's head finally lifts, and her eyes find mine.

I shake my head. "No, no. It-it is only a headache, I'll feel better soon–" I sputter, but another cough shakes my body.

Ever so carefully, my mother stands and begins to back away. "Pasiphae, get away from her now."

Pasiphae's gaze bounces between me and our mother, torn. And then she looks back at me, her hand pressed against her mouth. "I'm sorry," she whispers. And then she runs to my mother's side.

Yseult's hand lands on my arm, and she drags me outside. "Eliza," she says gently. "You must listen to me."

"What?" I wrench away from her. "I have done nothing wrong."

"You're right. You haven't." Her eyes darken. "But you are a threat to our clan now. The disease that killed your father has spread to you, and if it is not exterminated, it will spread to the rest of the clan."

"What are you saying?" My voice is flat, utterly emotionless.

"I'm saying you must leave this place."

Fever burns through me, consuming me, holding me in its fiery, relentless grip. My vision swims and my knees shake, and I am unsure if I am even moving at all. The trees around me are nothing more than blurs of green and brown, and the sun beats down on me, searing my face. The world suddenly lurches, and I slump against a tree. Everything is fading in and out and in and out, and I suddenly no longer have the strength to keep my eyes open, so I close them.

And I find that once I do, I cannot open them again.

I should have died that day.

I did not die that day.

I find the memory scribbled on several sheets of paper, tucked away in the deepest part of Victoire's drawer. I'd leapt at the opportunity to enter Victoire's bedroom again and dig around while both she and Fane were away waging war. It was my last chance to find something I could use against her. But through all the memories I've found within the depths of this desk, Victoire's personality and deepest insecurities have slowly revealed themselves to me, painting an image of someone completely unlike the demon she presents herself as. I almost feel bad for her. If every event of her life hadn't played out the way they had, she'd be a completely different person. Maybe she wouldn't even have become a demon. But there is nothing to be done about the past. I place the papers back where I'd discovered them and step away from the desk, exhaling deeply.

No more than an hour later, I've packed a bag and stolen a sword from the armory and slipped away from the castle, headed toward the battle raging in Guinyth and my fate. *Victoire's* fate.

CHAPTER THIRTY-ONE
ZHENGYA

THE SMELL OF BLOOD fills the air. I shudder as Catarina drops me gently onto the top of a small cliff. I sway for a moment, finding my balance and swallowing away my nausea from the flight. I creep to the edge of it. A massacre unfolds below us. It's a horrible mass of writhing bodies stabbing blindly at one another. Even from afar, I can see that everything is bathed in red. A flash of pale blond, almost white, hair catches my eye, and I see Victoire furiously slashing her way through the crowd of warriors. They fall like stalks of grass beneath her blade. *Bloody, bloody grass.* Fane stands right at her side, his shadows spiraling every which way. Catarina joins me at the edge of the cliff. Her sword is already in her hands.

"I want Fane," she says softly.

I look at her, hoping my expression is enough to convey more than words could. She looks back at me, and even though we say nothing, I dip my head in understanding. *Don't die. Be careful.* She leaps and swoops down the cliff and straight into the heart of the battle. I follow, sliding down the rocky slope and diving into the fray. Immediately, I am swept into a throng of sweaty, bloodied people. The deafening chaos of war is something I hadn't anticipated. Humans and demons alike shriek in fear and pain, others shout orders which are completely unheard. But my least favorite of all the sounds is the weapons. The unending crashing of blades against blades, blades against armor, blades against flesh, is broken up only by fiery explosions pounding the earth. Dirt and bodies go flying with each blow. I gasp for air.

I can't do this.

I spin around, searching desperately for a familiar body to cling to. But there is no one. *Where is everybody?* Everyone around me looks identical. Their teeth are all bared in snarls, facial features covered by blood, silver armor blinding me. Everything I've taught myself about battle, every familiar stance or swing or technique disappears from my mind, leaving me helpless. I retreat back to the safety of the forest with my sword still raised. I find a bush to crawl into, tears streaming down my face as uncontrollable, ugly sobs explode out of me. I crouch there for far too long, wiping salty rivers away and hating myself.

Stop being a coward. Go back out there. But I can't.

Battle has always been a glorious, fulfilling thing in my head. In reality it is a mess of bodies, wrestling in far too little space with far too much blood.

Suddenly, two demons land on the ground mere feet away from me. I spot the eyepatch wrapped around the head of one of them. *Catarina.* I stand, mouth opening to call out her name.

But then she tackles the other demon, knocking off the helmet shielding his face. It's Fane. He springs back to his feet, mouth twisting into a snarl. "I killed you," he whispers. "But now . . ." His gaze goes to Catarina's two black, feathered wings. "You're a demon." His expression has gone from one of disbelief to one of fury. With a roar, Catarina lunges at him.

He twists out of the way but drops his sword in surprise. But he doesn't try to retrieve it. "You're like a cockroach, you know. Resilient. But with enough force," he lifts his hands, "even cockroaches can be killed."

Shadows explode out of his palms and race toward Catarina with terrifying speed. Her eyes widen and I scream, barreling out of the bush and tackling her. I curl my body around her own. The full impact of the shadows slams down upon me, engulfing my body. My back arches as I bite my tongue and writhe, refusing to scream. Catarina crawls out from under me, a horrified cry ripping free from her. In a split second, she spreads her wings and gathers me into her arms and leaps into the sky. Fane lets out a snarl and opens his own wings.

"Let me go," I hiss, glaring up at her. "You can't protect yourself if you're carrying me." The entirety of my back is on fire, as if somebody has coated me in oil and set me ablaze. My body twists and contorts with agony.

"Do you really think I would do that?" she growls, instantly noticing and turning me onto my stomach to relieve my back of any pressure. I recognize how much stronger she must be now. We soar higher and higher into the air with Fane right behind us, but from her ragged breathing, I know she won't be able to escape him for much longer. Her wings beat frantically, determined to support the weight of both of us.

"You might as well stop now," Fane calls, much closer than I would've liked.

Catarina's wings dip, evading a quick, sharp stream of shadows that have been aimed at us. We head for the ground, her teeth clenched as her fingertips dig into my side and thighs.

"Let me go," I grit out again.

"No."

A scream from below pierces the air and I look down, terrified of what I might find. A girl I don't recognize holds Victoire with a knife to her throat. The two are tangled together, writhing across the bloodied grass as they claw and stab at each other. There is a wide hole gushing black blood in one of Victoire's wings.

"Fane!" Victoire spots the king and tries to twist, but her captor is strong. Behind us, Fane freezes, suddenly torn between me and Victoire. After another second of indecision, he lets out a snarl of frustration and dives for her.

Against me, I feel Catarina sag in exhausted relief. She looks down at me, concern etching every feature. "Can you walk?"

"Yes." The lie comes out far more smoothly than comfortable.

She gently lands on the very edge of the forest, kneeling down and placing me carefully on the spongy, damp ground, stomach-down. "Stay in the forest."

I shake my head. "No, I can—"

Her finger presses gently to my lips as her eyes fill with tears. "Please. I need you to be safe." I let out a hissing breath through my teeth. "You can't die, Zhengya. I won't allow it."

I nod once. She looks at me for a long time. "Promise me you won't go back out there," she whispers.

"I won't." I can hardly bear to look at the expression on Catarina's face. I don't like it. She cares so much. What had happened to Philan when he became a demon that made him so different than this? Why did Catarina get to retain her compassion? It hurt to see it. Especially directed at me. Her wings open once again, and she takes to the air. For one final moment, I look out at the battlefield. Fane and Victoire's capturer wrestle off to the side, and I consider them for a moment. The woman has icy blond hair, an identical shade to Victoire's. Tattoos cover her arms, reaching all the way from her shoulder to her wrists. I think back to the journal I'd studied, the one that had belonged to a demon. There'd been something about a group of people who'd allied with the humans in Cheusnys Battle. Something about a witch.

But my pain is far greater than the excitement of the discovery. I yank off my shirt. Even the soft fabric sliding across my skin agitates the infected area, bringing me to my knees. My eyes burn with tears I refuse to shed. I brush careful fingers over the very top of my right shoulder, shuddering. The flesh there is tender and inflamed. The smoke from the demons must be poisonous. *Wonderful*.

Carefully, I reach around my pack and find a small cluster of damp leaves. It isn't much, but it could ease the pain a bit. Slowly, I reach for the leaves and attempt to lay them wherever I can. Their coolness helps with the burning sensation.

And then a dirt-encrusted hand clamps around my mouth. My eyes widen, then narrow again as my mind clears and my muscles spring into action. My hand closes around a branch, and I twist, aiming to drive its jagged end into whomever is behind me.

"Stop!" I freeze, allowing the branch to fall back to the ground. "Zhengya, it's *me*."

"Brienne?"

Slowly, Brienne's hand falls from my face and I turn toward her. A sob of relief escapes her lips as she wraps her arms around me. "Are you okay?" she whispers, looking around fearfully.

The sounds of battle still ring in my ears, but even that has dulled to a faint buzz now that there is new hope blooming in my chest. I push carefully to my feet and look behind her.

Soren and Liserli stand there, exhausted and bloody but *alive*. I run to them, and for a moment, the three of us do nothing but hold one another and thank the gods that there have been no deaths. Yet.

Liserli finally pulls away, looking down at the layer of leaves coating me. "You're injured."

I shake my head. "I'll be fine."

Brienne joins us again and I grin. With these three people by my side, I feel unstoppable. But this rush of self-assurance fades as quickly as it had come. Two great, black creatures stand in a small clearing right before us. Their backs are turned. My gaze travels up, up, and lands on their riders. My mouth falls open and it takes all my willpower to hold back my horrified cry. Sitting atop one of the octilli is the one who'd taken my heart and shredded it a million times over.

Philan.

Brienne sees my expression and yanks me down behind a bush, pressing a firm finger to my mouth. "Be quiet," she whispers angrily. Soren and Liserli join us, their faces equally pale.

Philan wipes blood from his blade in disgust. Dead soldiers lay piled around him, their throats slit. I know him well enough to recognize the disgust flickering through his masked expression; I know him well enough to know that he hates the sights and sounds of battle, that he believes killing should be graceful and swift.

The woman beside him, King Fane's beloved General Izora Kizmet, wipes sweat from her forehead. "The humans are falling back. We need to take this opportunity to advance."

"Where is the king?" Philan asks. Just the sound of his voice drives a stake through my heart.

"A witch found her way into the battle and tried to assassinate Queen Victoire. Unfortunately, King Fane has not yet managed to kill her."

"I thought witches were our allies?"

General Kizmet swings herself onto her octilla. "Not this one. Hurry, Philan. The humans will not give up their home willingly."

Philan looks around and spots an octilla running rampant. Its rider must have been killed. Swiftly, he corners the frightened creature against a tree and twists the reins around his wrist before jumping onto its back. "Let's go."

My thudding heart calms the slightest bit as I watch them prepare to leave, and my grip around Brienne's hand loosens. I hadn't even realized I'd reached for her.

But then the general freezes. And then she smiles. Slowly, wickedly. "Do you smell that, Philan?" she asks softly. "There are humans in the vicinity." She turns around and puts a hand on Philan's shoulder. My heart seems to stop. "Now where could they be?"

He sniffs the air, and when he locates the smell, *our smell,* he lights up, too. "This should be fun," he says.

Both demons draw their swords, identical sneers twisting their faces. The low snickers coming from behind me send shivers down my spine, and the look on Brienne's face is enough to force me to hold back a cry of fear. Every instinct in my body is screaming for me to run. Instead I stand to face my fate.

Still crouched below me, Brienne lets out an audible sound of panic and grabs desperately at me. "What are you doing?" she hisses, desperate now. "Get the hell down." But it's far too late. My brother's gaze locks with mine.

"Philan," I say. My voice is dry and emotionless, despite the way my heart pounds and sweat makes my hands slick. Soren, Brienne, and Liserli stand up beside me, unable to do anything else. I watch as both he and the general take in the four of us, their expressions equal parts shock and delight. I raise my bow. I know he sees the tremors in my arms from the soft laugh that escapes his lips. "Put down your weapons," I whisper, not trusting myself to speak any louder. The general snorts.

"Who is this girl, Philan?" she asks.

"Nobody," he says, his attention solely focused on me. I stare at him, trying desperately to interpret him. "She is nobody." He doesn't lower his weapons.

Brienne's finger brushes my leg in silent reassurance, and I let out a shuddering breath before raising my bow. The wood is smooth and worn, its resistance familiar, but my arms still shake uncontrollably. My arrow trembles, a nearly imperceptible flicker of movement that I know the demons are instantly aware of.

"What are you going to do, Zhengya? Shoot me?"

The general's smile widens. "She's too afraid."

I can feel Brienne tense up slightly and hear Soren let loose a defeated breath, but it isn't either of those things that convinces me to release the arrow. It's the sneer on Philan's face, self-assured and entirely confident that he knows me, that he can read my every thought. I don't say another word, and as the arrow snaps free from the bow, time seems to slow. I can see every slight bend, every curve of the flexible shaft. Sunlight glints off the steel of the arrowhead as it zooms toward him.

The arrow buries itself deep into my brother's shoulder. His eyes widen as they meet mine, and simultaneously, our gazes both fall to his wound, black blood now blooming across his clothing. As if in a daze, he slowly reaches for the arrow and pulls it out, before letting out a small, pained sound and falling from his mount. Distantly, I hear the soft sound of metal sliding against leather, the familiar indication of a knife being drawn from a sheath, but I am too slow to react.

"Zhengya!" Soren's shoulder barrels into me, shoving me to the ground. The knife flies through the air, a millimeter from my head. It lodges itself in the tree just behind me with a dull thud.

General Kizmet draws another, and Brienne jerks me to my feet. "Go, go!" she cries. I sling the bow over my shoulder and run. The second knife grazes the skin of my thigh, and I grit my teeth. "Are you okay?" Brienne's voice calls from behind me. I don't bother answering. I can't.

"Don't stop," Soren says from somewhere to the left of me. A flash of red hair tells me Liserli is to my right. We crash through bushes and small trees, and I can't tell what we're running towards, but terror drives us forward. But then, there's the roar of an octilla behind us, and the pounding of its paws shakes the very earth.

Within seconds, Brienne lets out a shriek, and I can see her veering off to the side from the corner of my eye, narrowly avoiding the jaws of the creature. A cry of desperation rises in my throat, and I swing around a tree, knowing there is no way to outrun the creature. Before I can go even a step further, something catches on my thin jacket and tosses me into the air. I barely have time to scream before I'm falling. There isn't anything I can do to soften my fall, and I slam into the earth shoulder first, the impact sending a shock through my entire body and forcing my remaining breath from my lungs.

Above me, the general slides off the back of her octilla and draws a curved scythe. The steel is wickedly sharp, the inner edge serrated and already darkened with blood. "Zhengya," she says. My name on her lips is a promise.

"What do you want from me?" I inch backward, and my heels bump against the roots of the tree behind me.

Her octilla lets out a low growl, and she echoes it with a smile. "I didn't think you were actually going to shoot him."

"Then neither of you know me," I reply.

A laugh. "You'd be surprised," she says.

As I rack my brain for anything to say in return, anything to buy myself more time, there's a soft rustling above us. It could've easily be mistaken for a gust of wind, but the air is perfectly still, in a nearly suffocating way. Ever so slowly, I turn my eyes up.

Brienne crouches on the lowest branch of the tree, her arrow trained at the demon. Soren sits right beside her, pressing a finger to his lips. *Go,* he mouths.

I turn my gaze back to the General. Her smile remains. "What were you looking at?"

"N-nothing."

She walks forward a step. "Zhengya Lin, I have not known you for long, but I can tell already that you are a *horrible* liar." I hear a soft crunch, and then an arrow flies down from the tree, headed straight for her chest. Without ever taking her eyes off of me, her hand flies out faster than my eyes can process, reaching around the shaft of the arrow and crushing it without so much as a flinch. "And although you have not known me for long either, one thing you will learn soon enough is that I am *very* fast."

CHAPTER THIRTY-TWO

PHILAN

BLOOD HAS SOAKED completely through my clothing but the wound in my shoulder will heal soon enough. The only reason I was hit in the first place was shock; I could've easily crushed the arrow before it reached me. I hadn't realized how quickly my sister's love for me was fading – not only was she willing to disobey and manipulate me, she was willing to *hurt* me. Frustration burns brightly in my chest, and with a roar, I slam a fist into a tree, ignoring the way it makes my shoulder light with pain. Zhengya becoming indifferent to me was not something that I had even considered, but now that it is reality, worry gnaws at me.

Suddenly, there is a snap of twigs behind me, and I whirl. A figure is limping towards me. "Are you injured?" he asks. He wears a hood and his face is so smudged with dirt that I can hardly tell if he is a demon, but then I see the familiar lump of black folded wings jutting up on either shoulder.

"I'll be fine."

"We've just gotten new orders. Any injured demons are to advance, and any who are not are to fall back."

"Who said that?" I ask cautiously.

"General Kizmet?" His gaze flits from my eyes to the ground.

I step forward slowly, my hand tightening around the hilt of my sword. "I have been with the general for the past half hour, and she did not say a single word about new orders."

He backs away but stumbles on a rock, and his wings, which I now see had been raven's feathers glued together by tar and tied onto his back, fall to the ground. I sniff at the air, and underneath the scent of dirt and blood, I can smell human blood. *How did I not notice sooner?*

"Please . . . I'm sorry!" he says. "I was just following orders." His eyes are wide, and he quivers like a leaf, the metallic tang of fear filling the air.

I sigh. "I understand."

His face lights up and he moves toward me. "Oh my God. Thank you—" He doesn't get a chance to finish his sentence. My sword plunges into his chest.

"Sorry. I'm just following orders," I say lazily. I let his body fall to the ground with a thump.

"Philan."

I look over my shoulder. Victoire, Fane, and Minerva stand there, their armor still perfectly clean and their skin unblemished. Two soldiers stand between them, each gripping an unconscious girl.

My eyes narrow as I peer closer at one of them. A black eyepatch wraps around her head. *Oh,* I think. *Oh my God.* "Is that Catarina? I thought she was dead."

Minerva cuts me off. "That's what we all thought."

I tilt my head at the second girl. "And who is that?" Instantly, I realize why she'd seemed so familiar upon first glance. With pale blond hair and sharp features that appear carved from stone, she is an exact replica of Victoire.

"That one is a witch. She tried to kill Vicky," Minerva says.

"Don't call me that," Victoire snarls from behind her. "Philan, if you haven't already noticed, the lovely Catarina now has wings. And horns. And a tail."

"She's a demon," I breathe. "How is that possible?" Instead of anger or frustration, I find myself torn between shock and odd excitement. She'd been brutal enough as a human. What will her demon form be like? The idea sends tremors of eager anticipation through me. Catarina's destructive nature had been fascinating enough back then, but this new winged version of her utterly reeks of alluring power, even unconscious. And my soul, if I even still have one, seems to be drawn to it. Still, behind my intrigue is faint annoyance at myself. This girl was from my old life, and I'd been trying to distance myself from that life. I'll make an exception for Catarina. I want to watch her grow into her new being. I chide myself for letting her distract me from my new goals, but how could I not? *What an amazing creature.*

But then a thought strikes me. What if all my old friends become demons after death? What if they all joined me here in Ahuiqir? I reason that my fear only stems from the fact that I don't want anything from my human existence associated with me anymore, but a small, obstinate fragment of me insists that it's because they're far too good for anything Ahuiqir could offer them. They are far too kind and genuine. I think of Zhengya. Regardless of her waning love for me, she'd be seeking revenge if her inevitable death resulted in demonhood. No longer does she consider me family – she'd made that clear today.

Fane twirls his axe, the gleaming metal flashing through the air with glints of silver. "The universe just loves this annoying girl. Every single time we kill her, she comes back somehow."

"Then why haven't you killed her again yet?" I ask.

Fane's eyes snap to me, and I lower mine. "Show him," he says, gesturing at Victoire. She turns slowly, and I inhale sharply. A bloody gash runs from the top of her wing all the way down to the bottom, shredding through the glossy feathers and the leathery skin and the delicate bones holding it all together. No medic in the world could fix an injury like that.

"At first, the witch only made a small cut. But then the girl ran over and tore my whole wing open," Victoire says softly, dangerously. Her vast fury trembles the earth itself, shadows gathering and swirling in colossal quantities. They leak from her in waves. "And so they will both suffer the same thing I have," she says.

I study Victoire's gruesome injury, contemplating what it could mean for Catarina. The queen's threat is a death sentence. There is no way the girl can leave Liverraine Castle alive. And even though she's caught my eye, the urge to protect her is far less important than my new duty in the queen's court.

CHAPTER THIRTY-THREE
PASIPHAE

I AWAKE WITH A START, jolting upright with a gasp and hitting my head on the iron bars behind me. A dungeon. Victoire's dungeon. It all comes rushing back to me. The knife I'd jammed into my sister's wing and her blinding, beautiful fury. Someone must have slammed something heavy over my head as evidenced by the headache spearing my scalp. There's a demon on the other side of the small cell. She has only one eye, though it's closed at the moment. She's unconscious and her arms and legs splay every which way. There's a small pool of dried blood under her head, a sign that she's been hit with the same heavy object.

I snort humorlessly. I cross my legs and lean against the wall. She begins to stir, groaning and pressing a hand to her forehead. Her eye flies open, darting first to me, then her surroundings. She shoots to her feet. Terror clearly marks her face as she grips the cell bars and shakes desperately.

"*You're* Catarina Winyr?" I ask, feigning shock. Her eyes widen as she finally takes me in, no doubt noticing how much I look like Victoire.

"I'm not sure I understand what you mean," she says.

I snort. "I thought you'd be . . . prettier." A lie, but a fun one.

"Says you."

I fall silent. She stifles a smile. "Who are you?"

"A lowly witch of no importance whatsoever," I say inexpressively, waiting for her reaction.

"Are you sure?" Her eyes narrow as her mind works, clearly trying to pinpoint why she thinks I look so familiar.

"Certain."

"Are you related to Victoire?" she asks. Whatever sarcastic retort I had waiting dies in my throat as the door to the dungeon bursts open and footsteps thunder down the stairs. I don't have time to turn to see who it is before the door to our cell opens too. Catarina lets out a scream, and someone throws a black cloth bag over my head.

"No talking," a man orders.

I feel a rope snake around my wrists, the rough fibers painfully chafing the delicate skin. Something sharp jabs into my back between my shoulder blades and I stumble forward. The bag is suffocating and obviously coated with a weak poison. Each shuddering breath I take is excruciating, and the skin of my face burns. We walk in silence for what seems like an eternity, turning too many corners to count. Finally, the man holding my wrists stops walking.

"Take off their blindfolds," a familiar voice snaps. *My sister.* The man rips off my blindfold. We are in an even darker room than before, and the only source of light comes from a single lightbulb hanging from the low ceiling. A long metal table covered with knives, swords, axes, and vials of purple liquid sits in front of us. I risk a glance at Catarina. Her face is bright red and her pale brown eyes are glazed over with tears. Her nose runs, and she sniffles loudly. I know I look exactly the same.

Victoire gestures at the man. "Get out. And lock the door," she says. He hurries away, and the heavy metal doors swing shut with a bang.

She saunters over to the table of weapons, dragging her fingertips over them. She wears a deep vermillion gown that drags across the floor as she walks, and when she turns, I can see that the wing I'd cut through has been completely cut off.

She stretches out her remaining wing, yawning lazily. "You see that stump where my wing used to be?" She picks a tiny, intricately carved knife, and tucks it into her palm. "It's never going to grow back, no matter how many pills and concoctions I take."

"That was the whole point," I mutter in a tone that says, *Obviously.*

In a flash, Victoire's hand cracks against my cheek. The sound echoes in the stone room. Catarina's eyes snap shut, but I hardly flinch. The sting comes several seconds later, bringing with it prickling tears. I've always hated being hit in the face for that very reason. Even if it doesn't hurt, tears are almost certain to ensue. And the humiliation of crying is always far worse than the blow itself.

"Pasiphae, my sister. Why don't you repeat what you just said, but louder? I didn't quite hear you the first time," Victoire says. I can feel my mouth twist into something ugly.

"I *said,* 'That was the whole point.' To cut that wing right off—" I don't get the chance to finish. The small knife Victoire has been carrying slashes down, dragging a long, bloody cut down the side of my face. The shriek that escapes me is completely uncontrollable. I collapse to my knees and bow my head.

Victoire licks the blood off the blade slowly, turning to the girl. "Your turn, Cat." She steps closer, drawing the tip of the knife down the frame of her wing, just barely letting the tip of it break her skin. The familiarity of the nickname surprises me. "What do you think of this chamber, darling? Isn't it absolutely *marvelous?"* Even the slightest dip of her wrist would draw blood now. Catarina presses away from the blade, but it is no use. "You know, I don't think this knife is big enough. What do you think?"

"It's perfectly fine." She grits her teeth, shifting her bound wrists. Victoire pauses for a moment, and then throws the knife at Catarina's head. She jerks to the side with a gasp just in time. The blade still slices her forehead.

"No, I don't think so." Victoire flips her hair and turns back to the table, tapping her chin exaggeratedly. "Let me see . . . How about this one?" She holds up a sword.

"You could do better," Catarina forces out.

She laughs. "A brave one, aren't you? Okay then, what about this?" She grabs the hilt of a wicked, serrated dagger and the blades piled on top of it fall to the ground with a crash. The dagger gleams in the feeble, flickering light, and Catarina's throat works as she visibly swallows. Victoire looks at her hungrily. "It's *perfect*," she purrs.

I let out a soft groan, my hand coming up to touch my cheek. My blood has spread in a crimson halo around my head, seeping into the cracks in the floor and reaching Catarina's bare feet. Victoire looks down at the blood in disgust, as if she weren't the one who had caused it.

"How about this, Pasiphae? I'll make a deal with you. You're free to go."

My eyes open slowly. "What?" I whisper.

My sister nods, putting down her weapon and pointing toward the door. "Go! You're free!"

I lift my head to look at Catarina, whose eyes are wide with fear and uncertainty.

"What about—"

Victoire laughs humorlessly. "I was wondering when you'd ask that. My sister, we must reach an agreement. I will allow you to leave, but Catarina," she puts a hand on her head, "needs to stay."

"Go," Catarina snarls suddenly at me. "*Go.*"

"You know I can't—and won't—do that."

"You're making a mistake."

"I can't leave you here."

"One dead is better than two."

"I'm terribly sorry for interrupting your sentimental moment, but I don't have all day." Victoire places a finger under my chin, forcing our eyes to meet. "So, darling, what do you want to do?"

"Pasiphae, stop—"

I cut Catarina off, shooting a look in her direction. "I'm not leaving."

Victoire claps in delight. "Wonderful! Now that that's over with . . ." She lifts her dagger again. "Let's begin."

With a quick slash, Victoire slices through the fabric of Catarina's shirt, and it falls open, revealing a bare back lined with wiry muscle. Her knife digs into the spot where her wing meets her back, and slowly, she presses in. Catarina doesn't make a sound. I don't know how she is not screaming. The knife sinks deeper and deeper into her skin.

"You know, most people go their whole lives without feeling *real* fear," Victoire says lightly, as peaceful as if she was watering her plants. "Even if they think they have, in the back of their minds, there is always something telling them that nothing truly bad, truly evil can ever happen to them."

She has cuffed both Catarina and me to a wall with iron chains, our backs facing her and our faces pressed against the cold stone. A soft whimper escapes from Catarina's lips. Victoire laughs. "But today, you will experience fear. True fear. It's all right, darling. You can scream if you want."

The muscles in Catarina's jaw flex as she clenches them. The knife drags slowly down the wing, and a terrified, desperate scream claws its way out of her throat. My own body tenses, eyes slamming shut, but my sister has positioned us in such a way that I can't even turn my head to look away. Catarina's fingers find mine, and I force myself to open my eyes. Her face is utterly stony, frozen with fear. Her fingers flex, squeezing mine even tighter. I can't seem to find the strength to comfort her.

"End it," Catarina whispers, so softly that her mouth hardly moves. But Victoire, able to hear her perfectly well, only laughs. "Please," Catarina begs, sagging against her restraints. Her breathing is rapid and shallow, and in this moment, I've never hated my sister more. Victoire runs her fingers through the length of Catarina's hair, slender fingers working through strands crusted with blood.

"Trust me, Catarina, I would. But that would defeat the whole purpose of this exercise. You see, the point is to flood you with so much pain, so much fear, that your mind gives in. And when you are at your weakest, I'll make you kill yourself."

A small, helpless noise comes out of me. My hands tremble uncontrollably.

Victoire trails a finger up my arm, her skin cold and distinctly *not* human. "Don't think I forgot about you, darling. I intend to do the same to you too."

I find the courage to let out a shaky laugh. "I'm not scared of you, and neither is Catarina. I don't care *what* you do with me, but never will I let you win."

Victoire turns her full attention to me. "But you see, I've already won."

Her arrogant words irk me to my very core. "You haven't won until you've killed every single human in this damn world," I say.

Victoire clicks her tongue. "Don't give me ideas now, witch."

I look back at Catarina, who's gone still and silent. Her eyes are shut, face bearing an almost serene expression, even as her blood trickles down the length of her back, down the underside of her thighs, and drips to the floor.

When had simply existing become so painful? I turn back to Victoire, my mouth opening to scream at her to either kill or free us. But as soon as I face her again, her face pales, and she doubles over with a hand clamped over her mouth. I can only watch as watery, blood-tinged vomit spews from her mouth, and she collapses. Strangled screams of frustration choke out of her. Her body stretches and contorts as more liquid spills from her.

"Guards!" She manages to gurgle the single word. Two men dressed in black leather burst through the door, their swords up. "Put down your weapons," she growls, the sound almost unrecognizable. "Get them out of my sight."

One of the men unlocks me from the iron cuffs and I fall to the floor. Beside me, Catarina's half cut-off wing flops pitifully to the floor, and I wince, looking away. I can smell the festering wound.

And then a hand is wrapping around my throat and tangling in my hair, jerking my head back. Another black bag is thrown over my head, the cloth clean and free from poison. I breathe in the fresh air gratefully. The two guards shove us forward, and Catarina gropes blindly for my hand again. When I offer it to her, she squeezes so hard that my joints pop in protest but I don't pull away. Every step must be agonizing. Sure enough, she whimpers with every nudge of the guards. The guards lock us back in our cell and yank the bags from our heads. I settle into my own corner, but Catarina doesn't sit back down. She stands there, glaring at them, an absolute sight to behold. Every inch of her is covered in grime, but she still radiates a turbulent wrath. She'd been quiet enough in the stone chamber, but something has changed.

"Are all you demons really just heartless monsters?" Catarina asks. I can't identify her tone, but I feel her anger.

The guard with auburn hair turns slowly. "Excuse me?"

"Let us out," she commands.

"Aren't you a demon yourself?" he asks nonchalantly. "Or are you still confused about that?"

She hisses, lips curling back from her teeth. The expression is completely feral, and I'm reminded once again of how truly different demons are from humans, despite the similarities in appearance.

The guard laughs. "You really think I would just unlock this door and let you two leave?" The other guard says something under his breath, his gaze fixed pointedly at me.

Redhead snickers, and then taps on the cell bars with his knuckles. "If I were you, I'd get some sleep. When Queen Victoire starts something, she finishes it."

I clench my fists so hard that my nails cut little half-moons into my palms. "Wait."

Both guards look back. "Yes?"

"What do you accomplish by helping Victoire torture people?"

Redhead's gaze is cold and unflinching, devoid of mercy until his mouth twitches and something changes in his eyes. "You know, I never wanted to do this." I look up at him in surprise. "It's not as if working as a guard for a pittance is my life goal, my utmost pleasure. Even now, there's nothing I'd love more than to take the key and unlock the door to let you two free, then stalk up to Victoire and carve her heart right out of her chest."

The second guard, a dark-haired demon, looks at his friend in horror.

"The rule of a demon is bloody and cruel," Redhead barrels on. "Victoire and Fane have been ruling for so long now. The year of their ascension was torturous, filled with brutal murders and massacres. When a demon wishes to become the ruler of Ahuiqir, they must kill every single member of the family on the throne. And that's exactly what Victoire and Fane did. I still remember the queen from before, Ceiridwen Ladell. She was a lovely demon, but soft. Too gentle for this place. I'd worked for her, too. Her reign was short, especially for demon standards. Eight years of peace and calm. And then one night, Victoire snuck into her bedroom and cut her head off, and just like that, peace was over. The first thing Victoire did was declare war against a rival demon clan, claiming that they were threatening to steal Cheusnys Cave from her control. Victoire is beautiful too, but in a completely different way. She is heartless, just like you called me." He gestures at Catarina. "She is vicious. She is bloodthirsty."

The room falls silent.

"Queen Ceiridwen had a daughter," he says suddenly. "Zahiran Ladell. She was six years old when her mother was murdered. Her father died years before, and she'd never met him. But after the queen was killed, her daughter was nowhere to be found. People say that there is no possibility she's alive, but no body has been found. And she *can't* be dead. Because if she is, then Victoire truly has won already."

CHAPTER THIRTY-FOUR
ZAHIRAN

THE SIGHTS, SOUNDS, AND SMELLS of battle make me want to claw my skin off. It all brings back unwanted memories of my youth. But it's inescapable, burrowing into my brain through my eyes, nose, ears, It's nauseating. Snapping branches and crunching leaves nearby shakes me from my stupor. I turn toward the sound. Moments later, someone lets out a shriek and there's more commotion. I begin to pick my way wearily through the underbrush. I pull a knife from my waistband just in case.

Out of nowhere, three figures barrel past me, slicing their way through the forest. Their faces are pale and their eyes wide. The distinct, earthy scent they leave behind tells me that all four are humans. A demon rips past me in a full sprint after them, eyes blazing with feral hunger. When she spots me, she pauses and gestures impatiently at me to help before continuing on. Only then do I realize who the demon is: the infamous General Kizmet. I follow closely behind her. The humans have stopped in a clearing, a thick barrier of fallen trees and bushes full of thorns blocking their escape. The general slows to a leisurely prowl, teeth bared in a grin. I stay crouched in the cover of the trees.

The general unsheathes her scythe, lunging and swinging it at one of the women. The human rolls out of the way with a cry, but at the last moment, the general twists the weapon and catches the man straight in the head with the blunt end. He collapses soundlessly.

"Zhengya, get up!" someone screams. Zhengya forces herself to her feet, clutching a nearby tree for support and staring down at the man's unmoving body. The general lifts her arm to hurl her scythe, but the redhead comes flying out of nowhere, tackling her just as she releases the weapon. The blade spins sideways, heading in my direction. I move to roll away, but it only lodges itself harmlessly in a tree beside me.

The girl named Zhengya grabs desperately at the man. "Soren," she whispers through gritted teeth. "Get the hell up." His eyelids flicker, and she falls back on her heels in relief. I watch as she points to a spot behind a tree. "Stay there," she orders. "I need to help Liserli."

His head dips once as she stands, turning her attention back to the demon. The redhead is holding her ground as well as she can, but with every blow, her arms shake more and more. My eyes dart to the weapon still stuck in the tree and back to the human struggling under the weight of the demon. I shoot to my feet, hands wrapping around the wooden handle of the scythe and yanking it free. Zhengya's gaze meets mine and her eyes widen as she screams to alert her friends. I ignore her as I run straight for General Kizmet instead. With a grunt, I sink the blade of the scythe into the demon's back and push as hard as I can. She lets out a scream, throwing her head back in an attempt to shove me away. I widen my stance and use her own momentum to thrust the scythe even deeper into her body. Finally, she falls to the ground with a thump, lifeless.

Across the clearing, I make eye contact with Zhengya, whose mouth is still wide open in shock. Her two friends come to stand at her side, equally bewildered. Zhengya doesn't put down her sword; she points the tip of it at me instead. She's wise not to trust a demon, even one who has just killed her assailant.

"Who are you?" she demands.

"Zhengya! Liserli! Soren!" Someone comes charging into the clearing.

All three of them turn, nearly in sync. Yet another human appears, and they all dash for one another and meet in a crash of a hug.

"Brienne!"

"Are you okay? Is everyone all right?" the newcomer asks. Her eyes land on me and she stumbles backward, eyes like saucers. She thrusts a finger at me and turns to run.

Zhengya's hand lands on her arm, pulling her closer. "No, it's okay. She killed that demon." She points at the body slumped on the ground, and Brienne winces at the gruesome sight. The scythe is still buried in Kizmet's back.

"Where's Catarina?" Zhengya asks suddenly. All her friends freeze, three pairs of nervous eyes darting back and forth. "What?" she asks incredulously.

"Zhengya, didn't you know?" Brienne asks cautiously. "Catarina is dead."

She shakes her head in frustration. "No, you don't understand. She's alive! Fane killed her, but she came back to life as a demon. I was with her just a few hours ago. Did you see her?"

"Wait, stop." Brienne holds up both hands. "Why is she here? Who is she?" She gestures in my direction. "Why are we suddenly trusting a demon?"

I fight back my eyeroll. *I just killed Fane's general for you and you still—*

"Why would I ever hurt you?" I ask, batting my eyelashes. "I would *never*." With a sudden urge to be obnoxious, I smile a little to show off my fangs. She glowers at me, and I laugh.

Zhengya doesn't show any sign of amusement. "Where did Catarina go?"

"She was captured by Victoire," I say. Demon soldiers are surprisingly talkative, even in the midst of battle. The playful feeling in the air evaporates as the humans gape at me. I've misjudged Catarina's role in their lives. Are they trying to save her?

"What do you mean?" Zhengya's words are quiet but forceful. I chew on my lip, debating with myself how to navigate this conversation without being attacked.

"Your friend is as good as dead."

She stares at me for one long moment, entirely motionless. And then she turns back to her friends. "I'm going back to Ahuiqir."

"This is ridiculous," Soren blurts out. "The demon is lying."

I don't say a word to defend myself. I'd immediately realized Zhengya's combination of intuition and intellect, each trait only strengthening the other. She would know if I'd been lying. And when she looks back at me, I see my faith affirmed.

"She's not," Zhengya says. I fight the urge to nod smugly.

Liserli shakes her head slowly, as if in a daze. "You can't go back. You've gone there too many times already."

"What's one more?" She tries for a nonchalant tone of voice, but her words are far too high-pitched to be casual. Brienne, Soren, and Liserli share a look and an odd stab of pride shoots through me at Zhengya's fierce resolve. Silently, the three of them give up trying to convince her not to go.

Soren pulls the scythe out of the demon's back, testing its weight in his hands. "We're running low on arrows, and our weapons are no match against the demons. We might as well go into the cities and help evacuate the citizens while Zhengya heads for Ahuiqir."

Liserli's head lifts at his words. "And abandon the battle?"

"The demons are winning, there's no denying it."

"What are you saying?" she demands.

"We'll save more people if we go to the cities," Soren explains gently. His point makes perfect sense.

But the redhead's lips curl in disgust at him. "Are the lives of the warriors any less important than the lives of citizens?"

"No," he says carefully, "but in this situation, it might be more beneficial to try to save as many lives as possible, which could mean leaving the battlefield."

Brienne places a soothing hand on Liserli's arm. "I think Soren might be right."

But something in my gut tells me that nothing Soren says will change Liserli's stubborn, noble, *annoying* mindset, and sure enough, she explodes in a storm of fiery indignation.

"I'm staying here," Liserli declares. When nobody speaks again, she throws her hands in the air and storms away.

"Soren, I suppose it might be beneficial if you stay with her here," I say finally. The rest of my words go unspoken. It will be a death sentence to let her remain in the midst of a war alone. Maybe requesting that Soren stay with her will only result in his death, too, but he nods his agreement and immediately turns to follow Liserli. An unpleasant, almost awkward silence ensues.

Zhengya finally clears her throat and waves in my general direction. "Do you think you could go with Brienne to the cities? To help evacuate people?"

"Of course."

Brienne whirls to Zhengya to question the plan, clearly still untrusting of me, but Zhengya pays no mind. Instead she holds my gaze as she speaks: "If you get her killed, I'm going to slice off your wings and stuff them down your throat."

I almost laugh but manage to swallow it away just in time. She glares daggers at me, completely serious. "All right," I say.

She turns back to her friend, squeezing her hand tightly. Her knuckles are ghostly white. Then Zhengya slips into the forest and the green foliage swallows her whole.

The sky is on fire. I watch as horses and octilli streak by, their riders dead and their coats aflame; I watch as children cry over the bodies of their mothers and fathers, their little figures trembling and shaking. Brienne and I sprint into the city of Tegak, side by side. The great iron gates are wide open, and humans and demons alike stream in and out of the city. Many are screaming.

Brienne grabs a woman by the wrists and shoves a club into her hands. "Would you be willing to help us? We're trying to get as many people into Maarso as possible."

The woman twists out of Brienne's grip. "Are you crazy? We need to save ourselves first!" She hurries away, not sparing us another glance. Brienne's shoulders slump as she stares, defeated, at her disappearing form. I sigh, pressing one of my two daggers into her hand.

"Come on," I tell her. "A lot of families are hiding out in the marketplace, but the demons are sure to find them soon. They need to get out." I stride away, and she follows quickly. The knife in my hand is warm from my own body heat. Its bejeweled hilt is comforting and familiar to the touch. My heart settles a little as I squeeze the knife repeatedly as a meditation.

"What's the real reason you've decided to help us?" Brienne asks.

A rustling in the alleyway beside us makes me freeze. Brienne collides into me and her mouth falls open to complain, but I press a firm hand to her face. I lift my knife in warning that danger is near. A split second later, a demon leaps out of the darkness and runs straight for Brienne. Brienne doesn't have time to lift the dagger I gave her before his fangs are snapping mere centimeters away from her face, claws digging into her soft, human flesh. The smell of rotting meat and offal blows across my face as he sneers at her. With a hiss, I throw my arms around his neck, hauling him away from her and pressing my blade against his throat. He lets out a surprised shriek as he begins to tear at me. I am too quick for him to grasp. I jam my dagger into the space between two of his ribs with a flash of silver. Brienne pushes to her feet, eyes wide, as the demon collapses over my shoulder. I throw the corpse to the ground, jerking my knife back out.

"Thank you," she says hoarsely. I don't reply, wiping the black blood coating my blade onto my jacket.

We rush into the marketplace and my heartbeat refuses to slow. With each passing step I take, the feeling of impending doom looming in my chest grows and grows and—

My breath whooshes out of me. The market square is a ghost of what it once was. The colorful banners that previously advertised different foods and other merchandise are ripped to shreds. The wooden stalls have been bashed in. Rotting fruit litters the ground, their juices staining the stone faintly purple. I take a step forward and my foot touches something soft.

I force myself not to look down. A large, black tarp covers something large and lumpy in one section of the square. I reach for one of the corners, peer under it, and instantly throw it back down. I force my face to remain placid and mild, if only for Brienne's sake.

"What was that?" she asks shakily.

I wipe my hands on my shirt and look away. "Bodies. There's nothing for us here anymore. We should go." I begin to walk away, but Brienne's hand flies out and lands heavily on my shoulder.

"Did you say *bodies*?"

I shake her off. "Need I repeat myself?" I lean closer to her, so close that I can see the specks of gold in her chestnut eyes and hear her rapid breathing. "Everyone here is *dead*." She holds the weight of my gaze even as I step backward.

"You never answered my question earlier. Why are you helping us?" she asks. I search the depths of her eyes and find something similar to hopelessness.

My eyes flutter shut and I don't look at her as I say it: "My mother was the Queen of Demons."

Brienne's eyes go wide at that. "*Victoire*?"

"No, not Victoire. Before her." I pause, steadying my anger. "I never got to know my mother, though—the crown was taken from her when I was very small." I lean toward her again, narrowing my eyes. "Do you know what a demon must do if they want the crown for themselves?" She shakes her head, never taking her eyes off of me. "They must slaughter the entire reigning family."

"Oh," she says. She's quieter now.

"My mother knew what was coming." My mouth nearly opens to continue, but I look away toward the burning rubble around us and remember myself. "Let's just say I have my reasons."

CHAPTER THIRTY-FIVE

PASIPHAE

CATARINA PULLS HER KNEES to her chest, resting her head against them and letting her hair fall around her face. Slowly, I bend over, staring at the dirt-covered floor. My finger drifts down and digs through the grime, launching into the beginning stages of a drawing. I can feel Catarina's gaze pinned on me, but I continue without acknowledging her. My hand is as swift, my breath even. Shapes begin to take form in the dust: the sweeping curve of a willow tree's trunk, with its reaching branches and tiny thin leaves.

"Is Victoire ill?" Catarina asks, still watching me. I almost don't hear her question. The strokes of my fingers in the dirt are becoming more frenzied. "Pasiphae."

"Yes?" My head jerks up, breaking free from my trance.

"Has she developed an illness?"

"What are you talking about?"

"She was throwing up. I didn't think—"

My hand stills and I look at her incredulously. "Are you serious?"

Her brow furrows. "Why wouldn't I be?"

I dust off my hands, but dirt still clings to the underside of my nails in brown crescent moons. "Everyone has weaknesses. And Victoire Liverraine's only weakness happens to be herself."

"What do you mean?"

I lean back over my drawing. "She's addicted to poison. That fact was leaked years ago and within weeks, every demon had heard about it."

She lets out a laugh. "How is that possible?"

I lean back to admire my work. I've drawn a willow tree with someone lying under it. There is something enchanting about the simple image. Something dark. Catarina can't seem to look away.

"I don't know, but it was quite the scandal. She had to order seven executions before people would shut up about it. I think it started out as a goal she wanted to achieve. She wanted to build up a tolerance to poison, and eventually become completely immune to it." I sigh and plow my foot through the dirt, destroying the sketch, and she frowns. "And then it turned into a pride issue. She thought if she admitted that the poison was seriously affecting her, her people would think less of her. And now she just can't stop," I explain.

"...And you could be executed for saying that, too."

I jump at the sound of Fane's voice, but I don't give him the pleasure of seeing how scared I am. He is leaning against my cell, his arms crossed across his chest and a slightly amused smirk curving his lips. I don't even know how he got in here without us noticing him.

Unlocking the cell door and stepping inside, he takes up half the space. "How funny. She's angry, you know. Extremely angry," he says.

I somehow manage to roll my eyes. "When is she not?"

Fane turns to me slowly, and my breath hitches. But he only laughs. "I suppose that's true." He leans in closer to both of us, his wings caging us. I don't lower my gaze. "I almost feel bad for you two."

"Almost?" I ask as flatly as I can, but my voice breaks. He flashes his fangs in a smile. Catarina backs as far into the wall as she can, but I see the wince contorting her face.

"Of course! I'm not a selfish demon, but the wellbeing of my people unfortunately means much more to me than the wellbeing of humans."

I open my mouth to interject, but he places a finger on my lips and shakes his head. "Shh. Don't talk. I was just stopping by to check in on you two, but I've got to go now. Have fun," he says. I shove his hand away, and he clicks his tongue as if I'm a meddling child. "Don't make me angry now, Pasiphae." I freeze seeing the tiny wisps of smoke starting to waft from his fingertips. He laughs again and pats my head. "Goodbye."

He strides out of the dungeon, disappearing as quickly as he'd appeared. Catarina avoids my gaze, and the sudden silence is maddening. We sit for several minutes, completely void of words. I stare down at my fingers, twisting them together, toying with a strand of hair, anything to keep myself busy. Just when I feel like I might scream, Catarina turns to look at me.

"I still have no gift," she says.

"What?"

"I'm a demon, and I still have no gift." Her words are soft, even light, but the emotion behind them is clear. "I'm useless."

"No, you're not. Stop talking like that."

"Why?" she asks. "What is *wrong* with me?"

"Calm down," I say, warily watching how she now clenches her fists over and over again, how her mouth and eyes are tense.

"What is *wrong* with me?" Within several seconds, her breathing turns ragged as her hands begin to shake, and her eyes squeeze shut. My brow furrows with confusion, but I reach over, clamping my hands around her own.

"Calm down, Catarina. Very few—"

Every time I close my eyes, I remember my Embracing," she whispers. "It was humiliating" She looks at me frantically. "It's like I'm being strangled by the memory. *I can't escape.*" She pulls away from me, trying to hide the tears that well in her eyes. The longer I know the girl, the less I understand her. She isn't heartless, or a psychopath, but her emotions seem to completely control her, and she is powerless to nothing except herself.

"It's like I'm broken. Like each and every part of me is wrong, physically and mentally," she continues. I attempt to reach for her again, but she flings a wild finger at her eyepatch, then at her wing. "Look at me," she hisses. "*Look at me.*"

I grab her arm, pressing firm fingers into her skin to calm her. "Stop." *How could she have lived for this long holding such self-hatred within her?* "Catarina, very few demons have shadows." But my words are unheard, and I instantly realize that what she's feeling is far more complex than the desire for a gift.

"I don't have powers either, Catarina," I whisper in an attempt to pacify whatever storm is brewing in the depths of her. But now, she's staring at the tattoos covering my arm, whatever had triggered her sudden panic seeming to pass. The black ink twists from my shoulder blade, down my arm and ending at the bone near my wrist. She reaches to touch one of them but pulls away at the last second.

I shake my head. "No, it's fine." Her hand returns. She traces the fine lines, marveling at the sheer detail of the designs. Intricate flowers, snakes with bared fangs dripping with venom, and the outline of a woman with her own hands locked around her throat and tears streaming down her face. Even after so many years of having the ink under my skin, I still find myself amazed at them.

Her finger stops its path down my arm, lingering on the haunting image of that woman. "Who is she?" she whispers.

"I don't know," I reply, and somehow, that only makes it more emotive. "I was a little dramatic as a girl," I add.

"Do you have more?"

I nod, turn around, and collect my blond hair in my fist to move it away. I figure I'll start by showing her the willow tree inked into the base of my neck. It has always been my favorite, with its branches spreading toward the roots of my hair. Looking at it in the mirror has a sort of grounding effect, as if the tree itself steadies my mind.

"What is this tree?" she asks, and I know she recognizes it from the drawing I'd made earlier.

"Every witch has this tattooed when she turns thirteen. It marks the beginning of womanhood and is a symbol of loyalty to our clan." I let my hair swing back over the tattoo. She sighs and settles down; her tears have dried. I smile; could I have found a new ally in Catarina?

Several hours later, I watch as her eyes slowly drift shut. She's lying on the floor with her legs folded awkwardly to save space. She's shivering and her lips are turning blue. I shrug off my thin sweater. Carefully, so as to not awaken her, I drape the fabric over her shoulders. I make sure not to touch her hastily bandaged wing as I work. When I'm done, I settle back on my heels, beginning to wonder why Catarina hasn't healed yet. Could there have been poison involved? My fingers unconsciously reach for the willow tree tattoo behind my neck. For the first time since I'd gotten it when I was thirteen, the ink burns uncomfortably against my skin. As if it knows that I've betrayed my clan. Memories of myself at thirteen rush to the forefront of my mind.

Clink. Clink. The sound of Ganymede's tiny hammer as it tapped against the needle had evened out into a constant, rhythmic beat. My mother, Saskia Sandor, who had eventually returned to the coven after my father's death, was here now. She gripped my hand tightly. I can remember her face painfully clearly. It wore an expression of pride mixed with happiness. Her eyes were bright, and for once, her hair wasn't tied back into a stiff updo. It hung in soft waves down her back and reached her waist. She'd even changed out of her armor, which was usually all but fused to her skin those days. Ever since my father's death, it often seemed that something in her had broken, permanently, even when she returned home.

"It looks beautiful," she told me, looking over my shoulder.

Ganymede, the clan healer for as long as I could remember, finally lifted her hands from my neck. "My work is finished," she said, a tinge of pride in her voice.

My mother gestured at Yseult, who stood silently nearby. "A mirror, please."

Yseult yawned lazily and pulled a small silver mirror from her robes.

She'd gotten her first tattoo a century before, and by this time they snaked all over her body. My mother held the mirror up and I looked into it. The tree was almost identical to the one growing in the middle of our camp, and although my skin still stung, I reached for it in awe.

"You are now a part of the Coven of the Hyacinth, Pasiphae Sandor." Ganymede gave me a wad of soft cotton to press against the fresh tattoo. "In times of great need, call out to your ancestors. They will respond, and they will help you."

I stifled a laugh at the formality of it, and my mother's smile faded. "Do not laugh, Pasiphae. This is the most important moment of your life."

I stood, stretched out my sore neck with a satisfying pop, and dipped my head at Ganymede, who was cleaning up her pots of black ink. "Thank you, healer," I said. She grunted and waved me off.

Yseult clutched my arm in excitement. She'd always been so much older than I, and yet, she'd become one of my closest friends. She pushed up the sleeves of her robe to show off her other tattoos. "Next you should get a snake, and a rose, and maybe . . ."

It was so long ago that I was that age, but I know that I thought I ruled the world. Yseult had at least been the slightest bit more responsible than I. I press my fingers against the throbbing tattoo. The pain flares, but I keep my hand steady.

"Mother, if you're listening . . . I'm sorry. I have disappointed you." Nothing happens, but I don't give up. "Please, Mother. I need help." The last three words rush out of me in a breathless huff. I stand there for far too long, my fingers pressed against the tattoo, before I realize I must look like a fool. I let my hand drop, my cheeks burning with shame. *Of course. Why did I think that would work?*

"Pasiphae." A rough hand drops down on my shoulder, and for a moment, I can only stare at it, thinking that Catarina has somehow woken up without me knowing. But as my gaze travels up her arm, I realize that this woman is not Catarina. Her hair is gray and pin straight, unlike Catarina's soft, brown waves. And although she carries no weapons, the way she holds herself could command the attention of a million soldiers.

"Yseult," I breathe.

She shifts her arms, and for the first time, I notice blood staining the front of her robes and the hilt of a dagger sticking out of her chest. A horrified huff of breath escapes me. Her cold demeanor dissipates as a small smile curves her lips. "All dead souls look exactly the way they did when they died."

"Souls?" I echo. Somehow, she is still of preternatural beauty. She still has that faintly glowing skin and those pale eyes and gentle, sloping features. When she steps toward me, her feet hardly graze the ground. Her slight smile wanes.

"I am not here to talk about myself, Pasiphae. You've made a mistake, one that I don't think you can fix. Why did you kill me?" Her voice is forthright, just as I remember it to be. I let out a hissing breath.

"You were corrupt. You refused to see the evils that Fane Liverraine is committing."

Yseult tilts her head. "And was murdering me not an evil as well?"

I can feel myself turning defensive. "More people would have died because of you. You were going to let the demons take over Guinyth for the sole reason that you believed that Fane would spare the lives of you and our clan."

"You think he wouldn't?"

"I *know* he wouldn't. He is selfish, Yseult, despite all that he claims."

She leans down, so that our eyes are level. And even though she's only an inch or two taller, it still feels as if she towers above me. "Have you ever even met the King of Ahuiqir personally?" Catarina stirs, and Yseult casts her a quick glance. "I must go," she says.

I open my mouth to beg her not to leave, to tell me how to fix everything, but her form is already fading. My shock at her appearance is dulled only by the magnitude of her words. Was I hallucinating? But there was something about that specific memory of the day I'd gotten the willow tattoo.

"In times of great need, call out to your ancestors. They will respond, and they will help you," Ganymede had claimed. Were her words literal? I touch the tattoo, searching for any sign of magic, but the searing feeling I'd felt before is completely gone.

When I look back down at Catarina, she's gone still. But just outside the dungeon, I can hear the two guards talking.

"I wish Queen Victoire would let us watch," someone complains.

I recognize the voice as that of Redhead's friend. "Watch what?" Redhead asks.

"The torturing, of course. What else?"

"Uh-huh."

His friend continues, unfazed by Redhead's blatant disinterest. "I don't understand why the queen and king are still so caught up on this Catarina girl. She's pretty useless."

"I've heard that she can resist mind control," Redhead replies.

"I don't believe that. They've wasted too many resources and too much time trying to capture her," his friend declares. "So much effort for a giftless girl."

"At least it'll be over soon," Redhead interjects. "With Catarina dead, and Iesso Endyrdyn being the only person of the Pheorirya royal family still alive, taking over that city will be easy. And with Pheorirya in our control, Tegak will be much easier to capture. Perhaps it will fall first, even."

"Maarso might be harder. Their queen actually knows what she's doing."

"Taos . . ." Redhead says suddenly. "Do you ever have doubts about what we're doing?"

"What do you mean?"

"I can't help but feel guilty."

Taos laughs. "Just think of it as a game. As long as we have the advantage, as long as we're winning, everything will be fine."

"Can you be serious, even just for a moment?" Redhead asks. "Is this truly a game to you?"

There's a long stretch of silence before Taos's reply. "Laith, demons like you and I have *no choice* but to treat death as a game. We'd be dead too if we didn't play exactly how Victoire wanted us to play."

I can't stand to listen in on their conversation any longer. At that moment, Catarina sits up groggily. "You've finally gone crazy, huh?"

I jump. "What?"

"I've been listening to you talking on and on and on . . ." She flips a hand and almost collapses back down, as if intoxicated.

"Are you okay?" I ask. An all too familiar feeling of dread crawls along my skin.

She smiles drunkenly at me. "Why wouldn't I be?"

I stand slowly. "Turn around."

"What?" She flings a hand over her face, and then cups her ear, pretending she can't hear me.

"I said, turn around."

She frowns and shifts so that I can see her back. "Pasiphae—"

My heart stops. Orange pus oozes through the thin cloth she'd wrapped around her wing. A noxious odor wafts from it, and bile rises in my throat. How did I not notice before? I press my palm against her forehead. It's burning hot, but what else had I expected?

She puts a quivering hand on me, but when she speaks, her voice is steadier than it's ever been, and her soft hazel eyes are clear. "We are all supposed to die sometime, Pasiphae. Even demons, it seems, if we're wounded badly enough. I've accepted my own fate, now you should, too." She pauses. "But I must admit, I'd always thought Victoire would be the one to make the final blow. Not this slow rot."

She looks down at her hands. Her claws are yellowing and peeling from her flesh. "That blade must have been poisoned, too. A shameful way for a queen to die. How ironic. I don't know if you know Philan, Philan Lin. He is . . . he used to be a friend of mine. But he died from a poisoned blade, too. He's a demon now."

As she rambles on and on, I pace back and forth, twisting my fingers together. And then I freeze. "Catarina?"

She hums cheerfully, blissfully unaware of my panic. "Yes?"

"Kill Victoire."

"What?"

"You must kill Victoire."

Catarina doesn't even turn. "Of course I must. I've known that since the beginning. It's a little easier to say than to do, though."

I lean in, gripping the front of her shirt. She winces, and I let go instantly. "I-I'm sorry. I didn't mean to hurt you. But what I meant is that if you kill her now, you could become Queen of Ahuiqir," I say.

"And how will that help me?" She still isn't interested.

I look around, making sure the guards aren't near. "Catarina, the magic you'll obtain will heal you, and—"

Her hand clamps down so hard over my mouth that I stumble back.

"Pasiphae, don't you see? I am perfectly *fine* with dying. In fact, I *want* to die. Aren't you sick of all this? If I somehow do manage to kill Victoire, Fane will kill me. And if Fane doesn't kill me, all the demon citizens will. I'll never be queen. My death is inevitable, and I am so, so tired of fighting it."

I stare helplessly at her. "What? Why?"

"And besides," she goes on, completely ignoring my question. "Zhengya will come save us."

The bars to the cell open. But even as the guards knock us to our knees and cuff our wrists, her frigid gaze never leaves mine until the black bag comes down over her head.

When the guards drag us back into the dreaded stone room, there's another demon, a servant, in the room, trembling in the face of Victoire. "There have been sightings of a human girl running about Liverraine Castle," he says shakily.

Victoire's eyes flash to us before turning back to the servant. "I'll deal with it later," she says dismissively. "Get out."

He scurries away instantly. This time, Victoire doesn't smile or laugh at us. "Tie them to the wall," she says. The guards obey. Catarina is silent, but I watch as her face contorts with pain. The rough ropes are digging into her wing. “Get out.”

The two guards walk out, but I notice that the one with red hair is more hesitant. He stands there, his back facing us. For a second, hope blooms like a hesitant flower struggling to break free from the vines of fear wrapping around it. Perhaps he'll turn against his queen and save us. But then he slams the door shut. *Time. All I need is time to think, to plan.*

Desperate, I press my feet against the wall and push, straining against the ropes. But all they do is scrape against my wrists and ankles, tearing my skin. Something cold and sharp presses against the nape of my neck, right where my tattoo is. I force my limbs to still. Victoire doesn't even speak. The blade drags slowly down the flesh of my back, and my blood runs red and true. When she's finished, she leaves me hanging there. My throat is raw from screaming and my back burns with pain I've never experienced before.

When she strides over to me again, I see that her face and clothing are completely covered with thick, coagulating blood. *My* blood. Her eyes lock with mine as she drags her finger through a streak of red, then brings it to her mouth. “Delicious,” she whispers, and I shudder.

CHAPTER THIRTY-SIX

SOREN

I FIND LISERLI standing above the burning ruins of Greensbriar Manor. A ball of fire collides with one of the last spires that remain standing, and the explosion hurls pieces of stone and burnt wood at us. She turns to look at me. Her black cloak is singed and her face is streaked with ash and blood. Her hair is ripped free of its tight braid. My mouth falls open as I stagger forward. I turn slowly, surveying my ruined home with nothing but empty numbness filling my heart. Everything I'd built, gone.

"I was so sure we were going to win, Soren," she whispers. I step toward her. My entire body is shaking. My home, gone. Completely destroyed, like everything else that those demons touch. But she turns away, dodging my touch and adjusting her black cloak. "There are things to do," she says softly. "I hid three girls in the woods on my way here. I need to go get them." And so we begin to make our way through the rubble, pushing away the fragments of our old lives that get in the way.

Their tiny faces should be filled with fear, but instead, the girls are completely numb and unresponsive when we find them. The oldest girl grips the other two, who seem to be her sisters.

"What happened?" I whisper.

"Demons. They-they killed their parents." Liserli cannot hide the tremor from her voice. She gestures at the three daughters, and then pulls away a little. "I killed them all, but I was too late. These girls' lives are ruined, Soren. They'll never survive without protection." She casts her scythe to the forest floor, running a hand down her face in exhausted frustration. "If I'd come seconds sooner, maybe I could've saved them, maybe they'd still be alive."

She trails off, and I put down my bow to comfort her. "There's nothing you can do to reverse time, Liserli. It's all right."

She buries her head in my chest and I sigh softly. For a moment, we do nothing but hold each other. Our breathing gradually slows and our hearts pound in sync. And then I hear the distinct *click* of the shaft of an arrow knocking against the wood of a bow. Slowly, I push out of Liserli's grip and look around. Six demons surround us, their mouths stretched into wide smiles. One of them holds my own bow, and another holds Liserli's scythe. The others all carry wooden clubs the size of my body. Fear is a given. I have been afraid many, many times in my life. And yet *nothing* could have prepared me for the fear that I feel now.

I don't feel like myself. I am a stranger looking down at me, watching the scene unfold. I see my mouth fall open. I see Liserli's shoulders shake. I see the demons and their flashing fangs and gleaming claws and thrashing tails. And then I see the exact moment that the tears stop slipping down my cheeks, when I realize that I am going to die and there is nothing I can do. With that realization, my shoulders relax and the frantic beating of my heart calms, just a little. Liserli notices the shift in my face.

Without a word, she touches my hand, and we move closer to the three children still huddled behind us. They look up at us with wide, wide eyes. "Do not be afraid," I whisper. "Close your eyes. And whatever you do, *do not open them.*"

Their eyes do not close.

The demons are circling around us now, mocking us. "Are you scared?" they tease viciously. "Are you terrified? Are you praying for someone to save you?"

I start to turn away, but then the oldest girl reaches up to grip my hand. "Are we going to die?" she asks, her face calm. She already knows the answer to her question.

"Yes."

"Okay."

"Okay," I repeat, choking over the word.

Somehow, she finds the strength to smile. I look down at Liserli and I find that she's already looking up at me. Her eyes shine with tears, but they don't spill over her eyelids. "I wish . . ." she whispers, trailing off. "I wish I could've told the others not to worry about us. I wish I could've done the things I wanted to do."

"I know."

Mutual understanding shines between us. Slowly, my fingers tangle in hers. Our arms lock around each other, hands desperately clutching at dirty fabric to pull the other closer, closer. The embrace is not passionate, not heated. It smells of tears and blood and grime and it's filled with despair. In that moment, we are the only solace we have. She finally pulls back and the look on her face is truly remarkable. A long cut snakes down the side of her cheek, and the red of her blood mixes with the red of her hair, and every inch of her is covered in grime, but her eyes are infinitely bright. Slowly, she bends to pick up a branch from the ground. I do the same, and then together, we move closer to the three girls.

"Do not be afraid," I say again. They each pick up their own branches, wielding them like swords. The youngest's arms are shaking so badly that she can barely hold on to her weapon, but one of her sisters places a steady hand on her shoulder and smiles down at her.

Liserli looks at me one last time. I dip my head at her. And then she whirls, charging toward the nearest demon. The five of us, each carrying pathetic little sticks as weapons, move together as one. I drive my own branch into the soft flesh of one of the demons with a roar. The demon snarls, then turns and slices the wood I hold in my hands clean in half.

I am left with nothing more than a jagged shard. Somewhere beside me, Liserli lets out a scream and falls. I do not hear her get back to her feet. *Oh God,* I think. *Oh God.*

Suddenly, a small hand inserts itself into mine. I look down. The youngest girl is standing beside me, her eldest sister on the other side of her. The second sister is nowhere to be found and I swallow back horror.

"Don't be afraid," the little girl murmurs.

And so, when the demons come surging toward us, an unbreakable wall of black, we hold one another's hands tight, and we stare death straight in the eye.

All the way until the end.

CHAPTER THIRTY-SEVEN

PASIPHAE

VICTOIRE TURNS TO CATARINA, shaking droplets of blood from her fingertips. She lifts her head and curls her lips in a sneer.

"Do your worst, *Vicky,*" Catarina says.

With a snarl, she flings her knife at Catarina and it lodges deep into the back of her leg. She throws her head back, but no sound of pain leaves her.

"Is that all you've got?" Catarina taunts, rage seething through every word she utters.

Victoire stalks over to her and wrenches the knife from her leg. I squeeze my eyes shut, my head feeling as if it's been stuffed with wool. This time, the knife lands right in her infected wing and her back arches, jaw clenching tight.

Yseult, I whisper in my head. *Come back. I need help.* The witch doesn't appear. A second knife appears out of nowhere and embeds itself into Catarina's healthy wing. "*Please,*" I say aloud, not caring if Victoire hears. "I need you."

"After I'm done with this," Victoire whispers, "I'll wear one of your wings as my own. And I'll keep the other as a trophy." She places a hand on each knife and pulls down. *Hard.* Catarina's eyes flutter shut as she begins to lose consciousness. I grit my teeth, *willing* Yseult to appear. "Not so mighty now, princess?" Victoire's voice taunts.

"I never had to try to be mighty," she whispers. "Unlike you."

Victoire laughs a real, genuine laugh. "You truly have too much confidence in yourself. What was it that your father called you? Ah, yes. An ignorant, selfish child. Your friends have put their faith in someone who believes herself to be an almighty god. Instead, all they got was an ignorant, selfish child. Catarina, if anyone is a god, it's me."

Tears leak from the corners of Catarina's eyes.

"I need you," I beg Yseult as I search for any sign of her. My tattoo begins to prickle and my heart leaps into my throat. Victoire saunters closer to Catarina and pulls out a small iron key. My eyes widen as she unlocks the chains pinning Catarina to the wall. She collapses to the floor with a groan.

"I have a proposition for you, my dear." Victoire draws a slim, ornate dagger from a sheath strapped to her waist and places it in Catarina's hands.

"What is this?" Catarina whispers.

"I want you to kill yourself. I have decided to be merciful, my dear. I will give you one chance to do this. I promise you, death by your own hand will be more humane than the alternative." She turns the dagger in her hands so that the blade points toward Catarina's chest.

The willow tree tattoo is burning now, and when it almost becomes too much to bear, Yseult materializes silently beside me. I nearly let out a cry of relief. She surveys the room, eyes widening as she takes in all the blades piled on the table and the two other women. Somehow, neither Victoire nor Catarina have seen Yseult's phantom form yet. I look pleadingly at her and point at Victoire and the girl slumped at her feet.

Kill her, I mouth, praying she understands. *Kill Victoire.*

Gladly, she mouths back. And despite everything, I allow myself an exhausted smile. *Thank you.*

"Will it still hurt?" Catarina says, as she stares down at the knife in her hands.

"Of course it will," Victoire coos, sounding almost reassuring.

Yseult soundlessly floats over to the table bearing the obscene amount of blades and selects one while I stare intently at Catarina. Her face is the essence of exhaustion, her expression that of a woman finally losing the battle raging in her own mind.

"I'll do it," Catarina says, and my gaze flies over to Yseult.

Hurry, I mouth. Yseult nods, moving to position herself directly behind Victoire.

The queen smiles down at Catarina. "Wonderful. You're making the right choice, Cat."

She wraps both hands around the hilt of the dagger, positioning it to plunge straight into the space right below her ribs. "Thank you," Catarina whispers, "for allowing me to make this decision."

But then Victoire lets out a soft sound of surprise, and Catarina's eyes flick up. Instead of herself, Victoire is the one with a blade protruding from her stomach. Victoire falls face-first on the floor, black blood spilling from her back. She is twitching, but not breathing.

Yseult floats over the body, pulling the knife from her back and placing it in Catarina's hands. "Remember, *you* were the one who killed Victoire."

And with that, Yseult fades away into nothingness, returning to wherever she'd come from. Catarina's face has gone slack with shock as her gaze turns to me, searching for answers.

I point at Victoire's body. "*Pretend you killed her,*" I snarl.

"What is happening right now? Pasiphae, *what did you do?*"

But I don't get the chance to answer. The metal doors of the room slam open, and the two guards explode into view. For a moment, everyone is silent. Catarina stares at them dumbly, still holding the knife Yseult's ghost had shoved into her hands, and they stare back. In a moment of wild realization, Catarina rears her arm back and plunges the bloody knife into Victoire's body again, close to the heart. The body stops twitching.

The guards drop their swords and slide to their knees reverently. Redhead's eyes are wide, filled with wonder.

"All hail Queen Catarina," he says.

A third guard lets me free from my constraints and I fall to my knees, letting out a gasp of relief. My wrists are bloodied and scraped raw from the chains, but my injuries are far less severe than Catarina's.

The doors suddenly burst open, revealing a panting, dark-haired woman in the doorway. She lifts her bow as she steps in, and then lets out a cry of horror as her gaze lands upon Catarina. Catarina's bare back is facing the newcomer, revealing angry red gashes slicing down the muscled surface, and strong wings that have been cut right at the stem hanging on by mere tendons.

She rushes for us, bow still drawn and pointed straight at the guards. "What happened?" she whispers, kneeling down at Catarina's side. Redhead turns to look her up and down, a lazy smile curving his lips.

"Who are you?" The woman aims her arrow at his face, poised to shoot.

"Stop!" Catarina calls.

The dark-haired woman freezes. Their gazes meet, and I'm nearly stifled in the heat that is exchanged simply by their eye contact. Fire sparks between them, stars live and die, universes are flung into existence.

"Who did that to you?" the woman snarls, sheer, animalistic wrath coating every word.

"Zhengya," Catarina whispers. "I knew you'd come."

"Of course I came."

Catarina lapses into silence, lowering her gaze. The second guard slowly removes Victoire's crown of black iron from her head, then approaches Catarina from behind and places it on her. She jumps in surprise, and Zhengya jumps up to confront him, but the new queen's hand flies up to grab her wrist.

A strange gleam has glossed over Catarina's gaze, and a sinking feeling settles heavily in my gut. Zhengya sees it too. Her eyes widen as she kneels back down, reaching for Catarina. But shadows are already embracing their new queen, curling around her body and mending the marred skin and severed bones. The sweet, festering scent of magic in the air is enough to make my stomach roil. It doesn't seem to bother Catarina. She only stares, smiling at the other woman as the magic finally dissipates and reveals freshly healed flesh, freshly repaired cartilage.

"Who did that to you?" Zhengya asks, disoriented by the look in Catarina's eye and the secretive half-smile on her face. The sinking feeling in my gut only deepens, and all my instincts are suddenly urging me to *run, run, run.*

"Victoire," Catarina replies finally.

"I will *kill* her—"

"I already did."

"*What?*"

Catarina gestures at a black lump on the floor, her eyes glowing with triumph. "As I said, I already did." Victoire's remaining wing has been flung over her shoulder, covering her torso in a feathered blanket. Her pale eyes are as wide as her mouth, which is frozen in a scream.

Zhengya attempts to reach for her again, but Catarina shifts away. "Zhengya, it looks like you are no longer needed," she says.

Zhengya's mouth falls open. "W-what are you talking about? I'm here to save you."

For a moment, something wild flickers in Catarina's gaze, before it's quickly swallowed by the odd darkness seeping from the iron crown and into her. "And I'm telling you, I no longer need saving," she says.

"So you're just going to stay here? With *them?*" She gestures incredulously at the two guards that flank both sides of her. Catarina considers her for a moment longer, and then murmurs something in the guards' ears. They leave the room without another word and the door falls shut with a deliberate *click*, leaving the three of us alone. I duck into a shadowy corner to watch the scene unfold, heart pounding. It wouldn't have mattered if I stayed anyway. Catarina and Zhengya seem to have completely forgotten my existence.

"What are you doing?" Zhengya asks incredulously.

Ever so slowly, Catarina stalks closer to her. "That is none of your concern."

"Call off the troops," Zhengya says softly. "You can save Guinyth now."

Something is wrong. Something in Catarina's expression has changed. Something in *her* has changed. And Zhengya seems to realize it too. It's like she doesn't feel any pain. But it's more than that.

"*What happened?*" The words come out of her in a breathless rush. Catarina's lips twitch upward yet again, but the smile is not a pleasant one.

"Spar with me," she whispers.

"What?"

Zhengya doesn't have a chance to prepare before silver flashes in the air. Two blades slash down in quick succession around her waist. I flinch, almost jumping out of my hiding spot to help her, but she seems well trained. Zhengya arches away, and the knife grazes the space a millimeter from her skin. She lifts her knee, poised to drive it into Catarina's abdomen, but the demon is no longer in front of her. Zhengya whirls, sucking in a sharp breath. She is too late.

The hilt of Catarina's blade slams into the back of her head. With a gasp, Zhengya falls forward. A warm trickle of blood slides around the curves of her ears, stopping at the corners of her mouth. As she reaches up, feeling for the wound, she stares at Catarina in disbelief. My own heart wrenches in two at the sight of her face. It is a total betrayal.

Zhengya braces her palms on the cold floor, but even from afar, I can see that her muscles are shaking too much for her to push herself up. "Why?" the poor girl on the floor chokes out.

"I am no longer on your side," Catarina says. Her eyes are alight with victory as high and bright as golden flame. She lifts her arms, and death itself explodes from her hands. Whirling black sandy shadows spill from her, swarming across the floor and up the walls, making the lone source of light hanging from the ceiling flicker and sway. The shadows gather in throngs like storm clouds preparing to wreak havoc upon the earth. As she stands there, wreathed in shadows that now curl around her arms and legs, I shudder at the resemblance she bears to Victoire. She looks *evil,* her eyes glowing with a heinous sort of wickedness.

"*Who are you?*" Zhengya sobs. I hate the way that her voice breaks, I hate the tears that flow freely down her cheeks.

"I am the Queen of Demons," Catarina breathes. "And you will bow before me." To the guards, Catarina says, "Take her to the dungeons."

Zhengya makes no move to free herself when the two guards return and advance on her. There is no fight in her. They drag her away, her body scraping against the rough stone floor as she hangs limp between them. Then big arms wrap around me and something heavy slams into my head. My vision flickers before going completely black.

CHAPTER THIRTY-EIGHT
ZAHIRAN

A HAND COVERED in dried dirt and blood reaches out toward us from the darkness.

"Help us," a voice rasps. A mother, a father, and their two sons are crouched beneath the scant safety of a bridge, its once graceful arches now destroyed and smoking. The woman is cradling one of the sons in her arms, his head nestled in the crook of her neck and his eyelids twitching with feverish sleep. His brow is soaked with sweat.

"Help us," she repeats. "My boy needs help." She hardly glances at my wings and horns, which I'd stopped bothering to hide with my hood, ignoring that I'm a demon in hopes of helping her son. The boy's shirt is completely red with what I can assume is his own blood. The father helps to peel the soaked cotton away from his body, revealing an arm crisscrossed with so many lacerations and claw marks that it's hard to realize that clean, soft skin had once lain there.

"Help him, help him, help him," the mother moans over and over again, her head bowed as she rocks back and forth on the floor with her child's head now resting in her lap. The other son, who is only the slightest bit older than his brother, keeps his gaze pinned straight at the floor. The father stares unseeingly into the trees.

We cannot help the boy. He goes still moments later.

"The demons destroyed the entire city," the mother, whose name I've learned is Casilie, gasps out through sobs so hard they send tremors through her entire body. "They killed my *son*."

"It's all right. It'll be okay." Brienne's empty, whispered words go unnoticed.

The father's arm is tight around his wife's shoulder. "King Hanying and Queen Liuxiang are dead. Tegak is completely gone."

"There are no others," Landon, the remaining son, breathes. "No other survivors."

"There's—" Brienne's voice breaks, but I can see her forcing herself to try again. "There is a manor in these woods that we can find shelter in. I can lead us there."

I am the only one who stands, attempting and failing to smile. "Brienne is right. We'll be safe there."

Landon stands next, offering a hand to each of his parents. My eyes fall shut for a moment and I sigh bracingly. Then, I stretch out my clenched fists and readjust the weapons strapped to my body. "Let's go," I say.

Without any horses or octilli, we are forced to walk to Greensbriar manor. Casilie carries Landon on her back the entire way. Even when her feet grow so swollen that she can barely stand, she refuses to let go of him. The father, Polaris, is as silent as ever. I cannot help but dislike him.

Brienne's pace quickens and her face brightens as she looks at the woods around us. She looks like she knows where she's going all of a sudden. Despite everything, I almost smile at the childish look of anticipation on her face.

"You know what's up ahead?" she asks me softly.

"What?"

"Home. And safety. We'll be okay."

But then Casilie stops dead in her tracks, her hand fluttering to her mouth, and I whip toward her, worried.

"Is something wrong?"

She doesn't reply, and I follow her gaze to the forest floor. At first, I don't see anything. But when I look closer, my legs give out beneath me. Five bodies, all piled by a tree. Two of them have arrows sticking out of their backs, and I recognize Liserli's fiery red hair and Soren's black curls. Three girls, much too young to have been ripped from this world already, lie squeezed beneath them. A small, strangled sound escapes Brienne's lips, and I watch as she stumbles over and reaches for Liserli's hand. The body rolls over, and Brienne stares, open-mouthed, into her cold, lifeless face. Her emerald eyes are empty, the warmth completely gone from them. Soren is the same.

I hadn't known these people for long at all, but even these two deaths are enough to shake me. These people were special to Brienne. More casualties of the demons' bloodlust. Beside me, Brienne's arms begin to shake as she lets out a scream of complete and absolute torment.

And then something else catches my eye.

"Oh my God," I whisper. I push aside a tree branch, revealing the clearing where Brienne's home should've been. But instead of a huge, stone manor, all I see are burning piles of rubble. The head of a gargoyle has been knocked clean off the rest of its body and rests in the dirt right by my feet.

Brienne turns, slowly, as if she can hardly bear to. She falls to her knees, trembling with the force of her fury as she throws her head back and screams at the sky, cursing it, demanding answers it doesn't have. But the sky remains unresponsive. As it always will be.

"This is my fault," Brienne moans, tearing at her hair. "If I hadn't let Liserli run off like that, things would be different. But now they're dead and gone and my home is destroyed."

I open my mouth, but I can't seem to find the words to comfort her. How does one comfort a girl who has lost two of her closest friends and her home in the span of a minute? She rocks herself back and forth, tears falling from her cheeks and into the dirt below her. I have every confidence she would stay there forever, curled into a pitiful ball, and so I drag her up from the ground and cover the five bodies with leaves.

"Screaming and crying will not bring them back," I tell her, not unkindly. She blinks up at me unresponsively. I sigh and place a tentative hand on her shoulder. "Do you think they'd want you shrieking at the sky? No. They'd want you to avenge them. Make their deaths mean something." She looks anywhere but my face. I let out a soft breath, tilting her chin up with a finger and forcing her gaze to meet mine. "Stand up for something, Brienne. What's it going to take? Another friend to die? Another city to fall?"

"No," she whispers.

"Do you promise?"

"Yes."

"Good. Say goodbye to them."

It takes her a moment to realize what I mean. I gesture impatiently at Casilie and the rest of her family, and they disappear behind a line of trees without another word. Brienne turns back to the mound of bodies, her eyes wide as she stares at them. Someone's hand is peeking out from under the layer of leaves I've covered them with. Their skin is the same shade of grayish brown as the earth on which they lay. A half-suppressed cry escapes her.

There is no time to bury the bodies or cry anymore. So, slowly and methodically, I uproot a handful of white flowers growing at the base of a nearby tree and I lay them upon the pile. Their paleness is stark against the dullness of the dead, wet leaves and decomposing flesh.

After the others have fallen asleep that night, I find Brienne sitting under a tree, staring up at the sky. When she sees me, she sighs and I settle beside her. The evening air is pleasant and cool enough to dry the sweat lingering on my skin.

"Why do you think this is happening to us?" Brienne asks softly. "I've been a good person all my life. I've been kind and generous and caring. So why—"

"There's no point in thinking that way," I say, just as quietly.

"Don't tell me that there's a reason for everything," she says bitterly, turning away from me.

"No, no," I say quickly. "That's not what I meant."

She wipes at a tear. "What could you have possibly meant?"

"None of it is your fault."

She lets out a frustrated breath before looking back up at the sky. "I have begged the universe for answers countless times. Nothing."

"What answers are you searching for?"

"Answers that would tell me why everything has been stolen from me. Why them? Soren and Liserli were so . . . and why did I have to be the one to find them?"

"Do you truly think that any answers the universe could possibly provide would make you feel any better?" She falls silent, and I gaze down at the ground. "The universe is always cruel. It's how we respond to it that makes a difference."

Brienne nods wordlessly, and I shift my weight to place both hands behind my head. I lean back to rest against the trunk of the tree.

"When I was younger, I used to beg the universe for answers, too. About my mother's death. But I've grown to realize it's a waste of time," I say.

"What should I do instead?" Brienne asks desperately. "Every time I close my eyes, I see Soren and Liserli. When I open them, I can only see the horrible world around us. Catarina is still gone, and Zhengya is bound to be captured, and Victoire is on the brink of utterly dominating the entirety of Guinyth. A few weeks ago, I couldn't even imagine harm coming to me or the ones I love."

PART TWO
HELL IS EMPTY

CHAPTER ONE
PHILAN

EVEN BEFORE I STEP into the room, I know that something is different. The air itself seems colder. Filled with something dangerous. I push open the stone door even though my hands are shaking.

Catarina is wearing Victoire's crown. Her head is thrown back as she stands in the middle of the room, eyes shut and mouth curled into a perfectly victorious sneer. When she raises her hands, the shadows lining the barely lit room seem to peel off the walls, bending and twisting to her desire. She summons whirlwinds and typhoons and vortexes of power, enough to make my head spin and my breath grow shallow. She lets her hands slide up her body, eyes still shut, as she *bathes* in her own shadows, drinking up their energy like a starved animal. A siren cloaked in all the darkness of the universe. Tendrils of shadows slip free to wrap around her neck and arms and legs, and she leans into them. It's as if she was born to wield this tremendous power. When I am finally able to tear my eyes away from her, I notice the two other guards lifting an unconscious woman who I recognize as the witch from earlier, and a body in the corner. *Victoire's* body.

"Get out," Catarina says softly, shaking me from my shocked trance. I turn, but she's only speaking to the two guards. They nod quickly and haul the witch out of the room. When the door has shut behind them, Catarina turns all of her murderous attention toward the woman slumped on the other side of the room.

"Catarina?" I dare to breathe, but she hardly spares me a glance. In a flash, she crosses the room, too swiftly for my eyes to register, and slides to her knees beside Victoire's corpse. I watch in horror at the exhilarated look on Catarina's face. What does she want with the body? Victoire is gone. But Catarina's smile only grows as she pulls a knife out of the scabbard around her waist.

"You once stole something from me," she whispers to the body. "I'd like to take something from you in return."

Her blade traces lightly down Victoire's cold face, across her forehead and around her temple before coming to a halt at the corner of her left eye. I look away when she plunges the blade in, unable to watch.

Several hours later, General Pythea, sister of the late General Kizmet, and I walk into the throne room, where Catarina perches on the throne that Victoire had once occupied. Her gaze remains steady as we approach her. Cold, cunning, beautiful. A shiver runs down my spine as I take in her new eyepatch: metal-plated and black.

"Catarina, it's been far too long. You look as stunning as ever." My words are true, but my tone, lofty and vain, is formulated to test her limits. But if she heard me speak, she doesn't show it.

"Sit," she orders, gesturing at two ridiculously small chairs before her. "We have much to discuss."

I frown at my seat, preparing to complain, but the general gives me a small, firm shake of her head before settling into her own. I sigh and relent.

"Fane has been captured and is currently being held in the dungeon," the general starts. "His execution is to be set for whenever you wish."

"In two days' time," Catarina replies without a moment's hesitation.

"And you need a king yourself," the general adds. Catarina's face visibly twists with disgust, and the general sighs. "It's simply customary, My Queen. There need not be a romantic bond between you and your partner." *Had Victoire married Fane out of love?* I suddenly wonder. The thought of Victoire and Fane even being affectionate with each other is almost unbearable. I let out a soft snort, and Catarina's eyes flash to me.

"Philan?" the general asks. "Do you have anything you'd like to say?"

"No, general."

She rolls her eyes at me before turning back to Catarina. "My Queen, do you have someone in mind?"

"I have already chosen." She is the embodiment of haughtiness, her chin held high in the air and her back stiff and straight in her throne.

My mouth stretches in a smile so wide it reveals every one of my fangs. "And who might that be, my dear? Who shall be the new King of Demons, equal only to the queen herself?"

General Pythea shoots me a piercing glare that could've sliced through steel, but I ignore her. Instead I stare at Catarina, taunting her. She bares her teeth at me and I watch her, waiting for her anger . . . but for the briefest of seconds, her lips only press into a thin line and something troubled clouds her unharmed eye. She looks almost sad. Then, as if nothing happened at all, she's returned to her signature unruffled annoyance.

"You, Philan."

The tips of her ears go bright red, and I feel the gaze of General Pythea fall upon me as she observes us, eyes narrowed. "Philan?" the General says.

I widen my eyes with feigned shock, even as my heart flutters in my chest. "Your Majesty, I know nothing about ruling a kingdom. I couldn't *possibly* be up to par with your standards."

Catarina genuinely laughs. "You really think I would trust you to rule? Philan Lin, *I* am your ruler, and nothing you do will be without my permission."

"As you wish, my dear." I play lazily with a bejeweled ring encircling my finger, still smiling with placid amusement. There's something burning in her gaze I can't identify. General Pythea clears her throat, shifting awkwardly.

"When do you want the wedding ceremony to be? He will be crowned as soon as you'd like."

Catarina's entire face goes up in flames. I've never seen her so uncomfortable, even when we were humans. I almost laugh but decide not to for the sake of my own safety.

"As soon as possible." Catarina's words are no more than a whisper.

"As you wish, My Queen."

Catarina is physically recoiling now, slumping down farther into her throne. General Pythea's lips quirk to the side as she struggles to rein in her own laughter.

"Must there be . . . a wedding?" Catarina asks, utterly mortified. No one could have expected this girlish embarrassment. The general seems to collect herself a bit, swallowing and forcing her face back into a perfectly neutral position, a truly commendable feat.

"Nothing will happen that you don't wish," she says stoically.

"Then I don't wish a wedding."

The general's cackle of pure entertainment is caught in her throat as Catarina glowers at her, eyes nearly flinging daggers.

"Of course, My Queen. Philan will be crowned as king alone." She looks at me with a ridiculous half-suppressed grin on her face. "What on earth have you done to make her detest you so much?" her eyes seem to question. I shrug in response, and that only seems to humor the general more.

"I want every single acquaintance of Victoire and Fane's to be executed as well," Catarina says suddenly and desperately, as if wanting to escape from the previous topic of conversation as quickly as possible.

"Of course. And how do you wish to proceed in regard to the war raging as we speak?" Once again, the general somehow manages to calm herself.

"Begin the transition to Pheorirya." Catarina has regained her composure now too; none of the nervous embarrassment from before lingers.

"And what do you want us to do about Iesso Endyrdyn and your former allies when we inevitably come across them?"

"I want you to kill them all," she says.

The three of us continue talking of strategy, war, and death, but the whole time, Catarina looks at anything but me.

That night, I retire to my new bedroom. Fane had once shared this space with Victoire. The walls are matte and unadorned, but somehow still elegant. The massive bed pushed against the center of one wall is large enough to host a demon with their wings spread. Catarina is nowhere to be found, but the room smells faintly of rose petals combined with something deeper, a scent that reminds me instantly of her seductive, powerful femininity.

I change into the nightclothes a servant laid on my bed before my arrival and slip under the black silk sheets, but sleep evades me. The day's events whirl chaotically in my head. Everything in my life has been flipped completely around. Again. A part of me is almost thankful for Victoire's death. Her every wish was my priority when she was queen. She would've had me killed if it wasn't. I'd also begrudgingly admired her power. But now I feel free. I'm free to explore my emotions and my new role as king. My mind wanders to Catarina. The way she'd brutally butchered Victoire's body in the throne room with experienced hands. Her face had been just as terrifying, a mask of violent rage I'd never seen worn by anyone before her. How could someone physically be so resentful of someone else? Of course, I'd known that Victoire had been the one to drive her to gouge out her own eye, but was that the only cause for her wrath?

I think through everything I know about her lack of a gift as a human, the eventual murder of her parents, and everything I'd observed about her at Greensbriar. She must blame Victoire for every single thing that's happened to her, regardless of whether Victoire was truly the instigator. Was it simply a coping mechanism to deal with insecurity? Unless Victoire has been with her longer than her parents' murder.

I let out a sigh, shifting so that my wings don't prod into my shoulder. *What an odd creature.* And as my eyes finally begin to drift shut, I can't help but wonder what her new shadows will change in her. The very thought of it is thrilling. If she is a siren cloaked in darkness, her shadows are the enchanting songs that lure me in until I crash on her shores.

Early the next morning, a servant awakens me to take me to my coronation. I am officially bound to Catarina. Even if she did not choose to attend my crowning.

CHAPTER TWO
TONTIN

THE ENTIRETY OF THE COVEN of the Hyacinth sits in Saelmere Castle's great hall, each witch staring at me. My cheeks burn with the weight of their stares.

"Please don't say you want us to help your city again," one says. I recognize her as Zara, one of Yseult's closest advisors. "We've already done so to the best of our ability." The others around her murmur their agreement and some eyes dart toward me accusingly. I shake my head, putting my hands up.

"No, no. That isn't why I've called you all here today at all."

"Then what is it?" the same witch demands.

"What do you know about Fane?"

Zara rolls her eyes. I suspect she might be the leader of the coven now. "Why should we share any information about him?" she asks.

"I have fears about Catarina wanting to take his healing gift," I say. The room goes completely silent. "I'm sure that you have all heard the news of her ascension to the demon throne. This means only two things. Either she has already killed Victoire and Fane, or she has only killed Victoire so far, wanting to spare Fane's life for his gift. I know she's heard the stories about it, and I know her. She will want the gift, especially now that she holds the power in her situation."

Zara is quiet. The witch behind her leans forward to whisper something in her ear, and she nods slowly. Finally, she looks back at me. "What do you want to know?"

"Tell me about his gift," I say.

She exhales slowly. "King Fane of Ahuiqir wasn't raised like a normal demon. Yseult, Pasiphae, and I stole him from his cradle when he was only a baby. We took him into our clan to raise him as one of our own. There'd been prophecies of a demon wielding an all-powerful, world-bending gift. And selfishly, we wanted to have the child to ourselves. And the instant his gift revealed itself, we knew that the prophecy had been fulfilled. But as he grew older, he became more than a weapon. He became a true part of the coven, loved by every witch."

When I look around the room, tears are welling in the eyes of many witches.

"When it came time for him to leave, Yseult's reluctance to part with him no longer stemmed from the desire to keep his power in the coven. He'd become a son to her," Zara continues.

"Would it be possible for Catarina to steal this power?"

Zara looks at me, a grave expression clouding her face. "Even if there isn't, Catarina will find a way. You must not underestimate her."

My heart thuds dully in my chest. "And what would happen if she were to steal it?"

"The delicate balance of the magic system in this universe would be left askew. Even witches cannot withstand the magical force of universal imbalance," Zara says. "She isn't *supposed* to have that power. The universe bestowed it upon Fane, intending for it to be used by him, and him only."

"So what could possibly be done if Catarina were to take it?"

The witch doesn't reply but looks around at everyone. For a moment, there is silence. And then someone else speaks. "Surely you have heard of the Sisters of Night? Keres and Merikh?"

I nod in the direction of the voice. "I have," I say. Of course, the tales of their descent from the heavens to Guinyth have been pounded into children for centuries, and I was no exception.

"If anybody could reverse a situation as dire as that, it would be them. Their gift is to steal gifts."

CHAPTER THREE
ZHENGYA

IN THE CELL ACROSS from me sits Pasiphae. Her knees are tucked under her chin as she rocks back and forth, pulling at her hair. It can't have been more than two or three days since Catarina's ascension to the throne, but every minute feels like an eternity. I'd known a completely different life only weeks earlier, before my brother's death, and both his and Catarina's transformations into demons. Before the complicated but fascinating girl I'd known had become a complete stranger willing to turn on everything she had left for a taste of power.

Pasiphae looks up at me through wispy strands of her icy blond hair. "I've made a mistake."

I don't reply.

"Did you know her well?"

Still, I say nothing.

She lets her head fall against the stone wall. "Weren't you two friends?"

"Yes." More than that. *Or so I'd thought.* My heart aches to the point of pain. She seems surprised I'd even spoken, and my mouth draws into a thin, bitter line.

"This has nothing to do with her magic," she says suddenly. My head whips around, but her gaze is fixed on the floor.

"What?" I demand. "What do you mean?"

"Every ruler of Ahuiqir has worn that same crown for the past three thousand years; every ruler of Ahuiqir has possessed the same dark magic as her. And yet, those two things were not the reason they were the antagonists of their stories."

"I—"

She traces a tattoo on her leg. "You know why some people become demons after death and others don't, right? Ahuiqir is a place for scarred humans to let go of themselves, to enjoy the things they didn't or couldn't in their mortal lives. All for the hefty price of losing every ounce of humanity. Many of them are glad for the excuse to hate humans and lust for their blood, simply because they want revenge on those who'd wronged them in their past life."

My mind runs at a million miles an hour, processing her words.

"You must understand that, Zhengya. They hated humans even *as* humans."

"So what are you saying?" I ask breathlessly.

"Catarina was raised to be proper, well-educated, and eventually a queen," Pasiphae says, her eyes narrowing at me. "And yet, that didn't work out for her. She was mocked, ridiculed."

"I'm not quite sure I understand what—"

I can see her jaw work up and down as she struggles to rein in her own temper, fueled by her frustration in the situation and exhaustion.

"I'm saying that she is the best example of pure wickedness, Zhengya. She is sinister deep down in her very soul, and nothing anyone could attempt to do will ever change that. She works to twist things to her own liking; she strives to rule the world, when in reality she was under-qualified to be even Queen of Pheorirya. It factors in to her egotistical quest for glory." Every word she utters is a throwing knife, finding its target in my heart with deadly accuracy.

"I don't—"

"I am not blind," the witch says sharply. I don't flinch, don't even have the energy to do so. "I have seen the way your eyes go glassy when you talk about her, Zhengya, but you must let go of whatever feelings you still have. She is a power seeker. She is *bad*. Being Queen of Pheorirya would never have been enough for her."

My eyes narrow at her bluntness. Her words worm their way into every memory I'd shared with Catarina in Greensbriar Manor, sowing doubt in every happy moment. Had any of it been real? Who had she been, back when things were "normal?" Did I ever know the real Catarina Winyr? Try as I might, I can't seem to find anything to prove Pasiphae wrong.

"Then what do we do?"

"Nothing. We do nothing."

"What the hell does that mean?"

A shadow darkens Pasiphae's face. "Zhengya, by staying completely neutral, my clan has managed to stay out of harm's way for centuries. I suggest you and your friends do the same. It'd be the best for everyone, Catarina included. So if you truly love her—"

"You do not know me, nor her. So don't speak as if you do." My own clipped, terse tone matches hers.

She laughs quietly, humorlessly. "She will slaughter us all if we don't stay out of her way, and I think that's all I need to know."

"So I should just let the demons invade Guinyth?" I ask, incredulously. "This is *your* home too."

She jabs a finger into my chest. "Yes, but as I said, since we've remained neutral, the demons have had no reason to kill us. And if you join me now, they may allow you the same freedoms."

"You shouldn't have to be given permission to live. That's ridiculous—"

She moves even closer, so that our noses are almost touching. "It may be stupid, but it is the main thing that has kept the Coven of the Hyacinth alive. Why do you think there are so few witch clans besides mine, and none nearly as powerful? They interfered in human and demon interactions. And so they had to pay the consequences." A pause. "The last war our coven was in was Cheusnys Battle. We lost too much."

"Ignoring everything makes you just as much of a villain as the demons," I say.

She turns her back on me. "I've decided that I'd rather live neutrally than die trying to be a hero, Zhengya. The desire to preserve your own life is a mindset you need to learn to have, selfish as it may seem."

I gape, shocked at her. If she's beginning to think this way, others must be too. My blood begins to boil. "People who think like that are the reason we are losing this war."

"At least I'll be alive." She isn't listening to me, not anymore.

"Would it really be living?" I ask desperately of her. "Would it really be living if you merely existed in constant fear of your life?"

Her shoulders suddenly slump as she turns back to me. "I'm less afraid of that than death."

"You're a coward," I whisper.

"I know." We stare at each other, both breathing hard. "I'm so scared," she says finally, and the disgust I'd felt toward her only seconds ago dissipates. I want nothing more than to reach through the bars and comfort her.

"It'll be all right," I say blandly. How am I to comfort someone else when I don't know if I believe myself?

CHAPTER FOUR

ZAHIRAN

"We need to find Pasiphae, and Catarina, and Zhengya," Brienne says, absentmindedly toying with a sprig of tiny white flowers as she slumps against the base of a tree. I shake my head and let my eyes shut. I am an exhausted husk of the person I used to be.

"As long as they're more helpful than those two," I say, thrusting out a hand to point at Landon's parents.

Polaris's eyes narrow. "You have promised to help us, yet all you do is throw half-baked insults. When will we reach safety? How do we know that you're not working for the demons too?"

"I may have wings and horns but know this, Polaris," I say, leaning toward him, a half-delirious smile on my face. "There is nothing for me to win by allying with the demons. My own mother was killed by Victoire. I want her dead as much as you do." Brienne is listening carefully now, but Polaris barrels on without a second thought.

"So then why have we not reached safety?" His lips curl into a sneer, and the gesture is kindling to the fire burning in my chest. I have never wanted to strangle someone more, and the sudden urge to expel all this energy ricochets inside me.

"Because you're horrible and your constant complaining slows us down," I say calmly.

Casilie puts her hands on Polaris's arm. "Maybe if we all just—"

With a roar, Polaris rushes at me. It seems he feels the same. The breath whooshes from my lungs as he collides into me, and I collapse to the ground. The sour scent of his breath and sweat blows across my face as he leans in close, wrapping his fingers around my throat. I bring my knees in close and thrust him off my body. It is too easy. Although he is large, he's also weak. My fist locks around his throat, and the point of my knife finds its way to his neck. I can feel his veins pounding beneath my hands. I can see the strength leaving his limbs and his eyes widening and going wild with fear. If I just squeeze a little harder—

"Zahiran, stop!" Brienne's shoulder collides into me, and I roll into a crouch. "Fighting will do us no good!" She turns to Casilie, who now holds Polaris in her arms. "We'll find shelter, and safety, and everything else. But right now, we need rest. It's been a long day for everyone."

Polaris's chest heaves as his lungs ravenously gulp in air. His lips peel up in an odd smile, revealing crooked black teeth. Fear suddenly courses down my spine. *How far is too far?* I ask myself. *Have I reached the limit of his patience?*

"Zahiran." I whirl around at the sound of Brienne's voice. "We should keep someone on watch." Nobody speaks, and she blows a breath through pursed lips. "I suppose I'll take the first shift."

Landon moves first, helping his mother and father find a comfortable spot. The three of them curl around one another to sleep.

Brienne puts a hand on my arm, smiling tiredly. "Get some rest. I'll wake you up in a couple hours for your shift." Always trying to help. It's sweet. I almost resent her for it.

But I obey her and sit down, leaning my head against the rough bark of a tree. My knives lie heavily across my lap. Their comforting weight is the only familiar thing about this whole place.

I awake in the middle of the night without Brienne's interference. When

I glance at her, she's slumped against the tree beside me, completely asleep. Even in sleep, her jaw is wound tight as a spring and her fingers are clasped tightly in her lap. I lean over and settle a hand on her arm, rubbing up and down. Every muscle in her body is taut and poised for battle. She seems to relax into my touch. I let out a soft laugh as I stand and shake the drowsiness from my limbs.

Somewhere to the left of me, Polaris shifts a little. A twig snaps beneath his weight. Our gazes meet in the hazy darkness. He is sitting with his back against the trunk of a tree. His eyes gleam strangely bright, almost yellow, in the light of the moon. He does nothing but watch me, a faint smile curving his lips. Eventually, he settles back into his bed of leaves. My eyes remain on him for far too long. Finally, when I hear the telltale sounds of deep breathing coming from him, my muscles loosen enough for me to move.

The night is pleasantly cool and beautiful, silent save for the hesitant chirps and calls of wildlife. I make my way through the forest around us. I'm suddenly desperate for a moment all to myself. But as I travel farther and farther into the emerald dimness; it seems fate refuses to let me forget the destruction in the land. Entire groves of trees have been flattened by shells fired between demons and humans. The earth bears deep, brown, ugly scars as evidence. The leaves of the bush beside me are tinged with red. The branches have been compressed enough that I can deduce someone was thrown on top of it. Shivers crawl across my skin as bile rises in my throat. I return to the others, hoping I don't see anything else.

When I return to the clearing, Brienne is sitting up, already waiting for me. "Where did you go?" she whispers.

I settle back down beside her, careful not to wake the three others around us. "I wanted to clear my head."

She doesn't reply for a while, staring at her hands. "I'm terrified," she whispers finally. "Zhengya should be back by now. What if Victoire has captured her again?"

I nod silently. Losing Zhengya would mean the loss of every single one of her closest friends. And she's already known nothing but loss. She drops her head between her knees, sighing.

"I hate the uncertainty of it all," she breathes. "Like I can't control anything that happens to me. It's all just whizzing by in a blur."

CHAPTER FIVE
FANE

I'D ALWAYS IMAGINED I'd live forever. Barring that, I assumed I'd die in a battle. It is a cruel joke to sit here rotting away in my own dungeon. Victoire is dead, and I feel that I am destined to follow. Her death had been an unexpected relief. It was a freedom from something I hadn't even realized was completely unwanted until it had lifted from my shoulders. The power-hungry days of my youth, during which I'd felt utterly mature and in control, had in reality been days of ignorance. There has been so much I've learned in the centuries since that a younger Fane Liverraine would've scoffed at. I eye the door, wondering if I could somehow force it open with my shadows, but the motivation and energy needed is not within my reach. The two guards standing just outside the dungeon could easily overpower me.

"What's going on today?" one of them asks the other suddenly. I recognize his voice as Laith's, the ginger-haired guard who had once worked for me.

"The new queen is intent on invading Pheorirya," replies the other. I recognize his voice as Laith's companion, Taos. I let out a low, hissing breath.

"Have they left yet?" Laith asks.

"I think so. Last I saw, Queen Catarina was choosing her octilla."

"What do you think about our new queen?" Laith asks carefully. "Her advisors blatantly disobey direct orders. Did you hear about the advisor she killed?"

His words catch my attention and I sit up straighter for Taos's reply. Has Catarina's ascension not been welcomed? I'd always thought that she'd be as well liked as Victoire had been, and that the demons would've been attracted to her viciousness.

Taos hesitates for a moment. "I did hear of that."

"Why do you think they don't like her?" I say.

"I think they have some sort of prejudice, regarding her lack of a gift as a human. I hear citizens mocking her every time I go into the city."

I almost sympathize with Catarina. While Victoire's frigid persona had drawn me in, my marriage to her had initiated an onslaught of backlash from some of the citizens, many of whom believed I'd only wed her because I couldn't accomplish anything without her. Although the rise to power is always something thrilling and heady, the end result never satisfies one's cravings. There's always more to want. And so I'd stepped back, allowing Victoire to take the spotlight and shine in the eyes of her subjects. But something deep within me knows that Catarina is absolutely *not* the sort of person to do such a thing. Criticism from other demons will only make her more resentful and willing to do exceedingly more and more barbaric things to win the favor of her people. To prove herself.

Taos and Laith continue talking, but I tune them out and stare down at my hand. Memories of childhood flood me. I think of the witches with their dragons and the healing gift they'd cherished me for. I open my palm and exhale slowly. The center of my palm begins to glow. When the light has traveled through every inch of flesh, the light begins to grow in intensity, lifting from my hand in a shapeless ball of white light. My shadows have always felt sinister, as if even possessing them is sinful. But this pale orb is forgiving, gentle, and soft. It feels like *life*. I curl my fingers back over it and press my fist against my chest. It washes over me, traveling down my arms and legs, healing all my bruises and cuts as it goes. When it finally fades, all the aches and pains in my body are gone, completely chased away by this light amidst all the darkness.

Of course, although Victoire had known about this luminescence, it had been an unspoken rule to never use the gift in front of her. She was insecure, just like Catarina is. Any display of power stronger than hers would've been perceived as a threat. I'd been happy to hide away my gift. It had always seemed more significant than my shadows, something I didn't feel I needed to prove to others. It is rare for a king to have something he can keep to himself.

I can recall making my way through the forest as a boy, squatting by every yellowing flower I found and wrapping my hands around it. It delighted me when the blooms brightened and unfolded at my touch, no matter how many times I did it. I loved healing the other witches' small cuts and bruises far faster than their bodies or the healer could. In return, they'd slip small confectionaries into my hands behind Yseult's back. It had all given me a sense of affirmation that I, indeed, had a role in the universe. But that feeling ebbed away after years of existing in Victoire's shadow. Maybe her insecurity and her desire to impress others with her strength had been a far greater problem than even I'd thought.

I remember her staggering out of the dungeon recently, sending tendrils of smoke after the servants. I followed closely behind, an amused smirk on my face. "Tell Laith and the other guard to put them back in the dungeon," she gasped, sliding against the wall for support.

"Vicky, how many times must I say this? You don't need to pretend you're stronger than you are in reality. Nobody cares."

She shoved through the doorway leading to our bedroom. "Don't call me—" Another convulsion rolled through her, and a clot of black blood slid down her chin.

I snapped my fingers, and a servant appeared out of nowhere with a bowed head. "Yes, sir?"

"Get her an antidote."

"No," Victoire whispered, shoving her hair out of her face and hauling herself into the marble bathtub. "I don't want it."

The servant's head whipped back and forth between the two of us, unsure what to do. "Your Majesties—"

I didn't even look at him, rather turned all my attention back to my wife and threw my hands in the air. "You can't keep playing this unbreakable, callous person anymore. So why do you?"

She squeezed her eyes shut, as if that would help ease the pain. "I can't stop."

I watched her silently.

"Shouldn't you be out there, fighting alongside your soldiers?" she asked bitterly.

"Shouldn't *you*?" I said. She didn't reply, and I sighed. "We are winning already. Why should I waste my energy?"

"Mm-hmm." She picked at her fingers.

I turned to leave. "Well then. Have fun with everything, Vicky—"

"Don't call me that."

"Fine, Victoire. I'm going to check on those lovely girls."

The memory surfaces like a buoy, and all the signs of Victoire's crippling lack of self-confidence—however hidden to outsiders—become clear. I sigh. It's a waste, letting this power go unused. But my death is inevitable, and the luminescence will be lost. I pull half-heartedly at the iron chains binding my wrists, casting another look at the dungeon door. Even if I could somehow escape, what would be the point? I have nothing else to live for. So I rest my head against my hands and do nothing.

Later, I hear a door slam open from the floor above me, accompanied by shrieking and something crashing to the floor. My eyes open groggily as I sit up.

"Your Majesty, I was instructed to escort you to the war room as soon as you returned," someone says loudly. I hear a cry of frustration, distinctly recognizable as belonging to Catarina.

"I don't care! Let me go back, let go of me!"

Footsteps pound across the floor.

"You are careless," someone spits. "We'd never have lost this battle if Victoire were still here."

They lost the battle in Pheorirya? My eyes go wide. Hadn't Pheorirya already been weakened?

"Queen Victoire will always be a better queen than you could ever be," the voice from before continues on.

I squeeze my eyes shut, willing him to simply stop talking. I know what's coming next.

"You are useless. You are—" His voice cuts off suddenly, and my shoulders curl inward, bracing myself. Sure enough, half a second later, a loud thump that sounds suspiciously like a body hitting the ground echoes through the dungeon.

CHAPTER SIX
ZAHIRAN

"WHEN DID CATARINA leave for Ahuiqir?" I sharpen my daggers with long, swift strokes against a flat stone I'd found on the forest floor. The sun has only just begun its journey through the sky. At this early hour, it is a deep navy tinged with the faintest shade of pink.

Brienne watches with almost childish intensity, distracted from my question. "Where did you get those knives?" she asks.

I frown. "They were my mother's," I say as dismissively as possible. The question strays a little too close to the topic I don't want to think about, much less discuss with her.

But she doesn't relent. "Your mother's . . . they are very fine."

"Yes."

"What . . . what was she like?"

"I don't know."

"But you must have heard stories, from the friend who—"

"Stop asking!" I suddenly shoot to my feet, dropping the sharpening stone and my knives to the ground with a clatter. She looks up at me, wide-eyed. "All I asked was for you to tell me when you last saw Catarina."

She blinks rapidly, clearing away the film of tears coating her eyes that threaten to drip down. "A week and a half ago? Perhaps?"

She reaches for me but I flinch away. Regret suddenly gnaws at me—the look of sorrow on her face is unbearable.

"I'm sorry," she whispers, reaching for my fallen daggers and handing them back to me.

"Thank you."

She wrings her hands, staring down at them. "I really am sorry. I just like knowing about people; I don't know why. I can never seem to think before I open my mouth and—"

"It's all right. It's fine."

She continues to rub her arm in an unconscious self-soothing motion, and I sigh, watching her.

"I've always had to hide my . . . heritage," I finally say. For so long, I've kept the various stories of my childhood hidden deep within me, not wanting to wallow in self-pity. She looks up hopefully. I let my cloak slip off my shoulders a little, revealing my wings. "Why do you think I'm able to keep my wings mostly hidden, when it'd be impossible for other demons?"

"They're a lot smaller," she realizes.

"As you'll have guessed, my mother, Queen of Demons, once controlled the same cruel shadows Victoire does now. What you didn't know is that she fell in love with a human."

It had been quite ridiculous, really; how could a demon possibly love a human? It was unheard of. But my mother, with her big heart and wide eyes, did. It was only through finding her old diaries and hearing rumors that I learned about my father. I could nearly recite, word for word, everything my mother had written in those diaries. After all, they are the only things I have left of her.

Eoin. His name seems to have found its permanent home on my lips; the syllables are as familiar as the precise feel of his fingers laced with mine, the exact shade of his warm brown eyes.

Eoin Ladell, a general in the Pheoriryan army. Never before have I met a kinder soul. He radiates everything good in the world without so much as a thought for himself.

This is fate, isn't it? I have been destined to love this man, and he has been destined to love me. And yet, we are forced to creep about at night, exchanging disguised letters and brief embraces that are never, ever long enough. He's a human, and I am a demon. The two should never mix.

But as long as we're happy, as long as we're together, nothing else matters.

–Ceiridwen Lovell

"His name was Eoin Ladell," I tell Brienne, "and he was a general in the Pheoriryan army. My mother was . . . different. She was not like other demon queens. She was a dreamer."

When I steal a glance at Brienne, she's staring at me, absorbing my every word. I smile a little, despite myself. I could be spinning completely false tales right now, and she'd believe me without a moment's hesitation.

"When he asked her to marry him only several months later, she immediately agreed. Their wedding was secret, unlike the extravagant weddings that the union of a demon queen and her king normally call for, and her ring was tiny, because Eoin was far from wealthy. She didn't care, though. That was just the kind of person she was—passionate, loving freely and easily."

Brienne is still focused solely on me, and I can't help but wonder if she knows how much that simple fact means to me.

"Only a few days passed before her marriage was revealed. Her subjects were furious, and there was talk of a young human-turned-demon who wanted the crown." I pause, making eye contact with Brienne. "Victoire Sandor." She lets out a breath of understanding, and I continue on. "They said she was oddly ambitions for her age, that she was a sadistic, unrelenting murderer. My mother was terrified, but she had faith in her people, and in her love. And then I was born." I recall from her diaries:

I have a child now. What a strange thought, but it is reality. A beauti-

ful girl, with hair as black as midnight and warm, dark skin, just like her father. But she has my eyes, a coppery chestnut color with streaks of brilliant gold. She has smaller wings and horns than most demons.

I once wondered if I'd ever love someone more than Eoin, and I have now found my answer. Yes, yes, yes. This tiny girl with chubby arms and legs is my entire world. I love her more than life itself.

My baby, sweet little Zahiran, who shall someday grow to become the strongest, bravest being the world has ever known.

–Ceiridwen Ladell

My eyes begin to burn slightly, and my voice quivers a little when I speak again. "She thought that the situation with Victoire would resolve itself, and for several years, nothing happened. But then, Victoire challenged my mother for the crown.

"What does that mean?" Brienne asks softly.

"It's just a formal way of making your intentions clear," I reply, swallowing away the thickness in my throat. "Not many do so. It's far more common to assassinate the ruler swiftly and without warning, and my mother could respect Victoire for not doing so."

"What happened next?" Brienne asks.

"My father ran back to Pheorirya." The tremors in my voice can no longer be disguised as I remember the writing from her diaries.

I have been a fool, a complete fool.

Eoin has left me, blinded by cowardice. He has retreated to the safety of his own home and while I resent him for that, I understand why he went. If I could, I would run, too.

This situation is almost humorous. I remember so clearly that he'd once said he'd sacrifice anything for me. Why is it that when it comes time to make these sacrifices, he cowers in the safety of his homeland?

The fear has not yet left, and I doubt that it ever will. But I no longer fear for myself. I have accepted my doomed fate, and now understand that my life as a whole was simply not meant to be. But now, I fear for my daughter. She is far too young to be in the face of such imminent danger. There is no way for me to protect her from it, and I despise myself for that.

–Ceiridwen Ladell

"So, my mother devised a plan to keep me safe." Now, my voice is hoarse, and from the corner of my eye, I can see Brienne struggling to decide if she should reach for me or not. "She had an old childhood friend, Mirita Burgess, a demon she'd grown up with. Mirita was to be by my side every second of the day, watching and waiting for when Victoire inevitably attacked. My mother also ordered her not to interfere when Victoire eventually . . . murdered her. And when she did, I would be raised by Mirita, hidden in Guinyth."

If everything goes according to plan and I am eventually killed, Mirita will bring Zahiran to her private academy deep in the forests of Guinyth. Zahiran will hate it with every ounce of her being, but even that would be better than her dying. And so there is nothing else for me to do except sit and wait for my inexorable death. This may be my last journal entry, ever. Zahiran, if you are reading this, know that I never wanted you to grow up without parents. More specifically, without a mother. I wouldn't want my daughter to be raised by a damned weakling father anyway. And know that I will love you forever, through this life and the next.

–Ceiridwen Ladell

Angry tears finally spill from my cheeks, and my words spill faster and faster.

"My father was a coward. Instead of protecting my mother from Victoire, he ran back to the safety of Pheorirya. He left his wife and baby to die, Brienne. He left *me* to die." Brienne silently stares at me. "And my mother was mistaken. Her idealistic mindset doomed us all."

I get the feeling Brienne's reevaluating everything she'd thought about me prior. My mouth tightens into a bitter line. I must seem like a whole different person, a far cry from the poised demon she's known me as.

"I'm sorry," she whispers. "I never knew."

We sit there in silence a little longer, Brienne clearly still mulling through everything I've said. "You know," she says finally. "Humans and demons are similar in how complicated they are, even though we pretend to be simple or easygoing." And perhaps I'd misunderstood the intention behind her words, but my fists clench with frustration.

"I-I don't think resentment toward your parents will do any good at this point," she says.

My eyes shut. "Every day, I'm reminded of what I could've had by everything and everyone around me. And it's just a suffocating feeling, knowing that all these things were direct effects of the mistakes of people before me, mistakes I had no control over and can do nothing about now."

"That's precisely my point. Let go, Zahiran. Like you said to me when we found Liserli and Soren, you have no control over things of the past." The optimistic confidence she has in her own words is infuriating. "You need to let go, you need to move on—"

"How can I move on? This is my life, Brienne. I am constantly torn between my hatred for demons and my hatred for humans." I cut off, suddenly horrified I've revealed so much of my life.

"You're just scared," someone says quietly. I whirl around. Landon sits right beside us, shamelessly eavesdropping. He'd been completely silent the first several days after his brother's death, but now, the bags under his eyes have diminished and he seems slightly more energetic. His slow recovery has seemed to help his parents cope, too. "You're scared of moving on. It'd uproot everything you'd ever told yourself you believed."

Brienne's eyes widen at him.

"How would you know?" I demand. But even to me, my voice is whiny and pathetic.

He shrugs, and the maturity of the things he'd accused me of only seconds prior slips away, revealing the child he is again. "I don't know. It just seemed like it."

Brienne makes a flicking motion with her wrist, gesturing for him to leave. He obeys instantly, ambling away to find something else to do.

But my mind lingers on his words.

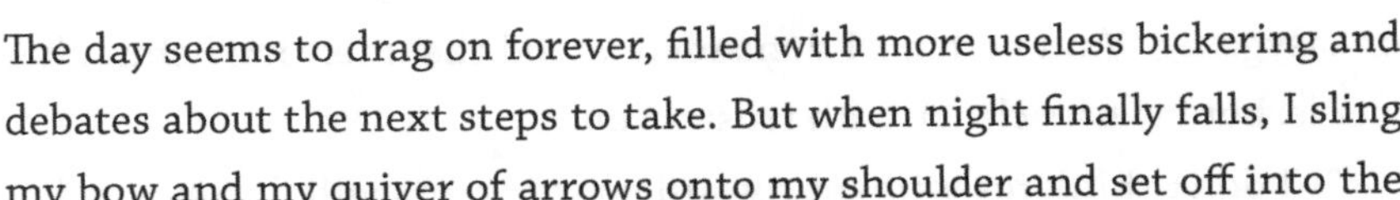

The day seems to drag on forever, filled with more useless bickering and debates about the next steps to take. But when night finally falls, I sling my bow and my quiver of arrows onto my shoulder and set off into the darkening forest. I let out a breath, a smile stretching slowly across my face. It's been far too long since I've been alone.

Even though the air still smells like burning leaves and blood, I allow myself to drop my defenses, letting my heartbeat slow and my senses sharpen. I hear the cries of birds calling to one another in their own melodious language, the scuttling of small rodents in the leaves beneath me and the wind rustling through the trees. Then, the rustling of a deer pushes through the underbrush of the forest. I creep toward the sound, careful to watch where I put my feet. Lady Burgess had been the one to teach me how to hunt long ago.

I see the deer standing in the middle of a small clearing. The light of the moon reflects off his glossy coat and it seems as if he's glowing. For longer than I'd like to admit, I feel like a disgusting person for even considering taking his life. But all life ends one way or another. Death by an arrow to the heart would be much more humane than whatever this world might throw at the poor creature. I shake the feeling off and draw an arrow, my eyes trained on him. His head suddenly jerks up. I freeze. His big, dark eyes lock on me, and his head tilts to the side. But then he dips back down to continue grazing at the clumps of grass scattered around the hard patch of dirt. I let the arrow fly. It sinks deep into his side. For a moment, he sways there. And then he collapses. I rise from my crouch and run toward him. Sweat slips down my neck against the cool air of the night as I haul the deer all the way back to the makeshift campsite and dump it onto the ground.

As I work on rebuilding the dying flame, Brienne carves out slices of meat and skewers them with sticks she finds on the ground. She passes me the skewers, and I arrange them above the fire. The smell of cooking meat fills the air, briefly covering up the stenches of war.

We eat silently, leaving several strips of meat for later.

"We need to go back to Cheusnys Cave," Brienne says finally. I meet her gaze over the still-smoldering fire, nodding in silent agreement. Zhengya and Catarina need help. I don't let myself think about the possibility that we could already be far too late, that both women are long dead.

Polaris's head jerks up. "What?" Casilie and Landon stop eating, too.

"We have two friends stuck in Ahuiqir," Brienne explains calmly, slowly. "We must save them."

Casilie swallows. "How are you even going to get through the barrier?"

"I have royal blood," I reply, mimicking Brienne's matter-of-fact tone of voice.

"And you expect us to follow you there?" Polaris asks incredulously.

His wife gives him a long look, before moving closer towards him to whisper in his ear, seeming to forget I can hear everything they're saying anyway.

"I want to stay with them," Casilie says softly. "Look, they can hunt for us. They can protect us at night. And this girl is a demon. Other demons would hesitate to kill us if we remained with them."

"So we must go wherever they tell us?" Polaris doesn't even bother to whisper.

"Polaris, I'm saying we have no choice. We will *die.*" He rolls his eyes, and his wife looks back at us. "We will come," she says.

"We're sorry," I reply blandly, but even Landon's eyes are narrowed.

CHAPTER SEVEN

TONTIN

"YOU HAVE DONE well, Iesso." My voice sounds tired, even to me. "Pheorirya will be safe yet another day."

"We can't keep doing this, Tontin. You know that. We're just wasting our resources and praying to survive."

"We have no other options. There is nothing to be done."

"Even if there is nothing to be done, we must do *something*, we can't just . . ." She throws her hands in the air, frustrated. "You heard about Catarina during the demons' attack today, didn't you? She has that black magic now. Perhaps all rulers of Ahuiqir gain that gift as well. I don't know. But my point is that she isn't just a pesky nuisance anymore, prophet. We can't overlook her strength."

I let out a rasping cough, and her hand flies to my shoulder. "Are you all right? You should lie down if—"

I shake her away. "I'm perfectly well, Iesso." I fall back into silence, my eyes scrunched closed. "She may be physically stronger now, as Queen of Ahuiqir, but she still has the same flaws she had as a human."

"Which are . . ." Iesso prompts.

I settle heavily into an armchair. "Queen Simone and King Kairos came to me when she was born, and again when she was ten years of age. Both times, they wanted me to see into her future." I inhale sharply, struggling to hold back more coughing. All the pressure has begun to take a physical toll on my body; every inch of me is exhausted.

"You are not well—" she begins, but I cut her off.

"I assure you, I am fine. I sensed darkness in that girl, Iesso. When I looked into her eyes, I saw nothing. No love, no life. And she did not utter a single sound the entire time. She did not cry or laugh. I was *terrified* of that baby."

"What did you tell the queen and king?" she asks.

"I lied, Iesso. I told them that I saw brightness in her future, that I saw great strength and beauty. While I *did* see that she would grow into a beautiful woman, I also saw a thirst for power that could never be quenched . . ." I trail off.

"So what are her flaws? What are her weaknesses?"

I smile, a little wistfully. "I can so clearly recall Catarina as a baby. Within the embrace of her parents and the comforts of her palace, she led a good life, perhaps *too* good. It has made her unaccustomed to independence. It has also made her used to all the flatteries of her people. This makes her extremely insecure when she is without those . . . luxuries."

Iesso thinks for a moment. "My sister had a specific temperament that I think only works out for select people. She was harsh, as you know, but she had an unmatched sense of right and wrong, and she only used her harshness in situations where she believed it was needed. I think that same harshness rubbed off on her daughter in a negative way."

I shrug. "Perhaps. Or it's always been in her."

"I don't believe people are evil for no reason. And I have faith that she can change."

"She is also used to being in control. And so if she feels any sign of her power slipping, she will completely fall apart. In fact, I do believe that to be her greatest fear. Being helpless. We need to exploit these personal weaknesses."

I can tell she knows what I'm talking about. Catarina's confidence in herself, the assured jut of her chin, the small, haughty smile on her lips as she pushed Iesso away. Followed by disbelief. And then fury. Fury not at herself, but at the people around her. As if it had been their fault that she had failed by having no gift at the Embracing, even when they'd offered her all the love and support in the world. It hadn't been enough for her, none of it would ever be. Fiery, unyielding fury made up for the powers she had been unable to summon.

I'm reminded of a memory. "Saoirse, Clan Leader of the Coven of Clarity, always claimed that magic was rare. That all the queens and kings and demons had a false magic that was simply given to them. I remember there was one specific instance she was teaching me a spell. Her hands drew intricate designs in the air, never stopping. And when she was done, she leaned back on her heels to admire her work and looked at me with an incredible brightness in her eyes. She said, 'Perfect. Now watch, child.' She lifted her hands, so that they hovered just above the drawing. The sand began to glow a hot white, so bright that I had to avert my eyes. She rotated her hands in a circle. The design seemed to float off the sand and rise into the air."

"'What do I do now, child?' she asked me.

"'Push it into the vase,' I replied excitedly."

Iesso smiles faintly.

"She nodded, smiling," I continue, "and with a graceful flick of her wrist, she sent the glowing design crashing into the vase. It shimmered for a second, and then the faint gleam faded.

"'Go ahead,' she said. I asked if she meant me. I was so surprised by her invitation—her trust. She just laughed sweetly at me and said, 'Of course! You are ready, Tontin.'

"I aimed my hands at the vase and she placed a hand on my shoulder. 'Calm yourself,' she said softly. 'Magic is very much influenced by your emotions. Absolutely nothing can cloud your thoughts, otherwise things could go horribly wrong.'

"I ignored her voice, all my attention trained on the vase. Ever so slowly, it began to wobble into the air.

"'Yes!' she exclaimed. 'Keep it there, now.'

"I steadied my mind and the shaking stopped. For several moments the vase hung in the air, and then it began to float back down. The ceramic settled against the wooden table with a soft clink.

"'Amazing. You will make a fine prophet someday.'

"I flushed with pride at her words, but then her expression darkened. 'But Tontin,' she said, 'remember this always. Never let the magic go to your head. It is a beautiful thing, but in the wrong hands, with the wrong mindset, it can turn deadly.'

"'Isn't that true of all things?' I asked.

"She smiled broadly. 'Wise words. I suppose that's true. But it's especially so with magic.'"

When I finish telling Iesso the memory, she is still smiling at me.

Like every other prophet in the world, I was a sign of a glorious new beginning for my kingdom. I was also destined to crash and burn in my magic, but I was certain I would find my way out of the darkness. And I would learn from it. Nobody, not a single soul in the world, can see the future with total accuracy. All we have are watery guesses. I prefer the uncertainty, even as a prophet. The world is beautiful in that way, filled to the very brim with potential and opportunity.

But right now, all I can do is predict the future of Pheorirya. Iesso watches me draw my fingers through a small pile of sand like Saoirse had shown me all those centuries ago. Of course, I am no longer the clumsy child I was then. My hands are sure and steady. When I am done, I rise slowly from my knees. My joints let out a series of snapping sounds. I stifle a groan.

"What are you doing now?" Iesso asks. I have grown to like her. She appears to most as a frivolously anxious woman, but there is substance underneath that not many are willing to uncover. Her timidity is what everyone associates her with. They haven't experienced her unwavering kindness, her trust in humanity, or her tenderness. There'd been countless moments over the years where she'd disappear for the entirety of the day, returning late at night with dirt smudging her face and clothing, leaves tangled in her hair, and nothing but joy shining in her eyes. The only explanation she'd ever offer was that she'd been observing wildlife. I flip my hands palm up. The design in the sand peels away from the ground, now tangible.

"Magic comes from within," I say, not bothering to answer her question. The glowing drawing suddenly morphs into a ball of light that grows bigger until it fills half the room. The brightness intensifies uncomfortably. It doesn't stop until it's swallowed me and Iesso, along with everything else in the room.

When I finally dare to open my eyes, we are no longer in Saelmere Castle. Iesso and I stand amidst the stars. A billion tiny drops of light scattered in an endless sea of shifting hues of blues and greens and purples shimmer around us. Planets and galaxies pepper the sky in the distance, each ball of swirling, brilliant color a song soaring through the expanse. This spell has always been my favorite to perform. It's the last I ever learned, and it still reminds me of the nervous, buzzing energy of being a young magician.

"What is this place?" Iesso said. Iesso's voice is wonderstruck, and I do not blame her. She may never have seen a star or planet without a viewing glass until now.

"This is our universe, Iesso. The beautiful, endless void in which our world floats," I say. "Knowing the future is not possible, at the moment, at least. But we *can* see different pathways, alternative endings. It's complicated, really." I lean toward her. "This is how prophets are able to 'see the future,' Iesso." With a wave of my hand, the sky itself seems to part and give way to a sliver of light. The sky falls back into place like a curtain, but the slip of light remains. I reach for it and it curls around my hand like a comforting friend. "Show me," I say.

It takes a moment for the spell to jump into motion. It breaks apart into tiny shards of light, and then comes back together to form a body. "Fane," I whisper, recognizing the wings and wicked eyes. There is a lifeless heap at his feet, a demon with a single wing and blood staining her skin. Victoire. Another figure forms, slightly smaller in stature and wearing long, embroidered robes.

"Is that . . . you?" Iesso guesses, stepping closer. Something begins glowing and pulsing from the core of Fane's body. I can sense the sheer force of that light, all-consuming and utterly beautiful. But then Fane is reaching for Victoire's corpse at his feet, allowing a singular tendril of the luminescent power to curl around her. It lifts the limp hair around her face, cradles her lax limbs, and breathes life back into Victoire Liverraine. Her pale, hollow cheeks flush with color as her eyes open wide.

But then my figure places a hand on Fane's arm. For a moment, there is nothing. And then, everything. The golden light that makes up Fane's body blows away into the dark wind. Another woman is there. Catarina. Catarina, who laughs cruelly with her head thrown back and arms spread wide, basks in the light that now transfers to her. Suddenly, everything disappears and we are left in darkness. Even the stars have vanished. The sky has somehow lost its beauty, leaving behind a deep, dark vacuum waiting to suck us in.

"What was that?" Iesso demands. "Why was Catarina there?" I wave my hand, my heart racing. The sky drops away, and then we are back in Pheorirya. Iesso slams her hands down on a table for support, her breathing as ragged as my own. "Tontin, what in god's name just happened?"

"I really don't know," I confess.

CHAPTER EIGHT

FANE

"FANE," MINERVA WHISPERS. I don't reply. "Fane!" she repeats, sharper this time. I can't seem to conjure up the energy to reply. She chokes on a faint cry, burying her face in her hands. And then she's sobbing, fat tears rolling down her cheeks and falling to the stone floor. She plunges her fingers into her hair and massages her scalp.

"It's always been Victoire, huh?" she asks. Slowly, I look up. "Even now, I mean nothing to you. But when have I ever? Victoire, the *magnificent* Queen of Demons, will always be your first choice. And I will always be the second. Vicky, Vicky, Vicky. Always Vicky."

I want to lie to her, to tell her that I'd made a mistake in marrying Victoire, but I'm simply *too tired.* I'm tired of the lies, of everything happening instantaneously. So I do nothing but let my head fall between my knees again.

"Okay," she whispers. My head snaps up, sensing a change in her voice. Her dark eyes meet my own, unflinching, uncaring. She braces two hands on either side of her head, and I shoot to my feet.

"Minerva—"

"I love you. I always have."

Just then, Catarina pushes aside the bookshelf covering the entrance to the dungeon and saunters down the stairs, and I'm almost grateful for the interruption.

"Fane. How lovely to see you," she says. I say nothing. "You're to be executed in two hours," she continues.

I nod slowly. "I'm aware, Your Majesty." Minerva stays silent in her cell as well.

My voice is neither bitter nor taunting, but she frowns. "Do you not care about anything I've taken from you?" Catarina asks. I see it fully now: her intrinsic desire to matter.

"No, not particularly. Minerva means nothing to me, Victoire never truly loved me, and being King of Ahuiqir had already become irksome before you arrived." My words are carefully crafted to bother her by making it seem as if her actions have no effect on me or anyone at all.

"Don't you hate me?" she asks, bewildered and indignant.

"No." I cast a look at the lumps of bandages beneath Catarina's clothing. "I apologize on behalf of my wife for that. I never understood her lust for blood." She lets out a hiss from between clenched teeth; her shadows swarm behind her angrily.

"Why are you being so kind?" she demands.

I don't fight back. I compose my voice and give her nothing. "Because you remind me of Vicky. Both of you try so hard to make an impact on the world, whether it be good or bad, because you just want to be—"

With a roar, she lifts her hands in the air and all my confidence evaporates. Black shadows swarm forward through the bars of the cell, surging up my legs, around my shoulders, and covering me entirely. Distantly, I feel myself fall to the ground. It feels as if a million needles are stabbing into my skin repeatedly. I hear the clang of the cell door slamming open and through my blurred vision, I see Catarina step closer to me. The shadows leave a trail of fire as they crawl across me. A groan escapes my lips.

"I will not hesitate to kill you," Catarina says, so quietly I could've hallucinated it. And yet, the truth behind the words rings so loudly and clearly that I realize there's only one thing I can do to save myself.

I call upon the luminescence once more, but this time, I don't summon it to my palm. I let it grow from within my core until it spreads throughout my entire body, encapsulating me in a sphere of warmth and blinding white light. It cuts through Catarina's shadows effortlessly. Catarina hisses as she throws an arm up to block the light from her eyes. I stand up and rush for Catarina. She aims her palms at me with a snarl, but I wrestle her hands behind her back.

"I'm not trying to hurt you," I pant.

"What was that?" she demands, writhing in my grip.

"Don't try to kill me again." I slowly release her, my eyes trained on her the entire time. Catarina doesn't move to attack me again. I open a hand, my palm facing upward, and summon another ball of light. Her eyes widen. I nod, and she reaches out to touch the luminescence. When she does, I can see the physical effects it has on her body. Her shoulders instantly relax and her skin takes on a sort of shimmer as her eyes drift shut. The scars I can spot on her wings slowly begin to fade, diminishing from an angry red to a shade of pale pink.

Her eyes open and she suddenly rips her fingers away from the light. I can see from the gleam in her eyes that she wants more of it. I grimace.

"What is that?" she breathes.

"A gift," I tell her. "It can heal any wound, comfort any soul. Catarina, we could work together. With both powers of life and death, we would be completely and utterly unstoppable."

A short, harsh laugh escapes her lips, and I look at her in surprise. "That's pathetic," she sneers. "Do you really think I would spare your life for a gift of healing? Fane, I want destructive powers."

"But I have that also," I reason desperately.

"So do I, and so does Philan. You are nothing but a burden to me now," Catarina says. She turns to leave, but not before I catch the look in her eye. She's considering it. And I hadn't been lying. If Catarina possessed both the powers of life and death, there would be nobody left in the world strong enough to stop her from getting everything she wants. I hear her slide the bookshelf closed and clap her hands twice.

"How may I serve you?" someone I assume to be a servant asks.

"Get me General Pythea and Philan. I want them here."

The servant's footsteps pound across the floor as he hurries away. Only several minutes later, I hear more commotion. It's easy to hear through the cell ceilings on purpose; Victoire loved to stand right above her victims and talk to others about all the ways she'd torture them, so she'd had the cell re-designed to facilitate eavesdropping. A cruel inside joke, but today I am grateful for her audacity.

"Your Majesty," the general says, panting a little.

"Were either of you aware that Fane Liverraine possesses the gift of life?" Catarina asks nonchalantly.

"What do you mean?" the general asks.

Catarina's voice grows more hushed. "I mean that he is able to conjure balls of light that heal anyone, and perhaps even bring dead people back to life."

"That's not possible—" Philan interjects.

"I saw it with my own eyes," she says. "I'm pretty damn sure it's possible." There's a beat of silence. "See? My back and wings are healed."

"Oh," he breathes.

"Cancel Fane's execution but continue as planned with Minerva's. We will let him stay alive until I can figure out a way to use his magic."

I hear Minerva let out a soft, whooshing breath of air, and my heart aches for her.

"What?" Philan's voice is incredulous.

"I want that gift for myself."

"Why can't you just *not* kill Fane at all?" the general asks.

A moment later, I hear a cry of both pain and surprise, signaling that Catarina's shadows have found their mark.

"Because Fane is a threat now," Catarina says calmly. "And he would be more detrimental to our cause than beneficial."

Oh no. I've underestimated Catarina. The general releases a breath through gritted teeth.

"My Queen, doing that would be impossible," the general says.

"No," she replies. "You're wrong."

"But—"

"Bring me Prophet Tontin."

CHAPTER NINE

ZAHIRAN

I STAND BEFORE Cheusnys Cave. Brienne stands at my side.

"My God," I whisper. The cave is a huge, gaping hole carved into the side of a cliff. The endlessness of the dark cavern never fails to steal my breath, and looking sideways at Brienne, I see the same fear polluting her features. I remember the countless stories of warriors who'd entered and never returned.

"Be careful of the smell," Brienne says softly.

"I know," I sigh.

"Catarina said that the inside of the cave smells awful, and I trust that's true."

I put a hand on her shoulder. "Take care of those bastards," I say, gesturing at the family behind us. Polaris has been glaring at us since we approached the mouth of the cave.

"Don't die," she says, a little fearfully.

"I'll try not to."

She tries to reply, but I turn away and stride through the barrier. I've never liked long farewells anyway.

Just like Brienne had warned and I'd remembered, the cave reeks of damp, mold-covered stone and death. I hold my breath and bear it. The end of the cave is nothing spectacular, just a stone wall. But as I peer closer, I see thousands of initials engraved into the wall. An idea strikes me, and I find myself looking for my mother's initials. She definitely would have passed through the cave in her time. Alas, I see nothing. I loathe myself for even bothering to look. Why am I still so caught up on this woman who left me as a child? I drive everyone away from me, and I never let it bother me. So why does she? But I already know why. Because I'd never been the one to drive her away. *She'd* been the one to leave me. And that hurt like hell. Although I'd never admit it aloud, Brienne has been right the whole time. I need to move on. My expression sours. Brienne is always right.

The heat of Ahuiqir hits me hard. There is absolutely no moisture in the air, and each Breath feels like sandpaper dragging down my throat. On this side of the cave, Tillkasen Forest offers no relief from the sun. The leaves of its trees are long gone, burned away. But what always chills me the most is the complete silence. I hear no animals, and it seems as if even the wind is quiet. I hurry by, ripping off my sweat drenched cloak as I go. I pause when I spot the two knives tucked in the cloak's pocket.

I'd been honest when I told Brienne that they were my mother's. She'd told Lady Burgess to give them to me when I turned thirteen. They are excellent weapons, but I have grown to resent them. They represent a rich, pampered life that I could have had. It's an impossible life. For me, anyway. I think back to Aisling, Lilliana, Nicolette, and Nora, the four girls I'd left behind. They were the beautiful daughters of rich parents who'd simply sent them to Lady Burgess to learn self-defense. They would grow up to marry into even richer families, and if their cities are now destroyed, they can use that money of theirs and simply pack their bags and move away. They could escape everything.

My jaw clenches, and I get the knives out of my view. I'd wanted to be those girls so badly when I'd lived with Lady Burgess, and not a single thing has changed. The closer I get to Liverraine Castle, the more I fight the urge to turn and run the other direction. That'd been my home many years ago. I share my mother's immortality, both a blessing and a curse. And now, with so many years passed, I can hardly remember Ceiridwen Ladell's face. Back then, the castle had not been named Liverraine. Dannamoore Castle. Named after the first Queen of Guinyth, Lycoris Dannamoore. It was Dannamoore Castle until the Fane and Victoire Liverraine took over. I curse Victoire and Fane every way I know how. But only cursing them will do no good. So I pull my hood up and cross the wrought iron gates of Liverraine Castle, pulling my daggers out of where I'd buried them in the thick pockets of my cloak.

Four guards stand before the main entryway. I spot two more circling around from the left side of the castle. But the right remains surprisingly unprotected. I pull a cord from my belt. The material is sturdy yet flexible against my fingertips. It won't fail me. I stole it from a merchant somewhere, years ago. I tie the end into a noose and hurl it up. The small loop falls over one of the peaks of the castle, then tightens into place when I pull. A window is cut into the brick. *My entryway,* I think with a small smile. Letting the cord dangle there for a moment, I slip on a pair of gloves covered in small dots of glue I'd stolen from the same merchant. The glue will prevent me from sliding off the rope.

Mirita Burgess once said that I would grow to become as ferocious in battle as I was in spirit, but it's hard for me to believe that when I tremble this much simply climbing a damned rope. I have to stop for a moment and press the soles of my feet hard into the brick wall to remind myself that the rope will not give out. I force myself to continue, sliding my feet up ever so slowly. I reach for the next segment of rope, sweat dripping off my forehead and onto the rope.

And then my hand slips.

I am left hanging by only my left arm. I try not to scream. The glove on my right hand slides off my hand, falling to the ground and out of my sight. I hiss in frustration and clench my jaw. I will not let myself fall. I will not let *this* kill me, after everything I've been through. Shifting the remaining glove from my left hand to my right, I wrap my fingers around the rope. Night is falling, and if I can't climb up the rope fast enough . . . I don't bother finishing the thought. Even if I were to climb back down, it would mean that I'd have to wait until morning to try again. And I didn't know what tomorrow would bring, whether it would be guards capturing me or an animal digging its fangs into my flesh. That would make my mission a failure. And Zahiran Ladell does not fail.

I flex my arm to test my strength. Immediately, my muscles shake and I let myself hang once again.

"Goddammit!" I stick my hand in my cloak to look for anything that might help me. My fingers brush against the cool metal of my gem-studded knives. With a grunt, I shove the blade of the first knife into the small sliver of space between two bricks an arm's length above me. The sky has darkened even more, turning from a muted periwinkle to a deep blue. I glare up at the window in the spire fifteen feet above me. So close, yet so far. Groaning, I pull myself up using both the knife and the rope. But when I try to pull the knife out, it's stuck. I strain harder, pulling with all my strength and shoving at the wall until my fingernails are torn and my skin is raw and bleeding. I let out a rage-filled shriek, cursing at the sky. Realization dawns on me, as swift and hard as a slap in the face. If I am going to make it to the window, I will need to use both knives. That will render me completely weaponless when I enter the castle. I snarl and jam my second knife—my last—into a gap another arm's length above me. After pulling myself up, I look helplessly down at my two knives protruding from side of the stone tower. I swear to myself that I'll return and retrieve them after this mission is over. The sun finally dips below the horizon, but I am already shimmying my way up that final, tiny stretch of rope and into Liverraine Castle.

I land on the glossy marble floor of the bedroom as silently and gracefully as a cat. I feel exposed without my blades at my sides. I reach out the window and pull the noose into my hands. I note the way the silken sheets are perfectly made on the bed. Too perfect, in fact. I sniff the air. The air smells stale, as if nobody has been in here in a long time. I let down my defenses a bit and sag against a wall. My heart still pounds in my chest from the climb. I shouldn't be as rattled as I am. I should've been strong enough to scale that wall in minutes. I cast a grim look at the moon shining in the dark sky. I vow to myself I'll be better prepared next time. But I'm concerned. *The very first step of the mission—already nearly failed,* my mind chides. *Worthless, cowardly, weak.* With a start, I realize that it is not Lady Burgess's voice chiding me, but my own.

I clamp down on my fears, gripping the bedpost for support. Don't look back at the window, I tell myself. Just walk forward.

My legs tremble as I open the bedroom door and step out into the cold, empty hallway. Every piece of my childhood furniture has been replaced with harsh iron substitutes. There are no lanterns or candles. Even the golden chandeliers hanging from the ceiling are covered with a layer of dust and cobwebs and are obviously unused. I creep along the corridor, sticking close to the wall. All the doors are closed. I don't bother checking to see what's inside each one. *Where would Victoire keep Catarina?* I rack my brain, dredging up the routes through the castle I know from my year of serving Victoire. *The dungeon.* I remember now, a dungeon hidden behind a bookshelf in the library. I continue on, more confident than I had been only moments before.

As I go down the winding staircase and pass the throne room, a faint glow of light flares to life somewhere inside. My heart leaps into my throat. I look around desperately for anything to protect myself with. I grab a ceramic vase off of a table and dump the dried roses out of it. The light grows brighter, and I hear soft footsteps coming toward me. I brace myself for whoever exits that room and lift the vase above my head. The door bursts open and before I can even think to scream, shadows curl around my wrists and ankles and clamp around my mouth. My muscles are no longer mine to control, and the vase falls from my splayed fingers, shattering into a million tiny pieces. Several shards embed themselves into my legs. I open my eyes, but it is not Victoire who stands before me. Her skin is just as pale, but her hair is darker, her lips fuller. An eyepatch covers one of her deep brown eyes. I smile grimly, noting two guards appearing at her side. The woman must be Catarina Winyr, complete with a wrought iron crown and shadows that writhe before me.

"Zahiran?"

"I'm here to save you," I say, wriggling in her grip. She throws out her hands in a gesture of irritated confusion, but I still remain hovering several inches above the ground, stuck in her shadows.

"Why is everyone so desperate to save me? First Zhengya, and now you."

"You killed Victoire." It is not a question, and my voice is flat.

"Yes. Victoire is dead."

"I'm here to save you, Catarina. I was sent by Brienne, Brienne Addington? Your friend." Her eyes narrow, and I realize that she might not even have known her friend's surname. "Come back with me," I plead. "The war will end without a ruler in Ahuiqir."

She laughs, and the shadows around me clench tighter. I can't take a full breath of air anymore, and it starts to hurt when I try.

"I am the ruler of Ahuiqir," she says delightedly. "I would tell you to run home to Brienne, but I don't really want you to leave. Why don't you stay a little while longer?"

"What are you talking about?" I demand. "Is this a joke? It's *me*."

And then a tendril of her shadows curls around my neck, digging in, and my mouth snaps shut. "I really should get going," I whisper. Her fingers twitch and the magic tightens even more around me. I gasp, my throat constricting.

"I could crush you without lifting a finger," she says nonchalantly. "I recommend you reconsider."

I shake my head once and she smiles. The pressure only increases until stars flash across my vision.

"So, what'll it be?"

"I-I'll stay," I manage to say.

"Good girl," she purrs. But the magic does not give up its hold on me.

"Let me go," I say hoarsely.

"No." She snaps her fingers and a pair of handcuffs circle my wrists.

Catarina's idea of hospitality is throwing her guests into a cold dungeon. She slams the door shut. I peel up the sleeves of my shirt, careful not to shift the handcuffs. Bruises are already starting to form where her magic held me. I see bands of purple and blue materializing under my skin. My horns scrape uncomfortably against the low stone ceiling of the cell and I shiver. She's even taken my cloak. I wrap my wings around myself. At least she doesn't have my daggers. They're still stuck in the wall, but they're away from her. I begin to question Brienne's taste in friends.

"Hello? Is someone there?" A shaky, desperate voice rings down the short hallway of the dungeon.

Another voice joins hers. "Save us," the new voice whispers.

"Please! Save us." Her voice sounds so strained and weak. I fear for myself; will I sound like that after spending time down here?

"I can't. I am a prisoner here, too," I breathe, hoping they cannot hear. But they begin wailing so loudly that I press my hands to my ears.

"Who are you?" one of them asks finally.

"Zamara," I say. The lie comes out swiftly, mindlessly, drilled into me from all those years of living in Liverraine Castle. "Who are you?"

"Pasiphae."

"And who is—"

"My name is Zhengya."

"I was sent by Brienne to rescue you and Catarina."

Pasiphae begins to laugh. The laughter turns wild, and I wince away from it. These two women scare me.

"Do you truly believe Catarina will leave this place now?" Pasiphae asks.

"No." The word leaves my lips as no more than a breath, loud in the sudden silence. She'd been utterly unrecognizable.

"Do you have food?" Zhengya asks then.

"No," I repeat. "Did she take your weapons?" I already know the answer to that question.

"Of course," Zhengya says flatly. She does not bother to ask the same of me.

None of us speak another word for several minutes. "Why are you two here?" I ask finally. The two women are silent for so long that I begin to believe they've fallen asleep.

"Victoire was torturing me and Catarina," Pasiphae says quietly. "Zhengya was supposed to save us. And then something happened to Catarina."

"So what happened to Victoire?"

"Pasiphae summoned her mother's spirit to kill her," Zhengya says. "The one and only Saskia Sandor."

"So what are we going to do?" I ask softly.

A low wail tears from the mouth of one of the women, and she inhales in huge gasping sobs. Pasiphae, I realize.

"Pull yourself together," Zhengya snarls.

"How long have you two been in here?" I ask carefully.

"Days, weeks, I don't know. They're all blurring together." Zhengya's voice sounds so distant, as if she weren't sitting mere feet away from me. Pasiphae continues weeping.

"Has she fed you?"

"What do you think, *Zamara?*" Zhengya spits out my fake name as if it's poison on her tongue. "I tried eating my own clothing." She holds up a suspiciously tattered cuff.

"I don't have anything to give you," I say helplessly.

"Don't be sorry." Zhengya's voice has lowered into a growl. "You're doomed to the same fate as us."

"Can't you summon Pasiphae's mother's spirit again?" I ask.

"I've tried that. Many, many times. She refuses to answer me." Pasiphae's crying is as relentless as ever.

"Stop," I say suddenly. "Stop crying. You'll just dehydrate yourself even faster."

The whimpering stops. "I'm so hungry, Zamara. So hungry."

I exhale slowly, guilt building in my chest. "My name isn't Zamara," I say softly. "It's Zahiran."

"You lied to us?" Zhengya asks.

"You would have done the same thing."

I hear the sliding of fabric against stone, and a dull thud as Pasiphae lets her head fall against the stone wall.

"So this is it, huh? We're all going to die right here in this godforsaken dungeon." A pause, and then another thud. And another. I realize with a start that Pasiphae is pounding on the wall.

"You're just wasting your energy," I hear Zhengya whisper.

"What's the point?" Pasiphae snarls. "I'm going to die. I am truly going to die." The sound of her fists connecting with the wall accompanied by her quiet sniffling don't stop for another half hour. Zhengya doesn't attempt to stop her again. Pasiphae finally falls silent. "Zahiran?" she calls softly.

"Yes?" I reply.

"Who were your parents? You must have royal blood if you were with Zhengya's friends in Guinyth and yet able to get here."

I debate offering a vague, nebulous answer, but something inside of me trusts Pasiphae. "My mother was Queen Ceiridwen. Of Ahuiqir."

"And your father?"

My chest tightens, but I manage to let out, "My mother married a human. He betrayed us." I brace myself for a flurry of apologies from her, but she says nothing. I smile.

"Victoire was my sister. When she died, I thought she was gone forever. I'd never thought that she would become a demon. But now, she is gone. No escaping death this time."

My eyes widen, but I'd guessed it. I have never seen Pasiphae herself before, but even her *voice* shares the same sharp, haughty pride as Victoire's does. "Did you love her?"

"Yes."

I don't apologize to her for asking, either. Condolences don't take away the pain.

CHAPTER TEN
TONTIN

IESSO PACES back and forth, her hands clenched in her robes in frustration.

"If you keep going, you'll wear a hole in the carpet," I say.

"Aren't you worried?" She continues her pacing without missing a beat.

"Yes, I'm sure we all are, but—"

"But what? Since Catarina is queen now, we know for sure that Victoire is dead." She drags a hand through her hair. "Or *was* dead. But in that . . ." She waves her hands around, unsure how to describe the magic I'd performed. ". . . *place* you took me to, she was brought back to life. What was that light? Why did Catarina take it from Fane?"

"It was Fane's luminescence," I say distantly.

"His what?"

"Have you not heard the witch clan speak of his healing powers? He was given the gift of luminescence, something the opposite of the shadows demons have, even though he's a demon himself."

"Does this mean that Catarina knows about the power?"

"Probably." I glance at the servant in the corner of the room. "Can you call for General Tenebris?" I ask, tired. She dips her head, rushing off.

Iesso continues to pace back and forth. I wave a hand wearily, using the last of my energy to summon a gust of wind that knocks her gently onto a sofa. It takes much more effort than it should have. Yet another reminder of my growing age. She looks at me in surprise.

"All sorcerers and prophets are required to be trained in the art of each elemental gift. Obviously, I am no king. But I can do a little bit." I shake my head, clearing my thoughts. "That is beside the point. Iesso, know that I am perfectly aware of the dangers of this situation."

General Lilura Tenebris bursts into my study, sweat covering her forehead in a fine sheen. "You called me, prophet?"

I nod. "Yes. General, we have a situation. A problem, you could say."

She pales. "I don't like the sound of that at all."

I don't even have the energy to force my lips to curve upward. "Fane Liverraine has been spared by Catarina. There's only one thing he has now that she could want."

She blanches. "The luminescence? Th-that's not possible. How would she even . . ." she trails off. I ignore her statement and trace my fingers over an old book on my desk. Dust covers my fingertips, and I brush them lightly against my robe.

"How many guards can we spare?"

"Why?" she dares to question, but I can see in her eyes that she already knows.

"She wants to steal his magic from him to use for herself. And she knows that I know how." Memories of Catarina's Embracing flood through me. I wince at how foolish I'd been to share my own powers with her, knowing that single moment could now cost me my freedom.

"So she's going to capture you?" Iesso breathes.

"Precisely." I speak slowly, not allowing her to see any of my inner panic. "Therefore, I'll need—"

General Tenebris shakes her head. "No. I'll call for Regan Grimsbane, Maritess Riddle, and Ulrich Cromwell."

"It's too risky. If Catarina manages to kill you and the others and captures me, Iesso will be left alone."

But Lilura's eyes are stone cold and her mouth is pressed into a thin, hard line. "No. The alternative is even riskier. If you are captured, there will be nothing preventing Catarina from winning."

"Thank you," I say, a sudden smile twitching at my lips.

She doesn't return the expression, only puts a hand on the hilt of her sword, which hangs at her side. "I'll go ask them now." Without another word, she slips out of the room. I turn back to Iesso, who has been silent this whole time.

"I am *so stupid*," Iesso whispers.

"What?"

"You two speak as if I cannot be trusted to be left alone. As if me leading this city would be worse than losing the war itself."

"No, that is not—"

"It is."

I agree with her. Iesso Endrdyn has done nothing to prove herself worthy of the responsibilities required of her.

"If you die, I will be queen."

"Iesso—"

Her eyes are steely. "I have been cowardly for much too long, prophet. But I will no longer shirk from my fears." Her face softens a little. "Besides, it would be an honor to lead and defend my home in your name."

I smile at her. "Thank you," I say blandly, not knowing how else to express my gratitude.

"Don't say that."

"What?"

"Don't seem so surprised that I—we—would do that for you." She hesitates, and then continues on. "I know you don't like being called a ruler, but it's what you've become in Catarina's wake. And so we are obliged to serve you until our last breath, to protect you until we can no longer do so." For a moment, I consider correcting her and insisting that I am nothing more than a prophet, but to my horror, she dips her head and bows, low and deep. "My King."

Later, I sit at one end of a long table made of thick wood covered in scratches. Queen Aideen of Maarso sits at the other side, cupping a glass of wine in her hands. She wears a deep, iridescent purple gown that cinches at the waist. A slit in the side of the gown reveals a sliver of scarred skin. Thick corded necklaces wreath her neck. Lilura, Regan, Maritess, and Ulrich sit around me. I watch as Aideen lifts up her wine glass and drains it in one gulp, before setting it back down with a *thump.* A servant rushes to fill it again.

I raise my eyebrows. "A woman who can drink," I tease lightly. "Respectable." But no amusement flickers in her eyes.

"I understand that your city has been independent for many years," Ulrich Cromwell starts. Aideen's face is a mask of calm, unaffected neutrality. "Pheorirya has also held its own for a while. But I am asking you, humbly, to help us. Pheorirya—"

"No." She takes another swig of her wine. Maritess stiffens beside me, and Lilura gives her a small, almost unnoticeable shake of her head. "We are already running low on supplies as it is. Another city to look after would only add to our growing litany of problems."

"Queen Aideen, with all due respect . . ." Maritess throws me a glance, as if asking for permission. I nod, and she hesitates for a moment, thinking over her words. "If our cities unite and we work together—"

"Do not spout such platitudes," Aideen snaps. "I am not a naïve child, Riddle. I understand your struggles. But I am unwilling to sacrifice my own people for yours. And I'm sure that if our roles were reversed, you would feel the same way." The burning fire in her eyes subsides a little, and she slumps back down in her chair. "This is war, Prophet Tontin. We must make decisions that benefit ourselves."

"Your Majesty," Regan Grimsbane starts. "If you walk away from this room without offering even a shred of mercy or assistance, Pheorirya may be wiped off the face of Guinyth. Just like Tegak was." His voice is filled with desperation, and when I look around, I see that same hopelessness dulling the features of all my friends.

She flinches at his last few words and her eyes flutter shut. "Grimsbane, I have said this many times and I will say so again. I do not have the resources to help you in any way." She lets her head fall into her palm, her fair hair swinging forward, and only then do I realize how tired she looks. Her usually golden skin is pallid. Her delicate silver crown slides off her head and falls to the table. She doesn't bother putting it back on.

"Are you feeling all right?" Ulrich asks, his gaze following my own. She looks up, seeing all of our faces etched with concern. Suddenly, she presses her palms against the table and pushes up, her features contorted with seething rage.

"I do not need any of your sympathy," she snarls. Her cold gaze turns on me and she jabs a finger in my direction. "Please do not ask me again for help. I don't particularly enjoy wasting my time here when my own citizens require my presence."

Lilura leaps her seat and stops Aideen before she can sweep out of the room. "What's happening in Maarso?" she asks flatly. "You can refuse to help us all you want, but we do not wish any harm on you. And I can tell that there's something you're not telling us."

Aideen shakes free from Lilura's grip, her eyes wide. Lightning crackles at her fingertips, and every hair on my body stands straight up. I realize that she must have the gift of the skies.

"How dare you speak to me like that." She glares at Lilura. "I am a *queen*."

I push back my chair and join Lilura. "Even though the general could have phrased her words better," I shoot a look at Lilura, "she is right. Queen Aideen, you do not look well."

"I am perfectly fine," she insists, but her voice breaks a little. The charged energy in the air fades as quickly as it had come. Maritess carefully puts a hand on her arm and guides her back to her chair.

"You can trust us," I say softly. "We are on the same side of this war."

"That's true."

"Tell me, Your Majesty. I want to help you," I say.

She looks up at me slowly, as if in a daze. "We have completely run out of supplies. My soldiers are starving, and sickness runs rampant through my camps. We have no resources, no medics to treat those illnesses." She presses two fingers to her temple, letting out a breath. "And I believe I have caught one of those illnesses. If the demons were to attack right now, I have no doubt in my mind that they would destroy my city. Just like Tegak."

"Lying was a mistake, Queen Aideen. We could have helped you."

"I know." Tears glisten in her eyes and her hands shake as she presses them against her wine glass. In this moment, she looks far older than she is. Too young to have such pressure thrown upon her shoulders. Too young to be forced to defend a city and its inhabitants. Aideen was the youngest in Guinyth's history to have taken on the title of queen, only twelve years of age. And somehow, for the past decade, she'd led her people perfectly well. Aideen had done more than that, in fact. She'd built up an icy reputation and earned the respect of everyone around her. I am suddenly overcome by guilt, and I settle into the chair beside her. Her face is dry once again, but when I look more closely at them, I see that the whites of her eyes are stained a sickly yellow color. A rasping cough escapes her lips. She stands. "I should go."

"No." I point at a large mirror resting on a desk. "Have you looked at your reflection recently?" She shakes her head and I gesture for her to stand. With a ghostly pale hand, she traces her features in the mirror. As she scans her sunken cheeks and lifeless eyes, her shoulders cave in.

"I didn't realize I looked like this," she whispers.

I clap my hands and a servant pushes off a wall to come to my side. "Fetch the Queen of Maarso a cup of hot tea, please," I say.

She turns back to me, fingers wrapped around her throat. "I cannot lead like this," Aideen says.

The servant arrives with the warm mug of tea, and I push it into her hands.

"Drink," I order.

Aideen obeys, curling around the fragrant warmth of the cup. "Thank you," she murmurs. Maritess shrugs off her own shawl and drapes it around

Aideen's shoulders. She coughs again, and Maritess flinches away.

"Call for a healer," Ulrich suggests from his seat at the table. I nod at the servant. He dips his head, already turning toward the door.

The old woman runs her hands down Aideen's body. We have moved her into a guest bedroom, and Aideen looks even thinner when surrounded by extravagantly plump pillows. Maritess, Regan, and Ulrich wait outside the room at Hagatha's request. The healer's skin is wrinkle-free, thanks to her restorative abilities, but her dark, kind eyes shine with wisdom only a person of great age could have. The low thrum of magic fills the room, sweet and pulsing, and the window slides open. A waft of warm air slides in, bringing with it the sweet scent of cherry blossoms. Aideen inhales deeply.

The healer finally straightens her knotted back with a soft groan and the vibrations of magic in the air fades. "It is only a fever," she whispers in my ear. "She will recover. But it is not the fever that is hurting her, prophet. She is simply exhausted." A callous-covered hand lands on my shoulder. "Let her sleep." And with that, she hobbles out of the room.

Aideen lets out a low, delirious chuckle. Her skin is even paler now, stark against the deep ruby red of the sheets. "I don't need sleep. I need to save my people."

"And in order to do that, you need sleep." I stride to the door.

As soon as I've shut it behind me, a servant taps my shoulder. "Two more queens are here to speak to you," she says, panting.

The buzzing sensation of magic against my skin announces the arrival of the new, powerful beings. I hurry back to the meeting room, where two women now sit at the oak table. They introduce themselves as Keres and Merikh, the two Sisters of Night.

"We are the Queens of Ilyvalion," Queen Keres says, naming a section of Guinyth to the south of Pheorirya. "It is separated into two cities: Yllalin and Shylseserin."

The dark skin of the two sisters seems to be dappled in whorls of glittering pale stars, and I cannot help but stare. Their sheer beauty is overwhelming. If I've ever doubted it before, now I know for certain these two women are not from our world. Matching silver circlets sit atop their dark hair, coiled into braided coronets on their head. The most striking difference between the two is the color of their eyes. Merikh's are a shade of brown so deep they look black. But Keres's, on the other hand, are a color so pale that they could be mistaken for utterly colorless and are glossed over with a milky film. I look more closely at her and notice that she looks not straight at me, but slightly to my side. She is blind, I realize. Both wear long, silken robes of midnight blue that flow around their bodies, delicate and light as air.

"Yllalin. Shylseserin," I repeat slowly. The syllables are foreign on my tongue. "Thank you so much for coming."

"This is my city. Yllalin." Keres whispers reverently. She lifts her hands and the stars flecking her skin seem to peel away from her. They swirl together, joining into a clear blue sphere of pure power. I peer inside. I've never seen a more beautiful place. A city bathed in gold. Music drifts from the streets and pairs with the laughter of children. Small cafes, taverns, shops, and inns line the sides of the cobbled roads, their interiors warm and comforting. A glimmering castle of glass rises above it all, its spires reflecting the light of the sun. But all that beauty is nothing compared to the sky. A million stars, planets, and galaxies fill the pale blueness. They are visible even in daylight. They hang so close I feel as if I could touch them if I just reach high enough. I long to see what they would look like after the sun has set. Iesso lets out a breath beside me. I know that she is just as wonderstruck as I am.

Merikh, who has been silent the whole time, steps forward. Her own stars peel off her skin to form an almost identical ball of light. But instead of pale blue, Merikh's sphere is a cloudy black color. Her city, Shylseserin, is darker, but just as beautiful as Yllalin. Its buildings are expertly crafted from black stone. The full moon shines her pale face down at the slumbering city, and thousands of fireflies weave through the dimly illuminated streets. Merikh's castle is wreathed in dark mist.

"Shylseserin," she says. "My city."

But then she waves her hand and both images disappear, replaced with a burning hell. The buildings are destroyed, the cobbled streets ravaged, the glass castle of Yllalin shattered. The joyous cries of the children have turned into a harrowing choir of agonized screams. A legion of demons soars into the sky, devoid of all its stars. Their faces are marked with sneering, wicked grins.

"And this is what will happen if we stand by and watch the demons invade Guinyth. We want to help you, Prophet Tontin." Her stature is smaller than her sister's, but her eyes are infused with an icy-cold confidence that very few people possess. *Like Catarina,* I think.

"Of course," I say as warmly as I can. But Queen Merikh does not smile. "Are your numbers great?"

Her lips twitch at that. "Prophet, the Cities of Night are the smallest in all of Guinyth. No, our numbers are not many. But our warriors are strong and brave."

"Then you will find yourself most welcome among the Pheoriryan ranks."

Keres smiles at me. I can already tell that the two sisters are opposites. Keres has a sweet, kind temperament. And Merikh is filled with stony, unbreakable calm. I reach forward with my mind to summon my powers. But when I reach the threshold of the void containing her thoughts and memories, I am met with an unbreakable wall of darkness.

She looks at me carefully. "We are allies now, but that does not permit you to go snooping through my brain."

I almost fall back in surprise. "H-how did you know?"

She plays with a silver ring encircling her finger. "You didn't even bother hiding it, prophet." She leans forward on her elbows, her eyes narrowing. "You are weakening."

"What?"

"Your powers are nowhere near the strength I expected them to be," she says bluntly. "I could see the strain written all over your face."

"Do you know of Catarina Winyr?" I ask. "You almost remind me of her."

"The Queen of the Demons?" she asks harshly. "The woman I am offering to fight against?"

"Yes. You both have impenetrable walls surrounding your hearts."

"Such poetry," Merikh taunts. "I assure you, Tontin, my heart is unguarded." But even as those words pass through her lips, her arms remain crossed tight over her chest.

"Do not mind my sister," Keres titters from across the table. "She does not know when to keep her mouth shut."

I turn my gaze back to her. She would be the better option to discuss things with. "Queen Keres, when do you think you can transfer your army to Pheorirya?"

She tilts her head, even the simple movement graceful. "Ilyvalion is the southernmost point of Guinyth, so days, perhaps," she muses. *We don't have that much time,* I think, and Keres must sense my distress, because she slides a slender hand forward and touches my arm. "While it may not be possible for me to move my entire army sooner, I may be able to transport individual legions."

"How?" her sister asks. Her voice is not harsh, only curious.

"I think I've figured out a way to create a set of false wings that mimic those of demons." She waves her hand, and a large object wrapped in dark cloth thumps to the table. She carefully unwraps it, revealing feathered wings. "I studied a real set of wings for years before finally making this."

"Where did you get real demon wings?" Merikh demands.

"I cut them off of a dead demon," Keres replies calmly. I instantly like her. "But that is beside the point." She lifts the wings from the table, revealing a harness attached to them. "Feel it," she tells me. I run a finger over the inky feathers, over the harness. Both are made from the same weightless material.

"How do the wings work?" Merikh questions.

Keres smiles broadly. "That is precisely the genius in my invention. I designed them with a bit of magic to meld into anyone's skin. The wings will respond to your mind, just as any of your limbs do."

—∞∞—

Night has fallen when the two queens leave Saelmere Castle. They'd decided they would be staying at an inn down the road for the time being. After hours of arguing and debating, exhaustion drags at my shoulders and eyelids, and nothing calls to me more than a warm bed. But there is still much to do. I lift a hand, and four candles flare to life around my bedroom to illuminate my desk. I sit down heavily in the chair, pulling a sheet of paper closer to me. It's a map, labeled with all the cities of Guinyth. Pheorirya, Maarso, Tegak, Yllalin, and Shylseserin, along with others that I am not familiar with.

I cross out the name *Tegak,* not allowing myself to feel any grief. All that I can hope for is that its citizens died mercifully. I circle Maarso, Yllalin, and Shylseserin, marking them as allies. My brow furrows when I move my pen to the edge of the map, where there is a border of white, blank space. I write down my estimations of the sizes of each city's army and then add them together. I pause, then scribble out my numbers so I can rewrite them. *How could that be?* Again and again I run through the calculations, each time reaching the same answer. My writing grows frantic, the numbers turning almost illegible. I look back over my work. I made a mistake, I forgot a digit, perhaps . . .

But finally, the pen falls from my shaky fingertips and ink splatters over the map, three dark splotches. I did not make a mistake. Even with all of our new allies, Victoire's—no, *Catarina's* army is still twice as large as my own.

CHAPTER ELEVEN

CATARINA

MY SPIES BOW before my throne, their faces pale and fearful. "Speak," I say.

The woman raises her head, her two front teeth digging into her bottom lip to keep it from trembling. "Your Majesty. Tontin has acquired two new allies."

"Who?" The shadows around me swirl faster, as if in response to my emotions.

"Ilyvalion. The Cities of Night," she whispers. "Yllalin and Shylseserin."

"Who are their rulers?" My shadows thrum under my skin, aching to be released.

"Queen Keres and Queen Merikh," the man beside her says.

"Are they a threat to me?"

"Their armies are not, but the queens may be. Their magic is old and powerful, but completely mysterious." The woman's face glows with something that resembles awe. "However, according to the many children's tales written about them, they are able to steal the gifts of others."

Her words bring back a wave of childhood memories, of the stories my mother and father told me. "What can they do with the gift once it's in their possession?"

"They can either use it for themselves or simply release it back into the universe," the woman says.

My fingers curl into a fist. "I'll slaughter them all." The words come out quietly, under my breath, but the two demons before me hear anyway.

"Why?" the man dares to ask.

My eyes narrow, and he has the good sense to shrink from the shadows that strain toward him. I slide off my throne and hook a finger under his chin to jerk his head up.

"Because," I purr, forcing his brown eyes to meet my own, "I can. And because I want the rest of those pathetic human rulers to see what will happen if any of them dare to side with that old man. I want to kill the queens myself." My claws drag up the sensitive skin of the side of his throat, leaving behind a slim trail of red. The woman beside him stiffens, and I let out a delighted laugh. "Is she your lover?"

"No," he breathes. "She is nothing to me."

"My, my." I draw back, but neither of them relaxes. "I'm not sure how you don't know this yet, but I absolutely *despise* liars."

The girl finally breaks down, her thin shoulders shuddering with each breath she inhales. "Yes, yes," she sobs. "We're engaged, we have a child, we—"

"Would killing him affect your work ethic?" I ask her, gesturing at the man. The woman frowns, and then her eyes widen when she realizes what I'm saying. Her lover squeezes his eyes shut but does not pull away.

"Please," she begs. "Please, don't kill him."

I rein in my shadows, and step back. "Convince me, girl. Give me one good reason why I shouldn't kill him."

"Because if he dies, I die." Her eyes are steady, confident.

I almost laugh considering the two of them, curled around each other with hands clutched together so tightly that their knuckles shine white. "Fine."

I walk toward the door as if I've decided to spare them. I hear them both heave gasping, relieved sighs behind me. With a flick of my finger, a stream of shadows shoots from me and into the man. A minute later, I stride out of the room, letting my cerulean blue gown flare out behind me, now speckled with red. A smile curves my lips, and I do not bother to hide it.

Philan waits outside my throne room, a smile to match my own on his.

"Catarina." The shadows circling him reach out for my own, and they intertwine, twisting around each other in a dark, powerful duet. He'd been crowned King of Ahuiqir two nights ago. I reach up and adjust his crown, an identical twin to my own. The wails of the woman seep through the heavy wooden doors, and he brushes a lock of dark hair away from my face.

"Who did you kill this time, My Queen?"

"A spy," I say. He doesn't bother to ask why. I gesture at two guards standing stiffly at the entrance of the room. "Go get that girl, please."

They disappear into the room, and return holding her between them. She bares her fangs at me as tears slide down her cheeks and drip to the floor. "*You monster,*" she snarls, low and savage.

Philan regards her with cold disinterest. "Be careful with the way you speak to your queen." He leans in closer to her, rubbing a strand of her thin hair between his fingers. "She may have an awful temper, but I have a worse one." He looks down at his clean hands. "And I'd hate to get myself dirty. But . . ." A wicked smile flits across his face. "I'd enjoy hearing you scream regardless."

"You may kill her," my voice rings out in the silence, and I relish the way the girl's face pales. But before she can even think to say anything, a sword stabs through her chest and comes out the other side. She sways on her knees, then falls.

Blood seeps from the wound all over the floor, and Philan toes at the red pool in disgust. "What information did she offer you?"

The guards drag the spy's body away, and Philan's wings wrap around us. I allow myself to lean into their warmth, sighing softly. "Tontin has two new allies."

He smiles. "I trust that you'll deal with them, as you always do with your enemies."

"Have you heard of Yllalin and Shylseserin?" I ask. "The Cities of Night."

"Keres and Merikh," he says flatly. "Yes, I have heard about their supposed powers before."

I shove him lightly. "Why did you not tell me?"

He tilts his head. "I did not think that they were going to become relevant again."

"Again?"

He lets out a whooshing breath through his nose. "I read a book about them and their sacred lands. Surely you've heard the tales, too? Legends say that they were born from the stars themselves, that they are not of this world."

"What exactly can they do?" I ask, remembering the woman spy's words. Their magic is old and powerful, but completely mysterious. They can steal gifts of magic.

"They steal the powers of others," he says, confirming what the spy had told me.

"And what exactly does that mean?" With each passing second, the lightheartedness of the moment fades.

"When they absorb a demon's magic, they grow stronger."

I tilt my head at him. "So they are a threat?"

"Yes."

"Philan, why did you not tell me?" My heart lurches in my chest.

"We all knew the fairytales, I just assumed you knew the truth of them, as a royal yourself," he repeats calmly.

I push away from him and stalk down the hallway. I am furious but I'm also terrified. Could these two women's powers affect me? Am I stronger than them?

I reach a set of heavy metal doors and fling them wide open. Moon-kissed light streams down upon me, bringing with it air heavy with the scent of a rare oncoming rain. *Yes,* I tell myself. *You are young. You are strong. You are powerful.*

But as I stand there with my shadows still flowing around me in listless spirals, I am *lonely.* I find myself longing for Zhengya's warm touch, her gentle yet firm reassurance, an emotion that confuses me.

But I shake my head, as if physically shoving away all those frivolous worries. I am no longer the weak human I was when we met.

I do not need her.

I walk back to my throne room and pass Philan on the way. He trails behind me, wary of every flicker of my shadows.

"Get me General Pythea," I say softly. He nods and hurries away. I settle back onto my throne, curling my legs under me.

The general bursts through the door moments later, followed by Philan. "Your Majesty," she says, falling to a knee.

"Get up. I want Tontin. Right now!" The words rip out of me, harsher than I'd intended for them to be, but I couldn't care less.

"My Queen, my spies still haven't reported back to me. I am unsure whether or not it would be wise—"

"That. Was. An. Order. I don't care how many soldiers die. I don't care if it's unsafe. I want Tontin and those two Sisters of Night."

"Your Majesty, we have no idea what we'll be facing. It'll be a suicide mission."

"General, are you questioning your queen?"

Her chin tilts up, her eyes flashing with defiance. "Yes, Your Majesty. I believe it's foolish and . . ."

I release the leash on my magic. It hurtles forward in an unending black wave, heading straight for the demon before me. She screams and turns to flee, but it catches her around the ankle, and she falls to the ground with a thump and a gasp.

"Don't you dare question me again," I snarl. Inky black fingers haul her up, holding her by the throat.

"Can't . . . breathe," she chokes out. My finger twitches and the shadows disappear. She collapses, clutching her throat, her breathing ragged. Slowly, her eyes meet mine. I do not back down.

"Okay," she whispers. "I'll take my best men. We'll retrieve both Prophet Tontin and the two Sisters of Night."

As she limps away, Philan throws me a look, sneering cruelly. "And *that* is precisely what happens if you dare disobey Queen Catarina of Ahuiqir."

My smile matches his own.

That night, I dream of complete and utter darkness. I embrace it this time. I throw my arms out and enjoy the feeling of the whispers of mist against my skin. I savor the way my shadows swirl around me in a whirlwind of death.

And then Victoire steps into view.

"You cruel, wicked thing," she whispers, almost in awe. "How did you do it? How did you kill me?" I don't particularly feel like admitting that I was not really the one who'd killed her; I just dealt the finishing blow. But I'm sure she already knows.

"You cheater," she breathes, reading my face. "You *liar.* You didn't kill me. So who did?" I hold her gaze, but I do not open my mouth to speak. "*WHO DID?*" she roars.

"I am not obliged to answer your questions. I answer to nobody but myself."

"Foolish girl. I thought that way once." She leans forward, her deathly cold breath skittering across my skin. "I believed I would rule till the end of time. And you stole that from me."

"Do you even care what happened to your husband?" I ask incredulously.

"No, not at all." She tilts her head, considering me. "Have you found a way to steal his powers yet?"

"What?"

She laughs under her breath. "You really are stupid. Darling, I can see everything. I am no longer of this world." She waves her hand, and the void around us shatters into a million shards of darkness before revealing the night sky. A dark, inky blue swirled with gold and silver and a multitude of shimmering colors, all speckled with bright white stars. Absolutely breathtaking. "This is where that prophet comes to peer into the future."

"Tontin?" I ask. She nods in response. "So can *you* tell the future?"

Her expression closes off. "Somewhat." The sky disappears, and we are back in the darkness. I reach for her arm, but my hand goes straight through her. She chuckles. "I am not alive, Catarina. This is my spirit."

I snort, but step back. "So tell me what happens, then. In the future, I mean."

She lets out a cackling laugh. "You really expect me to hand it over that easy?" she asks incredulously. "No, of course not. The future is for you to decide, My Queen."

I shudder at the way she spits out the last word. "You know, I've grown sick of people talking in vague riddles. Just tell me, do I win?"

"Catarina, that is not how the future works. I can only see paths that you may or may not take. I do not see the entire map."

"So what are the paths that I might take?" I ask, frustrated.

"That is precisely what you need to decide for yourself."

I wrench out of my sleep, seething. Philan lays in bed beside me with his feathered wings curled around himself. At night, the sharp panes of his face look almost serene. I brush the dark curls of his hair away from his face and press a kiss against his warm forehead. Then I slide off the massive bed and step onto the balcony of our bedroom.

Night still hangs over Ahuiqir, A single tiny, white flower blooms from a brown vine creeping up the side of the castle, delicate and beautiful in contrast to the harshness of everything else. It eagerly stretches to the sky in the absence of the sun, but as soon as that flaming ball appears over the horizon, those pale petals will be burned. This is the nightly cycle of Ahuiqir, to breed hope and then kill it.

I lift two fingers to my mouth and I let out a low whistle. Moments later, I hear wings beating through the air, and my octilla, Inair, soars down from the sky, hugging the wall of the castle. Her dark scales are bathed in the silver light of the moon. I take her snout in my hands and press my forehead against it, letting out a soft sigh. Then I hurl myself over the edge of the rail.

I plummet head-first toward the ground, plastering my wings tightly to my body. I want to feel every moment of it. And then Inair's hard, muscled body is beneath me. She soars up, up, and I cannot help but let out a whoop of joy. The wind tears at my hair, ripping it free from the pins holding it in place, and I let it stream behind me in a long, brown ribbon. I lean to the right and Inair twists with me until I hang upside down. With a genuine, true laugh, I release my grip on her and let myself fall. She lets out an almost *exasperated* huff and swoops down to catch me.

Hours later, Philan waits for me in the bedroom. He is pulling a shirt over his bare chest when I enter. He casts an amused glance at me, his eyes raking over my gnarled hair and disheveled silk nightgown. "Did you have fun?"

"Yes," I breathe.

My prisoners are quiet in their cells when I sweep in. The witch and Zhengya lie curled around each other in one, while Zahiran sits in another.

"A quiet lot, huh?" I ask. Nobody responds, and I sigh. Instantly, black shadows spill from my hands and wrap around the throats of the three women. Zahiran and Zhengya hardly flinch, but Pasiphae shudders with pain. I tighten my grip around her, noticing the way she tries to stifle a groan.

"You're still injured from Victoire?" I croon.

She bares her teeth and I use my shadows to peel her shirt up. Zhengya's mouth opens, and then closes. An angry red V scars Pasiphae's otherwise smooth, unblemished back. *V for Victoire,* I think. And although I'd hated the queen with all of my heart, I cannot help but feel in awe of how terrifying she was. The wound reeks of infection. I drop her in disgust, and she collapses, the groan finally escaping her lips. Zhengya twists and turns in the grip of my shadows. Zahiran only hangs there, as if all the life has already been drained from her.

"I think I'm just going to kill you three," I muse. "I have no use for any of you anymore." I drop Zhengya and Zahiran.

Zhengya glares at me, and I almost step back. The gaze is filled with so much hatred. "Catarina," she snarls.

"What?" I ask, fighting to keep the tremor from my voice. *God,* I think. The sound of my name on her lips makes me want to free all of them. It's a revolting thought, but I'd quite like for her to say my name again. What she says instead leaves my shadows limp.

"I loved you once," she seethes.

"What?" I say. Even Pasiphae and Zahiran turn to look at us.

"I was in love with you, Catarina. But you're not you anymore," she whispers. But her voice is not gentle, and her eyes are not kind. They burn hot enough to melt through the iron bars of the cell she's confined to.

"*What?*" I repeat. The word is a whisper of disbelief. "What do you mean?" I am whining, I can hear it in my voice.

"I. Loved. You. Back at Greensbriar Manor, when things hadn't fallen apart yet. When we were happy. I thought you were the most beautiful woman in the world. I thought you were strong, brave, clever. But no. You are none of those things. You are a monster."

Each of her words is like a physical blow. When she falls back, all her energy spent, I find myself trembling. I turn for the door and escape her as quickly as I can. I withdraw to my bedchamber, my powers thrumming through the room, drawing on my emotions until I am nothing but darkness. I fall to my knees. My mind tunnels into a pathway leading to nowhere. Everything swirls around me in a blur of black and white. My power surges again, consuming me, consuming everything that I am. I am lost.

I lie in bed for hours, unable to do anything. But when I finally drag myself from my sheets, my despair has become fury. My shadows explode from my chest and hurtle around the room, destroying everything in their path. They shred the curtains, shatter the glass windows, splinter the wooden furniture. The chandelier above me explodes and rains shards of crystal and gold. I throw up a barrier of black shadows to shield myself. I let my power surge from me until it is completely depleted. As the last black stains fade away, I slip down against a wall and curl there, hugging my knees to my chest. There is nothing inside me anymore. No darkness, no magic, nothing.

I absolutely despise myself for being so weak. So emotional. *Zhengya's words mean nothing*, I tell myself. Nothing changes after this revelation. Not now that I am different. But I cannot deny her words had hurt. A small knock shakes me from my stupor. My back stiffens and I thrust out a hand, mustering the energy to summon enough shadows to crack the door open. Philan stands there with his arms crossed over his chest. He surveys the destroyed bedroom behind me, and steps forward to pluck a feather from my hair. It's from the mangled bed.

"Did your temper get the best of you?" he asks, not unkindly.

"No."

"Uh-huh." With a sweep of his hand, the pieces of the ruined bed float into the air. He opens the door to the balcony and hurls the scraps of wood over the rail. The pile falls to the ground with an ear-splintering crash. "Who was it this time?"

"Your sister," I reply, watching his half-hearted attempt to clean the room.

"What did she say?" His words are casual, but I notice the way he stiffens slightly and his eyes dart toward me.

I cannot bring myself to tell him the truth. It seems most of the words I speak to him are nothing but lies. "Nothing." And then, "I feel guilty." It's the truth. A part of it, at least.

"Guilty about what?"

"She was not a bad friend, Philan."

He pauses in his cleaning for a second before replying. "She was not a bad sister, either."

I study my hands, allowing black flames to spark at my fingertips. "Is this worth it to you?" I ask. I don't clarify if I mean the magic we now possess or something else. He doesn't ask.

"Yes," he replies without hesitation.

I smile. "Good."

"What about you?"

I lean in so close that our horns knock against each other's and our noses touch. "Yes."

"Good," he says, smiling. I smile, too.

"Philan," I breathe. "Tell General Pythea not to get Tontin. Or the sisters. I'll do it all myself."

Somewhere inside me, that vast ocean of magic deepens. I dive down to savor the brush of the cold, black water against my skin. Every once in a while, I think I see the bottom, but as I push forward, only more darkness yawns open past it. I smile, satisfied, and let myself float back to the surface. It is a long way up.

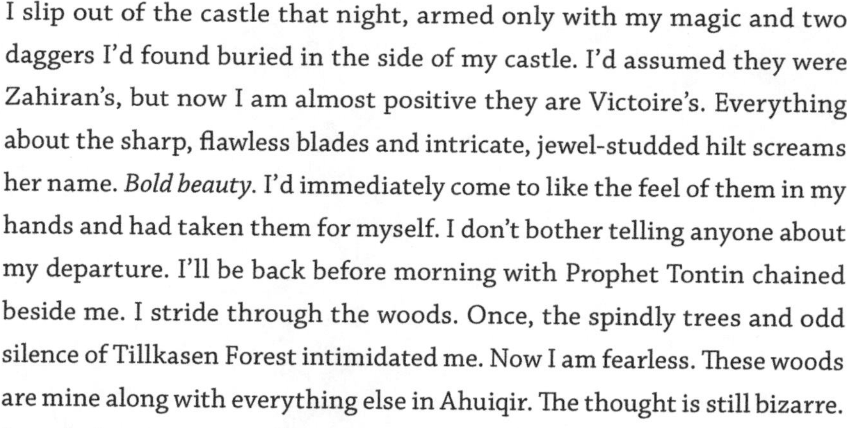

I slip out of the castle that night, armed only with my magic and two daggers I'd found buried in the side of my castle. I'd assumed they were Zahiran's, but now I am almost positive they are Victoire's. Everything about the sharp, flawless blades and intricate, jewel-studded hilt screams her name. *Bold beauty.* I'd immediately come to like the feel of them in my hands and had taken them for myself. I don't bother telling anyone about my departure. I'll be back before morning with Prophet Tontin chained beside me. I stride through the woods. Once, the spindly trees and odd silence of Tillkasen Forest intimidated me. Now I am fearless. These woods are mine along with everything else in Ahuiqir. The thought is still bizarre. I reach the entrance to Cheusnys Cave and I plunge through the barrier.

Although I hate to admit it, the cool breezes of Guinyth are a much-needed break from the heat of Ahuiqir. I gulp the fresh, clean air, then survey my surroundings. I still remember exactly where everything is. Tegak straight ahead, Pheorirya to the south, and Maarso northeast. I pass familiar streams. I see tree stumps that I'd rested on as a human, as a child. A strange, empty feeling gnaws at me, and I frown. Flaring my wings, I push off the ground and into the air.

Even from miles away, I can see the tall familiar spires of Saelmere

Castle. One of those spires flattens out into a small area large enough for two people to sit upon. I remember climbing out of my bedroom window and onto the roof with my father to watch the sun rise. I remember the cold, brisk cleanness of the early morning wind and the smell of searing meat and freshly baked loaves of bread wafting from the kitchens below us. I remember the way my mother would half-heartedly scold us afterward, and the way that my father and I would grin at each other, hair mussed by the wind and cheeks red from the cold. The empty feeling deepens, and I flap my wings harder. I land silently on the roof of the castle. I make sure to tuck my wings close against my back before hanging my legs over the edge of the roof and sliding them into the window directly under me.

Nobody is there to stop me.

CHAPTER TWELVE

TONTIN

I SENSE HER before she even steps foot in my study. The air goes cold and motionless. Instinctually, I throw up a shimmering golden shield of magic to protect us.

"What are you doing?" Maritess frowns. But when she looks at my face, her mouth snaps shut and her eyes go wide.

Catarina throws open the wooden doors.

My shields immediately sputter out from the force of her presence alone, and the five of us are left unprotected. Maritess, Ulrich, and Regan shift closer to me, and Iesso moves herself so that she stands closest to Catarina. She sneers, and my legs threaten to give out under me.

How has she grown up so fast? She's all sharp cheekbones and graceful collarbones and pristine, frigid beauty. Her skin has grown more tan in the blistering sun of Ahuiqir, and there are new lines marring the smooth surface of skin around her mouth and her forehead, but her remaining eye is clear and cold. She wears a dress of flowing mist and lambent, scintillating stars, covered by a thick black cloak. Her brown hair hangs in loose waves under her hood and her dark, feathered wings flare out behind her. Heart-breakingly beautiful, a replica of her mother. Catarina's finger twitches, and a wave of shadows spill from her and wash over us. Not enough to hurt, but enough to prove how strong she has really become.

"I assume you know what—or who—I'm here for," she says.

I see tears glistening in Iesso's eyes. I cannot even begin to imagine what she feels right now. I clear my throat, and everyone's gazes fall upon me simultaneously. "I'll go with you," I force out. Regan's hand clamps down on my robed arm instinctively, and Ulrich's eyes widen, darting between me and Catarina.

"How valiant," Catarina croons.

"I will willingly go with you. If you promise never to return to Pheorirya."

She tilts her head like a cat. "Tontin, Tontin. It's been so long, but perhaps you have forgotten? This was my home, you know."

"I am perfectly aware," I reply tightly. "But you are no longer welcome here."

She clicks her tongue in mock dismay. "What a shame. I was hoping for welcome-back festivities."

"Stop stalling," Maritess blurts out suddenly.

"You're right." A strange gleam enters Catarina's eyes, and her shadows swirl faster and faster around her. Beside me, Iesso's fist goes up in flame and I raise my own hands, but I know that I am no match for the Queen of Demons. Every single person in the room is throwing themselves back from the threat. They'd all seen the way she killed before. They all remember the woman she'd grabbed by the throat in the meeting room an eternity ago, when she was still only Queen of Pheorirya.

So, I drop my hands. I rise and look Catarina in the eye. "Do not harm these people and I will go with you."

"I thought you knew me better than this," she says, a slow smile stretching her lips. "I am not to be trusted to uphold promises."

"Just say you won't. Just say that you won't hurt them." My voice quivers as I speak. A tear slips down Regan's cheek and he wipes it away furiously.

"All right," Catarina says, and both dread and relief fill me simultaneously. "I won't." I step forward, so that I stand at her side.

"Catarina—" Maritess starts.

But then Catarina's arms lock around me and we disappear in a tornado of shadows.

Catarina soars through the sky with me gripping her hands with all my strength. The wind tears through my hair and rips at my clothes.

She peers down at me. "Not so mighty now, are you?" I don't reply, and she laughs. We arrive at Cheusnys Cave in minutes. Catarina's grip on me disappears and I drop to the floor with a grunt. She drifts down gracefully and strides through the barrier, gesturing impatiently at me. "Hurry up, old man."

"I cannot," I say. She was never one for details, so I gesture toward the entrance of the cave meaningfully.

I can see the realization dawn in her, but she feigns ignorance. "Just walk through the barrier. Are you dense?"

"I am not of royal blood." My cheeks burn with humiliation with the knowledge that seeing me stand there, completely powerless, sparks wicked joy in her.

"And what am I to do about that? Walk through the barrier."

I look at her, sheer hatred seething in my heart. "I can't."

"Just try, old man."

I no longer recognize the Catarina I once knew. Slowly, I take a tentative step into the barrier. The magic burns against my skin and I jump backward, glaring at her again.

"I thought you needed me. I won't be able to work if I am maimed." There is venom in my voice.

She tilts her head at me, pretending to think. "I suppose you're right. Fine. I grant you permission to cross." At her words, a shimmering mist settles over my body. When I reach for the barrier again, my hand passes through effortlessly. Catarina turns her back on me and begins striding through the cave alone. I struggle to keep up with her, and finally, with a sound of frustration, she throws out a stream of shadows to wrap around my waist.

"Why are you doing this?" I ask softly as she drags me through the pitch black of the cave.

"You know why."

"I'm assuming you need help acquiring Fane's power for your own."

She doesn't bother replying.

"How do you even know that I'll do it for you?" I ask.

"I don't. But if you don't, I'll kill you. I'm sure there are other witches or sorcerers or prophets out there who can help me if you can't."

"No," I breathe.

"What?" She turns to face me.

"I refuse to help you."

"That's not exactly an option for you."

"I would rather die than work for you."

Her shadows bind me and yank me toward her. She jabs a finger into my chest, and I see the flicker of satisfaction sparking in her eye when I flinch. "Tontin, I will say this one time and one time only. I will kill *everyone* you love."

"I love nobody."

"Somehow, I don't believe you."

"Kill Iesso, kill Maritess, kill Regan and Grimsbane. I don't care."

She considers me for longer than I can bare to look in her eye. "All right then. If you insist."

My eyes widen, and I reach out uselessly for her, but in a flash of black wings and shadows, she's flying back out of the cave. Headed straight for Saelmere Castle. I pace back and forth, tears flowing, cursing my stupidity. Dread pounds through my veins.

It takes her no more than ten minutes to return to the cave, Iesso screaming and writhing in her arms. When I see the two of them, my mouth widens in a silent O. Iesso looks at me fearfully.

"What have you done?" Iesso whispers.

I only shake my head and cry. Catarina watches us, clearly delighted. "Auntie Iesso, you'd be surprised to know that *Tontin* was the one who inspired me to go collect you." She inclines her head toward me, and I only shake my head again.

Iesso slowly backs away, her eyes trained solely on me. "Tontin, what is she talking about?" she whispers. I don't even try to defend myself.

"I am a fool, Iesso. An utter fool."

"Tontin, what is she talking about?" she roars. Flames burst to life around her curled fists.

"I was trying to see if she was telling the truth," I say softly.

Iesso shakes my thin, frail shoulders. "Telling the truth about what?" she demands.

"I wanted to see if she would actually kill you. I-I was wrong. There is nothing human left in her," I say softly. "She will kill us all without so much as a second thought."

"How are you just realizing this?" Catarina asks, putting on a mask of false offense.

Neither of us look at her, our gazes fixed on each other. "You were right about one thing," Iesso whispers.

"And what's that?" False hope flickers in me.

"You *are* a fool."

My face completely crumples. For once, Iesso's face does not reveal her feelings.

Catarina clears her throat, and Iesso turns back to her. "Kill me," she says roughly. "Kill me, and then kill Tontin." I don't even look up.

"No. I will not kill Tontin until he gives up the information I need. You, however, are expendable."

Iesso lifts her chin high into the air. "So kill me then, Catarina. Kill the only remaining person who still truly loves you."

"You do not love me."

"I do. I still believe that there is something good inside you, something that I will continue to fight for, even if you don't believe me."

"Then you are just as much of a fool as Tontin," Catarina sneers. "There is nothing good left inside me, Iesso. And it is just a matter of time until you realize that."

A muscle flickers in Iesso's clenched jaw, and Catarina only smirks as she watches her physically fight tears away. "I refuse to believe that. I still remember you as a human. You were kind. You were good."

"That is a lie, and you know it. I was never any of those things. Even as a human."

She doesn't reply, and Catarina sighs. "I have grown weary of this conversation."

Shadows spill from her hands and hurtle for Iesso's body. A monster inside of me awakens at the sight of her standing there with a million shards of black magic careening for her. Iesso's brown eyes are wide, like a startled doe. But she does not attempt to shield herself, even though I can sense the magic boiling beneath her skin.

With a roar of fury, I throw my hands out to either side of me. My singed flesh shrieks with pain at the sudden movement, but I grit my teeth and force my magic to flow from me. Time seems to slow. The magic inside me fights my commands, but I order it to bow to my will. I do not back down. My soul seems to rip in two at the strain, but I do not back down. Finally, the magic obeys. Brilliant, blinding light oozes out of every pore of my body, streaming toward the shadows that have almost reached Iesso. White clashes with black, and I am thrown backward from the explosion that follows. When I finally find the strength to open my eyes, Iesso has fallen to the floor but appears to be unharmed. I want to sob with relief.

Catarina looks at me, her eyes bright with wonder. And greed. "Thank you," she says breathlessly.

"For what?" I ask, stumbling to my feet.

"For proving that you indeed have the magic that I need to steal Fane's."

Catarina lets Iesso go back home by simply stepping back and gesturing toward the cave. After the harrowing few minutes in which I was sure I would watch my close friend die, the abrupt release is almost comical. I watch as Iesso casts me one last miserable stare, and then slips through the barrier. And when she finally turns out of sight, Catarina turns to me. "Do not underestimate me," she says quietly. "I hope that you now see what I am willing to do to achieve my goals."

"Your goals of killing everyone and everything?"

She smiles wickedly. "Precisely, Tontin. You know me too well. Now, where were we?" She taps a finger on her chin in exaggerated pondering. "Ah yes."

Her hand shoots out and grabs my own, too fast for me to see. Her nails cut into my flesh and a trickle of blood drips down my wrist. I try to jerk back but she holds me tight. She cuts her own hand and presses it against mine. "I will not set foot inside Pheorirya and I will not harm your friends. In return for my generosity, you are to serve me until your services are no longer needed. Only then will I let you return to Pheorirya," she says softly.

Our blood mingles, and a tingling sensation zings through my body. I can feel the blood oath sealing, traveling over my bones, and locking me to her word. Without another sound, she smirks and pulls away, wiping the blood on her hands on her cloak. When she saunters deeper and deeper into the darkness, I have no choice but to follow.

"It's beautiful, isn't it?" she says, watching me run my fingers over the cold, damp stone of the cave. There are intricate drawings and engravings all over the rough material. I trace a rough sketch depicting great lions and panthers chasing down their prey. My gaze shifts to the right, and I swallow. The next scene is of the prey being brutally mutilated. Of course Catarina would consider this beautiful.

"How old are these?" I ask.

"Centuries, millennia, who knows?" She waves a hand flippantly. The farther we walk, the more illustrations there are, until the red and black ink covers the entire surface of the stone. I see war scenes, hunting scenes, and more animals. When we reach the end of the cave, the carvings give way to writing. Thousands of letters written in different handwriting and language characters fill the stone walls.

"Initials," I breathe.

"Mhm." Even Catarina is transfixed by the writing.

"Haven't you seen these before?" I ask.

"I-I've never really stopped to look at any of this," Catarina admits. Her shadows have disappeared and there is a curious light in her eyes I have not seen for a long, long time. She hesitates, and then stoops to pick up a sharp stone off the floor.

She crouches, bracing a hand against the wall, and begins to write. *C.W.*, she scratches out. "I'd like to be remembered," she says.

For a moment, neither of us speak. We are humbled by how much primordial history is here within this cave. And then the warmth disappears from Catarina's face. She stiffens, and the shadows hiding under her skin reemerge. Without warning, her hand shoots out to grip my own and her other hand presses into the wall. A flaming, searing sensation engulfs me, and I have to swallow my scream. It's as if flames are raging within me, burning me from the inside out. But then, through the fiery hell I am trapped in, Catarina's hand reaches down. I reach up and grab it as tight as I can. And then she pulls me up, up, away from the fire.

Ahuiqir is no better. I gasp, clutching at my throat. The bone-dry air that enters my lungs is filled with sand and dust, each individual particle burning and burning and burning—

"Don't be so dramatic," Catarina sneers.

"Is it always so painful going through the cave?" I manage to choke out.

"No. It's not supposed to be. It's of the same magic that the barrier is made of. I could've granted you permission, but I didn't feel like it."

Any trust I had reestablished in her dies now. She leers at me, her white fangs flashing in the bright red sunlight. And then a shadow covers the sun. She looks up with a grin. A demon soars down from the sky. His great black wings are identical to hers. He lands, and she falls into his arms.

"Who's this?" the demon murmurs in her ear.

"Don't you know Prophet Tontin?" she replies.

The man looks at me for the first time but his gaze passes through me as if I'm an object.

"No, I'm not sure I do," he says, his arms tightening around Catarina.

"You have wed," I say blandly, noticing the silver ring on Catarina's finger for the first time. I had always imagined myself attending Catarina's wedding one day. That was when we were both devoted to Pheorirya.

"Oh, how rude of me. Prophet Tontin, this is Philan Lin. Philan, this is Prophet Tontin. He's going to help us extract the magic from Fane." Catarina's voice is a lofty purr.

He shoots me a lazy, predatory smile. "Is that so?" I immediately dislike him.

"No. I will not help—" I begin to say. Philan's shadows wrap around my throat and lift me into the air until I dangle above the ground. Catarina lets out a delighted laugh, watching Philan's shadows curl tighter and tighter around me.

"My, my. I've forgotten how fragile humans are," he says. "I can hear your blood roaring, magic man. Your lungs sound like they're struggling."

My throat is constricting, my eyesight is dimming. I can't see. I can't even think—he releases me, and I fall to my knees. My fingers wrap around my throat as I inhale huge, gasping breaths. Even the harsh, rough air of Ahuiqir is welcome. I drink it in as if I could never get enough. Philan and Catarina look down at my heaving form in distaste.

"Catarina told me of a prophet who could help us, but I didn't expect this." He nudges me with a toe and I almost fall over. I do not have the strength to fight back.

To my surprise, Catarina puts a hand on Philan's arm to stop him. "Don't hurt him," she warns.

"Whyever not?" His eyes are still on me.

"Because we need him." Catarina's voice is sharper now. "You will not harm him. Nor will anyone else."

At her tone, Philan instantly backs down. And I realize that even though he tried so hard not to show it, I see the strange gleam in his eyes. He is thoroughly afraid of Victoire. If even the King of Ahuiqir is terrified of his queen, what then? I shudder, imagining just how much power lies within Catarina Winyr.

The room I am locked in is absolutely beautiful in a cruel way. Everything is made of smooth, polished black iron. Even the sheets are of the blackest color. When I brush my fingers over the light fabric, it seems to leech the color from my skin. Vines of thorns climb up the stone walls, the impenetrable black interrupted by deep, silky red roses. A silver mirror is propped against the wall. Its border is made of black marble engraved with a language I don't recognize. Catarina clears her throat from behind me. I turn slowly. She twitches a finger, and four candles flare to life around the room.

"Whose room is this?" I ask.

"A guest bedroom," she replies.

"Why have you not thrown me into a prison?"

"Would you rather me do that?" She tilts her head.

Philan sweeps into the room, and I step back. "She's doing this out of the kindness of her heart," he says dryly.

"I can't use you if you're dead." She looks at me, and I suddenly see a glint flash through her eyes, signaling the spark of an idea.

"Go get Fane," she says, addressing her spouse. He nods, slipping away. "Come here," she says, turning back to me. I have no choice but to obey. She rolls her eyes, reaching for me in a flash and grabbing me by my collar. Before I can even think to defend myself, she swiftly rolls up one of my robe sleeves.

"Catarina—"

One of her viciously long claws seems to materialize from thin air and slashes down the length of my arm. I look down in horror as red sprays everywhere, dousing the rest of my clothing and the carpet on which we stand. But her cut had been expertly measured, breaking through only skin and avoiding vital arteries. Still, I yelp in pain. "Why?" It's the only thing I can think of to say.

At that moment, Philan waltzes back into the room. Fane enters behind him, wings bound with iron chains and handcuffed hands glowing with white light. "Kneel and heal him," Catarina's demands. Her tone leaves absolutely no room for compromise.

Fane obeys, kneeling beside my bed. A former King of Demons on his knees because Catarina Winyr told him to do so. I almost laugh at the horror.

Fane touches me and I force myself not to flinch at the feeling of his icy cold hands. And then I feel like I am floating. The smell of floral perfume mixed with a tinge of blood fills my nostrils. The scent of Clan Leader Saoirse, of my childhood, of my home. The feeling of stiff cotton washed in river water. The sounds of the witches singing around roaring fire pits, their long hair swinging and their hands clapping and their eyes alight with fierce joy. Tears spring to my eyes at the memories. I want to stay this happy forever. I want to bathe in the light that surrounds me, I want to drink it, I want to be it. And then everything fades. Including the line of fire seared into my arm. My eyes fly open.

Catarina stands over me with Philan at her side. She rolls up my sleeve to reveal newly healed skin. "Amazing," she murmurs.

Fane rises from his knees with his eyes locked solely on Catarina. She turns to Philan and gestures at the door. "Leave us, Philan." He complies and I am left alone with two of the most powerful individuals in the known world. Catarina turns back to me. "Touch him," she orders.

"What?" I say.

"Touch Fane. I want to know what you sense in him." I look to the previous King of Ahuiqir, now shackled and willing to obey Catarina's every word.

"Why are you cooperating with her?" I demand.

"Because I am a coward, Prophet Tontin. I want to live," he says. I understand.

Catarina nods her approval. "If you are wise, prophet, you will cooperate as well. Now touch him." I swallow and put two hands on Fane's bare arm. And then I jerk my arms away, my eyes wide. Catarina forces my hands back onto him.

"Do not stop until you've learned how you can capture it," she hisses.

Her eyes are wild. I dive back into the realm of Fane's gift. Magic thrums in his veins in huge, rolling torrents. I try to push forward, but the waves of golden flame rip and tear at me. I am stuck here.

"Let him in," I hear Catarina snarl at Fane. She sounds so far away.

The magic calms a little. I wade through it cautiously, marveling at the way it makes up Fane's entire being. He is the embodiment of power. In the distance, I see something darker. If Fane's healing magic is an ocean of golden light, then his shadows are a relentless storm of misery and suffering. I do not even attempt to go through it. And then, in the center of the storm, protected by the black, swirling wind, is a huge, pulsing white ball. *His mind,* I realize. His thoughts and memories and feelings are all locked away up there. Pure energy crackles around that white ball, streaking through the pitch black of the shadows surrounding it. And then I realize exactly what will happen if Catarina attains this golden ocean for herself.

Someone abruptly pulls me up and out of this world, wherever it is.

"What must I do?" Catarina asks breathlessly once I blink and rub my eyes. "What must I do to take his power?"

"Fane's mind is protected by his two gifts," I say carefully. I don't need to say another word. Fane's gaze snaps to mine, and he shakes his head silently, terrified.

Catarina's wings flare. "What does that mean?" she snaps.

"It means that you cannot take his magic without taking his sanity with it," I reply softly. I have never seen a demon cry. I've always assumed, based on what I've seen, that when a human turns into a demon, they are stripped of all their emotions and empathy. But Fane has now collapsed on the black marble floor and is trembling with silent tears.

"I-I made a deal with her," he manages to choke out to me.

"What did you agree to?" My hands turn cold and clammy.

"I swore that if she allowed me to be free after all this, I would let her take my healing gift. I never thought . . ." He doesn't finish the thought. He doesn't need to. I whirl to Catarina, who has been watching silently this whole time. A smirk curves her lips.

"Don't make me do this," he begs. "I never agreed to this."

"But you'll still be alive." Her smirk remains. *She knows exactly what she's doing*, I realize. Perhaps she'd even predicted this. Cruel, wicked demon. Always one step ahead of everyone else.

"I wanted to live," he says, his voice breaking. "Life without my sanity is not life at all."

"You swore an oath," she reminds him. Her smirk has turned into a broad smile, and I would like nothing more than to punch her across the face.

"Please," Fane begs softly, helplessly. Catarina sneers and puts her face so close to his that if she leans forward, just a little, their lips could touch. And she does, scraping her teeth across his skin. He shudders, not from pleasure, but from fear.

"No," she whispers, her breath fanning out across his face.

His eyes widen, first in fear, and then in anger. His wings buck against their restraints, but the iron holds fast. "Let me go," he snarls. Catarina only watches him. At that moment, both Fane and I realize that he is doomed.

Catarina's shadows flare behind her like a second set of wings. Fane tries to lift his shackled hands to shield himself, but it is no use. Her shadows seem to seep into his head. For a moment, he fights against her grip, his eyes crazed and his mouth open in a silent scream as his limbs jerk about. And then he stops. When I look into his milky, glazed-over eyes, I see none of the life that had been there before. He is now an empty husk of himself, a mindless drone for Catarina to control.

"What did you do to him?" I ask, utterly horrified.

"I made it easier for you to access his gift. You should be thanking me," she says. I do not thank her. Her expression sours. "Retrieve his magic for me," she orders, her voice barely more than a growl. And I have no choice but to put my hands on Fane's arm again and obey.

The golden waves lap pathetically at my ankles, greatly reduced from the towering walls of light from the first time I entered Fane's mind. Cautiously, I dip my fingers into the warm liquid. It covers my skin in a pearlescent coat. I cannot imagine all this belonging to Catarina, but I force myself to wade through the ocean.

It takes hours to reach the barrier of shadows surrounding his mind. Even the dark, swirling storm has stopped its wrath, and I am free to walk through to Fane's mind. It feels like an invasion of privacy, and even with Catarina's magic holding him in place, I can sense him straining against her. I can hear his faint screams for mercy, somewhere in his mind. The closer I get to that enormous glowing orb of light, the louder his screams get. I fight the urge to cover my ears.

"Don't do this," I hear him beg. "Don't take this from me."

"I'm doing this for my people's good," I say softly, unsure if he can hear me. "I'm doing this for my own good."

He spits a curse at me and I ignore it, because I know exactly what will happen if I return to Catarina empty-handed. Death, and neither a merciful nor painless one at that. So when I finally reach the orb, I don't hesitate to plunge my hands into the light.

Fane Liverraine is ancient. A million images—his memories—whiz past me: scenes of battle, glory, victory, love, loss, and peace. They blur together into one, but one woman is the constant thread linking nearly all of them.

Victoire, I realize, recognizing her pale hair, even paler skin, and striking blue eyes. I see the way in which Fane has gazed at her through the centuries, completely and utterly entranced. But with that adoration came jealousy.

The flickering images slow and a distinct memory forms before me, allowing me to observe as if it's happening in the present . . .

Fane watches as Victoire leans against a bed and pulls a gown over her legs.

"Help me lace this up," she says, and he complies. The dark, feather-light fabric skims over her skin, pale in contrast. He threads and tightens the delicate silver laces, covering the smooth expanse of skin on her back right between her wings.

"Turn around," he whispers in her ear. "I want to see how you look."

She turns, and his eyes widen as he takes her in. The dress is composed of layer upon layer of sheer black gossamer that together flows seamlessly down her body and around her wings. It cinches at the waist and wrists with strips of black leather. There are no adornments, no jewels, no sparkles anywhere on her. A glint of metal catches the light beneath the gauzy fabric. Two daggers are strapped to her thigh.

"I want the last thing Ceiridwen sees to be so terrifying that she forgets who she is," Victoire whispers as their eyes meet. "I want to be the wraith that haunts her, even in death. How do I look?"

"Beautiful." It's all he can say. She looks like death on swift wings, like bloodshed and war and the vengeful spirits of the dead.

The memory shifts forward a little. Victoire is nimble as a cat as she creeps through the hallways of a great black castle. This castle we are in now, I realize. But in Fane's memory it is known as Dannamoore Castle. Silently, Victoire unsheathes the twin daggers strapped to her leg. "When I kill her," she whispers to him, "let's rename this place."

"Stay focused," he tosses back, even as a smile twitches at his lips. "There could be guards."

"How does Liverraine Castle sound?" she muses.

He can no longer hold back his grin. "It sounds perfect."

There is no mistaking the queen's room. The door is decorated with gold swirls to complement the rich chocolate brown oak, and someone has painted colorful flowers and vines, which snake across the surface of it.

Victoire snorts beside Fane, and he presses a hand to the small of her back. "Do not be distracted. Remember, she knows the art of killing as well as you."

She turns and flashes a smirk. "I doubt that."

But Fane is thinking about how demons end up on Ahuiqir's throne – even gentle ones like Ceirdwen. And Victoire seems to consider it, too. Her cocky expression dims just a little.

Yet, Queen Ceiridwen does not even try to fight when Victoire leans over the bed and presses a knife to her throat. "Guess who," she says delightedly.

"Victoire Sandor," the queen says. "I've been expecting you."

"Victoire Liverraine," she corrects. Her hand curls tighter around Fane's, and his cheeks flush. Ceiridwen throws a lazy glance at their intertwined fingers.

"I suppose congratulations are in order?"

Ignoring her question, Fane turns around and takes in the full extent of the room. Empty shelves, a half-empty, half-open closet, an empty crib sitting in the corner. Everything is neat. Too neat. Something is missing.

"Where is your daughter?" Victoire asks, catching his eye.

"She is long gone," Ceiridwen says, completely unaffected. "And you will never find her. But one day she will return and slaughter you two. And she will take her place as the rightful Queen of Demons."

Neither Victoire nor Fane move for a long moment, their gazes locked on the queen. And then Victoire snaps. One of her knives slides into Ceiridwen's throat and the other finds its mark: straight into her heart. Ceiridwen makes a choked, strangled sound, and Fane smiles at the sight of her blood seeping into the white sheets around her.

"Remember me in Hell," Victoire whispers in her ear. And with a wet, crunching sound, her knives twist. Growling, she takes the knife from Ceiridwen's heart and slices it deftly across her throat.

Ceiridwen's eyes roll back and her head disconnects from her neck, falling to the floor with a dull thud and rolling. Victoire's foot stops it. Fane reaches over and plucks Ceiridwen's crown of black iron from her dresser. The crown has been passed down from the very first Queen of Demons and worn by everyone who followed her. Victoire falls to her knees before him, her daggers slipping from her hands and falling to the floor. Fane remembers this moment as the last time she will ever kneel before him—or anyone, for that matter. He places it on her head. The iron is stark against her pale blond hair. It suits her.

She rises, her face smeared with droplets of Ceiridwen's blood. Fane touches her face, scraping some of the blood onto his finger and dragging it to her mouth. She takes his finger between her teeth, licking the red off his finger, her eyes on Fane the entire time.

"Delicious."

Something in her gaze changes, something in the air changes.

She opens her bloodied palm and splays her fingers wide. A plume of smoke erupts out of her hand, billows to the ceiling, and swirls around the room. The plume wraps around Fane, curious and imploring but dangerous. So very dangerous. This is power unlike anything she's had before.

He falls to a knee before her, his head bowing and hands reaching up to clasp hers. "My Queen," he whispers. She laughs then, but the sound is not filled with light, love, or humor. It is filled with cold, triumphant victory.

Victoire is crowned Queen of Ahuiqir. Fane is crowned king two days later. Ceiridwen's daughter, Zahiran, is nowhere to be found.

An older memory materializes: The sky is filled with dragons of all sizes and colors, their wings casting great shadows on the ground. Roars fill the air. Their vibrations shake me to my very core. All around Fane, witches call out their bids, waving and pointing at the dragons they want. But something catches his eye. His gaze drifts to the ground, where four witches are wrestling with the ropes tying down a writhing mass of muscle.

"I want that one." Fane points at the black-and-gold dappled beast chained to the ground.

Yseult looks down at him with an amused half-smile. "You are too young to ride," she says.

"I want him." For a seven-year-old boy, his voice is surprisingly steady.

She considers him for a moment, then turns. "What is that one's name?" she calls to the dragon breeder standing beside the animal.

"Dusan," she replies. As if on cue, the dragon lets out a low growl and flares his mighty black wings. Fane tilts his head, observing the way Dusan's muscles flicker underneath his dark scales. His neck thrashes and flashes of gold catch the light of the sun.

"Why is he chained down?" Fane asks. "I want him to be free."

"He is too aggressive," the breeder explains. "If we allow him to be with the other dragons, he'll shred their wings."

"I want him," Fane repeats, and the breeder smiles.

"He is very expensive, young one."

"I want him," Fane says, more slowly this time and with unshakeable finality.

"What can you do to prove yourself worthy of such a magnificent animal?" the breeder asks. "He is a direct descendant of the great Ayere."

Fane remembers the legends; Yseult had recited them a million times over. Ayere had been a dragon with scales the brilliant golden color of the sun itself and claws the length of a human. Nobody had dared to ever ride him, and the witches say that when he died, he was reborn as a flaming comet that would soar through the unknowns of space until he found someone worthy of him.

"I'll ride him to prove my worth." Fane says. The breeder's words had been humorous, but he's determined now.

Yseult is beaming now, the sharp points of her teeth glinting in the sun. The breeder casts a look at the clan leader with wide eyes. She nods once, gesturing with a hand, and the breeder throws me a length of coiled rope.

"Stay up in the air for three minutes, and he is yours."

Yseult snorts, but Fane doesn't laugh. His eyes are on Dusan, and Dusan's eyes are on him. The witches around me clear a path. We all watch the beast warily as he paws at the earth, his claws scoring huge gashes in the dirt.

"Release him," Fane orders the witches holding his ropes.

"W-we cannot—" one of them starts, but with a single glare from Yseult, she lets go of the ropes and the others do the same.

The beast lets out a roar that shakes the earth, and his wings flare out. He towers above Fane, but Fane only grins. He leaps into the air, his own wings spreading and catching on a draft of wind. Dusan's eyes track Fane's path through the sky, talons poised to strike. Fane swerves just as one of those razor-sharp claws slices the air right beside him. He's reared up on his hind legs now, and Fane is almost certain he can hear his heart pounding, pounding, pounding. Another roar, but he's already landing on his back. The creature snarls and thrashes around, his tail whipping dangerously close to Fane's side. But he is too fast. He sprints up the spine of the dragon's back, feet digging into the cracks between his black scales. Unconsciously, he forms a noose with the rope in his hands. And then he throws it. It finds its mark, catching around the dragon's snout and tightening. He snarls and twists again, fangs bared.

Suddenly, they are in the air.

A gust of air hits Fane and he grunts, feet slipping. Just in time, he catches himself on a horn protruding from the dragon's back. Somewhere down below them, Yseult lets out a whoop, and Fane grits his teeth. Somehow, Fane clambers back onto Dusan's back. The beast bucks, but his grip on the rope is strong.

Dusan points his nose down, and Fane realizes a second too late what he is about to do. They fall straight down, Dusan's wings tucked in tight and a scream tearing loose from Fane's throat. He drops to his stomach, reaching for something, anything, to grab onto. They level out seconds before crashing to the ground, and Fane leaps to his feet at the opportunity. He clambers up the dragon's neck, grips his horns, and then wraps his legs around Dusan's snout. Their eyes meet. Fane loosens the noose still holding his snout shut; he's barely breathing. But the dragon does not attack. Fane slides down his neck, nestling himself in the hollow between his back and neck.

And then they're soaring, soaring through the air. A shout of pure ecstasy rips from Fane's lips and is immediately lost in the wind.

I am surrounded by all parts of Fane Liverraine. I see his happiness, I see his anger, I see his sorrow. The images swirl around and around, until I can no longer discern one from another. I want to keep looking. I want to rummage through this collection of everything Fane is until I understand who the demon truly is. It is a temptation I've struggled with every time I've looked in someone else's mind. Fatal, harmful curiosity. But that is not what I am here to do. I push past the images until I reach the pulsing core of Fane's mind. It's a tiny sphere of golden light, but the amount of sheer power radiating from it is staggering. My knees shake and I struggle to keep upright. *This is too private, it's not right.* I push the resistant thoughts out of my mind and stare at the orb. The nebulous surface is clearing. Black and gold, curling and twisting and bending together. *His two gifts,* I realize. I take the orb in my hands. Warm, soft, and comforting. And then I dig my fingers into it, inhaling sharply. It shatters into a million slivers of energy. Then it is gone.

"I have done everything you wanted me to do," I whisper. "Release me, let me go back to Pheorirya." Catarina is curled on her throne, her legs folded gracefully beneath her. Her attention is focused solely on the twin tendrils of black and gold streaming from her fingertips. I want to gag. The sheer amount of power thrumming off of her and into the air is astonishing. I can smell it, a sickening mix of decaying flesh and sweet vanilla.

"You're free to go," she says, waving a hand lazily in the air. "But remember, the second you step foot outside of Ahuiqir, I am free to attack your friends once again."

I whirl around.

She speaks before I can respond. "I promised I wouldn't bother your dear colleagues as long as you were working for me."

"But—"

"I took a blood oath, Tontin. And that was what I agreed to." Her smile is positively serpentine.

"I refuse!"

"Are you challenging the blood oath, Tontin darling? You're aware that could result in death?"

"I never agreed to this."

"Yes. Yes, you did."

I feel the oath pulsing in me, a reminder of what I have done. I ignore it with a clench of my fists. "I refuse," I say again. My voice comes out clear and steady, the exact opposite of what I feel inside. And then my blood is on fire. The blood oath burns through me, the sensation beginning in my palm where Catarina had cut it. It travels up my arm, across my chest, and into my brain.

Obey, it snarls at me. *Obey your master.*

I obey nobody, I want to growl back, but I cannot move my muscles.

I will not release you until you kneel, it whispers.

Against my will, I fall to my knees. "I will stay in Ahuiqir as long as you need me to," I tell Catarina flatly. My voice is not my own.

She smiles and gestures for me to stand. "I knew you would come to your senses."

CHAPTER THIRTEEN

BRIENNE

POLARIS AND CASILIE are growing restless and I don't know how to mollify their increasing impatience.

"Soon," I soothe. "Zahiran will be back, and we will be safe."

But I see the way Landon looks at me with a gaze much wiser than his age. He knows Zahiran has been gone for too long. He knows that I am only lying to myself. *Zahiran is dead,* my brain screams at me. But my heart tells me the opposite. And I know that if I listen to my brain, I will break. So I listen to my heart. *Zahiran is alive,* it murmurs to me. *She is only having minor inconveniences, but she will return to you.* And I force myself to believe it, because the alternative is too much for me to bear.

I have lost too many loved ones already. Tonight, as I lie in my bed of damp leaves, I allow myself to cry. I cry for Soren, for Liserli, for Catarina. And then I cry for myself. I grant myself the luxury of self-pity for just one night. When I finish, I wipe the drying tears from my face and stare up at the bright stars. I want to pluck them all from the sky, if only to illuminate the darkness here on the ground and in me. A small form settles down beside me. Landon, I realize, recognizing the smallness of his body.

"Stop crying," he says.

"What?"

"You cry every night. Stop."

I don't reply, utterly shocked at the flat tone of his voice, and he sighs.

"Don't you think that others might be going through the same thing as you? Don't you think that others might have lost their homes, their loved ones, their lives as well? Stop feeling sorry for yourself."

And then I realize that his tiny frame is shaking with anger. "Why are you so upset?" I ask.

"Because it's unfair, Brienne. Why do you get to cry? I want to too, but I don't let myself. I am grateful for every second of my life, especially now that I've almost died so many times. So why can't you be too?" He stands.

"I'm trying. You can cry too, Landon," I say, my voice breaking.

"No. You're not." He begins to leave, but then turns back. "Do you know what I see when I look at you?" he asks.

"No," I whisper.

"I see a girl who longs for adventure, a girl with wild dreams and an even wilder heart. But you don't fight for those dreams, Brienne. You don't recognize how lucky you are that you can even think about your own happiness." He hesitates. "I hate that."

Then he walks away, leaving me alone in the black silent night. Above me, a million stars shimmer as brightly as ever.

I do not sleep that night. My mind thrums with Landon's words, and I want nothing more than to close my eyes and let all my thoughts fade away into the wind and *sleep,* but I cannot. Because the little boy is right. *Selfish. Greedy. Ungrateful.* His voice echoes through my head like an endless chorus. I clamp my hands over my ears as if that will do anything. And then his voice warps into something ugly, into something more solid and sinister. I open my mouth to scream for help, but nothing comes out. I try to thrash my arms and legs, but I can't. My muscles are completely frozen. The voice in my head is growing louder until it drowns everything else out. I am suffocating in it. And then, against my will, my eyes shut and I am falling into the depths of unconsciousness. And there she stands in the darkness in all her winged, horned glory.

Catarina Winyr. She waves a hand, and the voice finally disappears. I can breathe again.

"What are you doing?" I ask. I find myself unafraid of her. I can see the slight twinge of guilt clouding her remaining eye, and the way her shadows curl around her more tightly than usual.

Good evening, my dear friend.

"I am not your friend anymore." Something like hurt flashes in her eyes. I almost feel guilty.

I wanted to deliver you some information, she says.

"What is it?" Now I am afraid. And I know from the way she smiles slightly that she can smell my fear.

Do you happen to know a demon by the name of Zahiran? she asks. *Zahiran Ladell?*

Oh no.

"No," I lie. My voice is calm, unaffected. It is so contradictory to the storm raging inside me. "I don't recognize the name."

She knows I am lying. *What a shame. She was a lovely young lady. I think you would've liked her.*

"Was?" Once again, I cannot breathe.

Don't worry, Catarina sings. *She isn't dead. Yet, at least. She has the fierceness of a well-trained warrior. She'd even make a fine general.*

"She would never work for you."

My words rip out of me in a savage snarl and Catarina lets out a delighted laugh. *Ah, so you do know her!*

"You are going to pay for all this." I do not recognize my own voice.

Oh, everyone says that. But somehow, I never do.

"What are you planning, Catarina?"

It would ruin the fun if I told you, Brienne Addington. But know this. She leans in so close that I can see the delicate points of her teeth and smell the faint scent of blood on her breath. I shiver. *It's going to be magnificent.*

Landon shakes my shoulder gently, hissing my name. I rub my eyes groggily, adjusting to the brightness of day.

"We're leaving," he whispers. I notice that he carries a small cloth pouch filled to the brim with leftover deer meat from days prior.

"What?" My mind is still foggy with sleep.

"My parents say that staying with you will do us no good. They were going to take the rest of your food, but I stopped them." I sit up so fast that I knock my head against the tree I am lying beside.

"Where are they?" I ask. He looks around fearfully.

"They left already. I stayed behind just to let you know."

I reach for him with my arms open wide, and he falls into them with fat tears rolling down his face. As he nestles in my embrace, his mask of bravery falls, and he looks like the young boy that he is.

"I don't want to die," Landon whispers.

"You won't." I pull back, holding him by his shoulders. "You are the strongest, most fearless young man I have ever met." He nods once, wiping his tears away with the back of his tattered sleeve. I hesitate, then stand.

"Wait." I pull out the rest of the dried deer I'd hunted with Zahiran. Five long strips, enough to last his family several days if they use it sparingly. I push it into his hands. "Take it."

His eyes widen. "What will you eat then?"

"I can hunt. Your family, on the other hand, cannot." He stares down at the meat in wonder. "Don't eat it all in one day," I say softly. "Watch out for demons. And just . . . stay safe."

"I will," Landon says. He turns away, the strips of dried meat tucked carefully into the crook of his remaining arm. I watch as he goes until the forest swallows him whole.

CHAPTER FOURTEEN

FANE

I WAS THREE YEARS old the first time I was able to harness and control my healing gift.

I remember being seated at the long wooden table inside the kitchen. Witches bustled all around me, transporting dish after dish of steaming food. A feast for my third birthday. Yseult's hands braced my chubby waist to keep me from falling over. It all seemed to happen in slow motion. A shriek from one of the witches, and then an ear-splintering crash. Zara had dropped a crystal vase full of bright red roses on the table right beside me.

"Don't touch anything!" Yseult told me firmly, before hurrying away to find a broom and leaving Zara to stand there, unsure what to do. I reached toward one of the larger shards of crystal, transfixed by the shimmery stone.

"Fane!" Zara said sharply, lunging for me. But it was too late. My pudgy fingers had already curled around the jagged fragment. The witch tore it from my fingers, horrified as black blood trickled down my hand. For an instant, Zara's eyes widened, as if she'd forgotten that I was a demon, before she snatched a damp rag from the table to press to my hand. And then she froze.

"How?" she whispered, her eyes clouded with confusion. There should've been a gash on my palm. There should've been more blood, I should've needed stitches. But instead, there was only smooth skin. Fresh, smooth skin. A faint pink line was the only indication I had cut myself, but even that was fading away by the second. She dropped my hand as if I was poisonous.

"A blessed baby," Zara breathed reverently. Her eyes were wide with wonder. Yseult burst back into the tent, a broom in her hands.

Zara threw the bloody rag to the ground and ran to the clan leader. "He has healing powers!" Zara cried. Yseult immediately understood, and the broom fell to the ground. Other witches were starting to gather around me.

"Tell me," Yseult demanded. "How do you know?"

"He cut himself with the vase, but Yseult, he healed himself, his skin just—" She threw her hands in the air, unsure how to explain what she'd witnessed.

"His skin just what?" Yseult urged.

"It just repaired itself!" Zara was shaking with excitement. Yseult hurried to me, determined to see for herself.

"Show me," she ordered. Zara took my hand in hers and pressed the shard of glass into my skin. I winced, but I let her do it. The pain was brief and dull, over in an instant. Black blood bloomed against my skin, and she pulled away. Yseult wiped away the blood, and her hands fluttered to her mouth in disbelief. Once again, my skin was as unblemished as ever. And instantly, everyone was reaching for me.

"Can you heal others too?" one witch shrieked, pulling at my clothes. Yseult shoved her away, but more kept coming.

"Can you heal my mother's broken arm?"

"Can you heal my sister's leg?"

"Can you bring my daughter back to life?"

"STOP!" Yseult roared. Her eyes flashed with rare fury. I almost flinched away from her. I had never seen her so angry. Instantly, the tent quieted and all eyes snapped to her. "It is my son's birthday," she said softly, dangerously. "And if I catch any of you touching him . . ." She left the threat hanging in the air, her piercing gray eyes burning through each and every witch in the tent.

The newfound magic inside me was nothing like the magic the witches possessed. Yseult had described magic as a river for anyone to draw from when needed—and only when needed. She had said it was beautiful and powerful, but also dangerous to both the enemy and the wielder. But the shimmering flower of abundance and health and joy inside me was nothing like that. Its roots stretched into my blood, planted themselves in my heart, buried themselves in my soul. It was not a river for me to draw from. It was me. I was the ruler of both life and death, the only one they both bowed to.

I burned with power.

But now I've never felt such pain. It burns through me until I can't breathe. The agony is something tangible, razor-sharp claws that grip my brain and shred it to pieces. I open my mouth to scream but nothing comes out. I writhe against Catarina's shadows, but she holds tight. Wicked joy is smeared all over her face. "Yes," she whispers. "Yes, yes, yes."

I am torn out of the memory with a sudden, violent jerk.

"No," I whisper. "No, no, no." The flower of life is plucked from me, taking with it a piece of my soul. I fight it, I reach desperately for its roots. But then it's gone. It's completely gone, and I am clawing at the emptiness it had once filled. Catarina's shadows release me and I fall to the floor, sobbing. I clutch at my chest, my head, my throat. It's gone. I scream as Tontin's eyes fly open and he leaves my brain. He presses a handful of light into Catarina's chest, and I scream again when I can sense the flower stretching its roots in her, nestling deep in a crevice it had once filled in my own being. When she holds out a hand, an ovoid ball of light sits atop her upturned palm, and then she's laughing with triumphant joy.

Tontin says something to her, but I can't hear or feel anything anymore because I am lost. The luminescence had been the one thing I'd selfishly kept to myself. The one thing setting me apart from others. And I'd built my entire being around that fact. Without the luminescence, who would I be?

Crushingly unexceptional. A king to be forgotten. Victoire's pawn, forever living in her shadow.

I shatter without the aid of my gift, like the crystal vase Zara had dropped. The fragments of me are mismatched and jumbled, scattered all across the floor in no apparent order. Irreparable.

CHAPTER FIFTEEN

IESSO

"LADY IESSO," Queen Merikh says lightly as she strides into Tontin's office, a place I'd found myself returning to more and more often. Her sister follows close behind.

"Don't call me that," I sigh, massaging my temples.

"I only refer to people as what they deserve to be referred to as," Merikh says lightly. "Now, why did you call us here?"

"It has been forty-eight hours since Tontin left with Catarina," I say. "He told me right before he left that if he did not return before two days' time, I should contact you."

"What does this mean?" Keres asks softly. I glance at her sister. Merikh's mouth is a hard line. The two queens' stars glow much less brightly today, the shimmering shapes dull and lusterless.

"It means that Tontin has been forced to help Catarina fulfill her wicked desires."

Keres's face tightens with understanding. "Catarina is not letting him leave," she whispers.

"Precisely." I brace my hands on Tontin's desk and stand.

"How is the process of moving your troops coming along?"

Her voice is sure and steady when she speaks. "The mechanical wings we designed have helped tremendously in our efforts to move our troops, but Lady Iesso, I must be transparent with you. It will take days to transport them all here."

I curse under my breath. "Is there nothing else we can do?"

"Not currently."

I look at the two of them. Even as they just stand there looking at me, the obvious magnitude of their powers is both terrifying and astounding. The air around them is charged with tension that skitters across my skin.

"What are you thinking right now?" Merikh asks me, meeting my gaze. "You look dazed."

"You both are incredible."

Keres laughs lightly, but her sister hesitates. "What do you mean?"

"I don't know. It's difficult to imagine."

Merikh's eyes narrow at me. "What are you saying?"

"Have you ever encountered a problem your gift couldn't solve?"

The queen sees right through my attempts to keep my voice neutral and nonchalant. "Lady Iesso, I do hope you're not suggesting my sister and I absorb Catarina's new powers."

Her words are harsh and her voice is frigid, but I barrel on. "You are the Sisters of Night. Dozens of legends have been written about your powers. Surely—"

"No."

I freeze at the tone of her voice.

"I will not, and neither will my sister. You cannot expect us to withstand that much power and survive. We could have done so before today, but not anymore. We will provide you with our troops and as much of our power as we can afford, but we cannot do more than that."

"I understand, Your Majesty."

Keres places a cold hand on my arm. "We really do wish we could do more."

The two queens leave for their inn, and I am left alone in Tontin's office.

Even in my sleep, monsters gnaw at the edge of my consciousness.

"How are you to win this war, Iesso?" they ask delightedly. "How are you going to rally enough troops? To provide enough supplies? How are you to win over the citizens of Guinyth and convince them to join you in your efforts?" They swarm over me, clambering and surging until I am nothing but the dread they are made of.

"Tontin will hate you if you fail. The Sisters of Night will hate you if you fail. The citizens will hate you if you fail." A gloating, malignant laugh. "Do not fail, Iesso Endrdyn."

A servant suddenly shakes me awake, and the flickering light of the candle she holds reveals I'm covered in sweat and tears. She looks away awkwardly as I wipe fruitlessly at my face.

"Somebody is here to see you," she whispers.

I look around, eyes still bleary from sleep. "What? Who?"

"Queen Merikh."

"Now?"

She shrugs. "She said it was urgent."

I groan, sliding out of bed and slipping the first item of clothing that I see around my shoulders to act as a cloak. When I reach the bottom of the stairs, Merikh has already let herself into the front door. She looks focused and determined despite the time. In the myths, Merikh and her sister were born as stars that glimmered in the dark sky with a radiance unlike any other. They played amidst solar systems and galaxies and universes and frolicked with the gods. Of course, in reality, nobody knows if they truly were *stars*, or minor deities, or even true goddesses. They fell to Guinyth regardless, burning through our world's atmosphere until their magic was allegedly stripped away layer by layer and human bodies were revealed. Immortal bodies, yes, but with not even a fraction of the strength their previous forms possessed.

"Why are you here?" I ask, still utterly confused. "What could be this urgent? How long did you travel to get here?"

She waves a hand in frustration. "The inn I share with my sister is only several miles away; it only took half an hour to ride here. That isn't the point."

The servant drapes a real cloak around my shoulders and I smile at her in gratitude before turning my attention back to Merikh. "Your Majesty, it is a pleasure, as always. But could this not have waited until morning?"

"I could not sleep, Lady Iesso. My sister and I have agreed to help you. We discussed it separately after our meeting."

"Help me with what?" I drag a hand across my face in an attempt to wake myself.

"You asked if we could consider absorbing Catarina's new magic. We have come to the conclusion that it is right."

I blink once, twice, hardly processing her words. "Queen Merikh, you must realize that I appreciate this news so much. But I really still do not see why this needed to be said now, at this hour."

"My sister and I fought about this," she says suddenly. "Do you think death is a very possible risk?"

"Your Majesty, this is war. Death is a given." My mind is clear now, all the fogginess of sleep gone. Merikh asks me questions like a child, and it confuses me.

"I do not want my sister to be harmed," Merikh adds.

"I cannot guarantee that. Did she agree to this first?"

Her gaze drops to the floor. "Yes. But Keres has always been like that, too eager to throw herself in harm's way."

"Your Majesty, I know that your sister is a wise woman. She knows exactly what she is agreeing to." I hesitate. "Why did *you* agree to this?"

"I have protected Keres for thousands of years," she whispers. "And I will continue doing so until death comes to rip me away from her."

"Is Her Majesty not capable of protecting herself?"

She stiffens, but my question was born of sheer curiosity. And after a moment, she speaks again. "One moment, Keres and I were graceful shards of light spinning and dancing through the folds of time and space, and the next, we were falling. All I can remember is the burning sensation and the feeling of Keres's hand clutching mine so tightly it hurt . . .

"'Don't let go of me!' she cried. 'Please.' And I didn't.

"We landed with an explosion of starlight and moondust. The earth trembled beneath our feet, but I managed to stand. Keres reached for my hand, and I pulled her up.

"'Where are we?' she asked me. She was afraid.

"I slid my hand into hers, casting her a forced smile that I knew she couldn't see. Gone was the lustrous beauty; suddenly, she was nothing more than a human girl with star-flecked skin. A sweetly scented breeze danced through my hair—it smelled like peonies, though I had no name for them then—and I finally looked at the world around us. The wind-swept land rolled with flowered hills and lush, emerald forests, birds sang to one another in the treetops, and deer pranced around in the soft, dewy grass. Beautiful, but nothing compared to the place we'd fallen from.

"'This must be a planet,' I said. I'd never been on one, I'd only seen them from afar.

"Keres leaned down slowly, wearily, and splayed her fingers into the young plants sprouting through the damp soil. 'Amazing,' she murmured.

"'Why has this happened to us?' I asked. Panic was starting to fill my chest. I felt as if I was bound by my ankles and wrists. This planet was not my home. But Keres was already moving away, wandering toward a tree with her arms outstretched.

"She touched the rough bark, her eyes wide. 'Come feel this, Merikh,' she whispered.

"I shook my head frantically. 'Are you out of your mind? Don't touch that!'

"She paid me no attention and pressed her whole palm against the tree. 'I can feel it,' she whispered. 'I can feel its life beneath my hand.'

I told her to stop, that she was spouting nonsense. When she didn't turn, I whirled away from her, turning my gaze to the endless blue sky. 'We need to leave this place,' I said.

"'No,' she said.

"I turned at the sound of her voice, horrified. I must have asked what she meant.

"She said, 'I'm saying that we should stay.' She was so calm. So certain. She said she wished to experience life as a mortal. That I could not expect to shield her from anything and everything for the rest of eternity. She told me she wanted to live."

Merikh shakes her head, clearing away the memory. I look at her expectantly, waiting for an answer.

"She is capable of protecting herself," she replies finally. "But—"

"Your Majesty, I do not wish to disrespect you in any way, but I believe that it would be best if you stop trying to control everything she does."

"I am only trying to protect her."

I reach out and place a gentle hand on her shoulder. She flinches but doesn't pull away. "Go back to the inn and sleep, Merikh. You can talk with her in the morning." I gesture at the servant, who hurries forward to see the queen outside.

CHAPTER SIXTEEN
CATARINA

AFTER LOCKING TONTIN in his bedroom, I creep down to the dungeon. Zhengya, Pasiphae, and Zahiran are all curled in pitiful balls. None of them move when I enter.

"Zhengya," I whisper at the barely twitching lump of skin and bones that is Zhengya Lin.

"*Zhengya.*"

Cold sweat breaks out across my skin. Unconsciously, light flares to life in my palms and illuminates the damp, dark dungeon. I banish my shadows to the darkest, deepest corner of my mind, their presence in me suddenly heavy and unbearable. Now is not the time for them. I throw open Zhengya's cell door and press my hands against her. Instantly, her pale, gray-tinged skin changes into a fuller color. Fane's healing magic works quickly. A soft sigh escapes her dry, cracked lips, and the relief that floods through me is almost palpable. I raise my free hand while keeping one on Zhengya. The healing light washes through the room, coating everything in a warm, golden glow. Pasiphae and Zahiran stir from their slumber. I turn my attention back to Zhengya. Her black hair is matted with vomit and blood, and her face is so gaunt I can hardly recognize her.

"Don't move," I whisper. And I sprint out of the dungeon. As soon as I can breathe in clean air, I lean over and retch all over the library rug. *What am I doing, helping?* Servants hurry to my aid, but I wave them off with a hiss of pain. "Get food. Lots of it," I tell them.

Servants carry tray after tray of steaming human food into the library. Once they finish, I send my shadows to chase them out. I stalk back into the dungeon and throw open the doors of all three cells.

"Get out," I snarl. "Before I change my mind." Zhengya sniffs the air, smelling the scent of the meal trays. Her gaze slowly turns to me. The gaze of a ravished, starved woman on the brink of death. She lurches to her feet, stumbling into the light of the library. Pasiphae and Zahiran follow suit. The three women throw themselves into the food piled on the wooden tables of the library. Zhengya inhales a large roasted chicken breast, juice dripping down her chin. Immediately, she gags and her stomach rejects the food. She collapses on the floor and vomits.

"Slow down," I say softly.

"No." Her stance widens, and her eyes turn predatory.

"It's all yours," I say, backing away. "I won't take it from you."

At that, she whirls away from me and continues eating, paying no heed to my warning. When the library reeks of vomit and all the food is gone, I snap my fingers. Two servants hurry forward. "Clean up this mess," I order. "And then prepare three rooms for these ladies."

Zahiran's crazed eyes snap to me. "You're not making us go back to the dungeon?"

"Don't make me regret my generosity," I snap. And then I sweep away, leaving my servants to clean up the mess of a library.

I want to scream. I want to burn down a million buildings. My shadows are my only company as I prowl into the depths of Tillkasen Forest. What am I doing? I don't know why I spared Zhengya. Or any of those three women. I do not know what came over me. I do not know anything. The dark flames swarm, froth, and seethe, spiraling from me in wave after wave of sheer power. They slice through brittle trees, leaving masses of splintered, destroyed litter in their wake. The moon stares down silently at me. Hot, fast tears spill down my cheeks. I throw my shadows over myself so that no one can see me. I am in my own dark bubble of fury, confusion, and misery. Useless.

I stumble back toward the castle, where I sit to rest, and I fall into a fitful sleep.

Zhengya Lin kneels at my feet, shackled and whimpering. I inhale sharply.

"Please," she pleads. "Do not kill me."

A knife appears in my hand, and she flinches even farther away from me. Her eyes are lined with silver tears. I watch as the silver slowly trickles down her cheeks and drips onto her thighs.

Kill her, my mind shrieks, and I move to lift my knife.

But I cannot. I cannot convince my muscles to bring the knife down into Zhengya's heart. I turn away, clenching my hands into fists to hide the shaking. When I finally turn back to her, she has somehow broken free of her shackles. Her tears have dried and left nothing but those breathtaking eyes that I could spend hours staring into. But something has changed in them.

"You can't even muster the strength to kill me?" she taunts. "I thought you hated me."

"I did," I manage to choke out. "I do."

"Then why haven't you killed me yet?" she breathes in my ear. I don't reply and she chuckles softly. "I always knew it, Catarina. You are weak."

Each word drives a stake deeper and deeper into my chest until I am gasping for air.

"Do it," she whispers. "Drive that knife through my heart and watch the life sputter out of me."

I shake my head and she laughs, reaching for the knife that still remains motionless in my hands. Her cold fingers brush mine. My heart flutters in my chest even at that slight touch.

She angles the knife so that it's pointing toward her. Poised to kill. "Do it, Catarina."

"No." My voice shakes as I say it.

Her eyes light up with wicked delight. "Oh my. Are you . . . are you in love with me, Catarina?" I freeze. "And here I was, thinking that the one and only Catarina Winyr was a little, emotionless monster. I see now. I was wrong, wasn't I?"

"I love nobody," I snarl, but even to me, my words sound the very opposite of convincing. Her free hand slides up my arm, twists in my hair, then travels back down to caress my face. I shudder, my body betraying me.

"Then wouldn't it be easy to just kill me?"

I drink in her smirking, proud, beautiful face for the last time. Then I snap.

With a roar, I drive my knife into her. She lets out a laugh, even as blood bubbles from her lips and her eyes roll back, even as I yank my knife out and stab her again, screaming in anger. And she keeps laughing until her chest stops rising and falling. I back away from her body, horrified.

I jerk awake, sweat pouring down my neck. I can still feel her blood on my hands. Then Philan is there, his hand massaging my back in comforting, soothing circles. I am just outside the remains of the parched castle grounds, but my shadows have long since dissipated.

"What happened?" he asks.

"Nightmare," I whisper breathlessly. A truth. I tell him so few of those these days.

"Why are you out here?" His arm snakes around my torso, helping me to my feet.

"I couldn't stand to be inside."

"Why?"

I freeze. "I wanted to take a walk and I got lost."

I know he can see straight through my hastily created fabrication. Thankfully, he does not pry. Something like affection flickers in me. That has always been something I've loved about him, that he doesn't need to know about every aspect of my life. My brief moment of peace is rudely interrupted when I remember Zhengya's words.

"Oh my. Are you in love with me, Catarina?"

The truth stands before me, plain and simple.

Nausea roils through me. I twist out of Philan's gentle grip. My abdomen constricts, but there is nothing left in my stomach to heave. What is wrong with me? Fane Liverraine had once been King of Life and King of Death, but I'd stolen all that from him. I should feel complete. *Is it enough?* I ask myself. *Is this enough?*

A servant hands me a small cup of something brownish and foul-smelling. "Drink, Your Majesty. It will help ease your stomach."

I snatch it from her and down the liquid in one gulp, ignoring its awful, bitter taste.

Philan puts a hand on the small of my back. "Are you feeling better?" he asks softly in my ear.

"I want to attack Pheorirya again," I reply.

"You do?" He pulls back slightly, and the servant leaves to offer us privacy.

"Tomorrow. We are prepared now, my dear." I almost want to throw up again. *My dear.* I feel disgusting for even trying to conceal the fact that I am a dirty, lying, cheating—

"I agree." Philan's voice snaps me out of my daze.

"You agree?"

"Of course, darling." He cups my cheek. "You are *Catarina Winyr.* You can do anything."

Somehow, that makes me feel infinitely better, and I brush a light kiss across his cheek.

"Gather the troops."

CHAPTER SEVENTEEN

PHILAN

I WATCH AS CATARINA stands outside Zhengya's bedroom, taking large gulping breaths before she knocks. I frown. What in the world is she doing? My presence has gone entirely unnoticed for the past several minutes.

"Yes?" a voice says. "I don't—I don't need assistance."

"It's me," Catarina says softly, as if half hoping she doesn't hear. But she does. *Why is she doing this?* I ask. It all makes absolutely no sense. Could it have something to do with the way I'd found her in the forest? There is a long stretch of silence.

"What do you want me to say?" Zhengya finally asks, so softly that Catarina is forced to press her ear against the door to hear. "I'm not sure what you could possibly want from me."

"I-I don't know."

Zhengya laughs, a short, harsh bark. Catarina slumps against the wall. "Why would you care?" she snorts. "You were the one who—"

"I'm aware of what I did."

"Am I supposed to forgive you?"

It's as if time slows. I can see every thought, every reaction that goes on through Catarina's mind. I can see her heart exploding into countless tiny shards of despair. I know that this will be the last time she ever allows her shields to come down, and that these new ones made of iron will no longer break.

"Yes. Yes, you're supposed to." Her voice is utterly frigid now. "I have offered you food, I have offered you a place to stay, I have offered you safety."

Silence. And then Zhengya throws open the door, hair mussed, fists clenched, bitter cold wind swirling around her. I'd nearly forgotten about her gift.

"I cannot believe you just said that." Her voice is dangerous. "Do you have any idea what it feels like to be locked away for days on end, begging someone, anyone, to end it all? I prayed for death, Catarina."

"I was tortured by Victoire," Catarina says softly. "Believe me when I say this. I know pain very, very well."

"So you do the same thing to your friends? What do you want? My pity?"

"No. I don't want anything from you." And then she walks out of her room, but it'd be impossible to miss the way she clenches her jaw to stop the quivering of her lips. I slip out from the corner I'd been hiding behind and grab her arm.

"Our troops are prepared," I say. "All we need to do is come up with a plan."

"How many soldiers are there?" The speed at which she can turn her emotions on and off is terrifying.

"Perhaps fifteen thousand."

"We won't need a plan."

"Why?" I ask, frowning.

"Pheorirya is weak, Philan. Their reinforcements haven't yet arrived, and they won't arrive for days. So, tell the troops to prepare for battle."

"I am not sure if that would be wise—"

"That was an order."

"Catarina, you're making a mistake—"

A single tendril of shadow snakes out from behind her and wraps around my neck. I let out a choked cry, eyes widening at her. "You may be King of

Ahuiqir, but you do not question my orders. Now," she saunters up to me, trailing her fingers up my arm, "is that clear?"

I force a wobbly smile onto my face. "Yes." I hesitate, and then add, "Your Majesty."

She nods, satisfied. Her shadows release me and I collapse. "Good. Now go."

I stand, dipping into a shallow bow before hurrying away.

She soars through the sky on Inair's back. General Pythea and I flank her, each riding our own octilli. Armor covers Catarina's chest, shoulders, and thighs. Blades of every size line the inside of her loose red gown, enough to be armor of their own. She pulls a helmet over her head. A bright red plume of feathers trails behind it, the exact same shade as the one cresting my own.

I watch Catarina evaluate the size of our army. Thousands of armed, muscled demons, all for her to control. Some sit upon octilli. Others stretch their own wings in anticipation of the flight to come. Their eyes track us through the sky, watching as the three of us land before them. The ground seems to rumble as every single one of those soldiers falls to one knee. A slow smile stretches across my face, and when I glance over, Catarina's triumphant expression mirrors my own.

"We are the strongest army in the world!" she calls to the legions. Her shadows carry her voice out into the field in which we stand, ensuring that each warrior hears her message. "And we will not be deterred by some weak city controlled by mortals. We will conquer all that there is to conquer!" Roars of approval. "And when we do, we will finally be unstoppable!" The army erupts in cheers and battle cries and shouts of excitement. "If any of you are unwilling to lay down your lives for your *queen,* leave now. Leave and never return," she adds, more quietly. "This will be your only chance to do so."

Her shadows sweep out over the crowd, lashing out occasionally at a random warrior. There are sharp inhales of breath and tensed muscles, and I can hear the way their hearts hammer in their chests. I can smell the sweat that drips down their backs. I can feel the fear radiating from every solider standing before us. Not one moves. Their faces betray nothing. The Queen of Demons smiles her approval.

General Pythea flies from my side, gesturing for her legion of warriors to join her. Hundreds of demons peel away from the rest of the army, taking to the sky. *What a sight to behold.* A mass of glinting metal, great, black wings, snapping fangs, and thrashing tails. The general shouts something I can't quite hear, and the legion falls into a close-knit formation. Another shout, and, with a flurry of black feathers, the demons begin to fly forward as our first wave of attack.

I slide a hand across Catarina's shoulder. "How do you do it all, My Queen?" I ask her softly.

"I hate losing. So, I don't."

"And how are you feeling on this fine morning?"

Her answering grin is enough to bring a smile to my own face. "I'm feeling unstoppable."

CHAPTER EIGHTEEN
FANE

I STAND OUTSIDE the castle, squinting into the sun. So bright, so very bright. Hot, too. I want to hold the sun in my palms. I want to soak in its warmth until the piercingly cold, empty nothingness in me is filled with light. I stare at it for a moment longer, until sweat drips down my nose and onto my top lip. I lick the salty bead away, and then turn my gaze down to my hands. I'd never realized how calloused my hands are until now. How interesting to not be a king.

The demon guards let me go after taking a single glance at my face, which had inspired a bout of laughter I hadn't understood. Is my appearance different? Has the theft of the luminescence had an effect on my physical exterior, too?

And then the light above me dims. I lift my head back up. A shadow has blocked out the light of the sun, a swarming, frothing shadow. I can make out the jagged edges of black feathers and the slight gleam of blades. I hear roars from octilli, and then before I know it, more shadows lift into the air. Thousands of demons blot out the sky until all I see is black. It's an image of nightmares, but I am not asleep, and this is no dream. Leading the army is none other than Catarina Winyr, Philan Lin at her side. My expression sours. The Thief who had stolen my entire life from me. The Thief who will steal the lives of many, many more.

I want to spread my wings and take to the air and slaughter her, but I cannot. After all, I am only a king knocked from his throne. A choking, hysterical laugh bubbles from my lips.

I stumble back into the castle. There are very few demons left here, only several guards tasked with watching my every move and making sure that The Thief's captives do not escape. I do not remember the names of the three women. I pause, tilting my head to think.

A guard leaning against the wall nudges me with the tip of his spear. "Get a move on it," he says.

I nod, dazed, and continue on. *I wonder if the captives are lonely. Do they want to escape?* As if in a trance, I find myself wandering up the great black staircase leading to the second floor. The captives' rooms are here, I remember.

I reach the first door. "Do you want to escape?" I call.

"What? Who are you?" The door flies open, revealing a pretty, dark-eyed girl. "Fane?" she whispers.

"Yes. I am Fane. I think. But that's beside the point. Are you The Thief's captives?"

"Who is The Thief?" She is confused.

I sigh dramatically. "The Queen of Demons is The Thief. Do you want to escape?" I repeat.

She is still confused, but she nods. "Yes, but . . . I can't. There are guards." She waves helplessly down the hall where four demons pace back and forth.

"I can kill the guards. But can you run?"

"Yes," she says breathlessly. "But there are two more people in those rooms. My friends."

"I can deal with that, too." I lift both of my arms, pointing one palm toward the guards at one end of the hallway and the other at the opposite end, where two more of The Thief's captives reside. They spot me. The guards shout to one another when they see my raised hands, but a stream of shadows bursts from my palm and slices through them. Even if my other gift has been stolen from me, at least this one never will be. Black blood explodes everywhere. I smile. "Promise me," I say to the girl. "Promise me that you'll kill her. Promise me you'll make her suffer."

She knows immediately who I refer to, and nods solemnly. Once I'd been envious of Catarina's cruelty. But none of that remains. I want her to cry as I did when she stole my life's purpose from me. I smile, satisfied. My other hand summons another swarm of shadows that burst through the two doors, fishing out the two women behind them. One looks strangely like Victoire and the other has dark skin and golden eyes.

"Run," I tell them. "Run and do not look back."

More guards are flooding up the stairs, but I kill them all with a sweep of my hand. The two women do not utter a word as they hurry past the carcasses of the dead guards and down the stairs. And then I remember I have forgotten about someone. The prophet.

My shadows fly from me, bursting through doors, windows, and walls as they search for him. They finally close around a figure and pull him to me. "Fane?" he asks fearfully.

"Can you ride an octilla?" I ask.

He gestures helplessly down at his frail, robed body. "No. I-I cannot. I'm sorry."

I point at the staircase, still littered with the bodies of the slaughtered guards, and smile as gently as I can at him. "Do not be sorry, prophet. There is no need. But you must run now. Run to Maarso or the Cities of Night, I do not care. But do not go to Pheorirya."

He nods once and turns away. And then he stops, dipping his head in a shallow bow.

"Thank you, Fane." He is the only one who has thanked me.

"It is my pleasure." I watch as he goes, and then something hits me. "Wait." He looks back. "I have one last gift for you," I say. "I grant you permission to pass through Cheusnys Cave." A shimmery golden mist settles over him before fading away.

His eyes are bright as he breathes, "Thank you."

Warmth blooms in me, sweet and comforting. This time, when more guards come running, I do not fight them off. Instead, I lower my hands and let the demons engulf me, let their shadows wash me away. A small, serene smile curves my lips even as I feel their hands lock around me.

I wonder if my death will come quickly and mercifully. I wonder if The Thief will be the one to strike the final blow. I wonder if it will hurt, or if it will be a warm wave of peace. Dark, warm peace at last. I think I'd like that.

CHAPTER NINETEEN
ZAHIRAN

ZHENGYA, PASIPHAE, AND I steal octilli from Liverraine Castle's stable and take flight into the sky. Before, I'd hated Fane with everything in me. Why had he released us? My thoughts are jumbled, and I can't figure out what to make of his sudden change of heart, except that he has a bit of compassion in him that I'd overlooked. But I don't dwell on him. Panic is cloaking itself over me as we fly. All I can think about is Brienne. I'd left her with no weapons and no protection. In the middle of a war.

Zhengya's octilla swerves in front of mine and I catch a glimpse of her face. Stone cold, emotionless. She is filled with burning anger and determination.

Pasiphae, on the other hand, shakes with fear. She catches my eye and offers me a wobbly smile. "I have never fought in a war before," she says.

I nod absentmindedly. The ground whizzes past a thousand feet below us, and the familiar hill in which Cheusnys Cave lies is up ahead. I close my eyes, granting Zhengya and Pasiphae permission the instant before we drop into a steep dive and barrel through the cave. Cool air meets my skin for the first time in days and I inhale gratefully, but I don't give myself time to savor it.

"Zhengya," I call.

She turns her head, her black hair whipping in her face. "What is it?"

"I need to get Brienne," I shout. "Keep going without me." She doesn't give me an answer and I don't bother waiting for one. They leap back into the air, the mighty wings of their octilli beating as hard and fast as the heart fluttering in my chest. I dig my heels into my octilla's flanks, and with a grunt, she presses on faster and faster. *Brienne*. I crash through the underbrush of the forest, searching for the place where I'd left her. I cannot find her. The panic that sears through me drives physical pain into my chest. Where is she? And then I collide with something warm, something solid. Something that lets out a soft grunt.

"Brienne."

"Zahiran?"

And then her arms are wrapping around me, crushing me into her chest. I think I'm sobbing, and I think she's sobbing, but I can't quite tell. She finally pulls away, teary eyed, and punches me weakly in the arm.

"I thought you'd died."

"Unfortunately, I did not." She manages a grin, and I grin back. "Are you okay?"

"I-I'm fine. I will be."

"Where is Landon? And the rest of that family?"

Her smile vanishes. "They decided to, ah, find their own way," she says.

"Why do you sound so sad about that?" I ask.

Her eyes snap back to my own. "You're not angry?"

"Why would I be?"

"I failed to protect them. I just let them go with no weapons, no protection, nothing."

"We can look for them after this is all over. But right now, we need to go to Pheorirya."

"What? Why?" She must not even know that Victoire has been killed, that Catarina is Queen of Demons. I snarl in frustration, raking a hand through my dark curls. "What happened?" she whispers.

"Catarina died, became a demon, and killed Victoire. She's attacking the city."

Maybe the war has made her less curious, because she's already running for my stolen octilla. She swings herself over its back and then helps me up. The creature lets out a huff and shakes out her wings before flaring them wide and taking to the sky. My heart has grown lighter, if only just a little bit. I tighten my grip on Brienne's waist, reminding myself that I am alive, and she is alive, and everything will be all right.

But we still have a war to fight.

CHAPTER TWENTY
PASIPHAE

SOMETHING IS WRONG. The river of magic containing the energy of the world has been drained, completely drained. I fall to my knees. *No, that's not possible,* I think. But then why can't I feel anything? Why can't I sense the comforting presence of the magic surrounding us all? I delve into the deep caverns of my mind, searching, calling. *Where are you?* I call. *I need you.* And then I feel something. An ember in the darkness.

I am here, the magic replies weakly. *I am still here.* I reach out a hand, and the tiny sliver of light curls around my fingertips. *Pasiphae, Pasiphae,* it sings. *I have missed you dearly.*

Show me, I demand. *Show me what is happening.* The magic complies. It shows me an endless, infinite river of soft, glowing waves flowing through solar systems, galaxies, and other distant universes. My breath hitches. *This is what the magic of the universe is supposed to look like,* it says softly. *But this is what it looks like now.* The voice falls silent for a moment and the image before me changes. I inhale sharply. The mighty river of gold has been replaced with a weak, feeble stream of magic that diminishes by the second. So, so frail in comparison to what it was before. *Do you know why this is happening?* the voice asks.

No, I reply. *Tell me.*

There were two very powerful people. Because there were two of them, and neither was more powerful than the other, everything was balanced.

Who were they? I ask.

The voice does not respond to my question. *And then something happened. The magic of one of them was transferred to the other. The magical balance of the universe was completely destroyed. A single being should not be able to hold so much power; it goes against the laws of nature itself.*

Who. Were. They.

Patience. I am surprised you haven't figured it out for yourself yet.

Fane and Catarina. When the realization dawns upon me, I somehow instantly know that my suspicions are correct.

Precisely, the magic purrs. *Catarina must be killed.*

What happened to Fane? I ask.

He is . . . alive, the magic says carefully. *But he is not himself. The prophet has made a grave, grave mistake. He's tampered with something that is best left alone.*

Prophet Tontin?

He was the one who helped Catarina steal Fane Liverraine's gift.

So, what must I do to stop this?

I'm sorry, Pasiphae. You must find that out for yourself.

No! I cry. *Tell me what to do.*

I have no mind. I have no thoughts. I simply observe.

You must be able to tell me something. Anything. Even in my head, my voice is pathetic and desperate.

I'm sorry, the magic repeats. *I cannot.*

I almost fall from my octilla. I feel a searing pain. I let out a shriek, my mount writhing in confusion beneath me. *Save me.*

And then Zhengya is there, her fingers an iron vice around my wrist. "Calm down!" she shouts. "What happened?"

But I can hardly hear her over the pounding in my ears and the frantic beating of my heart. I can feel the river of magic draining even further.

And as each drop is extracted, it feels as if a part of me is extracted along with it. *Catarina is using too much magic.*

Zhengya is shaking my shoulders, slapping me. "Pasiphae!" she shouts. My vision finally clears, and I jerk away from her. My octilla drops several feet, letting out a savage snarl. My stomach plummets with the drop.

"Control the damn beast!" Zhengya screams. Her own octilla is bucking with bewilderment, its paws flying about and its tail lashing. She struggles with the reins. I manage to tangle my fingers in my own reins and tighten my grip on the creature. She finally levels out and glares at me. "What happened to you?" Zhengya demands.

"Catarina has arrived in Pheorirya," I pant. The ringing in my head has not receded, and my vision still swims with red. "She's going to kill them all."

Zhengya's piercing blue eyes narrow to slits, her head turning to face forward. "No, she's not." And she digs her heels into the furred sides of her octilla to spur him on faster.

I dive back into my own mind to search for the river of magic again. Since the beginning of time, witches have been the caretakers of the river, responsible for its wellbeing and ensuring that no singular being gains too much power at once. But I'd never imagined that such a thing could even happen. *Perhaps this is why demons exist*, I think. The universe tends toward chaos. Maybe things have simply been orderly for too long.

We are only minutes away from Pheorirya when the stabbing pain returns, signaling further drainage of the river. I let out a gasp, and this time, I do fall off my octilla. The air rips at me, tearing at my clothes and clawing at my skin. I feel empty. There is no trace of the great, mighty river of gold, even though the world around me seems to feel no change. The damn birds still sing, and the sun still shines. Time seems to slow as I near the ground, but I feel no fear for my own life. What will happen now that Catarina is truly the most powerful entity?

Zhengya screams my name from above, and I catch a flash of black feathered wings as she forces her octilla into a sharp plunge. But she will never reach me in time. Gravity is pulling me down, down, and I allow it to happen. Death would be so much better than life now.

A gust of wind sweeps me into a glacial embrace and cradles me like a baby. The frigid cold seeps through my clothes and into my bones. My eyes fly open with a gasp. I am mere inches from the ground, and I look up to see that the only thing keeping me from falling is a gift of magic. Zhengya's hand is outstretched, and an icy wall spurts from her fingers. She soars down, her expression of desperation morphing into relief.

"How did you do that?" I breathe.

"Have you forgotten? I was once a princess of Tegak." She extends a hand, helping me back onto her octilla. I look up and spot the tiny figure of my octilla flying up and out of sight. We continue on our way. Zhengya's hands are braced firmly on my hips. "What happened to you?" she asks after a long period of silence.

"It's gone."

"The river of magic?"

"Yes."

"Catarina?"

"Yes."

She curses under her breath. I look down at the countryside passing by and see the green leeching from the earth as we fly. Entire fields of grass are turning yellow and sickly, crops are wilting, leaves are falling. Zhengya's gaze flits down for only a second before she looks away and blinks back tears. Below our flying creatures, the dying forest becomes a suffering city. Blood stains the stone buildings and cobbled streets. Bodies are piled haphazardly, with faces marred so horribly they'll never be recognized. The stinking pile attracts flies and maggots and demons. Too many of those bodies are human, and not enough have wings and horns and a tail. Most buildings are ruined, and even the ones that remain standing are smoking. The people trapped inside scream for help that will never come.

Catarina's demons are feasting upon the mounds of bodies, red dripping down their chins as they eat. Fangs and claws dig into human flesh and bones. They shoot us lazy, predatory smiles as we pass by. My stomach clenches in horror.

"Don't look at them," Zhengya says in my ear. A whimper slips from my lips. I can't tear my eyes from this massacre playing out below me. I can't do anything but watch as another city is obliterated. *"Don't look at them."* Zhengya's eyes are focused on the castle miles away, refusing to look anywhere else.

This time I obey, wrenching my gaze from the ground. Still, cold sweat beads on my brow and slides down my back. I shiver even in the warm sunlight.

"Zhengya? Pasiphae?" a voice calls from behind us. Zhengya whirls, her hands poised to strike, but immediately lowers them when she recognizes the approaching figures. Zahiran and Brienne are soaring toward us on an octilla. Bright, hopeful smiles are pasted on their faces. Neither I nor Zhengya attempt to smile back.

"We need to go," Zhengya says in that quiet way of hers.

Zahiran and Brienne's expressions harden. Zahiran gestures to the castle, a grim smirk on her face. "Lead the way, then."

CHAPTER TWENTY-ONE

IESSO

I AM FILLED WITH undiluted, violent rage. I want to *strangle* Catarina, the woman who is demolishing my home, my city, my life. The castle rattles with each hit it takes, and servants bleat in terror with each tremor. Merikh and Keres arrived only hours ago. They are just as frightened as the servants, their eyes glued to the windows, watching the black flames that tear through the city.

Catarina is a whirlwind of shadows, darkness, and night. She rains down upon Pheorirya with her wings spread wide and her shadows snaking across the land, and paints the world in red. The man I've learned is her spouse, Philan, dives down after her, and I hear him let out a whoop. Their blades flash and gleam in the pale sunlight as they carve into body after body. The demon warriors are an unyielding wave of black, surging forward and consuming all that gets in their way. When that wave falters, Catarina's healing gift is there to heal any injury and countermand any fatality. General Pythea slashes her way through a throng of villagers until she's back-to-back with Catarina. The humans fall beneath her blade like stalks of wheat under a scythe.

"Can't you do something?" I hiss. "If she is not stopped now—"

"Lady Iesso. We are quite aware of the situation." Merikh's voice is perfectly steady, but I see her fists are clenched. "However, if we go out now, we will be killed. There are too many of them."

A servant hurries by me and I grab her arm. "Where are our warriors?"

"They are still in their camps on the far side of the city. The last message we received from General Lilura Tenebris informed us that it will take another hour for them to arrive."

"Why were they not prepared for this beforehand?" I demand. But I already know the answer.

"None of us were, my lady." She looks around anxiously. "Now if you'll excuse me, I have many things to tend to."

I release her, and she strides away. I don't realize I am shaking with anger until Keres plants a firm hand on my shoulder.

"This is not Catarina's home anymore," she says softly. "She does not know Saelmere Castle the way we do, the way you do. We can try to trap her and weaken her. Then Merikh and I can absorb her magic."

"So let us go, then," Merikh whispers to her sister, turning away from me. "There is no use in staving off our inevitable death."

"Don't say that." Her sister's words are fierce.

"Would you rather me say we're *not* going to die? Would you rather I sugarcoat everything? Keres, I am simply stating the truth."

"I hate her." The three quiet words are infused with so much savagery that I almost step back. Keres has always been the gentle one.

"Then let us make her pay," Merikh replies softly.

Keres holds her sister's heavy, unseeing gaze. And although she cannot *see* the violence around her, I know for a fact that she can smell it and hear it. It seems that both of them have forgotten that I stand right beside them.

"All right then," Keres says. Silence. Another rattle shakes the castle so hard that I have to grip a bookshelf for support.

Below us in the streets of Pheorirya, a new wave of Catarina's army draws closer and closer. If I strain my eyes enough, I can make her out at the very front. The shadows around her are a living thing, striking when she strikes and shielding her unprotected sides. *Human Slayer, Black Assassin, Queen of Shadows,* I hear the demon warriors chant. *Run, run, run!* I hear the humans scream. She slaughters everyone in sight.

When there is nobody left in her path, she looks straight at Saelmere Castle, and for a moment, I swear our eyes meet. She flares her wings and takes to the sky. My heart drops to my feet. Arrows spiral toward her, but she simply plucks them from the air and hurtles them back to the ground in the direction of the archers who'd shot them. Someone approaches her from behind, and she whirls around, sword raised. I can see that it's only Philan, just as bloodied and sweaty as she is. I can't hear the words they exchange, but Philan offers her a flower, pushing aside tangled, blood-matted hair to tuck it behind her ear. She leans forward to whisper something in his ear, and he smirks at her before bowing and taking off once again. And she turns her attention back to Saelmere Castle. Even from my vantage point, I can see the wild grin that stretches her mouth. Her heels dig into her octilla's side as she spurs it on.

I hear an enormous explosion downstairs, and everyone in the room inhales sharply. The castle has been breached. "Don't panic," I say quietly.

People distantly begin screaming and I clasp my hands together, unable to stop their shaking. Slowly the screaming dies away, and my mouth goes dry as I realize the only thing that could mean.

"Auntie Iessoooo," Catarina calls loudly. She's in the castle, wandering the halls. "Where are you?"

I can smell the distinct, rotting smell of her magic, even from within Tontin's office. Her footsteps stalk down the hallway we're in, and someone lets out a moan of fear. I plant my palms face-down on Tontin's desk. My breaths are uneven and labored.

I can hear Catarina throw open each door one-by-one. She's getting closer. And then the door of the room directly next to ours slams open.

Save me, I pray. I can see Catarina's feet through the crack under the shut door, and seconds later, the door handle rattles side to side.

"Ah," she says, and I throw a desperate glance at the window behind me.

Could I jump out and end it all myself now? It takes all my willpower not to. "So this is where everyone has gone," she crows. "Auntie Iesso, I have come to pay you a visit."

I don't respond, and I can imagine the smile on her face growing wider.

"Wouldn't you like to come out? Wouldn't you like to greet your beloved niece?"

Someone chokes on a stifled sob, and Catarina laughs. "Now, now, no need to be scared. Don't you all remember me? I was the Queen of Pheorirya once. It seems so long ago."

Silence. And then I'm pushing my way through the room and throwing the door open before I can convince myself not to.

"I will give you one chance, and one chance only, to get the hell out of my home," I warn, feeling smoke rise from my fists. Catarina looks nothing like she used to, and still somehow exactly like her mother. I cannot even look into her remaining eye without seeing my family, my own sister.

"Spirited, aren't you?" She looks down at me in amusement. I snarl, and my hands burst into flames as I summon my gift.

"So, what'll it be, Catarina? Do you want to fight it out, or will you leave peacefully? Nobody else has to die today."

"Personally, I enjoy death. I relish it. And besides," she peers pointedly around me, looking into the office where perhaps twenty people are huddled under bookshelves and desks, gazes locked on us, "I think the people would like a show."

The sight of Catarina standing there, with blood dripping from her armor onto the fur rug and her eyes dark with maniacal, fiendish delight, is enough to make a stone cry. I think I am going to vomit. The orange and gold flames that dance around me seem like pitiable puddles in comparison to Catarina's roaring ocean of black fog and shadow. At that moment, I realize Tontin had been painfully accurate the last time I'd seen him. There is nothing human left in Catarina Winyr. But I can't let my fire die. I can't allow her to win without a fight. So I raise my hands and widen my stance and grin, beckoning her closer. She smiles back, cunning and wicked.

Shadows explode from her, engulfing the room. I brace myself for the burning pain sure to ensue, but none comes. Instead, the darkness drags down my mind, muddling my thoughts and clouding my memories. I scream at it to release me, but it holds fast. I am hauled down into an ocean of black.

When I open my eyes, I am floating in a dark abyss. Catarina is already waiting for me, picking at her nails and leaning casually on the hilt of a sword.

"Why did you bring me here?" I ask hoarsely. "Why didn't you kill me?"

"I wanted to have a conversation with you, Auntie. I wanted to talk to you without the company of your servants."

"Stop calling me that."

She curls a lock of hair around her finger. In this alternate world, she is wearing nothing but a thin black lace dress and there is not a speck of blood on her body. Her eyepatch is new and clean. Her thick metal helmet has been replaced with the crown of black iron, which sits atop her freshly washed hair.

"I'll call you whatever I like, Auntie." She leans in close. "I'm going to give you a choice. You have no idea how easy it would be for me to kill you, Iesso. Barely a twitch of my finger. I only spared you because I like playing sentimental. So I'm only going to say this once. Either give me Pheorirya or die."

Immediately, my mind is urging me to surrender and walk away free. Alive. I hate myself for even stopping to consider that option. Then again, what choice do I have? If I do surrender, Catarina will have free rein to all of Pheorirya, including the people inside. Including everyone I love. And I know she can see the war raging inside me because a smirk plasters itself on her face.

"So, what'll it be?" she asks me. "Certain death or eventual death?" She has no intention of keeping me alive at all, even with Pheorirya cupped in her hands. We are utterly at her mercy. The air inside my lungs is suddenly stale, and I think I'm going to be sick. "Don't fret, Auntie. You have all the time in the world to make a decision. Here, time is nonexistent."

"Where is 'here?'" I ask, desperate to delay whatever is going to happen to me.

"A hiatus," she replies. "A hiatus between life and death, perhaps." She hesitates.

There is a long moment of silence. "Are you happy?" I whisper suddenly. It is her turn to be confused. "I mean, are you truly happy? As a demon?"

"Why wouldn't I be? I have all the wealth, power, and ability I need—and more."

"Don't you think there's something more to living besides . . . killing?"

She lets out a genuine laugh. "My dear Auntie, I thought you knew me better than this?"

"Better than what?" Dread pools in my stomach.

"I do not need to be happy. I don't need anything besides my power and my own wits. Rip out my heart, for all I care. And then you'll finally see for yourself."

"See what?" My voice is no louder than a whisper.

"See that I don't have one."

"They've taken over you." I am unsure if I am still talking to her or to myself.

"Who has?" she asks, in a way that implies she knows exactly what I'm talking about. Her smile is stretching so wide that I have to force myself not to back away. Something flickers in her remaining brown eye, and I swallow a gasp. Black is spreading across her iris, and it doesn't stop until it's covered the entire surface of her eye.

"The shadows." I will myself to barrel on. They would explain the cold decisiveness in the ways in which she acted. She only smiles again, her shadows slowly billowing behind her like an endless sea of mist.

"Oh, I know."

My eyes widen, and then I fall to my knees in despair. She doesn't care about what she's doing with them, or what they're doing with her. "Catarina, they will kill you, they will destroy you—"

"And I am perfectly fine with that." She brushes an ice-cold finger along my jaw, and she is close enough that I can see how truly deep and eternal the black in her eye is. "I was always destined to die, you know." Her voice is no longer her own. It is harsh metal, something entirely inhuman.

My legs move on their own, propelling me back and away from whoever—no, *whatever* this thing is.

"You can't leave yet," she sings. She starts walking toward me, her steps unhurried. Casual, even. Like a predator stalking its prey. "You must still pick. Surrender, or challenge me."

Her face, her body, but not her, I remind myself. *This is not Catarina. This is not Catarina. This is not Catarina—*

"Neither," I call. *Time. I need time.* She blinks away from sight, and for a moment, I am left alone in Hiatus. And then she materializes right behind me. I cannot contain my scream. Icy claws dig into my back, but when I frantically whip my head around, she is not touching me. Her shadows are. I throw them off of me, tripping. Half crawling and half stumbling, I push myself away from her. "Don't touch me," I gasp.

"You still must pick. Surrender, or challenge me."

"No, no. I can't—"

"You still must pick. Surrender, or challenge me."

"Stop!" My voice is rising in pitch now.

"You still must pick. Surrender, or challenge me." She is only inches away now, and a dagger made of iron has somehow appeared in her hands, poised to stab me.

Something in me breaks. "I surrender! I surrender."

Both the shadows surrounding her and the dagger in her hands disappear. "Good."

And then the darkness around us falls away. Harsh, blinding light hits my eyes, and I clamp a hand over them. *So bright.* When I finally lower my hand and look around, we are back in Saelmere Castle. The servants are still in the office behind me, and Catarina still stands before me. We are in the exact same position we'd been in before. Catarina lifts her hands in the air.

"Iesso Endrdyn has officially surrendered the City of Pheorirya to

Ahuiqir, Land of Demons," she calls. The servants' gazes shift to me, shock and betrayal etched all over their faces. I burn with shame. "I shall grant you all two days and two nights to leave this city. But after that period of time . . ." she beams wickedly, "the demons have every right to tear the flesh from your bones. There is nothing left for you here."

A child starts crying behind me, and I can hear his mother desperately trying to quiet him. Catarina pauses. *Be quiet,* I beg silently. *Please.*

"My, my," she says, her gaze sliding to him. "How rude of that baby to interrupt me."

He continues wailing and wailing and wailing. I turn to look at him. His mother's eyes are hauntingly devoid of life, filled with incessant exhaustion and endless weariness, so contradictory to her wrinkle-free, slender face. She is young, far too young to have lived through a demon siege, let alone a demon siege with a child to protect. Her tired eyes turn sharp, razor sharp, as her arms lock around her son's thrashing body.

"You will not take my son from me," the mother snarls, and the words are filled with a feral violence I hadn't expected from a woman with as dull of a gaze as hers. A mother preparing to defend, to lay down her life for her child.

I want to fall to my knees and beg and beg and beg for Catarina not to do anything, but the people around the mother are already starting to inch away in fear, clearing a direct path for Catarina to reach her. I see the exact moment she realizes she is completely unprotected, because her mouth falls open in a soundless *O.*

"Please," the mother says. The single word is thunderously loud in the silent room.

"Unfortunately, disrespecting me is a crime I cannot forgive."

"He is only three months of age—" I hate that I can't hear any of the mother's untamed fury from a moment ago; all I can hear now is desperate pleading.

When I look back at Catarina, her eye is black with malice. I see absolutely nothing worth saving anymore. So when she lifts her palms to aim her shadows at the child, I leap forward and tackle her with a scream. My arms blindly wrap around her neck and my nails scrape at her skin. She lets out a cry of surprise, twisting, but I plant a foot on one of her wings to keep her from throwing me off. "I will murder you," I hiss in her ear. "I will—"

Something hits me in the chest with so much force that I fly off of her, all the breath whooshing from my lungs as I land flat on the floor several feet away, stunned and wide-eyed. She pushes to her feet, and I instantly know that I've underestimated this woman. Her eye is ablaze with black flame. She bares her fangs in a snarl, and her hair flies wildly around her. She lifts her arms as she stalks toward me, summoning the shadows lurking under her skin but also the shadows of the room and even the rest of the castle itself. They spill from every crevice, flowing in from the window behind me, from the door behind her, from under the walls. The room looks like a sinking ship. The shadows loom above her, contorting to her will.

She slides to her knees, one icy hand slipping beneath my neck to cup my head. "I nearly didn't expect you to do that," she whispers next to my ear.

"Don't touch me," I hiss, attempting to push away from her. But her other hand snakes up my body, closing around my neck.

"Or what?" she purrs. Her touch is burning hot and freezing cold all at once; I feel the invisible fingers of her shadows slide across my skin.

A low moan sounds from somewhere behind us, along with the sound of footsteps hurrying across the floor. I don't even have to look to know that everybody is using the distraction as an opportunity to attempt to escape the room. Catarina lifts a single hand. She only looks at me as she does it. A burst of black shoots from her palm, spiraling toward the open door and slamming it shut, and the group falls apart in wails and screams.

"I can hear your heart beating," Catarina whispers as if nothing has happened. "As a matter of fact, I can hear the hearts of every single person in this room beating. But yours pounds especially hard."

"Let go of me, Catarina." My voice carries an edge of hysteria that's perceptible even to me. I thrash in her grip, but the tips of her fingers dig into the sensitive flesh of my neck enough to bruise, and I stop for the pain.

"I think I've tolerated you long enough," she says, and I go rigid, my fear freezing into fury.

"*Tolerate?* I'm your goddamn aunt, how dare you—"

Her eyes flash and I hear the distinct sound of bones cracking. A million thoughts flash through my mind in the span of a second. At first, confusion. *Did I imagine that? Has she somehow killed someone else, even when both her hands are still on me?* Then, a flash of pain that dulls immediately into numbness, followed by realization.

Finally, I feel wrath. I hate my sudden inability to move, and the way she still gloats down at me, even as my vision dims and she blurs away into nothing.

Into the nothingness I descend, the blackness yawning open below me like a void. My body seems to fall faster, even as my mind stays stationary. It feels like I am separating and spreading through the abyss at an excruciatingly slow rate, giving me ample time to feel it all. Despite the lack of physical pain, the sensation of losing something vitally irreplaceable, bit by bit, is torturous.

I'm suddenly jerked away from the void. The shards of my soul, or whatever parts of me have dispersed, are thrust back together as if pulled by a magnetic force. I am in the same position as I'd been before, on the floor in the middle of Tontin's office. But everybody is staring at me, wide-eyed, mouths gaping open, as if I'd risen from the dead. And when everything hits me again, I realize that is exactly what has happened. *Catarina's stolen healing gift,* I realize with a soundless, sharp intake of breath.

And Catarina is only staring at her hands, which still glow with the remnants of the gift. She looks awestruck at herself.

"Oh my God," someone behind us breathes.

I whirl around. Merikh and Keres stand in the doorway, their mouths agape and their eyes wide. When my eyes meet Merikh's, I can see her terror. But then she looks away, instantly reaching for her sister's hand. Their fingers intertwine and both of their eyes flutter shut. Power flows between them, each woman's gift only strengthening the other's, until they are one. Golden light emanates from both of them, becoming brighter and brighter until Merikh falls to her knees, followed by Keres.

Catarina lets out a shriek and collapses. Nothing visible has happened to her. Then I see black mist lifting off her body and floating toward the sisters' golden light. Their magic finally reaches Catarina's black and gold, clashing and mixing into something awful. Keres curses under her breath, but the two women do not let go of each other as they absorb Catarina's magic. Merikh screams. The darkness is seeping from Catarina and pouring into their bodies, never-ending. With each second that passes, the sisters' faces grow more strained with pain.

I cannot even begin to imagine the weight of Catarina's power upon one's soul, something so evil and monstrous. And from the way that the sisters' backs arch as they take in more and more, it seems as if the shadows are scorching them from the inside out. Catarina is fighting back. She claws at the golden light, snarling and destroying surge after surge, but the sisters do not cave in. Their light is as unrelenting as the rise and fall of the ocean tide. I can see the precise moment Catarina begins to weaken. A bloodcurdling, furious screech tears free from her lips and her shadows begin to pull away from her in great, flowing waves. I know that she is powerless to stop it.

A burning smell fills the air from the sheer amount of power wrestling between the three entities. The others in the room cry out and curl together, shielding one another. I do not believe myself to be a cruel person. Yet, as I see my niece kneeling on the floor, her arms wrapped around herself, I want to do nothing but drive my blades into her body until she is an empty shell. The fiery storm of roiling, seething fury inside me is growing to the point of almost physical pain. Just this once, I will allow myself to be the evil one.

I have been the weak one for too long.

So I lift my blades and stalk toward the fallen queen. It is as if her very essence has been stripped away, layer by layer. She rocks back and forth, pulling her hair and suddenly looking utterly terrified. Is this what her greatest fear has been all along? Being powerless, vulnerable? She looks up at me, cheeks stained with tears and eyes welling with more.

"Aunt Iesso," she pleads. "Help me." They are words that have never left her mouth before, but she's clearly beyond the point of trying to preserve her pride. I do not think I have ever been filled with such blinding fury in my life. How could she think I'd help her now? Flames dance at my fingertips, but I restrain them carefully.

"Do you have any idea how long I've waited for this moment?" I whisper.

"What are you doing?" she breathes, trying to back away. A brief twinge of satisfaction ignites within me, knowing that she can see the rage burning in my eyes.

"Burn in hell," I snarl.

I drive my dagger up into her chest, past her ribs, and into her heart. She collapses with a small huff of surprise. Across the room, Keres and Merikh are still kneeling on the ground, their eyes squeezed shut.

"Release it," Keres growls at her sister. I watch as Merikh groans, gathering up every last ounce of energy she has. And then she pushes away the darkness and pushes away the light. Keres strains beside her, and finally, it all expels from their bodies and into the world with an explosion that rattles the castle and the earth below it. Sheer power blasts away from them in waves until finally, it is no more. And suddenly, abruptly, the heaviness in the air is lifted, and it feels as if I can breathe again. The downright relief I feel is so overwhelming that I fall to my knees, looking around in dazed shock.

"We've won," I whisper to nobody in particular.

Merikh finally releases Keres's hand with a gasp, looking at her thorough shock. "We've done it," she breathes, tilting unsteadily. But then I see the blood trickling from both ears, her nose, and her bloodshot eyes.

Keres looks exactly the same. "Merikh," she says hoarsely.

And then she falls over, her unseeing eyes rolling back into her head and blood bubbling on her lips. I let out a cry at the same time Merikh does, reaching for her. But then she collapses too, falling to the ground right by her sister. Three bodies lay around me in a circle.

CHAPTER TWENTY-TWO

ZHENGYA

WHEN I THROW OPEN the door to Tontin's office with Pasiphae right behind me, everything is wrong. Two women whom I assume to be Keres and Merikh, from the constellations glowing faintly on their skin, are on the floor, blood running in a scarlet river from their unmoving bodies. I don't know why they're even here, but I can't be bothered to think about it for more than a second. The scent of that blood fills my nostrils and muddles my mind, blurring my vision until all I can see is the destroyed room and the dead bodies and the—*Catarina*. Where is she? I whirl around, my eyes wild and my breath frozen in my lungs.

"Where is Catarina?" My voice is nothing more than a hoarse whisper, a murmur to add to the symphony of agonized wails around me. My fists clench and my eyes squeeze shut, and even then, all I see is red. Something buds in the pit of my stomach, heating the blood roiling through my veins and spreading through my body until it leaps from my throat.

"Where is Catarina?" I scream. But even then, it is not enough to capture the attention of anyone for more than a second. Finally, a single servant sees the furious tears that spill down my cheeks and her eyes soften. She points a finger at a shuddering heap in the corner of the room. And there she is. Everything else fades into nothing, and suddenly, all I can see, all I can perceive, is her. The once almighty Queen of Demons is now curled on the floor, her shaking wings wrapped around her. There is so much blood. Not a single shadow swarms around her, and she looks so young, so normal without her magic. Brienne, Zahiran, and Pasiphae hurry to the Sisters of Night, oblivious to my panic.

"Get a physician—a healer. Now!" Zahiran growls, and three servants leap up and rush away to look for one. But everything around me diminishes into nothing more than a fog of hazy commotion. Nobody is worried about Catarina. The blood coursing through my veins is icy cold. I sprint across the room, fall to my knees, and gently prop her head on my lap. Her eye flickers open, and I gaze into a familiar shade of warm, beautiful hazel, proof that she is finally free of shadows.

"Zhengya?"

"Catarina. Just hold on. I'm—"

"You know . . ."

"What?" My fingers stop brushing through her blood-matted hair.

"I don't think I'll survive this."

"Stop it."

"I can't." Her voice is so small and scared.

"Fight, Catarina. You've fought every single moment of your life, so just do it for a moment longer." I am angry, so unbelievably angry. How could she give up now? How could she allow that tenacious will of hers to die out, now? "Fight it," I snarl.

"I *can't*."

When has the Queen of Demons ever admitted defeat? The tears that flow down my cheeks and fall against Catarina's blood-crusted breastplate are ceaseless, and I clamp a hand over my mouth to hold back my sobs.

"Stop," Catarina whispers. "Don't. Just don't."

"You're leaving me again?" I whisper. "So willingly?" I can see the way she is struggling to keep her eyes open, and more tears threaten to spill down my face.

"Can I show you something?" she whispers.

"Yes. Of course. A-anything you want."

She lifts her cold hand and presses it against my arm. We are sucked into a black void. I clutch Catarina's hand, my heart clenching in fear, and she brushes her thumb against my skin in reassurance.

I am right here, Zhengya.

"What is this place?"

This is my mind.

The black surrounding us suddenly changes. *Paradise,* I think. It is the only word I can think of that comes close to describing this place. There are no buildings, no people, no demons. It is simply golden, light-bathed nothing. But within the nothingness is laughter, happiness, and joy. Promises of true bliss, promises of a better life. Catarina lets out a small gasp of pain, and my wonder vanishes. I grip her hand harder and she coughs. Even in this alternate world, tiny drops of inky blood spray from her lips and splatter against her clothing.

This is what the black waves are promising if I give in to them, Catarina's voice whispers. *Do you see why I don't want to fight anymore?*

"But there are so many things you still need to experience—"

I'm so tired, Zhengya.

"Are you really so unhappy?" I ask desperately. "Even right now?"

A slight smile from her. *No. Never with you.* Ephemeral relief fills me, disappearing before I have the opportunity to savor it.

"I don't think I can live without you."

You already have.

"It was torturous."

Have you not seen all that I've done, Zhengya? I've slaughtered entire cities. I killed my aunt, and then I brought her back to life only because I wanted to test the true strength of my power, and because I knew what you would think of me. All of you are better off without me.

"Stop, Catarina—"

She waves her hand, and then we are back in Saelmere Castle. Nothing around us has changed. It is as if no time at all passed in that strange, dark void. Everyone is still bent over the Sisters of Night, speaking in worried, hushed voices.

"Did I kill them too?" Catarina asks softly. Somehow, back in this world, her voice is even weaker.

"No, no. They're alive. I-I'm sure they'll be fine." Even if that's true, I can't care less if Keres and Merikh live or die. Because Catarina is still before me, her blood spilling in black pools over my lap.

"I love you." The words are so soft that I hardly know whether she truly uttered them, or if they are a figment of my imagination.

"What?"

"I love you," she says again.

"I know," I say. I don't say it back because I don't trust it not to break my heart. She sags in my arms, sighing. "What are you thinking right now, Catarina?" My voice is the barest of whispers, and I am unsure if she has even heard me until her gaze drifts back to me.

"I'm thinking that everything hurts. I'm thinking that I was fighting a losing battle from the beginning. I'm thinking that I'd like to kiss you."

I stare down at her, horrified. And then she cranes her neck and slides her hands up my arms. Our lips meet. I clutch at her desperately, as if holding her even more tightly would ensure she never leaves me. She tastes of sweat and steel and death, and only when I taste the blood coating her lips do I jerk back.

Catarina is not a good person. She has never been, and she will never be. I realize that as I look into her eyes and I see that cold power writhing under her skin, even without her shadows. Everything she said before is true. Catarina is capable of such unforgivable crimes, of stealing life after life, and she does it all with a smile. Even if I love her for it, she is evil. And now I have the chance to end that evil. Blood still drips from the hole right below her chest, a reminder of how little time I have left to choose. Iesso had never been a strong woman, physically. She'd missed Catarina's heart, only by millimeters, but if she received help right now, she could survive. She would survive.

My fingers find a small blade laying forgotten beside me. I am careful not to let her see, and even if she does, she doesn't say anything. "In another world," I say, "this would've all worked out in the end."

"Maybe." Her remaining eye is still trained on me, unwavering. Color flushes her cheeks, even as her breathing grows more strained.

"This isn't your fault," I say.

"Yes, it is," she says. A ghost of a smile lingers on her face. As I sit with her head in my lap and the silence stretches on and on, the grin fades bit by bit.

I drive the knife into her chest with a sob, throwing every ounce of my weight into the blow. The blade goes through her flesh as easily as any other. I'd almost expected it to feel harder. Could she really be killed this easily? Her eye widens, and then narrows as she realizes what I have done. I pull back as *I* realize what I have done.

"I'm sorry," I whisper. "I'm so sorry." As if words could atone for anything. Her breathing is so shallow, her face is so pale, her skin is so damp with blood. Only then do the words tumble from me.

"*I love you, I love you, I love you,*" I gasp. I can't speak them fast enough. As soon as the words leave my mouth, I know that they are nothing but the purest form of truth. If I do not keep talking now, I'll never be able to say the words I've kept within me for so long, I'll never be able to tell her how she's saved me from death, from pain, and from myself so many times. "I've loved you since the day we met, I'm so sorry, I—"

She only shakes her head, then breathes out softly as her chest stops moving.

Catarina, dead at last.

Tontin approaches me afterward, holding his hand cautiously outstretched. The reinforcements from the Cities of Night, each one of them wearing the mechanical wings that the Sisters had designed, arrived long after the bloodshed had ceased. Far too late to fight, instead taking to sweeping through the streets, clearing away the gore, and killing any demons who'd lingered for an easy meal or been too injured to escape. Later, they'll carry the countless, nameless corpses of humans to a mass grave. The war is over.

Catarina's body is already drastically changing. Her skin is fragile, as if even the gentlest of touches could break through it. I let myself hold her for a while longer, tucking my head into the hollow of her neck. I force myself to think back and tuck all the memories of *us* into a safe corner of my mind, but all I can concentrate on is how cold she is. How lifeless.

"I'd like to show you something," Tontin says softly from behind me. I turn and glare at him through tear-streaked eyes, my grip tightening around Catarina's cold arm. But his gaze is soft and something about the way he spoke convinces me to follow him. To my surprise, he takes me down to the castle stables, where two octilli look absurdly out of place next to the royal horses. He gestures at me to mount one.

We ride all the way back to Cheusnys Cave in silence. The sheer self-loathing I feel is enough to make me want to hurl myself off this thing. Why had I ever tried to bring my brother back? Why had I ever gone to Ahuiqir, why had I ever forced Catarina to come save me, why had I let any of the things that happened happen? I don't let myself cry. We round a familiar bend, and Cheusnys Cave looms before us, gaping and as large as always. Prophet Tontin looks at me expectantly. I mutter under my breath, giving him permission. He slides off his mount and strides in, still flinching even as his body passes through the barrier without struggle.

I follow. "Why did you bring me here?" I ask.

"I did not know you loved her," Tontin says, deliberately not answering my question. I don't respond, instead turning my attention to the walls of the cave—to the paintings covering every inch of the cold stone. And even though it is clear that the ink has been here for many, many years, the brilliant colors are still as vibrant as if they had been painted only yesterday.

"She said something to me that I'll never forget," he says suddenly. "When she kidnapped me to help her steal Fane's powers. She said, 'I'd like to be remembered.' And she didn't say anything other than that, but I think, at that moment, I understood. I understood why she's done the things she has, why she's said the things she has." His words are not unkind, but not gentle either. I am grateful for that. He stops walking and turns his wrinkled face to me. I scan his perfectly neutral gaze for any hint of pity, but there is none. He'd felt no sympathy for Catarina, and therefore no sympathy for me when she died. But this was still a kindness he was doing for me.

"She was only a child, Zhengya," he says. "And yet she felt so pressured to be perfect. And when she couldn't do that, she made herself perfect in other ways. She made herself strong, she made herself into something that people feared, demon or not."

"Why are you saying this?"

We have reached the end of the cave. One wall is covered with engraved images from legends of both Guinyth and Ahuiqir's pasts, but the other is covered with thousands of tiny letters.

"Do you feel all the spirits of the past queens and kings? Do you feel Catarina's spirit? This cave is not just a portal between two worlds," Tontin says softly. "It's filled with memories and history." He slides to his knees, brushing his fingers over two of the countless letters. "Look."

And I do. *C.W.*, carved out in Catarina's distinct, flowery script. I fall to my knees beside him, tears finally slipping silently from my cheeks to the hard, stone ground.

"Why did you love her, even after everything she'd done to you and your friends?" His question is genuinely curious, not critical at all.

"I don't know." It is the truth. "I think I'd like to be remembered too."

Tontin only offers me a small smile, as if he knows something I don't. He gestures to the wide expanse of stone before me. *Go ahead.* I pick up a sharp stone from the ground. With shaky fingers, I etch out the letters *Z.L.*, right beside Catarina's. Then I fall back on my heels, sighing. It feels as if a million wet, woolen blankets have been lifted from my shoulders. I can breathe again.

"What are you thinking right now?" Tontin asks. I'd asked Catarina the same thing.

"I'm tired." The grief I'd felt before has died away to a dull ache, if only because of the heavy exhaustion rooted deep in my bones.

He considers me for a long moment. "I want to grant you a wish. One wish, anything you want."

Of course, I want nothing more than to be able to feel her with me again, but I am not a fool. The magic needed to do that is long gone, and even if it weren't, Tontin would never agree to delve into such dark, unnatural energy again.

"I want to go inside her head," I say finally. "I want to see what she was like on the inside."

He smiles softly, gently. "Yes, my dear. And so you shall." He waves his hand, and I am thrown into darkness. At first, nothing. And then everything...

You are an ignorant, selfish child, pathetic, failure of a queen, better off without you, weak, feeble, defective, Human Slayer, Black Assassin, Your Majesty, My Queen, My Queen, My Queen. I have possessed powers that have made the gods themselves tremble in fear. I have possessed powers that have bent the ultimate ending of death to my own will. My feats shall be extolled far after my death, they shall be sung in prayer and told to young children curled, shivering fearfully, in their beds. I am hated. Revered. Worshipped.

The words and phrases blur together in swirls of black and gold until my vision swims and my head pounds. I glimpse snippets and snapshots of all her memories. Dark memories. A boy named Cam from Tegak. The violent dreams she'd had and the demons that haunted her sleep. The day she'd murdered her parents against her will. The feeling of Fane's blade pressed against her neck, her death. And then the feeling of coming back to life as a demon with new wings and sharp horns and a lashing tail. I see the day she'd become Queen of Demons. I see the way that the shadows spilled through her like a tidal wave. More recent memories flit by. I see myself.

"Did she have the chance to tell you what the shadows were doing to her?" Tontin asks softly. His voice sounds so distant, faraway.

"No," I whisper, unable to force my lips to form more words.

"They were taking over her mind."

"Why?"

"Because she was letting them. And do you know why?"

"No," I breathe. I am terrified of his answer.

"Because of you. She was furious with you."

I stifle a sob.

"But also, for herself." He looks at me carefully. "You loved a selfish, selfish girl."

Once upon a time, a girl fell in love with a girl. They held each other. And they refused to let go. They cared about each other more than anyone else in the world, but their love was not enough to divert the mighty river of destiny. They yearned for each other distantly, and they regretted every ounce of lost time, but only after it was too late. Because now, one of the two girls is dead, and the other is left in ruins without the other. I hate that I can still walk, talk, breathe. I hate that my heart pumps on relentlessly, I hate that my muscles flex and contract. Every tiny, minuscule movement, every part of ordinary life, reminds me that I stole those very things from Catarina. I do not deserve to live. But there is something I must do.

CHAPTER TWENTY-THREE

PHILAN

IT HAS BEEN several hours, yet nobody has come to take away Catarina's body, nobody has even come to dispose of it. Keres and Merikh began to stir several hours after Catarina's death and were immediately tended to. Teams of surviving servants have been coming in and out, clearing away bodies and debris. And yet, Catarina's body still lies there, untouched since Zhengya left. Nobody has even spoken of how it will be disposed of, as if her name itself has become a curse. She still lies there, her hands folded on her chest, her fingers carefully positioned by Zhengya to cover up the gaping hole beneath them. Her lips are tinged blue and her skin is an odd gray color, but even in death, her brow is furrowed in concentration. Fury, even. As if she is angry that she was finally defeated. The Queen of Demons has finally met as much of a violent end as she bestowed upon so many others. The tiny white flower that I'd tucked into her hair in the midst of our siege is somehow still there, almost untouched. I kneel down, grazing my fingers over her face. She looks so normal. Like just a girl.

I pluck the flower from her hair and turn it in my fingers. The pale, velvety petals are unblemished, not a speck of dirt disrupting their clean surfaces, and it still smells faintly sweet. I put it back in her hair. For a moment, it looks as if she exhales lightly, but it is only the wind blowing through the shattered windows of the room. I breathe in deeply. Somehow, even after so much bloodshed and war, the breeze is still pleasant, carrying with it the scents of grass and flora. The smell of a new beginning.

It had always been the Queen of Demons and her king. I'd stood at her side, and she'd dictated my every move. She'd never belonged to anyone. She'd held the world in her claws, and she'd loved every second of it. But now I'll get the chance to experience life without the presence of the steel-hearted, sharp-eyed girl I'd saved from a dungeon in her own castle. What would life have been like if I'd left her in that cell? I don't know, and I don't care to ponder it. All that matters is that I am free.

I haven't been free in a long time.

"Philan Lin."

I turn towards the gruff voice of a guard.

"I have been instructed to escort you back to Ahuiqir."

His belt is stuffed with several knives, and a sword hangs at his side. Sighing, I hold out my wrists for him to bind.

"Your wings too," he says, and I turn around, allowing him to secure thick ropes around my wings. They are far from comfortable, but I don't complain.

"What about Catarina's body?"

"Somebody will bury it—"

Suddenly, somebody bursts into the room. I turn to find Zhengya standing there, her eyes wild and sweat dripping down her chin, as if she'd just been running. "I want to do it," she says. "Let me do it."

I look at the guard. "May I go with her?"

His eyes narrow as he thinks. Zhengya is already striding across the room to Catarina, taking her limp body in her arms. "Fine," the guard finally says. "But the second you even think about escaping, I will not hesitate to kill you." He waves at two other guards standing in the corner, equally well-armed. "And they will come with you."

Cots have been set up for the injured in the spacious dining hall of the castle. Both humans and demons lie upon them, black and red blood mixing. The air is filled with the sound of suffering. Muffled screams, pained moans, nurses yelling for assistance. A demon leans over the side of his mattress, writhing and twitching in pain. Pale bones are protruding from his bloodied, bent wings, and the once-glossy black feathers have been burnt to ashes. If by some miracle he lives, he will never fly again.

"Help," he pleads. His arm shifts, revealing a long gash down the front of his body. I swallow back bile. His organs are peeking out of the inflamed flesh around them, barely covered by blood-soaked bandages.

"I cannot help you," I whisper.

He falls back against his thin pillow, his eyelids falling shut. "Did we win?"

I realize two things: First, this demon will not live through the night, and second, that he has not yet seen the dead queen behind me. I exhale slowly. I do not have the heart to tell him the truth. So, I lie.

"Yes," I say softly. "We won. Our forces are already moving farther into Guinyth."

"Good," he breathes. I look back at the four guards behind me. They nod, understanding what I mean. The dying demon's wings have been slashed, his horns chipped, his stomach cut open, and yet a faint smile still curves his lips.

"Why are you still here, My King?" he asks me.

"I don't think I'd want to die alone," I tell him. "So, I'm not going to let *you* die alone."

"What are you talking about?" He tries to laugh, but only a horrifying, choking sound comes out. "I'm not going to die." But even as he utters those words, the light in his eyes fades further.

"Don't talk," I whisper. But he pulls away from my touch, reaching for something in his pocket.

"I have something to give you," he says. I hurry to help him, but he shakes his head, pulling out a small sack of coins. The metal clinks softly as he presses the pouch into my hands. "There is a portrait in there," he whispers. "Of my family."

"Why have you given me this?"

"Because I know you are lying, sir," he says. My eyes snap to his. They are glossy with pain, yet crystal clear. "I know we did not win. Please give them that money. Tell them that I love them all." He coughs, and blood slips out of the corner of his mouth.

"Yes," I say. "I will."

"Thank you," he breathes, and his hand falls back to the bloody cot on which he lays. And then his chest trembles and his eyes widen and then shut for the last time. One of the guards behind me inhales sharply. I sigh and pull the flimsy blanket covering his legs over his face. I make my way back to the other soldiers and Zhengya, who still holds Catarina.

The people hurrying around us pause to stare at us, giving us a wide berth, but are quickly drawn back to tending to the wounded after seeing the guards surrounding me, and my bound wings.

"Where are we going?" one of the guards asks.

"A graveyard down the road," I tell him.

"No," Zhengya says. "We're going to Cheusnys Cave. She'll be buried there."

"Zhengya—"

"Don't you think a Queen of Ahuiqir should be treated with respect?" Her gaze is fierce.

"Of course," I reply.

"Then shut up."

We continue in silence after that. Eventually we stand at the entrance of the cave, staring into the gaping, dark hole. The setting sun throws rays of soft, golden light across the treetops. Pale clouds drift across the horizon, carried by gentle gusts of wind. The pale face of the moon and a countless twinkling stars are already starting to appear in the sky. Birds call out hesitantly to one another, as if afraid to break the deathly silence of the early evening.

Zhengya sets Catarina down with heartbreaking gentleness. "Dig," she orders the soldiers. They obey, scooping away the damp earth with branches they find on the ground. Zhengya folds herself over Catarina. I watch as Zhengya simply stares at her, tears dripping silently down her cheeks. It finally occurs to me that they might have been more than friends. She is not mourning the loss of an acquaintance, but of a loved one.

One of the guards taps my shoulder. "The grave is finished," he tells me.

I turn in Zhengya's direction and call her name.

She does not turn as she speaks. "Go back. I want to do it myself."

Her voice carries with it a gravitas that I know there is no use arguing against, so I motion for the others to join me as I stride away.

I never expected to return to Ahuiqir as its only ruler. I am king.

That sudden realization hits me like a physical blow, though I do not let my soldiers see. They will revel tonight in the brambles of our dry forests and celebrate surviving. Demons do not mourn the loss of war, they only celebrate the bloodshed. A loss for us is never truly a loss because thousands of humans will die with hatred in their hearts and join our ranks.

Even though I'd lied and cheated and tricked my way to this position, even though there is nobody here to witness my victory, I roar my triumph for the world to hear and I bask in the glory of it all.

I'd been mistaken as a teenager, not wanting to burden myself with the responsibilities of becoming a king. As I stand here, still processing what the deaths of all those who have commanded me like a peasant mean, I finally begin to understand Catarina's insatiable thirst for power. The high is addictive. I look around, feeling the thrum of my shadows under my skin. I already crave more.

CHAPTER TWENTY-FOUR
CATARINA

DYING IS NOTHING like the stories. It hurts. It burns until you are nothing but the pain, and the pain is nothing but you. You are powerless against it. I am left to writhe in silent agony, alone.

Death feels dark and unwelcoming, but not in the way that my shadows had been. This feeling is turning my muscles to jelly and blurring all my thoughts, memories, and feelings until I can no longer distinguish one from another. I think I'm falling to my knees. My vision is darkening. Black waves are calling out to me from the edge of my consciousness, enticing me, tempting me, seducing me. I edge closer to them.

"Catarina," they say. "You have a weary, weary soul."

"What?" I ask softly.

"Come rest. Come sleep with us. You deserve it."

"Where did my shadows go?"

"That is beside the point, Queen of Demons. You must rest now."

"I don't *want* to rest. I want my shadows back."

The waves are angry now, and they crash harder and harder against me. "Obey," they hiss. "Give in."

"What will happen if I do?" I ask. I hate how weak I am now. I am nothing without my shadows.

"You will be granted peace," they breathe. "You will be granted quiet tranquility, at last. Isn't that what you crave most in life, what you crave even more than power?"

Yes, my mind sings. *A million times yes.* And although I do not utter the words out loud, the waves seem to know what I am thinking.

"So come to us, darling. Bathe in our waters, drink us in until you are washed away to a happier, *better* place than this world you call home."

"What will happen if I don't?"

The waves pause. "You will suffer for all of eternity."

"Are you sure?"

"Yes. So come to us," they repeat.

Has this been a good life? I ask myself. *Have I learned and loved and lived to the greatest of my ability?* But I know the answer almost immediately. No. I have not. Angry, hot tears prick at my eyes. Why couldn't I have been gentle like Brienne, who'd always tried to be kind to me? Why couldn't I have been like Soren and Liserli, who died honorably, trying to save the lives of children? Why couldn't I have been like Zhengya? The strongest, smartest, bravest, most compassionate human being I've ever known. The only one who truly saw me—replete with all my flaws—and was still determined to help me. The radiance of my life, the light to my shadows.

But what if being benevolent and courageous doesn't equal a good life?

I am far too exhausted to tackle that thought. I can't resist anymore.

"I think that'd be nice," I say to myself.

I am wreathed in sweet, balmy light instead of darkness. I lie in fields of golden flowers instead of fields of blood. And somehow, even after Zhengya's final betrayal, I am smiling. Soft blades of green grass tickle my cheeks as I stir. A warm breeze dances across my skin. Gentle, imploring, curious, smelling of sweet sunshine and cool morning dewdrops coating summer lilies. *Welcome,* it seems to breathe in my ear. I wear a soft, white gown that flows around my legs as if it is made of air. Such a precious fabric would have been sought after in Guinyth. Merchants would've sold away their lives for a single yard of it. I shake my head, casting away the thought. That is no longer my life. My life is here, or rather my afterlife.

My hair is loose and when I reach up to touch my head, my fingers find a heavy band of cool metal. The crown I'd worn as a human queen. Even my eyepatch has disappeared, and my left eye is completely unscathed. I have not been able to see from both eyes in so long. But most importantly, I do not feel the rough horns that had adorned my head before, or the familiar weight of my feathered wings. I am no longer a demon.

Somehow, the realization doesn't make me as happy as it should've—a part of me misses the inherent power that came with being a demon, but I cast the thought of my head. I'm supposed to be happy here.

"Catarina Winyr," someone murmurs. "It is a pleasure to be in your presence."

My eyes snap up. A woman of ineffable beauty stands before me. Her skin is iridescent, shifting through every hue of the rainbow. One of her eyes is black, the other colorless. Her long, braided hair is as white as snow, but her face is free from the effects of old age. She wears a dress similar to mine, but somehow it looks as if it were the finest gown in the universe on her body. She wraps her white feathered wings around herself and smiles gently. An angel.

"Is paradise exactly what you imagined it to be?" she asks. Even her voice is enchanting. Lilting and delicate, full of secrets waiting to be discovered. I turn, looking more carefully at the land around me. Perfectly green grasses, clear rivers, groomed mountainsides. It is nothing like the harshness of Ahuiqir, and nothing like the wild beauty of Pheorirya. It is completely and utterly *flawless.* Yet it leaves a strange feeling in the pit of my stomach.

"Yes," I say quickly. "It is beautiful."

The woman tilts her head, her bright smile fading a little. "Why do you lie to me, Catarina? You can tell me the truth. Here, in paradise, there is nobody to judge you."

"I'm not lying."

"My darling, please. Do not disrespect me in this way."

"This doesn't feel right."

"I'm not sure what you mean by that." She gestures to the wide expanse of green land behind her. "Is all of this not to your liking? Is possessing a human body once again not your greatest wish?"

No. It is not. "Yes. Yes, it is. Who are you?"

"I do not have a name. You may call me whatever you'd like."

"This doesn't feel right," I repeat. My voice is no more than a whisper.

Her eyes narrow, and her mouth twists into a sneer. "Why are you saying these things, Queen of Demons?" Something in the tone of her voice has turned dangerous.

"I want to go back."

"You chose this," the angel snarls. Her voice pounds through my head, the sound like nails dragging over a chalkboard, no longer containing the sweet cadence it once had. Her teeth are elongating, turning to sharp, rotting points. *Fangs.*

"I want to go back home."

Her skin is losing its luster, and her soft white gown is melting off her body in scraps of black, burnt fabric.

"Let me go home."

Her body suddenly wrinkles, cracking and splitting as it goes. Horns erupt from her white hair. The pristine white feathers of her wings fall off to reveal black, leathery skin. Talons spring from her fingers, and she screams as her bones shift and snap, morphing her slender, youthful body into something ugly. Deep purple veins snake across her thin, frail skin. Her back hunches, her eyes bulge, her fingers turn knotted. Her hair thins and then seems to dissolve, revealing a spotted bald head. The golden heaven around me disappears. It is as if the entire land is collapsing in on itself. The rolling mountains flatten, the flowers disappear, and the grass parts to reveal a fiery, ash-filled hell.

I choke on a panicked sob. "What are you?" I cry, backing away from her. "What is this place?"

The elderly woman, once a beautiful angel, cackles and splays her twisted wings. "Did you really think that a vile creature like you could ever have a happy ending? My darling, this is where you belong. This is where you deserve to burn for all of eternity."

"What? But—"

"But what? You were promised a paradise?" The hag lets out another delighted, braying laugh that fully displays her yellow fangs. "All of that was a lie, Catarina Winyr! It was all an illusion. And you are trapped here. Forever."

"Let me go back." I shove her, panic clawing its way up my chest.

"My dear, you are dead. And while there are many things you return from, death is not one of them." She pauses. "In fact, that is one of the reasons I enjoy death so much. It is the only thing you can count on in life. It is final. It is inevitable. And it is ultimate. Such an amusing contradiction, isn't it?"

"Please," I beg.

"Don't you want to know who I really am?" she asks, still grinning.

"No," I whisper. All my energy is spent, and I want nothing more than to collapse on the floor and cry.

But then the hag's form begins to shift again. Her hair lengthens once more, taking on a pale, golden color. Her wrinkled, blemished skin turns smooth, young, and flawless again, and her eyes shift into an icy blue. Black feathers explode through the leathery skin of her crooked, sinewy wings and her bones straighten. I am staring at the cold, perfect, beautiful face of someone I'd hoped I'd never have to see again.

"Hello, Catarina," Victoire Sandor breathes. "It seems that after all this time, I have finally outsmarted the Almighty Queen of Demons."

My legs give out and I fall to the ground before her. "Why? How are you—"

She flashes her fangs again. "You killed me, and I was thrown into this hell. And when you have nothing to do but burn in hell, you have time on your hands. Lots of it. All I needed to do was realize that you are much, much stronger than I'll ever be. Physically, at least. However, you have a weak soul, Catarina."

"Victoire, let me go. I'll do anything, I'll—"

"You know," she interrupts. "I've always respected you." I freeze, shocked. "We're both deeply ambitious women, Catarina. And there's only a select few of our kind in this universe." She lifts a strand of my hair. "Not many will go the lengths that we did for power."

And a part of me agrees, despite everything. "I respected you, too," I whisper.

She offers me a sad smile. "You see? We could've worked together, Cat. In another lifetime. We could've truly been unstoppable." She clicks her tongue. "What a shame."

And some miniscule part of me whines in agreement. *We could've been.* She looks at me, an odd expression suddenly furrowing her eyebrows.

"You know what I first thought when I visited you in your dreams?" I shake my head silently, and she laughs quietly, bitterly. "I was relieved, knowing I wasn't a complete anomaly of nature." She leans closer. "You were just like me. And I felt as if I needed you to stay." I gape in surprise. "I didn't want to let you go."

"So let me go back now," I whisper. I don't want to think about Victoire's words and the strange tone with which she'd said them.

She circles slowly around me. I can feel her gaze burning into my skin, branding me. "I *can* offer a compromise. I will let you go. I'll revive you, but only if you agree to let me bring Zhengya Lin here. A life for a life."

"No."

Her answering smile makes me clench my hands into fists. She'd known I'd never agree to that, and that was the only reason she'd even asked. "Well then. You'll be staying here a long, long while. So get comfortable, my dear."

Fear takes hold of me in an unshakeable grip then, as deep and dark as my shadows had once been. I slump to my knees, utterly defeated. I suddenly cannot seem to remember the feeling of knowing I was more powerful than anyone else. Victoire only watches and laughs.

EPILOGUE

AT THE VERY END of Cheusnys Cave, if you've dared to brave the magical barrier and stench and darkness, lies a shrine of animal bones. It's not a large thing, but it's unmistakable, made entirely of skulls. The one at the very top is the largest, a stag skull with antlers spanning several feet each.

Pay attention to the stretch of wall between the shrine of skulls and the massive murals stretching from floor to ceiling. If you'd been alive a century ago, that space would have been blank. But now, do you see the carving that looks the newest? The grooves are sharper, not worn down as much by the elements and time. Do you see her wings, her tail, her eyepatch? Her shadows? Look at the way they curl around her, obedient only to their master. Look at the way her eyes are closed, the way her arms are stretched out to the sky and her mouth is curved with delight. If you know anything about history at all, it is clear who this demon is: *Catarina Winyr.*

Although she will never been remembered as the perfect queen she was expected to be, her name will *not* be forgotten.

ABOUT THE AUTHOR

A.J. YANG is a high school student in Ann Arbor, Michigan where she resides with her insufferable siblings, incredible pets, and relentlessly supportive parents. Besides writing, she loves playing piano and cello, ballet, and tennis. She also loves working on her podcast with fellow student and cohost, Zach. When she isn't holed up in her room, working on her writing till way too late at night, you can find Ms. Yang sleeping (which she loves just as much).